SCION OF CONQUERED EARTH

Books by Michael J. Allen

Scion Novels:

1. Scion of Conquered Earth
2. Stolen Lives

2.5 Hijacked

3. Unchained

Dumpstermancer:

1. Discarded
2. Duplicity

Bittergate:

1. Murder in Wizard's Wood
2. The Wizard's Bane

Guns of Underhill:

1. Fey West

Delirious Scribbles:

- Wyrm's Warning
- Chrysalis

Liz
Watch your head!

SCION OF CONQUERED EARTH

SCION: BOOK 1

MICHAEL J. ALLEN

Delirious Scribbles Ink

Delirious Scribbles Ink

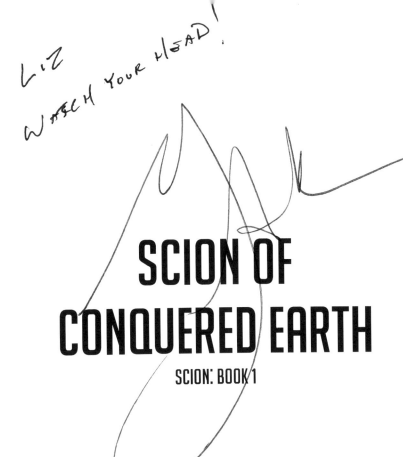

This is a work of fiction. Names, characters, places, and incidents are a product of the author's imagination or are used fictitiously. Locales and public names are sometimes used for atmospheric purposes. Any resemblance to actual people—living, dead or in between, businesses, companies, events, institutions, or locales is completely coincidental.

Delirious Scribbles Ink
P. O. Box 161
Fortson, Georgia 31808-0161
www.deliriousscribbles.com

Interior Layout ©2017 Delirious Scribbles Ink
Author Photo by Jim Cawthorne, Camera 1
Cover Design ©2017 Delirious Scribbles Ink

ISBN 978-1-944357-01-6 (hc)
ISBN 978-1-944357-00-9 (intl. tr. pbk. 1st ed.)
ISBN 978-1-944357-31-3 (intl. tr. pbk. 2nd ed)
ISBN 978-1-944357-02-3 (epub)
ISBN 978-1-944357-03-0 (kindle)

Printed in the United States of America
10 9 8 7 6 5 4 3 2 1
Scion of Conquered Earth / Michael J. Allen. – 2nd ed.

For B, B & J.

Sorry for turning you into captive sounding boards in all of those amusement park lines.

1

FLIGHT

"Pain is gain!" The high pitch cry told him the aerobics instructors were about to eat him alive—literally.

Lost more ground than I thought. He cursed. *Got to move faster.*

Loose tile and smashed brick slid beneath his soles. He went down, catching himself on ruined buildings and shattered glass with an already bloody hand. He scrambled back to his feet and pushed another burst of speed from his body.

"Pilates are life!" another woman shrieked.

He didn't look back. He raced toward less cluttered streets. Blast craters in the roadway and the discarded belongings of a city's fleeing population forced him to dart this way and that. He jumped onto a hover taxi smashed into a new career as an accordion, scrambled across its hood and leapt to clear a bloated corpse.

"Let's go ladies! Feel that burn!"

The teen reached a relatively clear stretch and risked a backward glance. Too-long uncut brown hair obscured his vision and filled his mouth with bitter reminder of how filthy he was. Not even half a block behind him, five women pursued dressed in leotards and sweatpants shredded enough to give him an eyeful he might otherwise have enjoyed if they hadn't been trying to eat him.

A section of torn asphalt shifted under one foot as he glanced back.

Like lipstick applied in an earthquake, dried blood stained their mouths beneath wild eyes and haphazard ponytails.

He cursed and raced between a pair of destroyed cars, blackened by laser blasts from invasion fighters. The sortie left a dozen burned out vehicles in his way like a morbid obstacle course. He ducked into the back seat of one and over half a child's skeleton too fused to the frame beneath it to be pried loose and gnawed on by feasters like the ones on his tail. He slammed the opposite door from his way and darted over the roof of the next car.

Road fell away several stories on its opposite side, revealing a vehicle graveyard hosting another feaster camp with a dozen crazed looking lawyers.

"Get your body bikini ready!"

"I object," a lawyer yelled back.

"Me too," the teen gasped.

He spun left. His shoulder clipped a side mirror, stealing his balance. He regained it in time to leap atop the next nearest car.

"Why don't you guys do lunch without me," he jumped again, edging the crater in an attempt to escape from both groups. He gestured to his loose hanging golden jumpsuit. "See, not enough meat for the effort."

"Carbs are the enemy!"

"Bailiff, restrain that man!"

He cleared the traffic jam and darted through a series of bomb-gutted storefronts. He dug into long exhausted reserves for a bit more speed. He knew he didn't have it, knew he couldn't keep up the pace.

Something had told him to avoid the bombed out gym, but he'd been desperate for something to eat or drink. He'd found food all right, some poor animal—he hoped it'd been an animal—roasted on a makeshift firepit surrounded by deranged aerobics instructors seated on half-flat exercise balls.

He cleared half the block and darted down a tight alley.

Tattered suits and shredded leotards pursued him, getting into each other's way and tearing into one another. It wasn't their fault they wanted to eat him. The invading aliens—Welorin—had done things to them. No one knew what went on in the re-education camps, but the terrifying byproduct craved a meal of anyone the camps didn't produce.

He'd been desperate. He'd been careless. Put simply, he'd been stupid and stupid led him into not one but two of the feaster camps in the same chase.

He tripped on something he'd rather not think about, sending him tumbling into an old trashcan. The can careened off brick, clanging like a dinner bell and bowling its way through a pile of rain melted boxes. The makeshift hiding place disintegrated. Its occupants, a woman and a small boy, shrieked.

He scrambled back to his feet and ran three steps before cursing and whipping back around. He snatched up the can. "Run. Go, now."

He hurled the can back the way he'd come, snatching everything at hand and hurling it at other debris in a rushed attempt to clog the alley. He hurried in the pair's wake, knocking over anything that came within reach.

The debris-clogged alley and the feasters' amplified competitive natures tangled his pursuers into a clawing, dogma-spewing Black Friday mob. He made it to the other street and shot glances both ways. Buildings lay at wrong angles everywhere. Reddish flames burned behind a putrid haze, ghost lights within diseased fog.

He caught a glance of the woman and child disappearing around a cluttered corner.

He probably should have followed and escaped pursuit ducking through broken buildings. With his luck, he'd stumble into another feaster camp, or worse, lead his pursuers to the pair he'd sacrificed time removing from their lunch menu.

He ran the other direction, taking advantage of the clearest roadway to both gain whatever extra lead it would afford him and draw the feasters after him.

He made it almost a full block before they fought their way out of the alley. A frazzle-haired woman in a tiger striped leotard shoved her way to the front. "First!"

Her near twin shouted behind her. "Second!"

"Hearsay, I object!"

A patent leather briefcase hurdled out of the alley. It slammed the ponytail of the lead feaster, sending her sprawling. "Sustained!"

The other lawyers chuckled, and the melee resumed. A robe-bedecked woman broke from the fight and pointed after him, "The accused is *not* dismissed!"

They chased him down a street bracketed by wrecked buildings leaning like stubborn dominoes against one another. Varied degrees of ruin mimicked his pursuers—some in far better shape than others.

He cut across a parking lot and headed down another street, ignoring shrieked oaths of those already demented then tortured into madness. His pace slowed. He ordered his limbs to keep moving, but they resisted the haste he demanded.

His heart thundered in his ears, rising above the following mob. It got louder, resolving into explosions accompanied by a low whistle which pricked the back of his head.

He whipped a glance over his shoulder. The feasters—restrained by who knew what brainwashing from eating one another—fought their way up his wake, making better time than he, oblivious to the danger racing their way.

He stumbled to a stop in a debris-littered parking lot, his legs still feeling in motion.

Ash rained once more from a putrid looking sky. He stared, shielded eyes raised. Unhealthy swaths of green and yellow streaked ever-present thunderheads horizon to horizon. Metallic grey death cut through the putrid skyline toward them.

Three triangular fighters streaked up the street. Green lasers ripped up the city on a direct line to him. Some sort of energy bolt seized derelict vehicles and building chunks, wrapping them in a corona of sparks and lofting them upward.

Blasts cut into the feaster mob. Bolts hit them, launching several screaming toward heaven.

He gaped as their bodies curved a lazy arch through the air back toward the ground—and him.

He fled. "There has to be some universal law against lawyers raining from the sky!"

Several feasters fled for cover. Others charged in his wake before deciding easy meat was better than dinner fleeing through a fire zone. They fled toward cover as fast as they could drag their fallen comrades home for dinner.

A ruined gas station offered his first real cover in a hundred yards—other than the hover cars the Welorin used as Hacky sacks. The huge blown out crater on its far side suggested it'd already been a target. It shared a fallen-in storefront with some kind of hair boutique. Opposite a small alley another building had been demolished. A sign stood in the wrecked parking strip advertising a combined air force and star force recruiting office, a tattoo parlor and a sandwich shop crushed like a Panini.

The fighter blasts strafed over him, exploding street and debris. Heat washed past him, singeing his hair and partially regrown eyebrows. A chunk the size of his head blew sideways, catching him in the midriff and knocking him into the smoking hole.

He scrambled from the mini-crater, hands burning on still hot concrete, and paused at its edge. The fighters turned a lazy bank in the far horizon.

"Yeah, come on back. You might have missed a mailbox or something."

<They're coming back to see if they missed you, little brother. Time for hide and seek.>

He froze as the voice rolled through his thoughts. He didn't remember a brother, though he knew the nameless voice. It was right. He had to get out of sight if he wanted to survive the assault.

He checked his back path. No feasters barred his way, but there were at least two camps that direction. The horizon around him was a mass of jagged broken buildings and ripped up streets. Any could have provided shelter, but also a target.

If they're even empty.

He examined the little crater. It was hot enough still he might lie in its burning recesses and the Welorin would think him dead—or an easy target. The alley seemed the best cover. He'd have two avenues of escape even if it wasn't.

He bolted toward the gas station, running around the long way in hope it'd misdirect the fighters when they came back for him—assuming he survived the next strafing run.

Laser blasts and lofted debris rained down toward him. He counted the blasts as they raked the roadway, trying to sense their firing pattern. At the last possible moment, he ducked back the way he came.

He fell.

A laser blast cut through where he should've been standing, sucking the air from his lungs and leaving his exposed skin sunburnt.

He didn't check the fighters.

He scrambled to his feet and limp-ran across the blasted front of the gas station.

The fighters streaked overhead, their blasts centered where he'd fallen.

He jumped behind a large plastic sign reading: Shella's B*U*Tique.

The fighters swept overhead again without firing a shot.

He ducked out from under cover and rushed into the alleyway. Mounded debris clogged it, turning it into a V-shaped valley—not the cover he'd hoped to find.

He flopped down against the boutique wall and cursed.

Every decision seemed the wrong one. Even minor victories turned wrong. With his luck, his interference had left the mother and child he exposed roasted on a spit for some shark in a torn business suit.

He shuttered and his gut knotted. It gurgled at him, reminder that he hadn't eaten either.

Not that there's much I can do about that.

He wondered about the sandwich shop. After so many months, anything not crushed or spoiled had been looted. The recruiting place might have had some food. It was the places that didn't actually sell food that he'd found the tidbits that kept him going.

Fighters swept the area again. A hover van lofted into the air and fell toward the ground—toward him. He scrambled over the hill of debris and down the alley. The van crashed down on his heels, crunching metal and crackling power drowned everything else in his ears. It rocked, nose on the building, then toppled off with a crash.

The teen eased toward it, careful not to touch the clinging energy field. It flickered away. He touched the side of the van, jerking back his hand.

It was cool to the touch.

Whatever power launched it airborne cracked the chassis like an egg. A reek of rotten flesh escaped its interior. Holding his breath, he eased into the gap for a look. Everything inside stank, scorched by laser and cooked in summer heat. An ice blue duffle bag lay wedged beneath the feet of a child's corpse and the seat in front.

He tugged at it.

He pulled.

He braced a hand on the seat back and yanked. It came free, breaking the child's leg in its path.

Bile rose in his throat. "Sorry, I didn't mean to, well, you know."

The bag held a menagerie of small stuffed animals. Other than something to pillow his head or burn he didn't have much use for them. He eased them from the bag and set them in the child's lap.

An adult's skull dropped away from its neck.

He jerked in surprise. His breath froze.

A light gleamed through the spiderwebbed windshield.

He scrambled out of the van and up the debris pile to gaze through a dirty window at an electric light shining within the remains of Shella's.

He smashed the window open with a brick, taking care to clear the broken shards along the edges of the window. He slipped inside, assaulted at once by a palatable wall of perfumed hair products. He gagged and choked, poking his head out the window to catch a cleaner breath then turned back to the light.

It shone like a ray from heaven inside a small bathroom. He rushed across the shampoo-slick floor, ignored the shattered sink and threw open the commode.

Thick black slime clung to the water's edge, spots of who knew what made up a galaxy of ick. He cupped two hands and lowered them into the bowl. The slime attached itself to his fingers, but he raised the water to his lips. Bitter, warm water quenched his thirst, the scent of weak chlorine tickling his nostrils.

He drank the bowl empty, relishing his slimy quench of heaven.

A blast shook the building.

A heavily laden hair product rack fell sidelong, slamming into the bathroom door and closing him in with a smash. It didn't worry him at first. Instead, he collected a wealth in paper towels, liquid soap, and oh-so-precious toilet paper.

He struggled open the tank, arms weak with hunger. Chlorine scent to rival the perfumes reeked from the stagnant water. An army of thumb-sized roaches ringed the water's edge. He snatched at the bugs, several fleeing through the water before he caught a slippery, flailing morsel and shoved it into his mouth. Still moving legs tickled his throat, but meat was meat, and things were desperate. He tried for another, but they slipped out cracks he couldn't. He filled hands with heavily chlorinated water. It burned his throat, but he drank his fill. One of the shampoo bottles might serve as a canteen for the rest.

He opened the door.

It didn't budge.

He cursed. *Of course, I should've known it was too good to be true.*

<Poor little brother, always so put upon.>

"Shut up."

He shoved and strained until his breath fled. He drank more water and fought the door some more. He finally wrestled it open enough to slide out an arm. He reached through the gap, finding a rack and myriad bottles against the door. He dug them away, eyes closed and seeing with his hands.

The door shifted more.

He dug.

The door opened enough for him to squeeze through. He took one last drink from the toilet tank, threw the duffel through the gap and crawled after it.

He'd have to remove the fallen rack before he could canteen the rest of the water and risk flushing to see if the pipes had more perhaps cleaner fare.

He turned toward the fallen rack.

"Holy heavens."

The outline of a door, painted over and previously blocked by the shelf stood sentry in the wall between the boutique and the gas station's convenience store.

Food.

If the power was still on beyond the door, there might be a feast of foods awaiting him. If nothing else, with no other entry to the store, it'd be a place to hide, rest his ankle, and be safe for a while.

The door didn't budge.

He beat at it with a stool until he broke through its lower panel and crawled into the store. What remained above dangled dangerously from a twisted aluminum skeleton. Dead fluorescent lights hung from last tenuous threads of electrical wiring, illuminating the room with occasional sparks—that the building had power at all was something of a miracle. They swung back and forth slowly, pendulums of doom rocked by fighter craft barrages to spread seemingly infinite dust reserves. Cracks riddled the cavernous ceiling above the skeleton, chunks of concrete clung to rebar by their fingertips. Dust and shattered ceiling tile littered every surface. Shelves teetered drunkenly into their neighbors while others lay on the floor uncaught by their peers.

Food lay on their shelves and at their feet—a fortune in canned items of every description, crushed foil bags of chips, snacks and a few cans of powdered baby formula.

If Shella's or the store had working water, he'd rest. He'd feast like a king.

He glanced at the ceiling.

At least, he'd feast until the world crashed down on his head. The store had stood this long. Who knew how long it'd survive.

The sound of approaching fighters filled his ears.

"No!" He wailed. "No, no, no..."

He heard them fire.

The building rocked.

The ceiling fell.

He backpedaled, heel caught, toppled backward.

Everything went black.

2

SURVIVAL

"Wake up, my little alar, you'll be late to destroy a world."

An explosion shattered his dream, wrenching the teen from blissful oblivion. Panic wrapped wicked fingers around him, held at bay by some intangible source of control. A heavy blanket of rubble buried him. Flashes of recent memory crossed his debris-enforced blindness. There was no way to tell just how much wreckage covered him.

He choked on dust, but there was nowhere for it to go but back into his face.

His limbs were pinned. Harshly angled wreckage dug into his legs and chest. A collapsed rack even managed to get underneath him. He struggled and strained, shoving ceiling pieces, aluminum frame, and lighting fixtures away piece by piece. The whole effort made him feel very much like a magician's assistant trying to shove away swords stuck into his coffin.

An eternity later thick but cool air relieved his suffocation.

He looked around and moaned. "I'm cursed. Whole world to smash and they have to target my head—again!"

Wait, if the first hit took my memory, maybe this one...

He dug into his mind. An ache filled it. Lost memories thrashed around in his brain, angry beasts hurling themselves against some unknown barrier. Their pounding insistence was a constant throbbing headache, worsened by persistent thunder, Welorin fighter barrages, and the occasional falling ceiling.

He cursed, fighting back the urge to cry.

Missing memories ached like the gaping wound of a dead friend. He couldn't remember what had brought him to Washington D.C., but it had been a mistake. He didn't even remember his own name.

The initial invasion flashed across his thoughts in twisted, broken fragments: arrowhead-shaped fighters bombarding the ground, detonations deafening him from every direction, beings in toe-to-crown armor with heavy weapons running everywhere and blood misting the air. They'd tried to grab him, but he'd slipped from them and ran until he literally collapsed.

He wanted to escape. He had to get away—though to what he couldn't remember. Three months he'd ran, survived—if only barely.

Another round of fighter bombardment shook the ground, threatening to bring down more of the roof already burying him. He shot a glance upward. A massive ceiling section had been replaced by the nose of an ambulance. It hung above him, dangling by crumbling fingers of cracked cement.

He had to get out. He had to get unburied. He had to escape—now.

He struggled to rise. Foot-long pins and needles ran up and down his legs. Pieces of fallen ceiling and tumbled shelves kept his legs pinned. He fell back, nearly impaling himself on the collapsed rack beneath him. A deep breath beset his lungs with more dust, and they objected violently. Once he finished choking, he spit grit and curses.

He searched his surroundings for any tool that might free him. Debris littered the floor—the useful bits just out of reach.

He wiped dust from his eyes with stiff blood-caked fingers. At invasion's beginning, it might've concerned him—no longer.

He twisted to one side, trying to claw his way across the tile floor. The effort sent pain lancing up and down one leg. He dug his nails along a ridge of broken tile, gritted his teeth, and shoved what he could out from under his body.

He flopped down, breath ragged, and let the pain fade. His stomach threatened sudden revolt in gurgling defiant tones.

He studied the mess pinning his legs. He shifted them again. Pain lanced up one.

"Pinned," he grunted shoving debris off the pinned legs, "and talking to myself. Wonderful."

<At least you're not hearing voices, princess.>

One leg came free. He collapsed back down and panted for breath.

Yellow caught his eye.

Just beyond his reach under a shelf, several packaged cakes hid from casual view. Otherwise useless debris drew some within reach. He ripped the plastic with his teeth and shoved one into his mouth. He choked down lumps of sweet, pasty, disgusting heaven.

"Ugh, the bug was better." He gagged down several more.

The building rocked, groaning metal heralding the ambulance's pending arrival. Dust rained down, insult to injury by nonexistent fairies out to get him.

A giggle escaped him.

He swore.

Focus, stay focused. You're losing it.

He lost it.

Panic seized him. He thrashed about, yanking at his pinned limbs and causing himself mind numbing pain.

He blacked out.

His mind raced through days and nights, smoke and wreckage, blood and violence. Nausea filled his dream self as poisonous looking yellow sponges with eyepatches and spears danced around him. Sponges became brutal looking pixies throwing sticky dust in his face. Suppressed memories of carnage too real for the most violent horror vid played back around him from a dozen angles.

His mind swam through thick, lethargic darkness toward the surface.

<Always knew you'd just give up and die, wimp.>

He lurched to a half-seated position, shouting at memories, "Shut up. Just shut up."

He grabbed a nearby shelf and yanked it over on top of himself. Cans and bags tumbled onto him, some striking in extremely painful ways. He wrenched a shelf from its framework and positioned it into a makeshift fulcrum.

He pulled on it from below, but couldn't manage any leverage. He tried again. He wouldn't give up. His brother was wrong. He would *never* give up.

He combined his free leg and impromptu lever, prying once more.

Shrieking pain proved his only reward.

Another barrage rocked the building. Chunks of ceiling tumbled down around him. The ambulance's horn blared and didn't stop.

He swore and then swore more for good measure.

He levered the shelf off of the framework, shoved chunks of concrete under it for more height, hanging as much of his weight on it as he could from beneath.

Pain wracked his body.

He pushed it away.

The shelf's edges dimpled.

He shoved against debris with his free leg.

His vision tunneled.

His lever bent, moments from buckling.

He kept up the pressure, unwilling to give up. The rubble shifted a little to one side. He wrenched his leg from beneath the debris, scraping sleeping flesh across what felt like predator's claws.

The lever buckled, dropping all its supported weight onto his ankle.

He howled.

The ceiling groaned. What remained above him dangled with malicious intent.

His heart hid in his ears.

Cold sweat trickled down his back.

The ceiling stayed where it belonged.

A titter escaped him. He slid his ankle out of the garbage and examined it with practiced motions. A massive purple bruise, centered on his ankle bone, spread over the pale limb. Twisted and later slammed, it remained unbroken but burned like fire under the least pressure.

Using both hands and one leg, he crawled behind the store's counter and flopped against one wall. Clear of emergency medical squashing, he checked himself out more thoroughly. He found no other injuries and by some miracle after all he'd been through, his tough jumpsuit remained whole.

Glass doors lined the wall next to the counter. Occasional cracks shielded collapsed and toppled shelves bearing a myriad of assorted containers. He crawled to the first and threw the door open. Cracked glass panes flew from the door and shattered, distracting him from a faint sour aroma. Hands shaking with excitement rooted through yellow jugs. With a triumphant cry, he raised up an intact jug, ripped the top and poured its contents down his throat. It dropped from his hands. Side by side, he and the jug spluttered and coughed up white curd clumps.

He moved to the next door, sweeping shattered glass from his path with one sleeve. He searched through syrup tacky plastic bottles. He opened the first sealed bottle he found and sipped at the neon green liquid. A taste later, he guzzled the bottle, its carbonation burning down his throat. He repeated the process several more times, slowing to every other bottle.

He scrambled around his varied hoard and seized the next door. Door, frame, fragmented glass and the rack behind it collapsed atop of him. He jerked his head out of the way of a dagger-like shard of glass, avoiding impalement by a fingerbreadth. He covered his head and threw himself backward out from under an avalanche of dark glass bottles. He smashed into the hoard. Bottles careened in all directions, adding venomous hiss to the sound of shattering glass.

The ceiling groaned in empathy.

He cursed, resisting surrender to frustrated tears.

Recomposed, he scavenged what few intact bottles remained. He found a broken shovel in a corner and with enormous effort, stood. Limping and wishing the ambulance horn a speedy death, he collected anything possibly edible and his hoard of drinks into the blue duffel and a few plastic bags.

The store scavenged clean, he dumped the remainder from the yellow jug, reclaiming its cap. He limped down a short hall. A collapsed cooler lay across its end, blocking a rear door. Bathroom doors stared each other down. He considered the ladies' room door a few moments before grabbing the men's room handle.

Locked, of course.

The women's bathroom opened easily. A blinding swarm of flies exploded from the doorway. A monstrous stench of rot, feces and perfume wrenched the breath from his lungs. He staggered backward, covering his face. His bile rose, stomach convulsing, he scrambled forward, wrenching the door shut as he disgorged the precious liquids in his stomach.

Several minutes of just breathing passed. He gulped air, stench still in his nostrils and threw open the door once more. A tangled knot of bloated corpses dominated a small room of ripped clothing, writhing maggots, shattered porcelain, and standing water.

He stared, his mind buzzing louder than his ears.

A man's lilting voice entered his thoughts. *<What do you see, young sir? What story does the evidence spin?>*

His mind probed what his fingers desperately didn't wish to. He turned and threw up again. The buzz of flies lessened and beneath it, he heard a slow trickle of water. He turned back to the room, noticing for the first time the trickle pouring onto the floor from a fly mobbed broken valve. His gaze flitted to the bodies, stomach knotting.

I can't.

<Coward.>

I just can't. He reached for the door handle.

A stronger voice cracked like a blow to the cheek. *<You will stand, you will look, you will see.>*

He bristled, and his expression turned mulish. He pulled the door shut, realizing as it clicked the treasure buried in hellishness. He threw the door back open, eyes falling upon handle and blade concealed by fingers and flesh. He gulped a breath, choked on it, turned his face away from the bathroom and replaced the first. He rushed into the room before his courage fled and grabbed for the knife. Loose skin sloughed off beneath his grip, but the hand refused to let go. He tugged at it, his lungs tightening.

The teen balanced on his good leg, spun the shovel and drove its half-blade into the wrist. It stuck fast, and he wrenched at it, breaking hand from arm and freeing the knife. His lungs burned. He pulled the shovel away, and the knife wielder's body toppled. Lungs straining to exhale blew out their breath in surprise. A short club between the bodies, caked in ichor dangled a copper key.

He gagged on his new breath and rushed from the room. A dozen fresh breaths and twice as many pep talks later, he reclaimed the bathroom key, shutting the door behind him. He unlocked the other door, took a deep breath and opened it.

Beside a faint aroma of urine, the bathroom was perfect. He cursed.

Between half-remembered voices and buzzing flies, he hadn't realized the constant drone of ambulance horn had fallen silent. Behind the nearer silence, a deeper silence hung in the air, empty of laser barrage and explosions. Little hairs across his body stood up and screamed for him to flee.

His ankle twinged at the thought of flight. "No."

He stepped to the sink. "Not everything can go wrong."

He cranked open the tap. Cool, clean water flowed from the faucet. A laugh, hedging toward the hysterical, escaped his lips. He gathered his belongings and locked the door. He drank his fill. He rinsed and filled the jug. And he bathed for the first time in memory. Once clean, he ate and drifted off to sleep.

3

VILE ESCAPE

A resounding crash followed by a siren wail woke him. A shrill voice screamed muffled curses. “Mine. Mine. Mine.”

He bolted upright, catching his head on the underside of the sink. He cursed, grabbed the shovel/crutch and eased the door open.

Where he had been trapped, the smashed ambulance filled the store, doors wide. Before it, a tangled storm of dirty blonde curls rose up and down with each repeated cry and thunk. From behind, her frame seemed famine-stunted at the brink of adolescence.

“Uh... Do you need some help?”

She whipped around, face blood-flecked and eyes wide. A bloodied pipe wrench dripped upon an unrecognizable corpse. She smiled and whispered, “Mine.”

She charged.

He raised the shovel in defense and hesitated.

<Now, my little alar, we don’t hit girls.>

“That’s *got* to be negotiable.”

An instinctual cringe responded to her answering glower.

He bolted into the bathroom, slammed the door and locked it. Something heavy—and probably bloody—hit the door. “My store.”

Another blow struck. “My home.”

Another landed with each wail. "My stuff. Mine. Mine. Mine."

Cracks and dents peppered the wood, none well targeted. He glanced around his temporary refuge. Concrete block supported the wet wall. A quick mental image placed the walk-in refrigerator beyond the left. He swung the shovel at the right. The broken blade carved chunks of drywall and old, yellowed fluff. His blows fell into time with hers. Wide eyes watched him through widening wrench holes. He cursed and swung faster.

The shovel broke through, not to darkness, but light and several low growls. He shoved a chunk still hanging from its paper to one side only to jerk back as canine teeth snapped at his hand.

He growled back, running low on curses.

He turned his back to the door and speared the shovel into the grout lines between concrete blocks. The blade splintered, breaking clear of the handle. Hot pain stroked one cheek.

She giggled.

He thrust the shaft through a hole in the door. "This is the men's room, go away."

She yelped, and something heavy clattered to the ground. He shoved away the immediate surge of guilt and resumed digging through the right wall.

New holes filled with snapping teeth. The shovel collided with one, sending the creature yelping away. The wrench knocked a hole in the door, just shy of the knob. She reached in. He slapped her hand, hard enough to sting his.

He snatched up his bags and threw himself between the wooden frames, exploding into a well-lit storeroom. Loose kibble scattered liberally across the floor slipped under his feet. He caught himself, planting the shovel as a brace. Three dogs snarled from the feet of little miss wrench.

They charged.

Without thinking, the shovel handle spun in his hands and snapped out, striking two of the dogs in their noses. He caught the third's open jaw with the shaft. He shoved it back.

Little miss wrench snatched up an empty glass bottle and hurled it at him. "Don't hurt my puppies."

Behind him, he heard, "My puppies."

He cursed, scanning the storage room while dodging more rapid fire bottles. Bottle-girl snatched up a claw-hammer. He backed away, keeping the dogs at shovel length. "Look, we can all be friends. I have some food and —"

"*My* food."

"Our food, sissy," Bottle-girl said.

He reached around behind, fished out something small and tossed it to the nearest dog. He repeated the toss several times, adding one more for Bottle-girl.

The dog to his right snatched up the yellow sponge cake, biting through the wrapper. It spat the treat out and began to lick at the ground. A second dog sniffed it, pressed its ears back and snarled.

Little miss wrench pressed her way into the room, a new trickle of blood on her upper lip. She hefted the wrench.

He gripped the shaft in both hands. "Look, I don't want to hurt you."

He tensed.

The third dog, ignoring the sponge cake, whined and looked toward an exterior door. The second dog followed its gaze, ears flattening.

A loudspeaker crackled to life with a piercing feedback whine. A robotic voice he'd heard too many times drained the blood from his face. "Citizens of Earth,

"The Welorin Protectorate aren't your enemy. We've come to protect you from the wicked Alistari Empire. Surrender, and you will be sheltered, clothed and fed. Every citizen is vital to the rebuilding of your world. Every worker is valued."

He shot a glance at both girls, realizing in that instant that they weren't twins despite appearances, maybe older and younger sister. He chanced a look at the digital read out on his jump suit's left forearm. He met what he thought was the older girl's eyes. "We have twelve minutes."

"Hard work will be rewarded," the drone continued. "Generous rewards are provided for information leading to the apprehension of lawyers, aerobics instructors or cabbies. These evil puppets of the Alistari have corrupted your system and must be re-educated."

A shiver shot through him. Both girls hissed in unison. He couldn't blame them. Lawyers and aerobics instructors devolved into feasters terrorized wasteland survivors—though no one knew what happened to the cabbies.

"Look, unless you're desperate enough to go surrender to that spider drone, we need to just sit here nice and quiet." He offered what he hoped was a warm smile. "We can continue our homicidal tea party later."

"Mine."

"Right, yours." He checked his chronometer. Ten minutes remained. Fools enjoyed last easy breaths. The wise ran. He flexed his ankle—if able to run. They could hide. The store hadn't been searched—at least before an ambulance had opened it up to the world.

He eased himself toward the door. Dogs turned back to him, lips peeled from their teeth.

"I'm just going to check," he shot glances between the girls, the dogs, and the heavy steel door. He unlocked it and inched it open to peek out.

"Mine!"

She tackled him, driving both of them out the door. Her wrench flashed down, pounding divots in the concrete as she screamed and he dodged side to side. The dogs joined her attack, adding flashing teeth to his troubles while she struck with one hand and pulled at his satchel with her other.

He shoved it at her. "Take it, just be quiet a minute."

She squealed with glee, mumbling, "Mine, mine, mine."

The dogs rushed to her, more interested in her and her rummaging than him. He glanced up the street and let go his pent up breath—empty. He checked his wrist. Seven minutes remained. Maybe they'd been too far away to hear.

He rose to a crouch and checked down another street. The spider drone strolled away across broken streets and crashed vehicles as if its six flanged and bladed limbs strode upon rose petals. Its spherical body swept side to side, dark red eye sockets scanning terrain and reporting back to the real danger.

Did the drone hear her screams? Has it reported us?

He crawled to the store's other corner and looked up the way it'd come.

His heart fell.

Only two or three dozen humans comprised most snatcher teams. So few couldn't search everywhere. They missed people hidden well enough. The enslaved snatchers, bent under the weight of glowing orange collars, often did miss people.

He cursed.

The team coming their way numbered twice the average, and he couldn't spot a single orange glow.

He caught the movement in his peripheral vision, diving to one side and bringing his staff up in defense. The wrench swept into the building side where his head had just been.

"Mine!"

"Stars, shut up!" He pointed. "Don't you see them? They're *all* collarless!"

She blinked up the road, smiled at him and raised her wrench. Her assault drove them more out in the open. He swept her legs from her and considered living with the guilt of braining her just to make her stop. Leaving her unconscious would doom her to being caught and who knew what.

"I don't want to hurt you." He looked up to where the other sister kept the dogs restrained in the storage room doorway. "Either of you, but those are collarless. We have to be quiet, hide, *something*."

Little Miss Wrench rolled back to her feet and charged like a maddened bull. He dodged, knocking her from her feet once more.

"Stop her, damn it," he gritted his teeth. "Those people snatch for the Welorin because they *like* being cruel, like hurting people. Do you have any idea what they'd do to you and your sister? Stars, they'd probably roast your dogs to celebrate your capture."

Miss Bottle eyed the dogs and the snatcher team coming down the road. She shoved thumb and finger into her mouth and made an ear-splitting whistle—practically summoning the snatcher team.

Why aren't they more afraid? Don't they understand?

Wrench girl stopped her assault. She raced toward the door, stopping only to collect the blue satchel, and applied her wrench to a square manhole cover. It squealed from infrequent use but opened until support arms locked it that way.

The satchel went first, followed by Little Miss Wrench. Bottle girl climbed part way into its opening and then grabbed squirming dogs one by one, handing them down.

She paused after the last dog, watching him.

The sewers might provide him escape. The sisters seemed sure it would, or they'd have been more afraid. He'd seen others try sewer entrances for escape only to be yanked downward to who knew what horror.

At least two horrors and three sets of teeth awaited if he followed. He glanced toward the approaching snatchers, weighing his chances.

Bottle girl tossed back her sponge cake and decided for him. She descended, released the braces and closed the sewer entrance behind her.

He scanned the horizons. The fighters had done their job well. Apartment buildings and businesses around him were smoking ruins. There weren't any good hiding places left. He couldn't get far enough away with his ankle.

Three minutes remained.

Vehicles were out, as were dumpsters and blown open storefronts. They were always searched.

Catcalls and laughter rose in the distance. It was such a strange sound these days he glanced over his shoulder.

He rushed into the storage room. Loose kibble stole his footing. He crashed down onto the concrete. He cursed.

His pulse throbbed in his throat, each beat a second lost that might mean his capture.

He crawled back to his feet and locked the steel door behind him. The store had escaped search before, and the ambulance hole probably wasn't visible from ground level. Of course, the girls probably hadn't screamed their heads off the last time a team had passed it.

The gaping hole he'd left in the bathroom drywall displayed the smashed door beyond. If they entered the store, they'd search the cooler. They'd search the pristine men's room, find the back room and him inside it.

There has to be somewhere I can hide.

A horrible thought occurred to him.

<You haven't the balls, little brother.>

His gorge rose.

If he'd had the right clothes, he could've pretended to be a feaster. So many cruel bullies in one place might make them bold enough to attack him anyway, torment a flesh eater like a rabid animal.

He had the knife and shovel handle. He considered picking a defensive position that limited their numerical advantage and making use of them. He'd lose, but he'd fight.

<Or you could man up.>

I'm going to hate myself for this.

4

CAPTURE

He rushed through the wall into the store, casting around for the straws he'd seen earlier but hadn't needed. He grabbed a handful and rushed back to the bathrooms. Rather than turn into the men's, he sucked in a breath and realized how pointless the clean breath really was.

He heard the snatchers near, calling to one another, telling off-color jokes. He heard them tromping on the roof. They'd find a way in, leaving him no choice if he wanted to survive free another day.

He edged around the bloated mutilated flesh, glad trod maggots didn't scream. He unwrapped the straws and wrapped the papers around them to keep them together. He fit them into his mouth and crawled toward the rotting flesh, struggling not to vomit through his breathing tube. Three corpses provided just enough bloated flesh to hide beneath until the snatchers passed.

The thought sent him into convulsions. He spat out the straws and retched.

I can't. Think. Think!

He eyed the door that at any moment might fill with snatchers. He pulled the knife and rushed the door, pushing it partially closed. He pressed the blade to the drywall, laying his index finger along the back of the blade to help cut through the easy-clean plastic wallpaper. He juggled the numbers while he slashed. Assuming the wall the same thickness as the men's room, there ought to be just enough room between frames to squeeze behind the door in a way that no one should fit. The stench and bloated flesh would drive them back. They'd never look.

His knife sliced down and caught on something. He fought through it. A surge of electricity bit into his arm. He jerked back, losing grip on the knife as the lights all went out. A quick glance didn't find the knife, but he'd cut enough. He grabbed the drywall, glanced out the door and threw it into the men's room.

He rushed back behind the door, pressing his shoulders against the old insulation with the shovel handle held in white-knuckled hands.

He reined in ragged breath, trying for slow quiet breathes despite the sweet rot taste assaulting his tongue. Noises came from the store: jokes, curses and smashed who knew what.

He glanced left and saw his own face in reflected shadows.

He closed his eyes and held back the urge to scream.

Stay still or chance it?

He rushed out from cover and cocked the shovel handle back a moment before he realized just how much noise breaking glass might make. No time to debate, he shoved a hand into bloated flesh, dragging a handful writhing with maggots free and hurling it at the mirror.

He ducked back into his hiding place. Footfalls neared. He went still. Disgust and wriggling worms clung to his hand, but he fought the urge to wipe them clear.

A beam of light lit the room. It flashed off the dripping mirror onto the horrid tableau.

A deep chuckle echoed off the tiles. "Somebody tried to have some fun."

A nasal voice answered. "Didn't go well for them, though, did it, Burr?"

"Uncover your nose, Chris. You sound like an idiot," Burr said.

"It stinks."

Burr stepped forward without answering, his light reflecting oddly off of something

"Why would someone leave a knife behind?" Chris asked.

"They were in a hurry," Burr said. "You smell burnt insulation?"

"Over that?" Chris asked.

"Search the place. Someone's hiding."

The teen tensed.

"And check the breakers."

Footsteps trailed away with Chris's voice. "Boss says we've got a hider. Tear the place apart."

Squishing sounds preceded Burr's lowered voice. "Poor slobs. If you're going to take a woman, put enough fear in her that she never thinks to fight back."

The teen's jaw tightened. His hands flexed around the handle. He shifted slowly peering out enough to use the mirror to see Burr.

An enormous dark-skinned man bent over the bodies, one hand sifting through gore and heavy boots crushing maggots. A hunting knife hung from his right hip and some kind of rubber loop from his left.

The lights flickered back on.

A resigned voice filled his memories. *<Unnecessary brutality happens in war sometimes, son. Some men become their darker selves, but a good commander doesn't tolerate such atrocities. Not against women. Not ever.>* A shot followed and then a falling body.

Burr tsked. "Jumped an astromarine, dumb jackasses got what you deserved. Should've clubbed her first," he chuckled, "Or shared with more men."

Heat built up in his chest. *I should club him over the head or use him as leverage to get out of here.*

"Burr, Burr!"

Burr turned.

The teen jerked backward out of sight.

Chris rushed to a halt. "A girl just popped her head out of a manhole."

"Then go get her," Burr said.

"In the sewers?" Chris asked.

"If you're too big a woman to go after her, why did you come tell me?" Burr asked.

"You said if you found out we'd spotted someone but not told you—"

"I'd send you away for re-education," Burr chuckled. "You're safe. No one would believe you're smart enough for a lawyer."

Chris exhaled. "Cool."

"Get her, or we'll find out for sure."

"What?"

"Go."

Chris rushed off.

Burr chuckled. "I hate cowards."

The door whipped from in front of the teen, replaced by Burr's looming bulk. The lost knife came down. He ducked to one side and struck out with the staff. A jab to the face made Burr step back. He struck again at bare chest between sides of a pocketed vest.

"Surrender, maggot-boy, you're not a fighter."

He kicked out, following up with a low swing at Burr's fatigue-covered leg.

Burr took the blow and threw a left-handed haymaker which he barely ducked.

Burr shoved his left into the rubber loop, its copper-studded knuckles sparking blue. He slashed with the knife. A shallow cut burned across the teen's arm. The shovel handle clattered to the ground. He dove after it.

Burr's fist hit him in the shoulder, a subtle shock making it through his jumpsuit.

He grabbed at the flex conduit he'd cut into earlier with one hand and Burr's vest with the other. He yanked the bigger man off balance and thrust bare wires into his chest.

Burr yelped and jerked backward.

He followed the shock with clasped fists to the shoulder, sending Burr into a disoriented turn. He grabbed the staff and slammed Burr with an upward swing.

The big man fell face down into the bloated flesh.

He turned to run. He stopped, swore and traded the handle for his dropped knife. He grabbed Burr by the back of his hair and saved him from drowning in rot. He pressed the blade to Burr's throat and tried to pry off the taser knuckles.

"Should've left me to die, maggot," Burr slurred.

"I can still kill you."

Burr snorted, dislodging a maggot. "You're a coward."

"All I want is left alone."

"Not a chance."

"Why not? Why do the Welorin want us? Why won't they let us live in peace?"

"Don't care. I only know two things," Burr said.

"What's that?"

"Never hesitate to kill someone who wants to hurt you," Burr said. "And always bring backup."

Someone tapped his shoulder. He whipped around. His shovel handle slammed into his face.

Everything went black.

He awoke, head throbbing and wished the world would consider a target other than his skull. He peeled his face from concrete and a puddle his nose suggested he not examine too closely. Wheel-less shopping carts strung together with barbed wire surrounded him and about a dozen other males. Another several corrals filled a supermarket parking lot like moons in orbit of a bizarre modern day Romani caravan.

Shrieks and catcalls punctuated his thoughts. Beneath the resentful glow of a parking lot light over another corral, several men dragged a screaming woman toward the center camp. He pushed himself to his feet. Balance fled. He tumbled, falling hard to his rump.

"For the best." A slim hand behind a nasal tone held him from getting up once more. "Heroes don't last long in the camps."

He forced the hand away and rose again to face an older man, maybe mid-twenties. A head shorter but twice as gaunt, his long, tapered nose looked as badly broken as the taped glasses perched upon it.

"I've heard it said heroes that interfere with their games become the play toy."

"What they're doing is wrong."

He shook his head. "Wrong doesn't really matter anymore. Keep your head down, and you might survive."

"Not him, Marvy," a dark-skinned man drawled. "Burr's got a hard on for that one. That's why he's already collared."

Marvy's thin brows rose. "You're the one that almost killed Burr?"

He didn't answer, reaching up to feel a collar fitted around his throat.

Marvy shook his head. "Got a name for your tombstone, kid?"

He searched his mind, racing faster and faster to find it this time before frustrated anger grew into panic. Sweat dripped from his furrowed forehead.

"It's all right," Marvy said. "You can trust me."

The black man snorted.

Marvy shot him a dirty look. "Shut up, Terrance."

"Ask him where your food is, kid," Terrance said.

"Shut. Up."

Terrance turned back to the others in hushed conversation.

"I can't remember my name," he said.

"Don't pay any attention to that loud mouth," Marvy said. "You can trust me."

He regarded Marvy, just as unsure of him as his own name. The constant struggles to survive after the invasion had left him little time for introspection, but rising fear was all his mental scouring could turn up. Nameless voices plagued him, scolding, accusing and teaching in aching fragments. Through it all, true memory eluded him.

Marvy turned his back. "Fine, be that way."

Blood drained from his face. He shivered. "I really can't remember."

Marvy scrutinized his face. "You can't remember."

"Stars! Why would I lie?"

Marvy cursed. "Just get away from me."

The teen shifted toward Terrance's group.

"Forget it, kid, don't none of us want in on the trouble you're in," Terrance said.

Metal scraped concrete. The others backed away from him, fearful eyes behind him.

Burr marched into the corral, eyes narrowed. A muscled woman in similar fatigues followed with a digital clipboard in hand. She drew a stylus from a bun of dark red hair.

"Name," Burr asked.

The teen looked up, words failing him.

"Says he doesn't remember," Marvy interjected.

Burr turned on Marvy, shoving him backward into the barrier with a thick arm. "Shut up, worm."

Marvy's painful collision with the barbed wire resulted in only a quiet whimper. The small man retreated toward the other prisoners. They shied away from him as they did Burr lest proximity garner Burr's attention.

"Name or pain," Burr demanded.

His thoughts raced, but not fast enough to catch up with his missing memories. His dream sprung to mind. The woman had called him something he knew was and yet wasn't his name.

"Alar," he said.

Pain, starting at his neck, razored its way down his limbs. He jerked and convulsed, limbs contorting.

"You're a liar, maggot," Burr laughed. "You know it, the collar knows it, and now I know it. Lie to me again, I dare you."

The pain waned, leaving him gasping in his own urine. He reached up to feel the collar around his neck. Its clasp design inhibited easy removal by the collared.

"Tell me your name," Burr said.

He tried to remember once more, anything to avoid the pain. A soft beep escaped the collar. It beeped again then again more and more often.

"Tell me your name," Burr said.

The collar beeped and with each beep seemed to tighten more. It squeezed more and more painfully as he searched for his memories. It grew harder to breathe.

"I don't know," he spat, "I can't remember."

The mind-numbing pain didn't hit him, but neither did the collar stop tightening. A rapid beep seemed to thunder in his ears while he failed to inhale.

"He doesn't know," the woman said. "He's not lying."

"Why should I care?" Burr asked.

"You're going to kill him," she said.

Burr spun toward her. "So?"

A flat stare answered his anger. "Dead toys aren't much fun."

Burr smiled. He pulled a remote from his belt and pointed at the teen. The pressure released and he gulped air.

"Occupation," Burr said.

"I don't know," the teen answered.

Burr kicked him in the stomach. It knocked him backward. Barbs poked at his head and shoulders. Burr's huge hands dragged him to his feet. Standing face to face, there was only a half head in height difference, though Burr had double the width.

"I don't like liars," Burr said. He slammed a fist across the teen's face. "Name and occupation."

"You know I'm not lying!"

Burr smiled. "Name and occupation, slave."

He met Burr's smile with an angry glare. "I don't know."

Burr swung again, but the teen's hand shot upward and redirected the blow. Before he knew it, his fist raced toward Burr. He snatched Burr's knife from his belt, ready to repay agony for agony.

The woman's clipboard clattered to the ground. She leapt upon him, fighting to keep the knife from Burr's gut. "Let go of the knife."

He fought her, the collar around his neck tightening.

Burr shoved him off, seeming to swell in size. "Tell me your name and occupation, maggot."

"Maggot," he snapped. "According to you, my name is Maggot."

The collar loosened.

She got her arms around his, holding him in front of Burr.

Burr purpled. "Well, aren't you the little lawyer? Maybe we should send you for re-education."

"Kind of dangerous, isn't it? Using such big words with so little horsepower to move them?" he asked.

The other prisoners gasped.

The teen slipped downward out of the woman's grasp, leaving her to take Burr's blow. More snatchers rushed forward, seizing him.

"He's fast and slippery," she wiped blood from her face. "That's valuable."

Burr leaned down until he was nose to nose with the restrained teen. "You're going to suffer before you join the other lawyers, maggot."

The teen shuddered.

"He's too young to be a lawyer," Marvy said.

All eyes turned on Marvy. He shrank back only to find no others around to hide behind.

"Little weasel's right, Burr," she said. "But he's fast enough to outpace most runners. I say we force him to snatch."

His guts twisted.

Burr studied him. "Doesn't look like you like that idea. This is my camp. I run it. Until you hear different your job is to beg, bow and grovel to me."

"Kind of hard to bow to slime under your boot."

"Jesus, kid, shut up," Marvy gasped.

Burr turned toward Marvy. "Make sure he has a name and occupation for me when I come back."

"Why me?" Marvy asked.

"Cause you want to be his mama, and you might need to remind him when he wakes," Burr turned to the other snatchers. "Hurt him."

5

KINDNESS AND TORTURE

Consciousness returned. Rain pummeled his body, agony a drop at a time. Gummy eyelids resisted opening. He managed one eye open enough to catch a stinging raindrop. He opened it again to find Marvy's challenging glare perched over tin bowls.

"Food?" he mumbled.

Marvy scooped the last spoon from the top bowl and tipped both over for him to see. "Gone."

"So hungry," he moaned.

Marvy tossed one of the bowls, knocking him in the head. "Too damned bad. Weren't awake to eat anyway."

Bitter rain wetted his lips, burning his questing tongue. He tried to wipe his face, but his arm refused to move. "Can't move my arm. Hurt."

"Dislocated," Marvy said. "You got a name yet?"

"No."

"Best pass out again," Marvy said. "Or better yet die."

"What'd I do to you?"

"I'm stuck here, you little shit. I should've moved on to a training facility, but Burr won't let me go until you've got a name."

"Can you fix my arm?"

"Remember your name?"

The teen glared at Marvy through the one opened eye.

He spent the night trading pain for dreams of a bag full of food and a clean bathroom. Unremembered voices encouraged him to rise or die in turns. The corral opened, waking him from a feast and letting new prisoners enter. He glanced at Marvy to find two bowls in the man's lap.

"He got a name yet, worm?" a snatcher asked.

"Still out," Marvy said.

Footsteps approached. A boot slammed into his gut. "Wake up, maggot."

He opened one eye and looked up at Chris.

"Got a name yet?" Chris asked.

"Maggot," he mumbled.

Another boot caught him, then another. "Don't know why Burr doesn't just kill you."

He curled into as tight a ball as he could, protecting his head with his one good arm.

Footsteps retreated. Carts dragged across the concrete back into place.

"You okay, kid?"

"Leave him alone," Marvy said.

"He's hurt."

"It's his own fault," Marvy said. "Stay clear if you value your skin."

The unknown man fell silent.

The teen hid from pain in dreams until activity woke him. The woman with the clipboard handed food over the fence to the prisoners. Marvy took a second bowl and walked toward him. His stomach ached. He couldn't remember the last time he'd eaten. He tried to push himself up, managing one elbow.

Marvy stepped over him, settling at the edge of the corral far out of reach.

"That's the kid's."

Marvy snorted and shoved food into his mouth.

The other man strode into view. Tall, fair haired but not muscular, he glared through cracked glasses. "Give him his food."

Marvy smirked. "Give who his food?"

"The kid."

"The lump gets food when he's got a name," Marvy said.

"He's got a name."

"Really?" Marvy said. "What is it?"

Behind the bespectacled man, the snatcher watched in silence. The stranger shifted to lower himself and his food toward the teen.

"Stop," she said. "Marvy's his nursemaid until Burr says otherwise."

He turned to her. "He's hurt. The body needs food—"

"Only useful slaves get food," she said.

"He doesn't look strong enough to do anything. When was the last time he ate?"

"Who are you?" She said. "Name and occupation."

"Lane Oswald. I'm a third-year resident," Lane said.

She cooed. "You'll be very valuable. Begging the *doctor's* pardon, but he's just lazy."

"How can you say that," Lane said. "I doubt he could even sit up unassisted."

"Sure he can. Hey, maggot, I order you to sit up."

The teen struggled to rise. Despite his obedience, the collar's beeping started. He pushed up with one rubbery arm. He fell forward. The fall struck his dislocated shoulder. He cried out. The beeps accelerated.

Lane's footfalls neared, brought up short by the woman's sharp. "No."

He pushed up again. The collar tightened, little jolts of pain prodded his obedience. He struggled further. He gasped for breath, eyes screwed up as he fought to obey.

He made it.

"Good boy, maggot, good boy, sit. Now speak," she laughed.

His voice cracked. "What do you—"

"No," she said. "Speak like a good dog, maggot."

"What kind of monster are you?" Lane asked.

She whistled, summoning half a dozen snatchers. "Speak, Maggot."

The collar tightened around his neck.

The first snatcher shoved the corral open. "We get to beat the smartass again?"

"Not if he barks," she said.

"Then why'd you call us over, Silv?" another asked.

"Hurt the nice doctor, just body, nothing permanent," she said.

"What?" Lane said.

"Told you," Marvy said.

Snatchers grabbed Lane, lining up like he was a heavy bag for their workout.

Pain increased around the teen's neck.

"I command you to bark, maggot," Silv said.

The teen let out a weak bark.

"You can do better than that," She said. "Bark like a big dog."

He barked and begged and rolled over while they beat Lane, the only one who'd tried to help since his capture. When the snatchers got bored waiting for their turn at Lane, they beat him.

A hand shook him.

"Leave me alone," he moaned. "I don't want to destroy the world."

"Good to hear," Lane said. "Sit up."

Lane helped him to a seated position and handed him a smashed hunk of bread and meat.

He looked around, finding only the gleam of Marvy's dark eyes open and watching them. "Why're you doing this?"

Lane shrugged, wincing. "You need to eat."

"They hurt you because of me."

"No, they hurt me because they're monsters. Please, eat."

He fell on the food. Smashed, cold and globbed with congealed fat, he'd never tasted anything so good.

Lane poked and prodded him, touching with careful motions. "Slow down, you don't want to choke."

"Left shoulder's dislocated," he said through a full mouth. "I think they cracked two ribs on that side too."

Lane pushed, and he winced. "Good diagnosis. Had cracked ribs before?"

"I don't think so."

"So you really don't remember your name?" Lane asked.

He shook his head. "Concussion—couple of them."

"How long since you could remember?" Lane asked.

"Before the invasion."

Lane clasped his good shoulder gently. "It'll come back, be patient."

His fears tumbled out of his mouth. "What if it doesn't? What if I never know who I am?"

Lane smirked and took hold of the dislocated arm. "You'll just have to go around telling people you're a maggot. Relax, this is going to hurt."

It did.

6

BURR'S VENGEANCE

Marvy squealed to Chris the next day at breakfast. The snatchers beat Lane again while Marvy made off with three meals.

The teen struggled to his feet and stumbled to a standing position over Marvy. Fists balled and wobbling, he glared down at Marvy. "Give that back."

"Got a name?" Marvy asked.

He glared.

"Starve then," Marvy said.

The teen stepped closer. "Give me my food."

Marvy kicked out with one leg, sending him to the ground. "Oops."

Snatchers laughed.

He struggled back to his feet. "Give me back my food."

The teen stomped at Marvy's crotch. Before he landed the blow, Marvy swept his other leg. Marvy jumped him, slamming an empty bowl into his face. "You're nothing, kid, compared to my lifetime's bullies."

He swung at Marvy, hitting the man on the side of the head but without much force. Marvy hit him with the bowl once more.

"Why the hell is there a free-for-all in *my* camp?" Burr said.

"He keeps stealing my food," the teen said.

"You got a name, maggot?" Burr asked.

"No."

"Then you don't get to speak," Burr said. "Marvy, who told you to eat the maggot's food?"

"He didn't need it," Marvy said.

"He needs to eat to heal," Lane said.

"Seems he and the doctor think different," Burr said.

Marvy snorted.

Burr's eyes narrowed. "You not taking me seriously, worm?"

"N-no, Burr, that wasn't meant for you—"

"Who said you could use my name?" Burr asked. "Since when are we besties?"

"I-I...I'm sorry, sir," Marvy said.

"You interrupt my breakfast, play with my toys, think we're girlfriends, and all you can say is sorry?" Burr asked.

Marvy's mouth moved, but either fear kept him from answering or uncertainty.

"And who fixed maggot's shoulder?" Burr asked.

Words raced through the teen's mind, ordering and reordering until they formed the sentence he blurted. "Marvy told Chris that Lane did it so he could steal his food too, but that's not right."

Burr watched him, eyes narrowed.

"He's lying," Marvy said.

The teen tensed, concentrating on exactly what he'd said.

"Collar doesn't seem to think so," Burr said. "You trying to play us, worm?"

"N-no, Burr, I mean, sir, I d-did rat him out for fixing the maggot and feeding him too. I wanted the extra food, but I didn't fix his arm," Marvy said.

"He feed you?" Burr asked.

The teen nodded.

"He needed it," Lane said between blows. "Marvy was starving him."

Burr scrutinized Marvy. "You're looking a bit plump, worm. Your methods for getting the maggot to remember obviously suck. Maybe it's time you moved on to your next job."

Marvy smiled uncertainly.

"Starving him won't help him remember," Lane said. "Amnesia takes time to heal even for a healthy patient."

Burr glared. "Shut up, *Doctor*, before I have you re-educated as a lawyer like the maggot."

"Burr," Chris said. "The bonus for physicians—"

"I know." Burr chuckled. "Boys take the worm back to our camp so we can get him cooking on his new occupation."

Burr held him up by the formerly dislocated arm and began slapping his wounds with a malicious grin. "Got a name?"

Tears crept down his cheeks. He whimpered and shook his head.

"No name? What about some skill? No?" Burr dropped the teen like a stringless marionette and crouched down. "You know how they re-educate lawyers, maggot? They break them through torture, starvation, special experiments—kind of like what we've been doing to prepare you.

"Once their natural tendencies have been amplified and they want to eat anyone not in a suit or leotard, they're put into a suit and let go," Burr smiled. "What size suit do you wear?"

"I don't know."

"Leave him alone," Lane said.

"Doctor wants to help you," Burr smiled at Lane. "He will, in time. He might've been your first power lunch, maggot, if he weren't so valuable otherwise. Silv's right, you're quick and slippery. I'll bet you'll get quite a few survivors once trained. You'll be like an urban legend, chowing down on so many others that they'll come running into our arms and make me an overlord, just like they promised."

"Why're you telling me this?"

"Career guidance," Burr laughed. "Now, maggot, I want a name."

"Burr, Maggotlord, Prince of Corpse Kissing."

Burr purpled. "Tell me your real name."

He struggled to remember for the thousandth time, but no name came to him. He could just see the orange light from the collar glowing continuously brighter which each more rapid beep. It tightened. Pain struck his neck, growing like a rising heat until he wasn't sure whether it'd pop his head from his neck or burn through it first.

"Reset collar."

The pain fell away, leaving an almost icy tingling in his skin.

"Tell me your name."

He repeated the command over and over for what seemed like hours. Every few times Burr paced around his gasping body, regaling him with horrible futures in gleeful tones. Again and again, he threatened re-education but seemed in no hurry to send away his toy.

Finally, the questions ended. Cold and lingering pain seized him. The teen shook.

"Rest up, maggot. You'll need your strength to survive re-education."

Silv returned at lunch time with a bowl for everyone but the teen. She watched the prisoners eat like a cat fattening up mice.

Once all the food was eaten, she departed. Heavenly smells wafted from the center camp. Every stomach gurgled, but none so violently as his.

Bowls of stew arrived just before sunset, one for each prisoner except him.

"The kid needs to eat," Lane said.

"I know that, doctor." Burr strode through his men with a smirk and a platter of steak. "I've got his right here."

The snatchers snickered.

"Come here, maggot," Burr said.

He struggled to his feet, the collar beeping then quieting as he stepped forward. He eyed the steak, juice pooling beneath the steaming meat. He reached out, unsure if Burr might snatch it away. His stomach threatened open warfare if Burr pulled it from him after offering it.

"You'll eat this with your hands, maggot," Burr said. "I know better than to offer you another knife."

He nodded, took the plate and darted to a sitting position a few feet from Burr. He fell on the heavenly meat, barely bothering to chew.

"I order you to eat every bite," Burr said.

Snatchers chuckled.

He looked up, brows furrowed at the strangely kind order. He ate more, chewing more slowly as the group of snatchers grinned at him.

"Can I share it with the others?" he asked.

The other prisoners brightened.

"No," Burr said. "This is special, just for you."

His stomach whimpered under the sudden heavy load. His mouth ignored its objections, chewing savory, juicy bite after bite. Even the watching snatchers faded to the feast. At last, he forked in the last mouthful. Pain and stuffed satisfaction filled his gut. He licked every last drop of juice from the plate.

"Care for some more?" Burr asked.

He blinked up at the snatcher. "No, sir, I couldn't eat another bite."

Chuckles erupted behind Burr.

"You sure?" Burr asked. "There's plenty of Marvy left."

He stared at Burr.

He's screwing with me.

<You know he's not.>

Chuckles turned to laughter.

"Good plan, maggot," Chris said, "Fattening up old Marvy with your meals."

"No."

Burr grinned, eyes locked on the teen's reaction as if something primal in him fed on it.

I'm a cannibal.

<Enjoyed it too, didn't you, runt, licked the plate clean.>

"What kind of monsters are you people?" Lane asked.

He didn't make it all the way over before chunks of Marvy spewed from his mouth onto jumpsuit and ground. His gut heaved and spasmed, disgorging everything he'd poorly chewed to chorused laughter.

He lay on the concrete heaving and gasping, stomach sending little aftershocks to rid itself of the greasy little man. Empty, raw and feeling oddly soiled to his core he looked up from the puddle to Burr's smile.

"Food is precious, counselor," Burr pointed the collar remote at the vomit. "Eat it, all of it."

Lane rushed between them. "You can't do that. You can't force a human being to eat vomit."

Burr glared. "I can force him to do anything I want. I'm in control."

He stared at the vomit, orange glow and soft beeping forewarning of pain if he didn't do what Burr wanted.

Pain sparked.

The beeps sped up.

The collar tightened.

"But why? Do you know the damage you could do to him? What did he ever do to you that warrants this?" Lane asked.

Burr's eyes narrowed. "I don't need a reason."

The teen looked up, choking out an answer through his squeezed airway. "I beat him."

Burr's calm anger exploded into ravening fury.

"Liar! You never beat me." Burr clicked the remote with thrusting motions, each blast of pain savaged the teen in time with one of his stabs. "I'm in control. I own you. Eat the vomit, maggot, tell me your name."

The collar sent him into violent convulsions all the while beeping, squeezing, demanding he obey.

Lane tackled Burr, grabbing for the remote. The snatchers seized him, pummeling the doctor from all angles. The extra jolts of pain stopped.

Burr kicked Lane's pinned body. "Beat some respect into the doctor, then collar him. He's going to help Marvy strengthen up our lawyer-wannabe so he can snatch before he's re-educated."

The teen bent down, body shaking and licked up a chunk of Marvy. The acid burned worse going down than it had coming up.

"Maggot," the collar loosened, he drew in a ragged breath and rasped, "and I'll get this damned collar off and beat you again once and for all."

Chris shoved a plate into Lane's hand. "Make the maggot eat it all."

Lane tensed, glaring at Chris as his collar brightened.

The others shied away from Lane, keeping distance between themselves and the two troublemakers.

He wanted to help Lane, but he didn't know how.

"Didn't you say he needs to eat, *doctor?*" Chris thumbed the remote, sending Lane to his knees in pain. "Obey or die."

Lane dumped the plate on the ground, seizing his throat.

Chris scowled, forcing the corral open. He snatched up the plate and shoved it into the teen's hand. "I order you to eat every bite."

He threw the plate away as if it were a bomb. It careened off a shopping cart, spilling its contents.

"I'd rather die."

The collar reacted at once, pain burning upward in crescendo. He fought the pain. He resisted as hard as he could, but every measure he surpassed was replaced by more.

Chris pointed at the doctor writhing on the ground, gasping like a landed fish. "Going to murder your friend rather than eat the worm that starved you? Even after the beating he took trying to help you?"

<If he wants to disobey and die it's not our business.>

He helped me.

<His choice.>

He crawled onto unsteady feet, dizzy from the tightening collar. "Stop hurting him, and I'll eat it."

Burr strode up behind Chris. "You'll eat it anyway. Don't pretend you don't crave human flesh."

"Won't," Lane gasped. "Kill. Me."

Burr chuckled. "Sure?"

Pain strangled him. He shuffled across the pen to the spilled meat, the collar loosening as he moved to obey. He snatched the meat and raised it to his mouth. His arms shook. Nausea tightened his stomach and bile rose in the back of his throat.

He took a bite of warm meat that tasted like ashes. The collar loosened. He chewed in a rush and swallowed. "I'm eating, so he's obeying. Reset his collar. Please."

Burr darkened.

A change came over his expression that sent a hockey team skating up and down his spine.

"As long as you obey."

He took another bite of Marvy.

Lane's collar darkened. His spasms stopped, leaving him lying in a puddle.

The teen took a deep breath followed by another bite of Marvy. He eyed the other prisoners. Disgust and fear shrouded the gazes flitting between him and the ground.

"Eat up, counselor," Burr said. "The team ought to be back soon with new refugees."

He watched Burr's retreat.

What does he mean by that?

Burr and Chris brought a new group to their corral just before dinner. Fear haunted their gaunt expressions. Burr grabbed one by the shoulder. He flinched, jerking away from the snatcher and taking a fighting pose.

"This one's a scrapper," Burr said. "Teach him what happens to scrappers, maggot."

He stared at Burr. "What do you mean?"

"Beat him."

The teen looked at the other man. The older but thinner man shot fearful eyes toward him then the snatchers and back.

He opened his mouth to object, his collar already attacking him when Lane screamed. He whirled to see the doctor on the ground in throws of agony, collar lit like the sun.

Burr's smile told all he needed to know.

It won't just be me anymore who gets punished.

<He's got your number, little brother. Either change your priorities or be his bitch.>

It's my fault Lane's being hurt.

Another voice entered the argument. *<A man is responsible for what he can and cannot do, son, no more, no less.>*

"Now, maggot."

<Lane helped you, you don't know this man.>

I don't have any reason to hate him.

<Not hate, survival, runt.>

A smile flickered over his lips. He jumped the other man, hooking the other man's leg. They went down in a sprawl. The other man slammed him in the jaw with a fist. The teen elbowed him, driving the breath from his body.

"I'll pull my punches if you do," he whispered. "We just have to make it look good."

The other man's eyes widened. He nodded slightly and punched the teen in the stomach with only half the force of the earlier hit. They fought to a standstill, the teen finally crawling off the unconscious man.

He checked Lane first, out cold but no longer in pain. He looked to Burr to find the snatcher's eyes narrowed.

"Dinner!" Silv said.

The other prisoners brightened. One of the new refugee's grabbed for the plate of steak, but she whisked it from reach. "Oh, no, this is for our little counselor."

"Why the hell does he get special treatment?" the man asked.

Burr turned his smile on the new man. "You like eating your fellow prisoners too?"

7

FREEDOM

Days of torture and nights filled with slowly-rotting roasted Marvy filled his existence. In addition to his meals, the collar forced him to beat newcomers. Some pulled their punches, but others fought for their lives.

Burr press-ganged him onto the snatcher teams. Burr came by for his name infrequently, busied by unknown troubles that prodded sharp retorts audible throughout the parking lot. With Burr focused elsewhere, his missing name no longer featured in nightmares of half-rotted, half-eaten Marvy glaring at him as he chewed on the man.

Waking moments were nightmare enough on their own. His true self slipped farther from him every day, anchored by fading voices as the collar forced him into more and more horrors. His experience with the collar explained the ineffective efforts of the other collared snatchers.

Chris and Silv kept him on a tighter leash, eager to punish and delighted to send him running barefoot through the wastes after someone fleeing capture. Chris forced him to worm into unsafe buildings, through sewer pipes, and under destroyed vehicles. Silv treated him like a dog, making him run down survivors like prey and then bark when he caught one.

Prey for the snatcher teams grew fewer and fewer. They exhausted the supplies in the grocery store before they did prey.

They moved to a new store parking lot to expand their territory. Burr sent what was left of Lane away when they moved, replacing him with a pair of boys not even into their adolescence. He forced the teen to carry what remained of Marvy on his back.

He didn't know what fate awaited Lane or those that were relocated from the snatcher camps. Part of him feared the knowledge. He clung to hope like a lifeline that those he caught and sometimes beat went to better places.

Couldn't be worse than suffering under Burr.

The things he overheard encouraged him for Lane's sake, but Burr wouldn't send him away to any place better.

His thoughts dwelt on Lane as he stared from the back of a hovertruck, massaging bruised feet. To his right, an apartment building soared several stories. Its face sheered away by Welorin weapons, it resembled a life-sized doll house complete with charred furnishings. The bottom level housed a feaster camp, but the cannibals eyed them in queer silence without attacking.

Something Burr has on the truck keeping them at bay?

It didn't feel right. Human remains haloed all but the newest feaster camps, but he saw none.

A snatcher named Phillip called back toward the truck, "Maybe you can come back after your re-education and have a power lunch with them, eh, counselor?"

The others laughed, though less than they had when such taunts had been new.

"You should join us," he replied. "We'll all enjoy a nice chat, chew the fathead as it were."

Chris darkened. "Tell me your name, counselor."

Pain came from the collar almost at once. It dropped the teen from his perch on the truck. He collapsed to his knees gasping for breath.

Chris tossed Phillip the remote. "Don't keep him thinking too long. I want him ready for a chase."

Phillip pulled on a cigarette, watching him writhe and gasp. He lit and finished a second before he reset the collar.

Chris strode up to the feasters without the slightest appearance of fear. "I demand a writ of halibut corpus!"

Silence.

"Mistrial!" Chris shouted. "I'll have you all disbarred."

More silence.

"Fakers," Chris said. "Catch them all."

The feasters bolted, and snatchers chased.

"Hey, counselor, I order you to..." He scanned the upper floor.

The teen narrowed his eyes. Movement flitted across the top level.

"Up there, maggot," Chris tossed a coiled rope at him. "Get them."

He scrambled up the broken wall, exposed rebar enabling his climb. A dresser drawer fell out of nowhere. He swung from its path, his fingers slipping from the rough metal bar. He caught several pipes in his side but managed a hold that prevented a twenty-foot fall. He hung from an old water pipe, hands slick with sweat and breath ragged.

"Get moving," Chris said. "Get up there and toss down the rope ladder."

He struggled to regain a climbing position before the increasingly temperamental collar brought pain to bear. Several stories and none-too-few close calls later, he secured the ladder to a heavy oak bedstead piled with debris.

He'd literally tossed the rope ladder down from a building once and secured it poorly another time sending a snatcher back to camp broken and concussed.

Burr made sure he never repeated either.

Chris's weight pulled the ladder taut. The bedstead remained in place and the rope secure.

He turned toward the inner building and his ordered hunt. He found a worm way and squeezed through it. Furniture blocked the discovered hall in too organized an arrangement. He shifted furniture and debris. The building groaned. He paused long enough to catch a breath and for the collar to start its beeps. He squeezed through just before Chris climbed onto the top floor.

Three people huddled in an otherwise intact room. A boy his age stood in front of a freestanding mirror, shotgun in hand. Behind the young guard, a young woman shielded their ailing mother with her body—a body Chris and the other snatchers would enjoy at her expense.

He cursed.

I can't let them.

<There's no time to let them go.>

Chris's reflection squeezed into sight. His eyes swept the tableau. A cruel smile grew across his face. His reflection pointed forward. "Seize the shotgun, counselor. Kill him, but don't hurt the women yet."

He glanced over his shoulder. "Burr said," he licked his lips, trying to wash the bad taste of his next words, "not to waste prey."

Chris' smile worsened. He pointed the remote. "We're not going to waste them. I order you not to tell Burr."

He hesitated, looking at Chris's pointing reflection.

"Do it, now."

<Attacking someone holding a scatter weapon in close quarters is a losing proposition, young master. Don't close with such an adversary, but attack from a distance.>

Suicidal is a better phrase.

Fighting his own desire to save the family while trying to disarm and kill the frightened boy didn't seem like a winning strategy. He glanced back at Chris's reflection, his absently pointing finger, and hungry grin.

The collar tightened.

Killing is wrong.

Pain shot through him.

I'm not a killer.

<Sometimes a man has to make unpleasant choices to survive.>

"I won't."

Shock spread across every face. In that moment, he sprang forward. He seized the shotgun, shoving its barrel upward as it went off. He wrenched it free.

"Don't catch the women in the blast," Chris said.

He chambered a new round and shoved the boy down to give himself a clearer shot. "Not a problem."

He spun, swung the shotgun barrel toward Chris's neck and shoulders and squeezed the trigger. He didn't think. He chambered round after round until no new ones came forward to shred Chris. Blood dripped from every surface, some splashing into his mouth. The vile taste suited Chris.

"But, the collar," the sister said.

He checked his bloody reflection. The collar lights glowed lazily like a sunning panther with no indication it intended to pounce.

He snatched up the remote from Chris's remains, wiping it on his pants. "Careless pointing and word choice."

"You some kind of lawyer?" the boy asked.

His chuckle felt rough after so much time. He offered them the remote. "Please. Order me to remove the collar."

"Why should we?" the boy snatched the remote before his sister could take it. "With this we control you."

He tensed, hands tightening on the spent shotgun. "I just saved you."

"So what? You serve us now."

Words managed their way through his clenched jaw. "I won't be enslaved again. Not ever."

The sick woman rasped a mother's tone. "Nathan."

Nathan flinched.

"Give me the remote," she said.

"No," Nathan said. "We own him now. He's ours to fetch food and guard and whatever we want."

"He helped us," his sister said.

"He helped himself," Nathan said.

"Na-" his mother devolved into coughing spasms.

Nathan pointed the remote at him. "I order you not to take off your collar."

He inclined his head. "Yes, master."

Nathan beamed. "See, now we—"

He stepped in under Nathan's guard, grabbed Nathan's head and slammed it into a colliding knee.

The girl screamed.

His forearm clubbed upside Nathan's head. He stomped the arm holding the remote.

Nathan opened his mouth, but a descending fist aborted any order he'd intended. He snatched the remote from Nathan's grip and glowered at the dazed boy.

"Never again. I will not be forced to..." his gorge rose, but he forced it down. "I'll never be compelled to do someone else's bidding. I won't be owned."

He closed his eyes, reining himself in and handed the remote to Nathan's sister. "Please, tell me to remove the collar."

Her gaze flitted between him, Nathan and the remote. "Remove the collar."

"Thank you." His fingers scrabbled at the clasp. Try as he might, he couldn't find the right angle to work the mechanism.

She stepped toward him.

He tensed, jerking from reach.

"I just wanted to help," she said.

He took in her hurt expression and guilt hit him at once. He apologized to the floor. "Sorry."

She smiled and reached for the collar.

His gut squirmed. Rough but gentle hands fumbled at his collar. The tip of her tongue emerged while she fiddled with it. A pretty face lurked beneath concentration and weeks of muck.

"Sorry I hurt your brother."

She smiled at him.

Warmth rose to his face.

I can't let Burr anywhere near her...them.

"You shouldn't hide in one place. Chris didn't have a gun, so they probably figure the gunshots killed us both."

She stopped working to meet his eyes. "Then they'll know to stay away."

"They'll bring a spider drone here, and I used all of your shells." He chewed his lip. "Sorry."

"We've got more shells, but we can't move mama." She pulled the collar from his neck. "There."

His hand went to its place at once, rubbing the feeling of it away. "Thank you."

He bent over Chris's remains, tugging stumps from his boots. She offered collar and remote. He hesitated but accepted both. He looked from daughter to mother.

"Is there anything I can do?"

Matching smiles answered.

"You could take my children with you," the mother rasped. The girl opened her mouth, but her mother's hand forestalled her. "But they'd refuse to go."

"Especially after I hit one of them."

A soft chuckle escaped the mother. "Can I...uh, help clean up or something?"

"Go with God, boy. Be safe."

He turned toward the door.

"Wait," the young woman said. "I'm Sarah. Do you have a name?"

He flinched, not turning around. "No."

"Good luck anyway," she said.

He disappeared back into the hallway. He shifted more furniture, this time blocking the path to their secluded hall. He found a backless cupboard which proved tunnel to the stairwell, descending until he found it completely collapsed. A debris pile on the back of the second floor offered him escape. The streets seemed clear—either the snatchers were still chasing fake lawyers or they were trying to scale the building's other side.

Crap, the rope, but it's too late to go back for it.

He raced across the ruin, stopping just inside the next alley to look back up at the building.

I hope if Burr finds them Nathan gives him a face full of shot.

He made it only a block before more of the snatcher group came into view.

He paused, panting. "Uh, Keith, you see where she ran?"

Keith shook his head.

He cursed. "She shot Chris. Burr's going to kill me if I let her get away."

"Then get moving, maggot."

He bolted.

A horrible thought sent stabs through his gut.

If he'd noticed I wasn't wearing the collar, I'd be caught again. That was stupid.

It took patience and plenty of luck to escape the area without getting spotted again. Several close calls left his nerves strained to their limits. He huddled in an overturned dumpster beneath a dispirited solar street light as night fell. Using an assortment of apocalyptic debris, mostly featuring lost keys, he managed to rig the collar so that it would close without locking.

He turned it over in his hands, glaring at the hateful thing that'd tortured him into doing horrible acts. Aversion wasn't a strong enough word to describe how vehemently he didn't want to slip it back around his neck.

But it might be just enough to convince another snatcher team I'm already caught.

He opened the jimmied latch and raised it to his neck. His hands shook. He half expected the condescending voice to berate him, but his disembodied past remained quieter and quieter.

He bit his lip and forced it back into place. The clasp clicked. Panic seized him. He wrenched it from his neck and threw it.

Once his breathing slowed, he reclaimed the collar and put it on once more. The click sent his body rigid, but a quick check proved the clasp still unlocked.

When sleep finally claimed him, it proved short-lived. His nightmares replayed the day, waking him with Chris's murder each time he managed sleep once more.

8

DOGGED THROUGH THE RUINS

He made his way through ruins, following the ghostly light traversing the sky. Wasted civilization spread out without end. Gaping storefronts illuminated by burning piles of their merchandise lined the cluttered and ominously empty streets. His time with Burr had its benefits. He spotted the occasional face peering from hiding, angrier than popping and hissing flames.

He'd learned better how snatcher teams moved, their best tactics, and how they worked with the Welorin spider drones. He'd picked up hints about the feasters too. He'd gained an eye for worm ways, false rubble, and survivor booby-traps. In some respects, his confidence in the wasteland grew, though the ever-present shadow of the collar at his neck kept fear a close companion.

Hair stood double shifts, guarding his neck in ordered rows.

His new knowledge made eluding feasters and snatchers in new neighborhoods easier—though it didn't account for those that appeared in his wake. Drones dogged him. Snatcher teams appeared where they shouldn't. Fighters flew odd flightpaths.

Or I've gone crazy paranoid.

He traveled west, always west, searching but not sure for what. He skirted other survivors, staying safe from those that might do him harm at the cost of possible help or companionship.

He prowled through neighborhoods lined with buildings reminiscent of a monster's jagged teeth. Burned out vehicles, dragged into clusters, served as blockades or shelters.

The islands of desperation centered in supermarket parking lots grew fewer, farther between but larger. Spider drones and a roughly wedge-shaped vehicle three times the drones' size rested idly in their midst. Snatchers guarded only their corrals, leaving the outer borders open for any willing to stumble into captivity.

He glanced behind. Glowing umber reached around broken skyline like a fiery halo. He'd forged through the night, nightmares and hunger preventing sleep. He scanned clustered ruins for a place to hide before it stole shadows from him.

He edged his head out of the worm way, checking the street for snatchers or worse. His stomach grumbled. The newer apartment building had suffered little damage, but its occupants or later looters had cleaned out the few rented spaces. The less desolated area had offered hope with a double handful of anxiety.

He crawled the rest of the way out. Opposite the apartment a brick and glass office building squatted with only one upper corner blasted away. A half-melted playground separated both it and the apartments from a forbidding looking grey building.

A police station and adjoining crater-shaped parking lots took over the next several blocks. New materials of dismal grey stood three stories, tiny barred windows overlooked one of its vehicle graveyards.

He crouched behind a brick half wall and watched.

Nothing moved.

Nothing explained the tingle tap dancing through his nerves.

A police station might have food for prisoners, weapons, ammunition, even body armor. Despite that, the prime target looked unmolested excepting laser damage and a melted black and white teetering in the wind on its roof.

He checked the street once more.

No one.

He crossed the street in short spurts, rushing from cover to cover until he crouched beneath a directory sign just inside the office building's lobby.

Inside the damage became more apparent. The detritus of fleeing lives littered its tiles around those that never escaped. The stench differed from the convenience store bathroom. Open to the elements, it lingered only as a slightly cloying sweetness at the back of his tongue. Darkness swallowed the building's interior the further away from the windows he peered.

Just enough light slipped inside to scan the directory through squinted eyes.

2nd Floor: Heartlock, Trotter and Strike, Attorneys at Law.

He tensed.

Feasters explained much of what bothered him about the area.

Just my luck I...

His eyes fell upon the next section.

4th Floor: Suite Sweat, Executive Gym and Juice Bar.

No. There's no way my luck is that bad.

"Citizens of Earth."

He jumped, head jerking side to side in search of the sound.

"The Welorin Protectorate aren't your enemy. We've come to protect you from the wicked Alistari Empire."

A spider drone marched across the building's front.

"Surrender and you will be sheltered, clothed and fed. Every citizen is vital to the rebuilding of your world. Every worker is valued."

He knocked his fist against his head several times. "Not fair, not even close to fair."

He scanned the directory again. Two more law firms, miscellaneous businesses, and an Internal Revenue Service branch office populated its list.

"Hard work will be rewarded. Generous rewards are provided for information leading to the apprehension of lawyers, aerobics instructors or cabbies."

Up or out?

Hungry but in reasonable shape, he could run or hide. Snatchers might not search a building with so many possible feasters.

And I'm thinking about going right up into it.

"These evil puppets of the Alistari have corrupted your system—"

BOOM!

He jerked around to see pieces of spider drone launch airborne. His ears rang, almost sounding like screams for a brief moment.

He blinked.

He couldn't be seeing what he saw.

A ragged band rushed from the police station garbed in orange jumpsuits and flak vests. They hit the broken drone chunks with pipes, bats, and nail-spiked boards.

He stared at them, watched as they hooted and cheered around the destroyed drone.

He rose.

The hair on his neck rose, tried to yank itself free and run.

Another yell arose from the drone's back trail. A dozen men charged into view, their collars gleaming orange. At least ten flatbed hover trucks followed in their wake, loaded with prisoners and led by collarless snatchers.

His breath froze in his lungs. *Burr, that's Burr.*

A wedge-shaped vehicle three times the spider drones' size hovered on either side of him. Their metallic daffodil surface parted, revealing several deep violet crystalline shapes he didn't understand—at least until energy lanced from them to obliterate several attackers and a swath of street.

The refugees bolted, running a dozen pathways back toward the police station.

Another lance quartered their number.

Burr has tanks, Welorin tanks.

He glanced at the directory. "Screw it, my luck can't possibly be that bad."

9

NO ESCAPE

He raced into the shadows, scanning for the inevitable stair-well door. He yanked four times before it opened enough for him to squeeze through—heartening even if it did leave his heart racing in his ears. He yanked it closed, hoping the yelling and blasting outside muffled its slam.

He raced up to the fifth floor, stopping long enough for breath and to squint through the door's rectangular window at the darkness beyond.

He inched open the door.

He sniffed.

Something dead lingered in the air.

Strong enough for a feaster camp?

He crept out, ears straining for sounds.

BOOM!

He leapt back into the stairwell.

Outside, stupid.

He slid onto the floor once more. Soft carpet muffled his footfalls. Light colored walls barely visible to his adjusted eyes slid in either direction.

Something crunched under foot. He froze.

Please don't be bones, please don't be bones.

A pair of racquetball goggles lay beneath his shifted foot.

He let out the breath he'd been holding.

BOOM!

Whatever's going on, I hope they beat Burr.

He stalked further down the hall, turning with it. A crouching figure shifted into view.

He leapt back around the corner, assuming a fighting stance.

Nothing made a sound.

No one followed him around the corner.

He lay flat on the carpet and peeked.

No one crouched in wait, but something's head lay just beyond the glass doors.

He retreated back around the corner, regained his feet and stalked forward ready for a fight. Turning the corner, the other person leapt into view in a fighting stance. He rushed them, meeting their charge.

He slammed into thick mirrored glass doors with a *thwoong* and cursed the air blue.

Back on his feet, he opened the heavy door and peered into the gym. Darker shadows filled dim darkness accompanied by the faint scent of rotted meat, but nothing moved.

He rushed through to the other side, peering through the slats of heavy blinds. Outside, Burr and the snatchers took cover in the park. Deep thrums of power lanced at the building but did little to its exterior despite the Welorin firepower.

Must've been built to be attacked.

His stomach rumbled.

Right, the reason I came this way to begin with.

A quick search brought him to the juice bar. Without power, most of its goods were spoiled beyond use. He collected sealed containers of various powders and piles of foiled wrappers—glad in some ways not to find anything vaguely meat-like that he'd have to eat regardless of his feelings.

He shuddered. *I can't even think of meat without thinking of Marvy.*

He ripped open a foil packet and gnawed a bite from what felt and tasted like tree bark.

He crossed back to the window.

Refugees hurled objects down on the collared snatchers, engulfing them in flame. Tanks blasted away at the building, slowly pockmarking the police station. Burr stood in their middle like some kind of general. Prisoner laden trucks followed his gesture, hugging a right turn at the foot of his building.

Some kind of rocket lanced out from refugees on the roof. The blast overturned the third truck. Screams filled the street. Prisoners scrambled to escape their charred and burning fellows. A few bolted in random directions—including the office building.

He cursed his luck. *I'm not sure if I should wish them escape or hope they're captured fast to keep the snatchers out of here.*

A young woman cradled a half burned boy thrashing in her arms. Tree bark tumbled to the floor.

Sarah and Nathan.

Snatchers raced into the lower lobby.

He cursed more for good measure, scouring his surroundings. He raced to the barbells, stripped weights from a long heavy bar and hefted in his hands.

<No, son, you're too small for something that big. Pick a weapon that compliments your strengths.>

I was smaller then, sure of it.

He swung the bar. A grin spread across his face.

Some snatcher's going to lose teeth if he comes up here.

Another explosion. More screams.

He glanced at the window, itching to know what happened below while not wanting to leave his position inside the doorway ready to pounce.

He waited.

He tightened his grip on the bar.

He strained to hear the smallest sound.

Sweat trickled down one cheek.

A steady pull of gravity urged the metal bar downward.

His curiosity grew.

He glanced toward the window.

A door slammed open.

He whipped around, choking up on the bar.

"Leave me alone," A man said.

A familiar voice snarled back. "Get back here."

Footsteps pounded in the hallway.

Something hit a wall.

"Just let me go!"

Footsteps raced nearer.

"Jesus!" The man yelped. "Damn mirrors."

A man careened through the doors, past him and into the gym. Phillip followed a moment later with another snatcher on his heels.

He swung at the second snatcher. The bar drove the snatcher's breath from him with an agonized cry.

Phillip glanced back at the noise. "Chet?"

The teen heaved it into an upward swing, slamming it into the doubled man. Chet staggered backward into the glass door, pursued by another vicious blow.

"Maggot!" Phillip said.

His head jerked around.

Chet ducked. The bar hit the glass door with a shattering crash.

Phillip charged him, other prisoner forgotten.

He dodged Phillip's knife and jabbed the bar into Phillip's gut. Chet's snarling yell sprayed blood as he tackled the teen around his midsection. They slammed into a weight machine. Pain shot up his back.

He slammed the bar downward again and again. Chet slugged his gut.

An explosion rocked the building.

"Chet, keep him pinned there," Phillip said. "Burr wants this one bad."

The other prisoner slammed a platter-sized weight into Phillip's side, aborting the snatcher's charge.

He tucked his knees to block Chet's blows, kicking out with them into the snatcher's knees. The bar followed Chet to the ground. A sickening crunch heralded a spray of blood.

He gawked. *I killed him.*

Phillip's bloody knife missed him by an eyelash. He fled backward, abandoning the bar lodged in Chet's skull. He dodged around an exercise machine. Phillip chased.

Another explosion hit the building a floor down, shattering the glass wall.

He leapt the gutted refugee, catching one of Chris's ill-sized boots on the slow flailing refugee.

He stumbled forward, threw himself to one side to avoid Phillip's thrust, rolling into a collision with a stand of free weights. He grabbed a pair of bright pink barbells and crouched for Philip's next attack.

"I'm going to get you, maggot."

Words snarled from his throat. "Not alive."

"If I had a remote you'd sing a different tune."

His body tensed. His eyes narrowed. His jaw tightened.

"Burr's going to send you away this time." Phillip lunged.

He dodged to one side, bringing his weight-anchored fist across Phillip's jaw. He followed with his other fist, then another and another. A scream erupted from his gut, tearing his throat as he screamed at the snatcher. "Never. Ever. Again."

Bloody knuckles throbbed as he panted.

His eyes lifted to the shattered wall. He sidled to one edge. Below an armored hovervan sparked its way across the road, belching smoke. Refugees poured out of shattered doors behind it, piling on as Burr's tanks and a half dozen oversized and heavily armored spider drones fired on them.

They jumped atop the van in droves, rocking the vehicle until it teetered on its suspensor field. A tank blast sent it into a wild spin, throwing bodies from its back. It recovered making better time until more refugees piled onto it on the side opposite the guns. It scraped along the road, struggling toward escape tipped nearly half way over.

Another tank blast sent it toppling in a steam roll that smashed passengers not thrown far enough free to avoid it. Snatchers descended upon dead and dazed alike.

They'll be coming up here next.

He studied the room.

<What do you see, young sir? What story does the evidence spin?>

A grin rushed across his face. He grabbed Phillip, dragging him closer to the dead refugee.

He lifted the stabbed man, straddling him over Phillip.

"Sorry about this." He propped him up, shoving Philip's still-held knife into the corpse's wound. He let the corpse topple over and clunk his head on the floor. "Uh, for that too."

A quick search of the locker room provided a duffel full of horrid socks but no place to hide. He traded socks for fitness bars and raced up to the next floor. More offices left plenty of dark corners, but none that Burr and his people were likely to leave unsearched after Phillip and Chet's deaths.

Not that a lazy glance at the evidence won't tell them no one survived the fight.

If there was one thing he'd learned about Burr, it was that the snatcher didn't fall into lazy or stupid categories. The roof offered safety for the first thirty seconds it took for a fighter sortie to buzz the building. He pried open a vent panel on the elevator access shaft, climbed in and shimmied his way down its framework by feel until he came to the car.

On top is too obvious.

With exaggerated caution, he slid between the car and wall, scraping his back and bumping his funny bone twice. Once questing fingers declared him beneath it, he felt for the metal framework at its bottom. The dark made judging size harder, but he squeezed into it. For a moment, he found himself wedged. His breath jumped to light speed. Dark spots filled his already blind eyes. He shoved himself backward. He barely moved.

Ignoring the unknown depths beneath him, he clawed and struggled to exit tightening metal fingers. One moment, it held him in a death grip to squeeze his life away. The next his body plummeted, stopped only by a sudden death grip on the rails.

He hugged the rail, eyes squeezed shut and breathing out of control.

Where are the damned voices when I need a little help?

His grip remained even if the memories didn't return. His arms ached. He swung a foot out, finding purchase along the shaft wall. He focused on breathing, one breath then the next.

I can't hang here all day, and even if I could, if they bring lights they'll spot me for sure.

He climbed back up into the framework feeling for its center. It pressed against him as he squeezed underneath. It caught him tight for a moment. His breath rampaged, but he stopped, forcing slow, methodical—if not calm—motions. He freed himself, finding, at last, a cradle to hold him.

His breath sounded loud in his ears.

No sounds of a fight came from outside.

An image of Sarah cradling Nathan filled his imagination. She'd smiled at him. She'd asked his name, and not as some sort of torture. Burr caught her despite his warnings.

He hadn't seen her mother. She'd lost her brother. She was alone in a hell run by the Burrs of the world.

<Don't even think about it, runt.>

10

FOOL FOR A PRETTY SMILE

He hadn't realized he'd been considering it until the arrogant older voice warned him off.

But how could I get her away?

None of the snatcher camps he'd come across had contained the number of prisoners on Burr's trucks. He imagined the camps so many prisoners required, the amount of food it'd take to sustain them for only a few days.

What is Burr doing with so many? He can't possibly keep them.

A grunt drew his attention. Dim light filtered through the gap between wall and elevator.

"Empty."

"Check on top," Silv said.

His nose tickled.

"Nothing. Forget it, Silv, it took three of us to pry open the door."

It itched.

"I don't like it," she said. "It reminds me of what we found of Chris too much."

He wrinkled it.

"You're still on about Maggot?" he laughed. "You and Burr need a life."

Silence.

The itch worsened.

"Can't we just get out of here?" he asked. "We've got to catch up with the trucks."

"We're still emptying the jails," Silv said.

"Fine, maybe I'm uncomfortable in a building full of law offices, you know?"

"Coward."

"Say what you like, Silv, but I don't have a harmonic device like Burr to keep them back."

He grabbed his nose, squeezed it shut between fingers and held his breath.

"What was that?" Silv asked.

"Nothing." He lowered his voice once more. "I didn't say a word, you uptight bitch."

Carpet-muffled footsteps retreated.

The teen waited.

Darkness and silence closed around him.

He waited.

"Come on, Silv, there's nobody there."

She snorted and stomped away.

Trailing Burr's caravan proved simpler than expected. He lurked out of sight until the last of the trucks pulled away with its new load of orange-clad prisoners. The trucks never moved faster than its escorts, and the snatchers didn't seem to have a reason to rush.

He trailed it as far back as he could, using various ruins' debris to hide. Occasional glimpses of Sarah kept him on his nemesis's trail. She'd saved him. He couldn't do less. His imagination played at solving the riddle of their destination—the most horrible scenarios revolving around a massive food processing facility.

The last greys of dusk faded toward shadow. Railroad tracks ridged a broad, shallow valley. Putrid mire edged the tracks, leaving each embankment a foggy quagmire. Lights swam in the haze, backlighting railcar after railcar stuffed with squalling humanity. Shrieks punctuated the night, flooding from the caged occupants without any discernable reason.

On the right edge of the valley, the larger spider drones stood sentinel over Burr's delivered prisoners.

He edged forward to get a better view when every hair on his skin raced a wave of gooseflesh for total dominion. A moment later a floating soccer-ball-shaped drone drifted out of the mire like a shark fin cutting its way across a swimming hole.

Darkness engulfed him followed at once by the press of metal fingers squeezing the life from him. He bit his lip, clamping down upon the urge to scream out his terror.

The memory faded back into his mind's recesses. His terror receded. The spherical drone floated down the valley, disappearing back into the mist.

Another wave of shrieks filled the night far to his left. The floating glow of a spherical drone rounded the train into view.

He held himself still, watching its slow patrol rise and sink through the mist.

His instincts reacted a moment before the fear slammed into him. He bit his lip until he tasted blood, disbelieving the flashing horror of being submerged in rotting flesh that tasted like Marvy.

Reality remained on the edges of each blink, but it still took every bit of his will to keep from bolting out of his hidden vantage point and back the way he'd come.

The drone passed, and the fear ebbed.

Cries rent the night once more.

Those poor, poor souls. Subjecting someone to that over and over could destroy their mind.

His gaze shifted right, witnessing an empty truck pull away only to be replaced by the next.

Sarah's down in that, if not now, soon.

Sentinels, fear-mongers, snatchers and the wedge-shaped lancer tanks remained between her and any help he might offer. Shrieks traveled the trains in waves. With each, his resolve to help Sarah hardened only to be undermined when a fear-monger passed close enough to show him his inevitable failure and death in any rescue attempt.

The last truck pulled away, filled with Burr and his crew. The tanks followed with sentinel drones guarding their flank. Three fear-mongers floated around the train, weaving in and out of range to set off the prisoner's screams as if the robotic drone gained some pleasure from their distress.

Where're they taking all those people? Will they be slaves? Food? Is there even any way to help Sarah or the others?

He studied the fear-mongers. Their patrols weren't exact. One, in particular, tended to drift into range of the prisoners more often. The time between their circuits on the incredibly long train left gaps he might use to get to the train for whatever good that might offer.

Cargo carriers caused some of the breaks in the screaming. Whatever filled every fourth or fifth car wasn't alive—or at least not alive and sane.

Another wave of horror pummeled him.

Could my amnesia protect me?

Images flooded him. His pulse thundered in his ears.

No past, no name. I'm no one. I don't exist.

The defense lasted about fourteen seconds, but those few moments let him see the horrors for the thin illusion his body refused to disbelieve.

The drone edged away.

He followed it down the train's length, staying just close enough to feel the tingle on his skin. Once to the tail, he headed back up the train into the teeth of the next fear-monger. He counted the seconds between tingle and terror. Once clear of the second drone he continued up to the string of engines waiting to pull the train to destinations unknown.

No drones on the train. Why and why haven't they left?

He ran the circuit again, comparing his second count to the first. At the end of the train, he noticed the rearmost cars remained empty.

They're waiting for more prisoners. Heavens, how long are they going to make those people endure this? Better question, how long until the next load arrives?

He scanned the direction Burr's convoy had used as their approach. No lights approached in the distance.

Will the next delivery wait for daylight? Heavens, what kind of monsters were the Welorin?

He paced up and down the train again, enduring the terror to check for some new type of drone he'd not yet encountered.

Nothing.

Without drones, could I climb aboard and elude pursuit at last?

<Just fritter the night away lounging in the middle of a nightmare like some vid hero. Great plan, little brother.>

<My little alar would never leave others to suffer.>

<Sure, be the hero, runt. Just like you had the balls to hide under those bodies.>

He snarled. *You're ganging up on me now? Where were you when I needed advice?*

<Language.>

He flinched. "Sorry, ma'am."

Nightmare of disembodied voices falling from faceless mouths hit him like a hovertruck. The edge of a scream made it to his lips, but he covered his head with both hands and held it in with all he was worth.

<Can't even put up with a few bad dreams. How're you going to survive in the center of that?>

He pushed away the nightmare, replacing it with frantic mental scouring for his missing name. Before he could think about it too much, he launched himself forward in the fear-monger's wake. He darted through the fog, nose wrinkling at its underlying pungence. No prisoner could've escaped and gotten out of range before the next drone came into view, but racing into captivity the numbers in his mind claimed he could make a cargo carrier.

<Assuming you actually got a math equation right for once.>

He froze halfway up an embankment, head and shoulders above the mire and a dozen yards from the train. Pleas and demands for help assaulted him from the train.

He cursed and rushed ahead, diving into the next bank of fog before their noise brought a fear-monger's attention down onto his head.

His arms tingled.

He bit his sleeve and screwed up his face in anticipation. Flashes of Burr gloating over his recapture as he ordered him to eat Sarah's roasted flesh forced him into the tightest ball he could manage.

The fear waned.

The drone missed him.

He rushed the last stretch, heaving himself up onto a cargo car. He yanked on the door, missing at first the padlock hanging from it. He cowered under the car as the next drone sent him into a living hell. He waited for it to pass and the shrieks to start elsewhere on the train. Under cover of their terror, he slammed the lock with his blood-stained weight bar.

It took three drone passes to break open the lock. He squeezed through the barely open door into a dream come true as another nightmare struck.

He bit his sleeve once more as he shoved the door closed. It refused to close the last finger's breadth. He curled onto the car's floor and hoped the drones didn't notice. Inside the train, fear-mongers on either side hit him with nightmares time and again until he regretted his success.

Minutes, hours, days or decades later, the train pulled from the station carrying a sea of miserable humanity, a girl to save and a single teen, crying silently surrounded by a literal wall-to-wall feast he hadn't enough time to eat.

11

THE GREAT TRAIN ESCAPE

The last vestiges of induced fear fled.

He fell on the food, ripping open containers at every side. Foods of every description filled them. Cans, boxes, bottled drinks and packages of dried fruits and meats filled container after container. Emotional exhaustion and a full stomach hurried him off into thankfully dreamless sleep.

He woke, the thud, thud, thud of the train on its tracks somehow peaceful. He ripped open another bag, but hardly had the third bite to his lips when he remembered Sarah.

I have to find her.

He grabbed the door then glanced at the food around him. She'd be hungry. Everyone was hungry in the post-invasion ruins. He stuffed his duffel with food and dragged open the door.

Fighters streaked by the train, flying low enough to throw debris up in their wake. He jerked out of the way of a flying branch and hid behind the doorframe. The fighters buzzed the train several more times then vanished. He glanced at his jumpsuit forearm, reminded by the empty, broken fasten points that Burr'd ripped his processor pad off.

Then beat me when it didn't work away from the suit.

He waited.

Fear gripped him. He didn't want to be caught again. He couldn't face a real collar once more. He closed the door to a hand span and watched the countryside pass by, a mouse peering out its hole.

They appeared once more about an hour later, ripping up countryside with their low-altitude flybys. When the sorties ended, he stuck his head out the door. Wind roared in his ears, but he couldn't find the grey arrowheads in predawn storm clouds above.

He waited for them to return once more. Fighters flew over the train at regular intervals, checking on its otherwise ignored passengers.

If the livestock cars are locked like this one how do I free anybody without the Welorin seeing?

He opened the door more fully just after the third patrol. One hand on the door's handle, he leaned out, looking up and down the train. A ladder on the car's side led up but was a long reach in such stiff wind. He adjusted his food-stuffed duffel out of the way, took a deep breath, swung for the ladder and missed.

He hung beside the train, one foot hooked around the door, one slipping hand on the door's handle and his face pressed against the car's exterior. His heart beat so hard in his chest it threatened to catapult him off the train.

He dragged himself back up into the cargo carrier, pulled the door closed and collapsed against the food containers. He remained there, shaking and panting.

The train traveled nonstop through the dark morning. It passed through mountains and forests, along broken highways which almost looked normal save the occasional smoking islands of mangled vehicles. They traveled from mountains eventually to vast flatlands. Farms rose up on both sides of the rails, densely populated by downtrodden people and Welorin drones of half a dozen configurations.

Desire to find Sarah rose above his fear.

The train slowed slightly as he cracked open the door. The first signs of a major city sped past his view. Like Washington D.C., a smoking ruin remained the only evidence of former glory. Welorins promised food, work and shelter over massive loudspeakers as he passed.

How do the prisoners passing by feel about such lies?

He swung out of the car once more, this time catching the ladder. He crawled onto the car's top, keeping low against the wind. He sprang toward the livestock car behind his.

The jump went long.

He slid across the car's top, one leg sliding out over the side of the train before he got a solid grip.

"Sarah? Is there a Sarah in there with you?" He shouted.

"Get us out of here."

"What's in the bag?"

"Help us."

"Do something, boy."

He peeked his head over the other side of the car. "I'm looking for Sarah."

The state of the prisoners wrenched at his heart. He opened the satchel, grabbing food from within and shoving it through gaps between the top slats.

Chaos ensued.

People climbed atop one another to snatch food as he dropped it. Other's attacked those who caught it. One man standing atop two women seized his wrist, nearly dragging him off the train before someone just as greedy slugged the man making him let go.

The teen stopped, trying to figure out how to help them without dying to do it. Their screams reached riot ferocity. Many spat death wishes at him. The car behind, having witnessed his attempts to feed the first joined their pleas and curses to the tumult.

Handing food in an item at a time isn't going to work, but I only have one bag.

He eyed the sky, trying to guess the time he had until the next flyby.

He rushed up the train. Doing a bit of quick mathematical guesswork, he adjusted his jump. He landed on target back atop his cargo container. He repeated the process, car by car as fast as he could. At each, he called down for Sarah. A few answered, but none the young woman he sought. His mouth dried the closer he came to the engines. His palms stole that moisture for their own purposes.

Fear drained away with the third successful leap, but a slip on the fifth brought it back as caution.

He reached the engine.

What if there's a driver?

<Do what you must to survive.>

He crawled the last half car. He leapt down, fists up into an empty compartment.

Fighters streaked by a moment after he made it under the engine's canopy. He searched while they rocketed by, higher than before.

Maybe they're not the same fighters.

He found a few heavy flashlights, good for light and as make-shift weapons, a gigantic crescent wrench too big to carry, a first aid kit, an old pocket watch, and a ball-peen hammer.

A desperate plan grew in his mind. He thought through the physics, estimating the timing.

Once I start, though, there's no turning back. The Welorin fighters are bound to notice an ever shortening train.

He made his way back down the train. He climbed down the ladder of each cargo carrier, fighting buffeting wind and occasional branches to knock the locks free with his new hammer. As each pair of fighters reappeared, he hid in the nearest cargo container, using the watch he'd found to better time their approach.

Most cargo carriers contained only food. A few included bulky cold weather clothing. With each pause in the action, his thoughts went to the Welorin.

What do they actually look like? Why haven't I ever seen one? How will they react to my plan? What'll they do to the prisoners if I fail?

He continued down the train, breaking the locks on the cargo containers. Many an arm tried to grab him as he passed by above, some pleading for release, others demanding his hammer. He asked after Sarah but failed to find her at each livestock carrier.

He managed to unlock the last cargo container in line as dusk stole his light. He slid inside, warmed by a winter coat atop his jumpsuit. He ate, though guilt at others cold and hungry on the train muted its flavor.

Exhausted, he slept, built up his strength and watched for dawn. He used the daylight to check the couplings between cars. He made another pass at finding Sarah and another attempt at passing food out. Neither proved a success.

Daylight faded toward dusk. They reached a shallow uphill stretch braced by fields and foothills. Small clusters of trees offered possible cover.

The old stopwatch estimated an hour until the next air patrol. He climbed onto the train and scuttled toward the last car in line. He twisted his feet over the side. Something touched his leg, visions of being yanked downward seized his limbs. He forced himself to loosen his death grip on the car's top and climbed down.

A dirty man in once fancy business attire stretched a helping hand out through the slats. A girl with matching mahogany hair clung to his leg—her wide blue eyes a match for his.

"It's all right, son. Do your thing. I'll keep you from falling."

"Is there a Sarah in here?"

"Work, I'll ask."

He struck an offhand blow at car's padlock. Clumsy and buffeted by wind, it broke only after several blows.

Those inside wrenched opened the door.

A shoving throng of over-packed prisoners sent dozens out the door to unknown fates. Others yanked the businessman from their path. His daughter shrieked.

The teen swung forward, catching her around the waist. The hammer in his hand struck the next person. The accidentally injured man shoved girl and teen away. She screamed. He wrapped arm and hammer around her waist, hanging in midair by a slipping grip on the slats.

A strong hand pulled him closer to the car. A second slipped between him and the girl beneath the father's grateful smile. "Thank you, son. Sorry, no Sarah."

"Stay in the car. I'm going to uncouple you and a food carrier. "

Her father nodded.

He climbed up the car and raced to the next car. Its occupants demanded release, but none helped steady him. He swung out to strike the lock. He caught glimpses of prisoners leaping free from the previous car.

Good luck.

The lock broke.

The door jerked open.

"Sarah?!"

Bodies tumbled out.

Prisoners scrambled over him, fouling his grip and nearly costing him the hammer. He rushed to the third car but had to wait before leaping to its roof.

"Get out of sight, they're coming back."

No one paid him heed in their race for the cargo container.

His stopwatch warned of another patrol. He leapt to their car, pausing before jumping back to the cargo carrier. "I'll be back once the fighters pass."

If anyone thanked him, he couldn't hear it over the vulgar occupants. Bodies blocked his entrance into the cargo container. He fought to close the container, but men seized foodstuffs, shoving anyone coming near them out of the car.

"Stop it, I've got to close the doors, or they'll see."

"Who cares," the bully said through stuffed mouth. He shoved the teen. "Get out."

The hammer flashed forward, striking the bully's wrist before its swing grazed the man's head. He yanked the dazed bully forward, sidestepped and let the brute tumble from the train.

Horror gripped him between gasps. *What did I just do?*

He pushed it away, guzzling a sports drink and settling himself for his next efforts. He scaled the car as soon as the fighter flew past. The smart in car three prevailed over the selfish. No one tumbled out when their door opened.

More climbed up after him, nearly knocking him from the train in their rush to the food car. A woman suffering acute weight loss seized his duffel. They struggled. She slipped, tumbling from the train.

He climbed back on top and moved to the cargo carrier's forward coupling. He uncoupled the quartet, leaving them to slow to an eventual stop. Heat flushed his cheeks.

Adrenalin and fear fell to background noise after so many close calls. He scaled the next container and attacked the lock. He opened three of the four cars behind the next cargo container before checking his stopwatch.

He cursed.

He rushed passed the fourth car. "Be right back."

He repacked his duffel while waiting out the flyby, replacing what the woman had spilled out.

Probably last chance I'll get.

He set to work on the fourth car's lock when the fighters made an unexpected extra pass at slower speed. They returned almost at once, raking the cars with laser fires. Smoke billowed from the gutted cargo container.

Are they trying to scare us into staying? He raced through the smoke to the next coupling. "You suck at warning shots."

Their next pass ripped up the livestock container at his back. Shrapnel gashed his shoulder, a chunk bludgeoning one leg. He finished uncoupling the cars and raced to unlock the undamaged car between him and the next cargo hauler.

"Sarah?!"

A lucky hit broke their lock on the first strike. He skipped uncoupling and attacked the next lock.

The fighters roared overhead. Green blasts rained around the train, hitting many who tried to leap to freedom. A bolt sent a destroyed livestock container soaring through the air.

He unlocked the next and managed a second.

Lights enough for a major city sped toward them.

They'll have drones waiting, we have to go now.

He raced forward atop the cars. Lasers rained down around him. He managed to get four cars up the train, leapt down and unhitched the car. The remaining train of screaming prisoners raced away.

In a last rush of effort, he raced backward along the train. He passed the door, turning to unlock it from a position which would allow him to do the same for the next car. Desperate hands stopped what they thought was their abandonment. They snatched away his hammer and shoved him almost off the car's side. Their door burst open followed immediately by dozens shoved out by those behind. People scrambled on top of the cars and rushed for the cargo container.

"Sarah?!"

A fighter strafed sideways across the train, sweeping low to blast those rushing along its top.

Two locked cars remained, but the hammer had disappeared.

Another pass of the low flyers sheered the top from the cargo container.

He glanced at the ground, judging the speed for a jump. Dirt exploded between him and freedom, sending him back to clutch the car's slats. The hammer lay on the car's floor beneath fleeing feet.

He glanced upward.

<Time to go.>

I can open another.

<Think the feasters will eat you with any particular kind of sauce?>

He cursed, preparing himself to jump from the slow train.

No.

He leapt into the car and snatched up the hammer. He dove clear as lasers cut through the car. He landed wrong, rolling with the fall but still twisting his ankle. He hobbled to the nearest prisoner car, climbed up and struck off the lock. He spun toward the last lock.

A Welorin bolt launched the car airborne. It slammed down, cracking open for any still alive inside to escape.

Now it really is time to go.

He turned.

"Wait."

He whipped around, lost his footing and raised hammer as he tumbled backward. He fished a flashlight from his duffel and raised the light to illuminate two figures.

A hulking figure in denim overalls and cotton undershirt loomed over him, more intimidating than Burr on his best day. Twin to an ogre, he held a two by four as if it were some kind of souvenir bat.

A tiny girl with a haphazard ball of dark, dirty hair smiled at him

Next to him, anyone'd look tiny.

A silverish-brown jumpsuit very much akin to his own golden one hugged slight but alluring curves.

Survive now, date later.

"Come with us so I can patch you up." Her smile widened. "You saved us. It's only fair."

He gaped at her.

12

OGRES & PIXIES

A thick southern accent dominated her companion's tenor. "El, we gotta go."

"I think he's in shock, Jesse," she said. "We can't leave him after all he did for everyone."

"He ain't a stray," Jesse said. "If he don't want to go we shouldn't force him."

El bent forward, hand extended. "Come on, we should hurry."

"Not giving this up, are you?"

"We owe him our lives," she said.

"Fine," Jesse strode forward and bent to carry him.

"Wait. I can walk."

He stood. One leg folded half way up. Jesse caught him and helped him hurry away from the train.

El took his flashlight and led the way. The street's surface reflected its light oddly, but curiosity took second place to survival. They rushed deeper into the suburb along commercial byways almost as ruined as Washington D.C.

Laser blasts and screams continued behind them.

"How many do you think escaped?" El said.

"Three less if we don't find someplace to hole up," Jesse said.

Wrecked, formerly tall buildings teetered into one another like a group of drunken friends held upright by a single solid companion. Melted concrete and blasted tops crowned the revelers, debris vomited atop their squat supporter. A municipal bus impaled its storefront offering injury to accompany insult. A sputtering street lamp haloed it on and off like some bizarre sale spotlight. The convenience store's sign dented the bus's roof with a proud blood-colored glowing V perched atop a matching horizontal line.

He stared at the sign. *Power's still on.*

El ducked into the bus and yelped.

Jesse rushed in behind her, dragging him along into an all too familiar stench.

"Sorry," her cheeks colored. "I'm okay."

A wedge of half-decayed bodies, seats and bars writhed in the eerie flashlight.

"We could dig a tunnel maybe," he said. "Wriggle through then collapse it."

El's nose wrinkled. "In that?"

"We'll check the building first," Jesse said.

A bent security gate allowed access through a door's broken lower half. Gold-painted glass at its top declared its former owner a tax lawyer. He crawled through despite his apprehension. The office was ruined, but he found no signs of feasters. Jesse didn't fit through as easily. It took the teen and El pushing and pulling to get Jesse into the ransacked building. He cursed his ankle, and both he and Jesse cursed the narrow stairway more than once.

The top remaining floor angled into its neighbor, laser blasts cracking it open and filling it with an avalanche of building. They studied the steep debris ramp.

"I think I can make that solo."

"You sure?" Jesse asked.

He chewed his lip. "I don't want to unbalance you."

Jesse frowned at the slide. "I could maybe carry you piggyback."

He reddened.

"He's *sure*, Jesse," she handed Jesse her flashlight. "Go."

Debris shifted underfoot. A cascade of loose debris knocked downward by El swept away his footing just as he recovered. Boy, bag and hammer tumbled in all downward directions.

He belly flopped onto litter-strewn concrete, head snapping forward into the floor. A combination yelp and gasp for lost breath left him choking dust. He rolled over, head cradled in his hands.

Small hands pushed away his own, replacing them with blinding light. "Don't move."

He groaned. "No problem."

"Sit up slow," she said.

"He can't do both, runt," Jesse said.

"Help him over there," El said.

He tried to help Jesse, but his leg wouldn't support him. Jesse set him down on the clearer section of floor.

"Past time for introductions," she said. "The monster carrying you is my cousin Jesse."

Jesse inclined his head.

"I'm El."

"I don't have a name," he said.

Jesse scoffed. "Everybody's got a name, hell, our cows have names."

He stared downward. "I can't remember mine."

"Suit yourself." Jesse snatched the flashlight back and disappeared into the store's depths.

El sat next to him. "You really can't remember?"

He shook his head.

Jesse reappeared in the store room, scowling.

El glanced up.

"All cleaned out," Jesse said.

"You can't remember anything?"

"In my dreams, a woman calls me her little alar."

Jesse laughed. "Her little, winged thing?"

El scooted closer. "Ignore Mister Dictionary. What do you think it means?"

"No idea."

Her thoughtful frown rivaled puppies in cuteness. "Hold still."

Jesse reached out a hand to stop her, but she waved him off. "I don't think he's dangerous, Jess."

Her hands ran up his leg, pushing up his jumpsuit leg and herding blood upward and ultimately to his face. El's fingers probed, gently but painfully, into the area around his ankle.

"It's not broken," she said.

El peered into his eyes once more, not like some love-struck girl or a mother searching for lies. It seemed as practiced as the way her hands searched his head for injury.

Her gaze fell onto his left arm. Fresh blood seeped from a tear where the shrapnel hit him on the train.

Was starting to think this jumpsuit indestructible.

"Sprained ankle and a nasty cut but I don't think he's got a concussion," She said. "I should watch him at least for tonight."

Jesse glared at him. "Uh huh. Why don't you watch him from over here?"

"He's not dangerous, Jesse."

"I'm thinking his expression while you fiddled with his leg says different," Jesse said

She reddened.

He cleared his throat after the third try. "We might chance a fire. There're no windows back here, and smoke shouldn't be visible exiting the hole. Might even choke any snatchers trying to sneak up on us."

Her stomach grumbled. Not to be outdone, Jesse's answered all the more ominously hollow.

"I'm sorry, there's food in my bag if you want."

Jesse's gaze narrowed. "Saved us, offering your food, just what are you after birdman?"

"Nothing. You're hungry."

"Stop being so suspicious," El smiled at him. "He's a hero."

Jesse crossed the intervening space, snatching up the duffel and drawing El away to explore it with him.

"Did you check the bathroom for water?" he asked.

"Not a drop," Jesse said

"There're alcohol towelettes in there if you want to clean up," he said.

El fished out a box, then picked a roll of bandages from the bag and seated herself next to him.

"Thought we were eating," Jesse said.

"In a minute," she said. "This might hurt a little."

He nodded.

She expanded the sleeve's rip, revealing a shallow cut bleeding over a colorful metallic tattoo.

"Whoa, step away from him El."

Both of them looked at Jesse.

"Why?" she asked.

"I could believe he's got no memory, even excuse that collar, even maybe his heroics and narrow escape," Jesse held up a forearm to display a holographic foil barcode tattooed across his wrist. "But instead of one of these, he got some elaborate hidden mark. This some twisted Welorin experiment? You a plant? Did all those people die just to set us up?"

"Jesse!"

"What're those?" he asked.

"Don't play dumb, man, you know these are what prisoners get when they're processed."

"I've never been processed," he said.

"Which proves you're some kind of alien agent, maybe you're not human at all," Jesse said.

"You're way over thinking things, *again*," El said. "Of course he's human. Look at his blood."

Jesse crossed the room and dragged her away.

"Snatcher team that caught me never sent me for processing. They made me—" he hesitated. "Their leader, Burr, tortured me."

El stepped toward him, but Jesse held her back.

"Even called me counselor as a threat," he said.

"How's that a threat?" El asked.

Jesse rolled his eyes. "He talks like you, diplomatic like. They were threatening to re-educate him."

El gasped. "That's horrible."

He looked away.

"If you was captured and collared, how'd you escape?" Jesse asked.

He told them about Sarah and his escape.

"That's the girl you kept asking for on the train?" El asked.

He nodded.

"You telling us you jumped on that train for a girl that wasn't even your girlfriend?" Jesse asked.

"Shut up, Jess. You did some pretty dumb stuff for that girl Whitney, and then there was Riesa and of course—"

Jesse reddened. "We're not talking about me."

"You didn't find her, did you?" El asked.

"No."

Silence filled the empty store, broken only by an occasional pop from the fire.

El crouched down next to him and resumed cleaning his wound. He hid his discomfort poorly, drawing an impish grin from her. She wiped her hands on the last wipe. "Best I can do."

She joined Jesse and the food across the small fire he'd built while she worked. Jesse warmed tinned fish and soup for each of them.

"You from D.C.?" El asked.

"I don't remember."

El gestured at his jumpsuit and then her own. "All junior UN delegates were assigned these things, to honor the aliens' way of dress—though I don't remember who had yellow. You seem familiar, like I saw you at the kickoff party. We're down from Boston to observe the talks."

Jesse glared. "Ain't got no uniform cause I'm *chaperoning*."

"Why honor alien invaders?" he asked.

"Not the Welorin, the Alistari silly," she said.

He examined El's jumpsuit. *Must be silver under all the dirt.*

She reddened under his scrutiny, words tumbling from her in a rush. "I'll be eighteen next month." Her blush deepened. "Mom insisted Jesse keep an eye on me."

"Aren't you the same age?"

She sighed. "Double standards alive and well in the South."

"Damn straight," Jesse said. "El's a bit older actually."

"Thought you said you were from Boston," he said.

"Can't remember your own name, but you know Boston's not southern?" Jesse asked.

El shot him a look.

"Mom and Jesse's family are southerners. He's already in his second year at Massachusetts Institute of Technology." El sighed. "Mom's convinced that makes him mature enough to keep me out of trouble."

"Hard to believe, huh?" Jesse asked.

That he's mature enough to watch her or that he's an accelerated graduate in a tech school?

<Ask, runt, I dare you.>

Jesse handed a warmed tin to El and then reached over with the other. "Here ya go, Kent."

"Kent?" El asked.

Jesse beamed. "Well, he Kent remember his name, Kent remember what he's doing here, Kent remember if he's Junior UN, and Kent get back out of here without help."

"Kent might do," El giggled. "He's got that whole Superman chiseled jaw going for him."

Jesse scowled.

He chewed his lip. "I'm sure I'm not a Kent."

"Got to call yourself something," Jesse said.

El slipped her hand into not-Kent's, worsening Jesse's scowl. "Just wait for your memory. It'll probably return faster if you don't give up on remembering to be someone else."

"I don't know. Names are important I suppose, but I'm still me even without my memory," he shrugged, "mostly anyway."

"You'll remember. Just don't give up," El said.

Not-Kent gestured around them. "You're awfully positive all things considered."

El beamed.

"She can't help it. I swear she's part pixie. Nothing gets her down," Jesse's eyes lit, and he imitated El with a rough falsetto. "You're just not seeing the sunshine in this alien-ravaged countryside."

He coughed and continued with a slight rasp to his usual baritone. "Seriously, you can be whoever you want. Start over, invent yourself without anyone else to stop you. What about Heyou?"

They both made faces.

"Why are you being so nice to me now?"

Jesse shrugged around a tipped up can of soup.

"You fed him," she said. "So his stomach trusts you—that's most him."

Jesse snorted letter-shaped noodles from his nose.

He and El shared a laugh.

"How about Blade?" Jesse interjected. "Cool name, explains that tattoo, makes sense, right?"

El's nose wrinkled. "You can be such a *boy* sometimes."

Jesse drummed his chest with both fists and made gorilla noises. "He's got to go by something."

She smirked. "It's up to Kent-Not-Kent-Heyou-Blade."

He chewed his lip. "I guess if you have to call me something. It's better than maggot."

"Great, Blade it is then."

El's eyes lit up half way through a roll. "What about Eric?"

Jesse groaned.

"What?" She asked. "You saw what he did on the train. He rules!"

He frowned at them both.

"She's making fun of me," Jesse said.

"I don't understand," he said.

"She's sweet on a teacher back home named Eric, so she suggested that to make me worry about her being sweet on you," Jesse said.

"And for you defining alar," she said.

Jesse glared at her. "I suppose you're going to combine them so he's some kind of angelic king or something."

"Alar Eric?" he said.

She brightened. "Oooo, I like that."

"You do?"

"Yes, Aleric, but three letters from each, so spelled with an A instead of an E."

"And she calls me a nerd," Jesse said.

"You are."

"Alaric," he said. "It's better than maggot."

"And a lot better than *Blade*," she said.

"Hey, it fits him!"

"Does not," she said.

"Alaric," he mumbled. "But didn't you say I should wait to take a name?"

She set a hand on his. "Whatever you want, as long as I don't have to call you *Blade*."

She stuck her tongue out at Jesse.

"Where'd you learn medicine if you're not in college?" he asked.

El sat straighter. "I may not be in college, but there's plenty of brains on my side of the family too. I'm not some scatterbrained pixie."

Jesse grinned.

"I didn't mean anything," he said. "You seem so practiced at it."

"She's had lots of practice, playing doctor with *Eric*."

"Eric's an EMT. I'm interning under him as part of a pre-premed program because doctors only let you watch while EMT's are more flexible about..."

"Touching?" he asked.

Jesse darkened. "They'll let a girl who works her smile touch anything she wants."

"I'm almost eighteen."

"See why I had to come? *All* pixie." Jesse stretched out, cradled his head and closed his eyes. "Your turn to stay up, runt."

He opened one eye and glared. “Keep your hands to yourself, mister.”

“He can barely move,” El said.

“Then keep away from his hands, missy.”

She rolled her eyes.

13

TAKEN

She shook his arm some time later. He jerked awake.

"Shhh, it's just me, El."

He yawned.

"Mind if I curl up next to you?" she asked. "For warmth?"

Warmth crept into his cheeks. "Wouldn't Jesse be better?"

"He thrashes too much," she said.

"Yeah, I guess."

She settled into the crook of his arm, warm and comfortably uncomfortable. After a few minutes, he broke the silence. "What were you talking about before, the Alistari?"

"I guess you don't remember that either," she sighed.

"Sorry."

She straightened a little, gazing up into his face. "The Alistari revealed themselves to the UN, asked for a conference—something to do with transit permissions." El beamed. "Something happened behind closed doors, making them reveal themselves globally."

"Probably objected to someone trying to keep the Alistari all to themselves."

She tittered. "That'd be irony. Once the cat was into the nip, a bunch of groups demanded representation at the meeting. Jr UN got picked—probably as a lesser of evils—but I'm not complaining. Be part of a global meeting with peoples from another planet, what an opportunity!"

"Except the Welorin stepped in?"

"Stomped is more like it." She sighed. "Once in a lifetime opportunity blown all to hell, literally."

"You sure the Alistari and the Welorin aren't the same aliens?"

"I never thought of that." She shuddered visibly before apologizing under her breath. "No, if they're the same and we welcomed one, why invade like this?"

"Rivals of some sort?"

She shrugged.

"I'm sorry."

"Why are you sorry? You didn't blow up the meeting and order an invasion, did you?"

"I don't think so, but—"

"You can't remember," she finished. "Damned Welorin. You know, Jesse thinks he saw some of them, not just one of their drones or fighters, actually one of the aliens."

His stomach tightened. "Yeah?"

"He said they were tiny," El said.

He laughed. "Jesse's like twice your height. To him everyone's tiny."

"He is not *that* big," she said.

"Harder to tell from this angle," he grinned, "So, you're right here where I can get my hands on you."

She smiled nestling tighter to him. "If you decide you want to touch me, Alaric..."

He smiled at the sultry way 'Alaric' rolled off of her tongue. "Yes?"

"I'll break all fifty-four bones in those pretty hands of yours."

He awoke to El and Jesse discussing their next move.

"...make our way back to 'Bama cross country," Jesse said. "Ain't no way they'll find us in those woods."

"It's too far and too cold, Jess," she said.

Jesse rubbed his biceps. "Ain't that cold here."

"Wish we knew where here was," she said.

"Colorado," he said.

She turned to him, a smile illuminating her face. "Good morning, Alaric."

"How'd you triangulate that while counting Z's, Mister Sleepy Guard?" Jesse asked.

He blushed.

"Leave off, nobody's perfect, and we're safe," she said. "How do you know?"

"I saw a sign."

"That explains the cold," El said.

Jesse grunted. "That means mountains, ice, and snow. Crap."

El examined his leg. "Swelling's down, we really should get further from the tracks."

"Guess no more special treatment then?" He asked.

"Don't push your luck or I'll break both those just-for-warmth arms, boy," Jesse said.

He glanced at El.

"I explained."

"El's right," Jesse said. "We should skedaddle."

"You're coming with us, right?" El asked.

"I, uh."

Jesse scooped him up and chuckled. "I gotcha, Blade."

"Alaric," El corrected, gathering his bag.

She followed a few steps behind, dodging dislodged rubble. Jesse concentrated on every trudging step, tongue peeking from his lips. Their heads crested the ramp to find three snatchers—two collared—exiting the stairwell.

"Here're some more," the collarless snatcher yelled. "And they've caught one of our new scouts."

He pointed a remote. "I order you to help us fight him."

Jesse dropped him. "You backstabbing liar."

The two collared snatchers charged.

Jesse roared, his massive fists drove them back at opposite angles. He stomped down on the teen, missing by inches as he rolled to a crouch.

The collared snatchers tackled Jesse together. Jesse lifted one of them off the ground. The first's struggles and the man around Jesse's waist unbalanced him.

"Get him, get him," the collared man ordered.

The teen jumped to help Jesse as he fell backward. His ankle fouled his rush, and the big man went back down the ramp with his two adversaries.

"Go after him, idiot," the snatcher ordered. He turned his back on the teen. "Get some more help here. This one's a beast."

Alaric slammed a chunk of rubble into the snatcher's head then smashed the stone into the hand holding the remote. He snatched it up and struggled back to his feet.

Jesse emerged from the ramp, face redder than the blood on it. "I'll beat you until there's nothing more to beat."

The teen gestured at the collarless snatcher. "I'm on your—"

More snatchers rushed in from the stairs. He turned toward them as a huge metallic ball with six extendable arms crawled over the building's side. Dark red sockets glared beams onto Jesse's chest.

"Welorin Sentinel," Alaric threw one of the snatchers in between the sentinel and Jesse. Deep red beams ignited the collared prisoner.

His stomach knotted.

The sentinel shifted its beams toward him.

He pointed the remote at the other snatchers. "Destroy the Sentinel. Jesse, get El out of here."

The snatchers charged the drone, screaming battle cries as the orders drove them toward repressed desires despite their terror. He hurried to the ramp, throwing himself down it sideways. He rolled over painful rubble, descending faster than Jesse to hit the floor hard enough to empty his lungs.

Jesse grabbed him, fist raised.

"Jesse, stop," El said.

He pressed the remote into Jesse's hand. "Do what you have to, but get her clear."

Jesse glanced from the remote, to him, to the ramp, and to El in several quick rounds. He grabbed up a flashlight. "You get her out of here. I'll catch up."

"No!" El said. "That's a sentinel."

"And Blade just sent a bunch of snatchers to their deaths to save my ass," Jesse said.

"To give you time to get her out of here," he said.

"There's no other way out," Jesse said.

"The bus," he countered.

Jesse shuddered. "You do it while I keep them off of us."

"Stay with us," El said.

Jesse kissed her forehead. "Right behind you."

Jesse charged up the ramp. Metal hitting metal echoed down to them. Laser blasts shredded the air above them. A man screamed.

"My god, Jesse," El cried.

"It wasn't him. Help me here."

She helped him to the front of the store, every other step agonizing. The ravaged store's front matched Jesse's description, though he'd left out the overpowering stench.

"Help me over there," he pointed.

El yelped.

The driver's body was crushed up against the shattered but somehow whole windshield.

"Come on."

She helped him over the shattered storefront and several mangled newspaper boxes. Hand on the windshield to balance his one-legged stance, he slammed the hammer into the safety glass. It resisted his blows with minimal conviction. Holes grew in its pane until he handed her the hammer, grabbed the windshield and heaved.

Teeth gritted against a pernicious scream, he finally wrenched the glass away. He shoved hands into compressed rotting corpses and pulled slimy, putrid flesh away in squelching handfuls. Maggots writhed along his arms as he dug. He pushed their tickling wriggles from his mind with the rest of the things he was pointedly not thinking about and kept digging.

He and El gagged and choked.

Sliding stone and hasty searching voices came from the back room. He glanced toward it, cursing under his breath and wishing flesh diving wasn't one of the things he remembered.

He dug out several limbs, part of a spine and a woman's head. "You first."

"I can't," she said.

"Jesse told me to protect you. You have to go first."

She mouthed in horror.

He cursed, drove two arms into the hole and dragged himself through using a wedged pole. He reversed himself and swam back through death's womb, anchoring a knee. El retreated from his gore covered arms but dazed enough for him to catch her. He seized her and dragged her shrieking body through. He dumped her on the floor, vomiting and cursing him. He shoved bloated flesh into the hole, seized up stray bars and seats, wedging them into place to block pursuit.

"What about Jess?"

He swore and yanked clear the metal bones of his barrier.

He grabbed her wrist and dragged her from the bus, using her to catch him when he stumbled on the stairs down. They hobbled from the bus, heartsore and green to the gills. Pungent rot and a dislodged maggots trailed them.

A dazed El supported him though he led, keeping her pointed forward. Punctures dotted the roadway like ones he'd seen left behind by Welorin drones. They hurried around missing chunks of street, jagged but oddly hexagonal. She recovered herself, turned around and froze.

He tugged. "We've got to go."

"But Jesse."

"He'll catch up."

Her answer felt lifeless. "Okay."

He put barrier rather than distance between them and the snatchers, using what he knew of snatching pattern to anticipate what they expected of their prey. They hid in an apartment over a looted store, hunched in an overturned refrigerator when he could keep her head down. The third time she peeked her head out where she might be seen, he opened his mouth to scold her.

"Thank you, Alaric." Tears drew the only clean lines down her face. "We should've just ran, but you risked yourself to stay nearby so Jesse can find us."

He closed his mouth.

I'd love for him to find us, but he charged a Sentinel. Even with a half-dozen snatchers... "We can check the street every once in a while, but carefully. We'll double back once the coast is clear."

She wrapped herself around him, burying her face into his chest. He repositioned them so he could barely see out the window's corner. She pulled her knees in tight to her chest, shaking hard enough it made his teeth chatter.

They huddled and hoped.

Exhaustion claimed her.

Nightmare contorted her features while he wrestled ghosts of missing memories and others he wished he could forget.

I should've done more, saved him somehow.

He picked maggots from their hair and clothes, dropping them into an empty beer bottle. Impatience ate at him until he couldn't wait any longer. He eased himself from her grasp.

"Where are you going?" El asked.

"I'm...," he hesitated, settling for a lie. "I have to you know. Stay here."

Tears welled in her eyes. "Hurry."

He chewed his lip. "I'll be back soon. Stay out of sight."

"Maybe I should come with you, I need to too."

"No," he snapped, "Uh, I, uh, couldn't with you there."

"No sisters then," she said.

"What?" he asked.

"Boys with sisters aren't so shy."

Not sure that's right, but it'll do for now.

Her sobs followed him out, but he had to know. His leg hurt, but hiding had let it rest. He limped downstairs and up the street, hurrying from cover to concealment. Half way there he started cursing: his leg, the Welorin, distance in general and his luck.

He cursed how long it took him to manage even short distances.

His mind retreated into a hunting state, watching for too-quiet places, flickers from mostly covered fires and peeking faces. The neighborhood seemed empty, but he knew it wasn't.

They missed some of the survivors here. We must've hurt their team worse than I thought.

Images played through his mind—collared slaves engulfed in flames on his command. His stomach threatened to empty itself.

<Sometimes a man has to make unpleasant choices to survive.>

"I know."

He considered the people he'd encountered since the invasion—many just making the same kinds of choices he'd been forced to make. There were the Burrs and Silvs. There were the greedy refugees, killing each other, shoving little girls from a moving train to steal a yellow sponge cake. In some ways, they were worse than the cannibals.

Am I so different? Who knows how much damage I did to that refugee in the cargo container with my hammer?

For every Marvy or bag snatching woman, there was a Lane. For every crazy set of sisters, there were good if distrustful souls like Jesse and El.

Which am I? Where do I fit?

<With the rest of the sobbing little girls, man up, princess.>

"Shut up."

Welorin fighters streaked overhead, shaftless arrows piercing the night's eerie quiet. These didn't fire at him, though sounds of laser fire carried through the night.

He reached the bus. It'd been torn apart from the inside, its huge metal skin folded open like razor-edged flower petals.

He chewed his lip. *Bus or stairs?*

He chose the building and its narrow stairs. Bodies torn and burned littered the landing. A decapitated flashlight lay in their midst, opposite part of a flanged spider leg too big to carry as a weapon.

No sign of Jesse.

He cleared his throat. "Jesse? Are you there?"

Hollow silence answered.

"Jesse? It's, uh, me, Alaric? Blade? Whatever."

Nothing.

The storeroom awaited below a wide dark mouth that hid who knew what. *If I go down its climb up or...no it's definitely climb up.*

Peering down into the store, he hesitated. In the dark, on the injured ankle, the debris slope presented considerable difficulty. He glanced around for an audience, sat down on the pile of rubble and slid safely if indignantly down into darkness he knew he had to search.

He slid into the store's interior, rising when he hit bottom. "Jesse?"

Nothing.

His foot trod one something hard. It rolled, but he caught his footing. He bent down to find his flashlight, lost during their flight. He reached his thumb forward to turn it on but froze.

What if I turn it on and Jesse's ripped up in some corner.

<Coward.>

He depressed the switch.

Nothing happened.

Figures.

He slammed it against his palm. Light burst from it straight into his face, leaving him dazzled. Furious blinks tried to restore his sight. He panned the light over the empty room, the wall between storefront and storage room ripped wide by huge sharp cuts.

The sentinel.

No sign of Jesse lurked in the ravaged storefront.

No Jesse's better than a mangled corpse.

He panned his light toward the bus. The sentinel's search had torn off the bus's front and scattered several bodies' worth of corpse pieces. It'd forced its way out through the top, but its effort to hunt him left an unexpected boon: a narrow gap between rubble and metal.

About time I had some good luck.

<You're still alive.>

He doused the flashlight and squeezed through, succeeding scratched and bleeding but happy not to repeat his earlier exit. He rushed back to El, footfalls too loud in his own ears. Eyes he didn't see caressed his fine hairs to a standing ovation. He climbed the stairs and rushed into the room.

"It's me, El."

No one answered.

14

THE SEARCH

He searched the room with his flashlight, illuminating his duffel bag, various filth and a few wriggling maggots. Heart and stomach parted ways, one falling away and the other sticking in his throat. An itch developed behind his eyes.

"El?"

"Here," El stepped into the room behind him. "Where'd you get that?"

He turned out the light and hurried over to her.

"I went back to find Jesse."

She slapped him. "You left me here. I was terrified something happened to you, too. You should've taken me."

"I didn't want you getting hurt."

"You mean like how I'd feel if you..." Sobs peppered her words. "...disappeared and never came back even though you promised? Like Jesse?"

"I was trying to protect you."

"That's not your job. You're not Jesse."

He hung his head. "I have to try. It's my fault—"

Her voice went shrill. "None of this is your fault."

He couldn't look at her. "It is. If you hadn't helped me, you two wouldn't have been found."

"You don't know that."

A chill ran the length of his spine, leaving the hairs on the back of his neck tingling. "I've got a bad feeling all of a sudden." He glanced around. "We should move."

She sniffled. "What about Jesse?"

"He wasn't in the store. I don't know where he is."

"We need to find him," she said.

"All right, we'll figure out where the Welorin are taking their prisoners."

"Thank you, Alaric."

<*Oh, my sweet, Alaric, you're my* hero*!*>

"Shut up," he growled too low for her to hear.

They kept on the move for the next few days.

Unlike Washington D.C., the Welorin maintained a transit system in Colorado Springs. Buses, many of them school buses, moved collarless humans from one undisclosed location in the morning to another and then back that night.

"I think we should find out where they take them during the day," he said.

"Why not at night?"

"I'm betting they'll be under tighter guard at night."

"You're probably right."

El impressed him. He'd expected her to disintegrate with misery, but he hadn't seen her cry in days. Bright, resourceful and an ever-present warmth, she held back the gloom with pure force of cuteness.

They followed the buses deeper into Colorado Springs, holing up in buildings along the bus route when they fell too far behind to follow. Food and drinkable water grew elusive, and his duffel loomed emptier each passing day.

Cold added to their troubles, nearly betraying their position in white puffy smoke signals.

The deeper they penetrated the city, the more undamaged it became. Two weeks into their slow pursuit of Jesse and the buses, a clothing boutique offered up candy bars and tinned mints.

El beamed around a hunk of chocolate. "Come on, we can still catch the caravan."

"Not until I check the storeroom for more food."

"Alaric, we'll lose another day."

He held up both hands. "I know. Jesse could be hurt. He might need us. Well, we can't do much to help him if we're half starved to death."

"Fine," she said.

"Fine."

"Well, go."

"I'm going."

"Good."

He paused at the storeroom's entrance, ducking through once he had the last word. "Good."

She rushed in behind him. "Good."

He turned to counter when screams rent the air.

Hairs on his arms saluted. Fear rolled over them in waves. He seized her, pressing his hand into her mouth and biting down on his own sleeve just as the nightmares started. Her teeth dug into his hand, but it kept her screams to whimpers.

The screams quieted.

The nightmares faded.

He released his hold on her, realizing just how closely their bodies pressed together. She wrapped around him tighter. Warmth flooded his cheeks. He focused on his throbbing hand rather than the woman pressed into him.

"Oh my god," she whispered. "I saw them take you. They'd collared Jesse, and he stole you away."

"It's just a nightmare, a projection," he said. "It's not real."

"Don't leave me, please I couldn't live with this horror all alone."

He caressed her head. "I'm right here, El. Everything's going to be fine."

"Promise you'll never leave me behind."

"I promise."

She pressed her face into his chest and didn't let go for a long time.

Colorado Springs offered up different challenges than D.C. Welorin drones of all kinds patrolled more often. Snatchers neither kept rigid schedules nor stuck to a set territory. Sentinels and fear-mongers teamed up to corral the wayward.

They raced down the street, taking cover behind the many abandoned hover vehicles. They'd caught the buses earlier that morning, paralleling them a few blocks over. The caravan turned away from them.

"Come on," El said. "We've got to keep up this time."

He hurried behind her, as exhilarated by their success as he was her smile. A scream around the next corner alerted him with only a moment to spare. He seized El, dragging her into an abandoned copier store. He shoved half a leather belt between his teeth and pushed one at her. She grimaced but bit down, wrapping herself around him in a death grip. His thoughts raced toward fantasies rather than nightmares.

He peered out through the glass.

A crowd scrambled terrified down the ravaged thoroughfare. A handful of Welorin spider sentinels led the chase just ahead of the soccer-ball-shaped fear-mongers.

"I think we're out of range," he hesitated. "You can let go."

"Mmhmm."

Humans followed, staying well back from the drones. Most strode uncollared through the streets like they owned them while drones drove a fleeing gaggle of refugees before them. One snatcher edged too close to a fear-monger. The others tossed his collapsed form into the back of flatbed hovertruck like refuse on garbage day.

Beams of different colors shot from the sentinels. One cut a fleeing child clean in half. Another beam, some kind of stunner struck down a trio of girls. The flight turned down their street. He tensed and put the leather back into his mouth.

A woman raced into the copier store, freezing at its entrance when she saw the two of them. Her terrified eyes widened. Her mouth tensed, but before she could speak yet another beam struck, splattering her in all directions.

El squeezed him. He felt her silent screams pouring into his chest. He felt the telltale warning as a fear-monger drew into range. He heaved her off the floor and through the backroom door seconds before a nightmare hit them almost as bad as the reality around them.

Amidst the screaming of people and the jeering yells of the collared workers, he heard something that he didn't immediately understand: laughter.

El huddled in the corner, not even holding onto him anymore. Whatever nightmare she'd been subjected to left her huddled in a fetal ball in the furthest corner. Every attempt to approach resulted in shrieking.

I wish I knew what's wrong. His mind returned to a problem he could solve. *Why was laughter coming from the drones?*

<You're imagining things.>

The snatchers were too far back for it to have come from them. The Welorin machines had to be the ones laughing—unless it was piped through from some sort of remote control station.

He looted the next store over, piling torn clothing up in the box of some huge printer—making a cozy bed big enough for them both to hide inside.

"El?"

A harsh, hoarse whisper escaped her ball. "Leave me alone."

What now?

He gazed at the comfortable nest, sighed and headed toward the front of the store. "Okay."

"Wait!"

He whipped around. "What?"

"Don't leave me."

"You just told me to—"

Tears flooded her cheeks. "Please don't leave me."

He stepped toward her to offer her an embrace.

"No!" she said. "Don't come near me."

"But don't leave?"

She hid her head, pointing at the storeroom's opposite corner.

He sighed, trudged to the corner and sat with his back to the wall.

Words mumbled from the ball. "Don't look at me."

"What?"

"Please," she said. "Don't look at me."

Why can't girls make sense? Head shaking, he turned around. Déjà vu seized him. *Why do I have the feeling I've done this a lot?*

One of the remembered voices he thought of as an older brother sniggered.

He awoke with a start still staring at the corner. His neck ached and folded legs resisted moving. He turned his head, wincing at a massive crick. "El?"

The storeroom was empty.

He leapt to his feet, pounding pins and needles through his legs. He teetered to one side, but caught himself. "El?"

He rushed out into the storefront, heart racing. He ducked into the little employees-only bathroom. Paper poured out of the waste basket to litter the room. She'd used all of the paper towels, all of the remaining water in the toilet, all of the soap and then countless sheets of copy paper.

Okay, she's a girl, so I get the bathing thing, but she couldn't have needed this much. Why use all the soap? And why so much paper?

He scowled at the room a few minutes more before returning to the storeroom. The makeshift bed hadn't been used. The rear door remained barred from the inside. He spun, searching for clues.

Duffel's gone.

An ache settled into his gut.

She just left?

"Alaric?"

He jumped, whirling around.

El stood in the doorway with the duffel in hand, eyes cast down. She fished into the bag to reveal a handful toothpaste and gum samples. "I found a dentist office around the corner."

"You should've told me you were leaving," he said. "You scared me to death."

"Sorry."

He closed his eyes and took a deep breath. "You're safe. That's what matters."

He opened his eyes to find a sheepish smile perched on her lips.

"Does that stuff have any nutritional value?" he asked.

She shrugged. "It'll make your breath better."

"Have you slept?"

She shook her head.

"You've got to rest. I'll take that and," He reached for the duffel.

She flinched away.

"I'm not going to hurt you, El."

"I'm sorry."

I don't understand. He frowned at her. She shrank before his eyes, not at all the girl he'd grown to know since the train. "Get some sleep. It's my turn to watch, runt."

She stepped around him to the makeshift bed, forcing an uncertain smile as she settled into it. "Wake me in a few hours?"

"Sure."

She covered herself poorly, but he resisted the urge to help. He turned his back to her, cupped a hand over his mouth and tested his breath.

It's not that bad.

He didn't wake her. Whatever had her spooked might look smaller after a full night's sleep.

Maybe we should linger here a day or more instead of pushing harder.

His ankle no longer hurt, but it still felt weak after the continuous strain of staying on the move.

She won't let us linger too long, not while we still need to find Jesse.

After a while, the inactivity got to him. Mint toothpaste became unappetizing pretty much right away, but it filled his stomach in a queasy lump sort of way. He folded copy paper into half-remembered shapes, eating several to fight off hunger and an urge to doze off.

El poked her head out of the box. "What time is it?"

He glanced at his forearm. "No idea."

"You were supposed to wake me."

He smiled. "Was I? Damned memory, I guess I forgot that too."

She pursed her lips and glared. "That's not funny, little boy."

He cocked his head to one side. "Not even a little funny?"

"No."

He watched her.

She fought grinning with all her effort. She lost.

"See."

"Fine, but you need rest too."

"Sounds good to me." He gestured at a pile of toothpaste and folded paper. "Breakfast is served."

She darted to the pile of shapes. "Oh my god, these are beautiful. What are they?"

"Paper?"

"Where did you learn to do this?"

He shrugged.

"I don't recognize a bunch of these," she held one up. "This almost looks like a space ship."

He yawned, climbing into the bed box. "I probably screwed them up. I left you the last chocolate bar. Eat. Afterward, you'd better keep a close eye on me."

"Why?"

He closed his eyes. "I might do tricks."

She snorted. The sound was so sudden that his eyes sprang open in response. El laughed, snorted again, and covered her reddened face with one hand.

Better.

He closed his eyes and drifted off in the warmth.

15

WINDFALL

Days later the ever shining El barely managed to lift the corners of her mouth despite many attempts to recreate her laughter. The ravaged convenience store around them reinforced the reality of life in post-invasion Colorado Springs.

Once more, the building had power. A suspicion grew, poking his curiosity like a caged tiger.

Later, when we have more time.

Collapsed walls, a determined hammer, and his own stubborn methodical searching turned up a small cache of unscavenged foodstuffs.

A yellow box smashed beneath fallen shelves revealed a precious find of jerky disks from some place called Tillamook. Tough and dry, it improved on their diet of elusive winged and wingless rat. Moisture-disintegrated boxes inside a walk-in refrigerator held smashed snack cakes, three in five protected from soured cola by their wrappers.

Even sated hunger couldn't improve their opinion of the replenished stock of yellow sponge cakes, not even the chocolate covered ones. Some few soda bottles survived.

The value of the food notwithstanding, the real windfall of the half crushed store lay in an unobstructed view of the factory complex through a night security window. White smoke rose from the massive plant across the way. Sentinels, fear-mongers, wedge tanks and a heretofore undiscovered Welorin drone patrolled its perimeter.

It resembled an elongated diamond with the same golden skin as the wedge tanks. The floating shards circled overhead of the factory, slower than fighters but an aerial enforcement unit of some kind.

What's so important in there? Is this why most of the surrounding city isn't smashed?

"Ever wonder what happens to captives after processing?" El asked.

"Among other things."

"Think Jesse's still okay?" Her voice wavered no matter how many times she repeated the question.

The numbers they'd seen in no way accounted for the population of Colorado Spring's size—even taking into account those shipped in by train. He'd seen almost no survivors in the mostly undamaged miles leading to the factory.

He chose his words.

"People coming on and off the buses seem in decent shape, though it's hard to tell how well fed they are under the winter clothes the Welorin gave them." He smiled at her. "He's tough and crazy smart. They won't want him hurt."

"Unless he's too smart."

He chewed his lip, deciding to change the subject. "We've got three ways to learn more: sneak inside at night—"

"Through all that?"

"Follow the buses the other way, or leave."

"Or stay here," she said. "So close to that, what're the chances of a snatcher team?"

There's some sense to that, but why is she so sure they'd want Jesse for whatever they're doing in there?

"Bet there's a sewer line going under that," he said.

She shuddered. "Dangerous."

"Maybe not, not here anyway," he said.

"If they're safe, then they're patrolled."

"The Welorin can't be everywhere. Subjugating a planet has to be a severe manpower drain."

"Which's why they use all the drones."

He sighed, pulled a small disk of jerky from a pocket and chewed absently. "What do you want to do?"

She choked on her words. "Find Jesse."

"El..."

"I know," she dissolved into tears. "There's no way to know..."

He offered her a hug.

She shied away like she had every time since the copier store. He'd just lowered his arms when she bolted into them, embracing him with an iron grip. "Oh, Alaric, I'm just so frightened for him."

He held perfectly still, afraid that any movement might frighten her off.

He eased his arms around her. "Somehow, it's all going to be okay, El."

"You can't know that," she said. "There aren't enough people going in and out of there. For all we know, they're feeding the rest to the factory workers. Jesse could be..."

"Living fat and happy on barbecued Coloradoan? Tex-Mexican? Maybe baked Alaskan?"

Her face wrinkled, but she swatted him. "Stop it, that's gross."

"Bean baked Bostonian?"

<*Do you* ever *think before you speak?*>

She jerked away from him, pressed her face into a wall and sobbed.

"El, I'm sorry."

"Jesse was all I had left. I'm never going to see my parents or family again." Thick tears flowed down her cheeks. "I hate this."

"The water works here. We've got food." He offered another embrace, but she ignored it. "We'll do like you say, sit tight, rest and I'm sure Jesse'll ride by at some point. If you want, I can look around a little at night, too."

"I don't know."

"It'll be okay, El, I promise."

He spent the day rigging a loft above the drop ceiling, perching shelving atop pipes and girders. Unless she made some noise, no one exploring the store would notice their nest.

Rags and ripped clothes turned his jumpsuit into a camouflaged if shabby scarecrow. He left her their gear, taking only a small flashlight just in case.

His first night he circled the factory. Fewer drones guarded the dark, still buildings. Sentinels guarded high rises edging its south and west perimeters, bobbing up and down on their bladed legs.

A skeletal, half-finished building dominated a massive, empty expanse on its north side. Four gigantic space ships lay at its feet. On either side of each carrier ship, several pairs of triangular doors stretched open to launch drones the moment humanity begged for another round of exterminations. Others hid who knew what behind closed doors.

A series of concentric barbed wire rectangles contained snatcher camps around prisoner pens between the carriers and a rail depot at the property's northernmost edge. Lancers and skyshards patrolled both, imprisoning refugees and snatchers alike.

A close call sent him home long before sunrise, hungry and discouraged by the scope of the Welorin presence.

His next night he stuck to the buildings east of the combined occupation complex.

Despite his suggestion, he resisted exploring the sewers beneath them. He searched for food, clothing, or anything of use night after night. He collected small electronics and batteries in addition to the basics. His explorations ranged away from the compound a dozen blocks easterly, moving slowly north twelve blocks at a time.

El grew more frustrated by the day.

She refused to move to an apartment complex he'd found which still had water, power, and real beds. He jury rigged the convenience store water heater, giving them hot water for about an hour before it filled the store with smoke.

His trips took him north of the rail line. An airplane graveyard stretched as far as he dared go across the rail from the Welorin complex. Signs for some kind of aircraft tour pointed him toward an air and space museum somewhere at its center. He searched plane by plane, hoping for the means to assemble some sort of radio.

Weighed down by a dozen hopeful components, the sunrise caught him by surprise still in the graveyard. Miles of empty city and active Welorin separated him from El in the dwindling darkness.

I've got to try.

He used wrecked aircraft to shield him, weaving south and slowly east to stay out of sight. A parade of snatchers herded prisoners by the hundreds down the street he needed to cross.

He cursed his luck before realizing that it might not all be bad. *I can see where they take those shipped in on the train.*

He followed them to a series of buildings so plain as to be fit only for government use. The buildings clustered together cattycorner from the air and space museum complex—a huge thing of interconnected domes that could have swallowed a dozen shopping malls.

Using once sculpted museum hedges for cover, he knelt down to eye the government center. His gaze strayed to the sidewalk, more of the hexagonal tiles. He placed a hand on their surface.

<Is now really the time to get touchy feely with the sidewalk?>

He ignored the voice, listening with his hands to the tiniest of thrums. He dug fingers into the edge, trying to pull up one.

<Sure, just play in the dirt while the Welorin march right down atop of you.>

His gaze shot up. The street remained clear. He frowned at the sidewalk.

Later.

He circled the government buildings until he found a hiding place half way down an alleyway. He lifted a dumpster's lid and dove inside without looking. Fist-sized cockroaches scattered. A rat darted in from an unseen hole. They escaped it, and it hissed its frustration at him. He snatched up a bottle, killed the rat and eased the dumpster open once more.

Snatchers lined prisoners up on the sidewalk to a single door. He stared, watching as people disappeared into the building. Some time later, others emerged from a parking structure beneath the government towers. Snatchers helped or dragged most of them toward buses lining the street on his side of the block.

What're they doing to them in there?

Snatchers carried out a girl that might've been El's twin. His stomach lurched, forcing his heart to stall several beats. He glanced up to see the sun risen near to noon. He slammed a fist into his forehead.

If I hadn't gotten so distracted, I might've made it back to her. She might even worry enough to come looking for me.

<She's smarter than you are.>

You're right. She won't venture out for at least a day.

He watched, occasionally distracted by a launching fighter drone or carrier ship above and beyond the buildings processing all the refugees.

The day dragged on, his stomach noisily frustrated by his recent life choices. He glanced at the dumpster's corner.

I'm not eating raw rat. Not again.

His stomach argued, but he held firm.

I should've brought more food with me.

Night fell. It took all his restraint to wait out the last prisoner transport's departure before racing back to El. Two sentinels swept into view a moment before he came out of hiding, checking the building's perimeter. He waited another half hour just to be sure.

He crept back to her. The debris he'd set to obscure their entrance remained in place. He slipped in, turning to restore it. She tackled him.

He reacted to the attack, reversing their position and pinning her to the floor. He lifted his arms. "Damn it, El, you start—"

She yanked him to her and kissed him full on the mouth.

El's kissing me.

<Really, what was your first clue?>

We're kissing.

One kiss turned into a series of smaller kisses, soft, caressing and salted by tears.

<Better stop now, runt, before she figures out the dead rat in your bag kisses better.>

What do I do? I don't know how to kiss. Do I?

She pushed him up, one hand checking her hair. "Dear God, where were you? I was so worried."

"If that's the reward maybe I should get stuck hiding more often."

Her expression changed. Her fist slammed into his jaw. "Don't ever do that again!"

"Kiss you?"

"W-What? N-no," She reddened. "You know exactly what I mean!"

He rubbed his face. "Um, okay?"

She climbed to her feet, perched fists on her hips and glared. "Well?"

He raised both brows.

"God, you're such a dense...*boy* sometimes," she said. "Where were you? What happened?"

He told her.

"...so if I can get a better look—"

"No."

He blinked.

"You're not going back out tonight."

"But we might be able—"

"No."

He opened his mouth to argue, but something behind her gaze stalled him.

He smiled. "Okay."

She wrapped herself around him, sagging into his chest. "Thank you."

She slept against him that night, head on his chest and arms wrapped too tight for him to even slide an inch away. Her hot breath tickled his skin. She wrapped one leg across and around him, occasionally shifting in a way that kept him all-too aware of how her body pressed against his.

She let him sleep late, but stayed within inches of him.

A tickle woke him. Her finger traced patterns along his chest. He tried to meet her eye, but she stared at the finger in dour thought.

"Credit for your thoughts," he said.

She smirked at him. "I don't take credit cards."

He smiled. "What're you thinking?"

A sigh escaped her. "I don't want you going back out there, but I know you need to go."

"There are other places we can go."

"No. Not without Jesse."

"El."

"I'm not leaving him behind. He's all I've got."

"Thanks."

She opened her mouth, closed it again, a minuscule shake of her head proceeded opening it again. "I found a safe in the floor. I couldn't open it."

"You want to rob the place?"

She gestured. "Was there something here we weren't going to take?"

"Point to the pixie."

He took it in turns, watching the factory and fiddling with the store's floor safe. Small dismantled electronics ringed the floor around it.

An hour after night fell he heaved himself to his feet. "Time to go back out."

"Not tonight."

"I know you're worried, but—"

"I'm coming then."

He frowned.

Fear, need, and desperation warred for her eyes.

"Okay. Gather the important stuff."

He sacrificed new exploration to indulge her need to see all he'd described. Welorin base and camp, museum and government building, seeing them eased the set of her stance. A low corona edged into view to their east.

"Let's go back."

She tugged the other way. A semblance of her former playful smile lifted her lips. "Come on, let's go into the museum."

He returned it. "You're the boss."

Her smile widened. "Don't you forget it."

Neither invasion nor violence marred the museum. Flight paraphernalia overflowed exhibits. Planes and spacecraft hung from high ceilings. They stopped in a dome filled with a mixed forest of cafeteria tables and comfortable sitting areas instead of exhibits. Early dawn shone through the faceted glass skylight that crowned its upper half. Hallways spoked outward in six of the eight cardinal directions—restricted by dueling restaurant and souvenir shops.

Kitchen lights flickered on at their entrance, illuminating wire shelves stocked with molded bread, chips, condiments and canned cheese.

"Oh my God." She seized chips by the handful.

"Let's check the walk-in first."

She stared at the bags in her hands, looking almost as if he'd taken a warm kitten from her. She dumped all but one bag back where it'd come.

He opened the refrigerator while she opened the chips. He got his opened first. He gaped at its insides in silence broken only by the ceaseless, chainsaw-like chomping at his back.

"Wuh?" she said through a stuffed mouth.

Metal shelves bowed under the weight of box after box, offering French fries, cookie dough and meat patties of every flavor from simple to maple bacon cheddar. Frozen microwave burritos and hot dogs leaned against one another in large self-seal plastic bags.

He swept an inviting hand toward its frigid depths. "Ladies first."

She rushed past him, stopping long enough to kiss his cheek. "You're so sweet."

Just didn't want you eating me by mistake.

16

FAILURE

They sat at the foot of a little conveyor machine that took in frozen burger patties and returned perfectly grilled burgers.

El nudged him with her shoulder. "Now aren't you glad we came?"

He hesitated.

Her brows rose.

He chomped another bite of patty, nodding and smiling around it.

She beamed, leapt to her feet and grabbed his greasy hand. "Come on, let's go shopping."

That most of the store's contents had little use in post-invasion Colorado didn't seem to blunt El's exuberance. She led him through several racks of t-shirts, pressing them up against him with a pert little smile. She dropped two into his arms. She sorted through a bin of pilot travel kits, choosing a dark purple set to shove his way. She dragged him to a section of 'tour guide' mp7 players. She hung one around his neck and towed him to a wall displaying ball caps. She tried several on him, frowning until she finally rolled her eyes at him and put the final dark blue hat on her own head.

She dragged him to the nearby restrooms and shoved him toward the men's room. "Go clean up."

His brows rose.

"We've got hot water, stinky. We can bathe here."

He opened his mouth.

"I know, you kind of got that hot water heater working, but now we can get completely clean thanks to my detour here."

<Don't say it. Let it be her idea.>

"I've been trying to get you to move for days."

Her face fell.

<Idiot.>

"We could have moved into those apartments, had real showers, slept in real beds."

<Shut up, moron.>

"I'm *sorry* that I don't smell as good as you do, but I didn't figure you'd be happy if I came back to that store all clean while you still reeked to high heavens."

She wilted.

<You're officially the dumbest guy on this planet.>

He offered the second t-shirt.

She sniffed. "That's for drying off."

He looked at it, refusing to see her tears. "What about you then?"

She spun and marched back to the store.

<Don't chase, just go clean up.>

I should apologize.

<You think? Won't do you any good until she calms down.>

He sighed and entered the bathroom. Fluorescent lights flickered to life. He blinked at the pristine white and metal surfaces.

It's like another life.

He crossed to the sink, freezing midstride to match stares with the filthy stranger in the mirror's surface. The wall length mirror left him speechless before himself.

Another life, another me—whoever I am.

He leaned closer, staring into his reflected face and searched his own light violet eyes.

"Who are you?"

Loss and panic welled up as his question echoed away against the tiles. Burr remained thousands of miles away, and El didn't care if he remembered his name or not.

Did I forget or just not want to face the emptiness?

He shook away the pointless questions and stripped. He stuffed his jumpsuit into one sink while shoving paper towels into a second. He filled them both with hot water and turquoise gel from the soap dispenser. Towels, soap, and water, he set to work removing layers of Colorado.

Filthy, blood-matted hair transformed into fine, soft brown. Filthy hands revealed long, slender fingers. Days of dirt and toil drained away, leaving a too-thin naked man in his reflection. He dried himself with the two t-shirts. He scrubbed the jumpsuit next, sending water sluicing away until no longer brown.

Two thick and two thin cobalt blue stripes alternated down the jumpsuit's ripped left shoulder. He waved it and his under-things under a jet engine of hot air.

The door cracked open. "Aren't you done yet?"

He covered himself with the damp jumpsuit.

"No."

"Hurry up. I want to get clean too."

"Use the other bathroom."

"I was hoping you'd guard the door for me," she said.

He started to object, then thought better of it. "Sure. Wait outside a moment."

The door closed.

He raised the jumpsuit to the dryer. The door cracked open once more. "Nice legs."

He snatched his clothes back to his body, blood heating his cheeks.

Once the door shut again, he ducked behind it and pulled on his damp clothing. He exited to a frowning El.

"What?" he asked.

"You were supposed to wear the t-shirt."

"You said to dry off with it."

"One of them."

"Oh."

She shook her head. "Stay out here and guard me. No peeking."

"You peeked."

She reddened. "You were taking too long."

"So if you—"

"A gentleman would guard the door and absolutely not even think about peeking." She disappeared into the bathroom. A bolt slid closed with a click.

He thought about peeking, forcing himself to adjust the jumpsuit sticking to his skin.

She unlocked and opened the door a long while later. A souvenir t-shirt hung down over her to the tops of her thighs.

"I think that shirt's too big," he said.

She tugged at it. "Not big enough."

He looked down at the amount of visible leg, realizing his jumpsuit needed adjusting again. *Just not in front of her.*

"Where's your jumpsuit?"

"Drying."

"The dryer'll get it mostly dry."

"Oh, I just bet you'd love that, me waltzing around with my jumpsuit clinging to me like a second skin."

The image washed across his mind.

His smile grew until it ran out of face. "Well, yeah."

She swatted him, blushed and returned her hand to keeping the shirt pulled down as far as possible. "Take the tour or something. I'll catch up when I'm decent."

He put one of the two earbuds in and started the recording. It directed him to a spot just outside the gift shop. He glanced back to see El staring at him with a strange smile.

"El?"

She started, blushed and rushed back into the bathroom.

He smiled. *I need to get her to rush in that shirt more often.*

The recording led him through era after era of aircraft. Each collection culminated in a massive domed hub, like the food court, spoking off to other eras. Glass displays lined some halls, while windows in others opened up onto craft too big for inside display.

He climbed a spiral stair to the upper level of one dome, granting him an elevated view of a half-dozen fighter planes in a staged dogfight.

What I wouldn't give to have a working fighter in all this mess.

He continued around the display, attention wandering between the dogfight and a gigantic six-engine plane outside the dome, facing another spoke. He stopped at a display window, staring out at its back.

A voice made him jump backward. "The C-230VR represents the last generation of USMC tactical airlift vehicle." A holographic display of statistics appeared in the upper window. "This generation boasted a hyperdyne VTOL system carried on to replacement designs. The addition of experimental, rapid recharge alternating rail cannons to this model doomed the C-230VR to a short-lived, inglorious career.

"For more detailed information regarding high-cycle electromagnetic interference caused by the RRARC on the hyperdyne electronics, visit the main C-230VR exhibit in corridor thirty-four."

Wonder if there's enough there to jury-rig a weapon.

He descended to the floor and turned down a hall that should bring him to the C-230VR.

<Idiot.>

He glanced back.

El's supposed to catch up on the tour.

He gazed down the hallway.

A weapon like that would change things.

<Yeah, like break your back. It's a mounted cannon, moron, not a pistol.>

If I could get the plane running—

<Bulky aircraft launches in sight of space fighter squadron. Memorial services to be announced.>

"Jerk."

He resumed the tour.

One display held a mannequin in a leather bomber jacket covered in patches. He stared at it, read each campaign, airfield, and locale stitched into their design.

"Take it."

He whirled around, losing his footing. His eyes darted to her legs to find them covered in silver jumpsuit once more. His pounding heart fell.

She helped him back to his feet. She looked him up and down, smile growing. "You may be disappointed in what you see, but I'm not."

"Done inspecting me?"

"Turn around for me," she said.

He rolled his eyes but spun.

"Slower, I want to enjoy it."

"It's my back, what's to enjoy?" he asked.

Breathiness edged her reply. "Plenty. Turn around. What do you think?"

"I liked the t-shirt better without the jumpsuit."

She swatted his shoulder. "Too bad."

She unhooked a velvet rope from a brass pole, lifted it—teetering a bit—and swung it at the display. A crack shot through the glass as the rebound tumbled her.

"Give me that."

Glass splintered in all directions. An alarm bell trilled.

He cursed. "Come on, fun's over."

She snatched the coat from the display, bringing the mannequin toppling out as well. They raced to the entrance. He pushed open the door, forestalling her with a hand while he scanned for patrols. Lines of prisoners moved into the building across the way, but no heads looked their way.

"Stay inside."

He closed the door, and the alarm fell silent.

He opened it once more to hear it still ringing.

He stepped inside, scanning sky and street for drones. "Huh. Internal alarm."

"Let's find security and turn it off," she said.

"Probably shouldn't stay either way."

"We'll be able to see them coming with the cameras. I'm not abandoning food, clothing and warm water unless they storm the place."

He crossed to a freestanding map. Security wasn't listed on the directory. He memorized the exit pathways.

"Let's stay here and watch."

She pointed upward. "With that running?"

"I don't know where security is," he said. "If we could go straight to it, disable the alarm and watch the monitors that'd be one thing, but exploring blindly without knowing whether or not the alarm called Welorin just doesn't sit well with me."

"You're the boss."

He barely noticed the ringing alarm by the time he felt safe to abandon watching. It took a while to find security and more time to disable the display alarm. El watched the cameras while he tinkered. When it finally turned off, the silence felt surreal.

"There—"

A soft snore escaped El's chair. He laid the offending jacket across her overtop a security nightstick cradled in her arms. He settled into another command chair and watched empty hallways.

"Alaric."

He opened his eyes.

She smiled. "Let's eat and then finish the tour."

He glanced at the monitors.

"Still no one," she said.

They wound along the tour, stomachs full but still nibbling snacks. Their tour guide brought them to a section of early generation space stations which included crew quarters. El stepped over the ropes.

"You're going to set off another alarm."

She perched hands on her hips. "Am not."

"What're you doing?"

"Let's sleep here."

"What about the rest of the tour?"

"This place is huge. We're not going to finish it today."

"We could try."

"I'm full. I'm warm. I just want to rest instead of always being on the move."

He glanced around the hub, eyeing hallway entrances, "If you want to rest, we should go back to the store."

"This place is better."

"We don't know it's safe."

"We don't *know* if the store is safe. We've been here over a day, even set off an alarm. Nobody's bothered this place in all these months."

He grimaced. "That's what worries me. This place is a fat prize sitting in the center of how many snatchers and Welorin? There are too many access points, besides what about Jesse?"

"They're processing people across the street." She studied the space station in silence, circling it slowly. "If we're going to find Jesse, it's over there."

"You really want to sleep in there?" he asked.

"It's a space bed." She beamed. "Help me find a way in."

"You're the boss," he mimicked.

The station bed wasn't as big as their loft nest, but that had its benefits too. El pressed against him. He'd hoped she'd wear only the t-shirt again, but even without it, he could still imagine her bare, shapely legs draped across him instead of the clothed one doing horrible things to his sleeping ability.

He eased her leg from atop him and slipped from her arms. He jogged around the food court, taking it easy on his ankle, but otherwise burning away pent up energy. He returned to the module with a serving tray of grilled meats, baked cookies and warmed prepackaged cinnamon rolls.

He'd barely entered when her questing nose brought her out of dreams. She offered him a sleepy smile and purred. "Breakfast in bed? I think I love you."

His stomach fled for its life. His heart auditioned as an entire percussion section and sweat appeared spontaneously everywhere embarrassing.

She bolted upright. "Are you okay?"

Calm down, she can't hear it. Just smile.

He smiled. "Thought I heard something for a moment."

"Sit with me," she patted the bed. "Did you eat?"

"A little."

"What's wrong?"

"There's a lot here to like, but I dislike being so close to snatcher and Welorin activity."

"We were close across from the factory."

He nodded. "In a half trashed building that looked inaccessible."

"As opposed to a huge untouched museum."

"Right."

"I'm not frightened," she stroked his cheek. "You'll protect me."

"El, I can't protect me, let alone you."

"You're shaking."

"I like you, Jesse, too, but I *can't* wear another collar."

"What was it really like?"

"Worse than I told you, more horrifying than you can imagine."

"Okay, let me finish, and we'll leave."

He waited outside the station, staring at the wall. So many horrible things lurked in place of his lost memories. Her warm hand slipped into his, her other hand wrapping around his waist.

"You okay?"

"If I said 'not really,' would it disappoint you?"

"It shouldn't, but it might a little. I've got used to you being my angelic king, Alaric."

He sighed. "I'm all right."

They watched the processing center, waiting for the prisoners and their guards to clear the way back to the store.

"I think I should sneak into that building before heading back."

"All right." Her hopeful, hungry gaze rested on the building.

"You should stay here, it's too big a risk—"

"For a girl?"

He stood, not facing her. "For someone I'm terrified of losing."

"You'd come for me, I know you would," she said.

"I'm not some kind of super man."

"You'd come," she whispered.

"Let's just not find out."

She pulled him into a seat next to her, wrapped around him in a half embrace and kissed his cheek. They watched the building in silence until the sun went down.

El rose to her feet. "I'll get you some food."

Thank you. He slipped outside, darting from cover to cover across the intervening distance. He found the entrance unlocked but circled to enter through the parking garage. He rounded a pylon, coming face to face with a lancer.

He froze, scream caught fast in his throat.

Nothing moved.

He slipped back behind the pylon.

Nothing moved.

He crept around its other side. A panel different from the tank's weapon ports hung open.

Must be dead.

He crossed to it.

Too small for a maintenance hatch, could be they removed a processor module or something.

Part of him ached to disassemble it, use it somehow to get him and El to safety.

She won't leave without Jesse. He sighed. *Nothing could fit inside that anyway.*

The lowest office building floor had been gutted of unnecessary walls, cubicles, and furniture. Poles and ropes queued the emptied space. A stair took him up into a maze of cubicle walls. He rushed through it, anxious over the slightest noise. A small alcove attached to the maze contained medical supplies: cotton balls, gauze, and ointment.

He snatched a few vials of antiseptic and two rolls of gauze. First aid alcoves gave way to larger spaces, each containing a computer terminal and a portable barcode scanner.

He aimed one at the wall and depressed a raised stud where a trigger might go. Lasers burned the cubicle wall. The computer terminal beeped. Its screen came to life, displaying an empty photograph blank and biographical data form under a barcode.

He leaned toward the burned wall, nose wrinkling. Imperfect on the melted fabric, it resembled the wrist tattoo Jesse showed him.

A few minutes clicking provided a search function. He typed Jesse.

Did Jesse tell me his last name?

He hit search, hoping to narrow the results further. He browsed through thousands of pictures until the friendly giant's photo appeared on the screen.

He clicked on the details button. Blood drained from his face.

Subject: Jesse Archibald MacIntyre

Assignment: Candidate for stardrive micronization project.

Status: Subject intellect far exceeds population norm. Recaptured after escape attempt. Regional command orders punishment example for other prisoners. Relocation to medical facility twenty-three for surgical alteration before return to worker population.

Panicked fingers sped across the terminal controls.

This is my fault. I have to locate that medical center and rescue him before they punish him.

Medical facility twenty-three appeared on his screen. Its location read: Docked—Orbital Platform Four, Lunar Orbit.

He slammed his fist into the console, cursing the pain.

He ran a search for El, cross-referencing her through Jesse's family relationships when she didn't come up. He brought up her record. Cold sweat formed between his shoulder blades.

Subject: Rebecca Elle Thibodaux

Assignment: Detention center six, behavior insurance re: Jesse Archibald MacIntyre.

Status: Deceased.

Fury burned through his chest.

How could the Welorin relegate El, bright capable El as a mere prisoner to force Jesse to whatever?

Dread replaced fury.

How old is this status?

He glanced out the window to see dawn on the rise. He raced toward the stairs only to double back and clear the terminal display. He paused at the building entrance, gut knotted into a black hole. Impending terror tripled its gravitational force.

A Welorin Sentinel bobbed outside the museum's front entrance. Snatchers strolled its perimeter.

A herd of prisoners marched toward him up the street under the watchful menace of countless snatchers.

He raced the other way, up through the queues and back down to the parking garage. He scoured the surface of the lancer drone, but couldn't find remote control, panel access or even a way to yank free one of its guns to wipe out those between him and El. He gave it up, rushing through covered positions back to the dumpster he'd hidden in once before.

He hid, waiting out the day and hating himself for it.

Early nightfall found a pair of Sentinels perched on the lawn between him and the museum door. He waited hours, crouched just out of sight. He raced to the museum the moment they wandered away.

The museum doors lay smashed and shattered in the entrance. Scorch marks scarred the walls from energy weapon fire. A snatcher's body, blasted from behind, lay near a discarded nightstick, its upper quarter burned away.

He searched: food court, kitchen, gift shop, crew compartment. He pushed open the door of the women's bathroom, hoping to be scolded. He tried the security office, watching as monitors flickered from location to location. She was nowhere. El was gone.

First Jesse, then El, I tried to save them. But even my best intentions went sideways.

<As usual.>

I told her I couldn't protect her. It's all my fault.

<They might have survived happily for years.>

As slave and prisoner.

<You had to play the hero and now they're doomed.>

He seized the nearest chair and hurled it at the monitors, screaming at the top of his lungs. “Shut up. I never meant for any of this to happen.”

<A commander takes responsibility for his actions, young master, foreseen and unforeseen.>

<Only babies throw tantrums.>

“You aren’t important enough to remember. Just get out of my head and leave me alone.”

He paced the office, fingernails digging into his palms.

Think, think, there has to be something I can do.

17

ESCAPE

He crossed the food court, rushing beneath the enormous skylight toward the kitchen, oblivious to the grey light illuminating the emptiness around him. He stuffed himself with tasteless food, packing extra heavy in El's favorites.

Options and counters, plans and outcomes circled his mind. He seized upon one, rushing back to the broken entrance. A moment's scanning and he plunged into the darkness. His heart beat around a molten core in his torso. Every beat drove him to a quicker stride. He cleared the pillars and came face to face with nothing.

He cursed.

<A tank weapon isn't going to be much lighter than a plane's.>

He seized upon the next plan, exited the parking structure and slid to a stop on the tile just inside the museum. He stripped the lower torso of the mildly pungent snatcher, leaving only the man's underwear behind. He dragged what remained to the nearest closet and hurried to the souvenir store.

Despite his determination, he hesitated at exchanging his jumpsuit and instead, belted the snatcher's jeans atop it. An oversized t-shirt combined with the soil of a long dead potted plant and the pilot jacket finished his snatcher disguise. He stuffed ripped fabric into the too large boots. He dirtied hair and face before leaving behind the museum—perhaps forever.

Cover to cover, he snuck back to the administration buildings. He settled in a bathroom stall just inside the entrance and waited.

Temper eased from him as hours drug on, replaced by haunting images of El left much the same as the dead snatcher. Noises marched into the building just as he started to doze. He realized just as voices ordered people down the line that he had to use the bathroom.

He resisted the impulse for half an hour. *Time to go.*

<Ha Ha.>

He finished his business, flushing the toilet before approaching the sinks. He started at it and his hands. Washing would clean his hands of the filth so carefully applied.

Screw it.

He washed his hands despite a lack of towels or soap, wiping them on his jeans as he strode out of the bathroom wearing an expression he somehow knew trademarked by the obnoxious voice that called him runt.

Eyes seized him up and down the line. He shoved the closest refugee. "Watch it, Greatfather."

"Sorry, sir," the old man mumbled. "Wait, pardon?"

He glared back. "Keep moving."

"Sorry, sir."

He didn't enter deeper into the building. He had no interest in the computers that he couldn't satisfy later. He headed outside. An uncollared snatcher eyed him, opening his mouth in preparation for who knew what.

Alaric shoved a refugee and smirked at the snatcher. "Never can get over how pathetic they are, you?"

The snatcher sneered. "Sheep. Where'd you come in from?"

"D.C."

His eyes narrowed. "You one of Burr's lot?"

Alaric shook his head. "We've met, but I don't work with him."

"Lucky you."

"Tell me about it." He stepped through the door and outside. His sudden chill wasn't from the weather. *How does he know Burr?*

"You, in the jumpsuit," a familiar voice shouted.

He spun.

Silv yanked a woman in a silver jumpsuit from the line. Slightly longer hair and a head taller, for a moment he still thought the woman thrown to Silv's feet was El. Heat rose up in his chest. He took two hasty steps before he drew up short.

"Dogs, over here," Silv said. "You too busy smelling each other's asses to pay attention?"

Alaric slipped through to the line's opposite side.

"Jumpsuits go for interrogation, bark that you understand."

Two collared snatchers barked beneath glares.

"Good boys, take her back to Burr at the camp," she said.

He froze.

Burr's here?

"What're you staring at?" Silv demanded.

He lowered his voice to a growl. "An uppity bitch not worth a romp."

El's voice flitted through his thoughts. <*What do you think you're doing?*>

She darkened. "Watch it, meat, I've got pull."

He snorted.

She jabbed a thumb at the museum. "We were on the raid, were you?"

He laughed. "Wow, you crossed the street and what, caught a rat or two?"

"We captured a runaway—"

His heart thundered. "One? How impressive—"

Silv stomped up to him, knocking refugees from her way. "Go on over to the museum, meat. Take a stroll in there. I dare you."

The snatcher from inside the door leaned outside. "Knock it off, Silv, you're slowing down the line. You want him dead, mark him for a knife fight if you can take him."

"I can take him."

Alaric looked at her. "Thanks, you're not my type."

A sentinel marched around the corner, its bladed limbs pockmarking the hexagonal plates making up the road. It aimed dark red eye sockets at him.

"Enough mating rituals, return to base." It pivoted toward Silv. "Get the line moving, Earther."

Silv glared at him.

He shrugged it off, shoved hands in his pockets and marched in the collared snatchers' wake. Half a block down, he hurried his pace. A block shy of the camp, he caught them.

"Hold up there."

They turned, simmering anger in their eyes.

"Ignore that bitch. She's got no right talking to a man like that."

"Got a remote to enforce that order?"

"Jesus, Barry, shut up."

Barry gestured. "He called her a bitch, I didn't."

"This isn't a trick. I'm not going to punish you for what you say," Alaric jabbed a thumb back toward the administration buildings. "Sentinel ordered me to bring the woman back for processing."

"Why?"

"Hell if I know. Wrong jumpsuit I guess," he said. "Point is, I'll take her off your hands, and you can relax back at camp."

"Until someone else orders us to sit up and beg," Barry said.

"Nothing I can do about that, wish I could."

Barry's friend grinned. "You're not a bad guy."

<For a traitor to the planet.>

He marched forward and grabbed the woman's arm. "You're coming with me."

Their eyes met. Fear wrapped a core of resignation like a haze. He dragged her a block before shoving her into an alcove. She tripped, landing in the corner, eyes wide and skin drained of color.

"Please, please, don't rape me, not a—, plea—" her thick New England accent disintegrated into wracking sobs.

"Shhh, I'm not going to hurt you. Are you from Boston?"

"What?"

He pulled his t-shirt up enough to expose his golden jumpsuit. "Boston, that jumpsuit means you were part of the Boston delegation, right?"

"Yyeeess."

"Do you know where they're taking the delegations? Why you're not being processed with the others."

"Just rumors."

He waited.

"Welorin don't want diplomats with the rest of the prisoners. They're afraid they might—"

"Rally others. So where do they go?"

"If they don't have a useful skill they just disappear."

He frowned. "Like what kind of skill?"

She shrugged. "Engineering, medicine, the sciences."

He stared out of the alcove. *Will that save El? Where could they take the others away?*

<What with a whole solar system to choose from.>

Exactly, how do I find out?

<Don't agree with me, it's just weird.>

"What're you going to do with me?" she asked.

Alaric turned around, mouth open. "I don't know."

"You're resistance, aren't you? Can't you take me to your cell?"

He stared. "I'm alone."

Her color drained once more. "Alone?"

"El was with me until yesterday, and Jesse right after the train—"

"You knew El? Did they kill her?"

"I don't know."

She frowned. "You're not very good at this hero thing."

"Thanks."

"What're you going to do?" she asked.

"I'm going back."

"You're out of your god-forsaken mind!"

He shushed her.

"I'm not going back there."

He pointed. "That way to the processing or the other way toward the camps? You're dead center in there."

"You know somewhere we can hide, right?"

He nodded.

"Take me there, then do whatever the suicidal little voices in your head desire."

He snuck her to the apartments, glad to be rid of her. She'd known El but wasn't anything like the pixie. Over her initial fear with freedom on the horizon, she complained, ordered him around and generally made their flight to hiding a hundred times more dangerous than necessary.

That's it. I'm not helping anyone else—ever.

With Silv and the rest of Burr's snatchers in Colorado, he decided not to return to his snatcher ruse that day. He returned to the store. The waiting store felt cavernous without El.

She's alive. Silv let that much slip.

He buried his unease in the floor safe, fiddling with the electronics he hoped might help him unlock it. It beat him.

He returned to the administration building just after midnight. His gaze fell on the darkened museum. Guilt and stupidity waylaid him. Glass composed its upper half. They'd spent the night, enjoying light and warmth without thinking about what motion activated lights might look like from the outside.

I led them straight to her.

He pushed the thought away. El shared some of that mistake, but a possibility to repair their mistake awaited feet from him. He snuck inside, following the queues until he found an alcove with an active computer terminal. Though the terminal took moments to respond to his fingers, it felt as if he held his breath an eternity.

Subject: Rebecca Elle Thibodaux

Assignment: Detention center six, behavior insurance re: Jesse Archibald MacIntyre.

Status: Awaiting execution.

Fury burned through his chest. He kept reading, his vision blurring as their lengthy analysis of her value as a hostage versus an example droned on and on. The report's synopsis recommended continued use of her to keep Jesse doing whatever they had him doing, but a final paragraph dismissed the analysis in four short words: Execution mandated by command.

"The hell they will." His own voice startled him. "They're not killing El, and they're not treating her like some animal to make Jesse behave."

He took several moments, browsing through other records until he'd collected the information he needed.

A grin crept across his face.

He brought up El's record once more, wiped her history, family connections and the insulting report. He ordered her relocated to worker population housing and set her job assignment to the nearby factory.

His hand poised to finalize the orders. He added medical abilities to her skill list and submit the change.

Just in case.

He'd infiltrate the factory. Maybe not tomorrow, maybe not the next day, but he'd snatch her back.

His stomach bottomed out, and the room's temperature seemed to plummet.

I'm casually planning to infiltrate a heavily guarded factory in sight of a Welorin airfield and snatcher camps.

His hands moved to his throat. It tightened as if a collar squeezed it once more. He shifted baring the wrist still naked thanks to Burr's sadism.

<If Burr catches you again, it's going to be a whole lot worse.>

Revulsion brought bile to his throat. Burr's threats of re-education echoed in his mind.

<What happens if you free her and she's caught once more?>

Welorin subjugated the whole planet. There wasn't anywhere they could run that being captured again wouldn't mean her death.

<Leave it alone, runt. You've saved her life. Don't play the hero and throw that all away.>

Maybe she'd be better off if he didn't come to her rescue. His own words echoed in his thoughts. He'd told her he couldn't save her. Certainly not from so many Welorin.

Her face swam into his memories: hopeful, trusting gaze and confident expression declaring, even demanding that no matter what he'd rescue her.

He forced down a lump in his throat.

I have to try.

He waited, expecting the voices to berate him, call him an idiot. No memory challenged his intent.

He exited, returning unnoticed to the convenience store. He studied the factory until the sun rose again. He watched the drones, noting how their number and activity changed with arriving workers. His mind catalogued and sorted almost by reflex, searching for a tactical weakness.

He alternated his watch with troubled pacing. Fear dogged him, returning after he'd pushed it away. A nagging suspicion drove him. If the ones that wanted to see her executed discovered his change, they could order it once more. He had to save her before that happened.

By day's end, he'd discovered no apparent weakness.

He flopped down next to the store's floor safe, gnawed on some jerky and tinkered with it. After he didn't know how many tries, the safe opened up to him revealing bundles of useless money and a solution.

Down, beneath the building through the sewers.

He dug into the cash, thoughts running through possible scenarios that included refugees like wrench girl. He found a handheld taser, its casing orange with some sort of corrosion, a revolver and a sagging box of shells.

He hefted the dirty pistol. *What I wouldn't give for a compressed-quasar pistol.*

He kicked himself. He had a weapon, something that would've altered countless close calls. Against feasters or the knives and clubs of snatchers, a pistol reigned as king.

He entered the sewers the moment darkness allowed. He paused just inside it, distracted by the circuitry underneath the nearby road tiles. He shook his head and descended into the dark, smelly underworld.

He took a few deep breaths to force aside his fear. He wound through dank passages toward the factory, trusting his direction sense. Dead ends, collapsed sections, and misturns stole the hours away. He popped from access points like a confused gopher, darting glances to correct his course and scurrying back beneath.

He lifted a sewer access with shaky hands and emerged in a boiler room in the subbasement. A telltale clicking warned of nearby spider drones.

Dread rose within him, sending shudders through him that threatened to give him away with chattering teeth. With exaggerated care, he crept into the basement and lowered the access cover.

He crept from the room. He shifted from shadow to shadow.

<Don't you think they've got infrared sensors?>

He pushed the thought away. He poked his head up, jerking himself down mere feet from a drone's back. He scanned the cold, deserted building, wishing for some tech to help him see like they could. Conveyors wound throughout the building, supporting strange, massive engines in varied state of construction.

He sought a vantage point, overseer or supervisor's office, anything that might allow hidden surveillance. He scanned the girders in the ceiling, eyeballing spots near one of the big spinning fans for enough room to hide his body.

The drone whirred, legs clicking on the cement.

Every hair on his body rose.

It's facing me. Did I make a sound? Can it see through my cover?

He held his breath, moving only his eyes in a desperate search for anything he might use to shield himself from its lasers long enough to put a bullet through the control module.

It whirred again, legs clicking their way around the machines he used for cover.

He circled opposite it, rolling beneath a conveyor belt. He fought the urge to close his eyes, using his imagination to keep track of the drone he couldn't see. Instead, he searched for the second drone, the one that'd doom him.

The drone chasing him kept going, marching up the pathway he'd hidden in toward the building's edge.

He breathed again slow and quiet.

It'd either dismissed whatever noise he'd made or it'd all been part of its programmed patrol. Alaric darted to another position, watching its path and searching for its partner.

He only found one.

Its pattern wound through the factory in a long, complicated crisscross that covered every corner in a leisurely patrol.

He edged toward stairs leading up. He waited for the drone to turn away into one of the office access hallways.

He darted up the stairs to a platform over the main assembly line floor. Ringing noises announced every meeting of foot with metal step.

The drone swept back into the room, dark red sockets sliding back and forth.

Alaric grabbed the first door handle, shoved it open, bound through and closed it in a controlled rush. His heart thundered in his chest. The dark room exploded with light as every bulb in the factory lit at once.

Draft boards and tables circled the room, piled with blueprints and rolled plans. Holograms burst to life in the room's center, soft blue glowing replicas of the engines resting on the conveyors below and ships like he'd seen on the carriers nearby.

He stared, yearning to delve into the interactive blueprints and learn how the factory served the Welorin, but the sound of approaching spider legs made it impossible. Metal groaned outside. A crack like thunder proceeded ringing metal and a heavy crash.

He risked a glance out one window. The stair leading to him had fallen, the too-heavy drone upon it.

Alaric exhaled in relief a moment before lasers cut through the floor around him. He leapt into a forward roll. Near misses flashed heat across his legs.

He raced for the next office, springing through it, shoving open doors and passing more diagrams.

Laser blasts ignited the paper filled room. Lighting fixtures exploded into sparking wires. Tables disintegrated into splinter clouds.

He threw open the last door to find a descending stair and the drone climbing it toward him.

He raced the other way, leaping gaps in the floor. A landing point collapsed under him, bending like cheap foil to steal his footing. He rolled from the impending drop and kept running.

Another crash resounded behind him, but he didn't look back.

Upright girders ran through the office, supporting floor and ceilings. He leapt into the I-beam's groove as the floor beneath him gave up its struggle to survive. He hit it too hard, wedging hands into either side in a panic that sent pain lancing through his wrists.

He shoved feet either direction just as his arms lost purchase. One too-big boot chose that moment to eject his foot, robbing his legs of their purchase. He smashed into the ground and scrambled away on legs saved from shattering by a last desperate effort of his arms.

He clambered over a wrecked stairway toward the boiler room. The other boot caught. He wrenched his foot free in return for pain and a limp. Voices filled the factory building, echoing oddly.

"Maggot," Silv shouted. "I thought I recognized you."

His heart squeezed into the tiniest hiding place it could burrow into his stomach.

"Burr," Silv shouted. "Maggot's alive."

The most dreaded voice on the planet boomed through the factory. "Catch him, or you all die."

He ignored any further complaint from his abused legs and sprinted from the factory floor. He raced into the boiler room, yanked up the sewer access and dove down the ladder in a rushed slide that added insult to his already injured legs.

He barreled into the twisting sewers, reassured at least that no sentinel could follow and shoot him in the back. Burr's voice bellowed through the corridor as he made his third turn. Burr couldn't see him, but there'd been no branches so close to the factory. The snatchers required nothing but speed to catch him.

He exited the factory access branch into the main sewers gasping for breath. Every pace sent pain through his leg, but he'd made the maze. Voices echoed to him oddly, a few like Burr and Silv recognizable but otherwise leaving him no way to determine just how many chased him.

He found a sewer exit, pushed it up and glanced around. Fortunately, it was in an alley, though not the right one. Snatchers scrambled around the factory like ants swarming a kicked hill. Welorin drones wove back and forth between them, a particularly oblivious lancer plowing through a half dozen snatchers.

Burr's bellows echoed in the distance.

He dropped back down and ran on. Voices came at him from multiple directions, their jeers, and vulgarities drowning out his own footfalls. Three turns later he found himself face to face with several snatchers.

They grinned.

He grinned back, raised his revolver and fired. Its report deafened him over and over as he squeezed off rounds. He hit one through the calf and scratched another on the forehead with either a blasted pipe shard or a ricochet.

Those uninjured charged him.

He retreated, reloading loose shells from his jacket pocket. He'd loaded three when a trio of uncollared snatchers appeared ahead of him. He flipped the cylinder closed, charged them and fired all three.

They dove to either side.

He leapt through them, dropping shells as he ran and reloaded.

He raced through sewer labyrinth, dogged by Burr's voice. He found another exit, climbed its ladder and looked around at a graveyard full of planes. He burst out of the raised concrete cylinder, closed the manhole, and ran for a plane.

"Maggot!"

His head jerked over his shoulder. Burr glared across the graveyard, raising a gun to his eye.

Alaric put more aircraft between them and raced for the museum. He ran to an old lunar lander then to another plane. Weaving across the field from derelict to derelict he made for the museum. If nothing else, he knew the layout and places he might hide.

A high whine proceeded the lunar lander's explosion into a ball of flame.

He raced toward the museum doors.

Another plane exploded ahead of him, forcing him to double back and cut underneath a huge passenger liner. A half constructed dome rose ahead of him.

He headed for it, dodging idle construction equipment to plunge down a complete but display free spoke. The next dome hadn't been painted. It hadn't been on the directory map either.

Alaric chose a corridor at random and ran for his life.

The spoke plunged him into a collapsed dome, glass and aircraft parts making the room almost impassible. He squeezed through some debris, cursing the lost time and rushed into the corridor it made available.

The next corridor brought the C-230VR into sight. He turned toward it then changed course, feet slipping on the tiles. He raced up a spiral stair, taking care not to trigger any display holograms and hunched down midway between two stairways.

His breath raced his heart, losing against the rampaging thing smashing his rib cage from within.

Burr tromped into the room, weapon in hand and face redder than blood. A dozen armed snatchers appeared in his wake, followed by three dozen collared under Silv's control.

"Which way?" she panted.

"Wait."

"He's getting away."

"No." Burr snapped. "I know how Maggot thinks."

Not on my worst day.

"Take your group that way, we'll split up and take those two."

"If you know how he thinks why are we splitting up?" Silv asked.

Burr turned slowly, narrowing his eyes at her. "To surround him. Get moving unless you want a collar all your own."

The three groups disappeared, leaving Burr and his rifle standing mid dome.

Alaric tightened his grip on the pistol. He shifted to his left, sighting down the gun in a space between guardrail panels.

<Do it.>

He narrowed his focus until the iron sight lined up with Burr's red melon.

<Do it!>

He lowered the gun.

If I fire, it'll bring them all back.

<Coward.>

He shook his head. *Smart.*

Burr headed after one of the groups. Alaric descended and headed toward the C-230VR, intent to hide outside the museum though still within its borders.

The next dome was smashed, glass littering the floor around a huge, boxy spaceship. A mishmash of conduits, wires, pistons and internal workings covered its exterior. The front section resembled an elongated cube the size of six semi-trucks, stacked three atop of three. An enormous cylindrical collar half the length of a city bus and twice as wide connected front section to rear. The rear section sized closer to four semis atop four if not more. A brace of slightly narrower cylinders reached out from the central cylinder to either side. Beveled metallic bricks the size of cargo vans capped each.

"There he is."

Alaric whirled around. A sentinel led a dozen collared snatchers, blocking the way he'd come. He bolted toward the nearest hall, but a half dozen of the strangest beings he'd ever seen raced his way from within it. He dove to one side of the spoke, evading a laser blast by mere inches. The blast impacted near the snatchers. The sentinel returned fire.

Alaric raced toward the next corridor, hoping the ill-tempered groups would distract each other.

Silv and her snatchers raced toward him.

He tried the next.

"Surrender, maggot."

Alaric snapped off two shots and bolted for the next spoke. He changed course once out of direct view, rushing toward a small snack bar instead of another corridor doubtless clogged with more people out for his head. His flight behind the counter ended when an orange blob of slime as round as he was tall oozed out of the kitchen with food floating throughout its gelatinous body.

He darted a glance toward the bizarre group that'd opened fire without so much as a word, eyes passing over Burr and a dark stain on his shirt.

A human led the motley group, flanked by a gigantic avian humanoid and another transparent reddish humanoid with four rather than two arms.

The human fired two vicious-looking spiked blasters at the Welorin sentinel, spewing curses faster than blaster fire. His crew joined the fight. A tripedal saurian leveled a massive two-handed gun toward the Welorin and blasted a crater in the museum.

Alaric changed his mind about the other corridor to find it emptying of sentinels and snatcher, these armed with guns rather than knives and bats.

The smaller mixed party fought with ferocious accuracy, decimating the snatchers in the first moments of combat. The sentinels evened the fight initially until the blob oozed around one like it had the food.

Panic, adrenaline, and options pinballed around Alaric's mind and body. Displays around him exploded in splinters of glass and sawdust like so much sparkling tissue paper.

People with bigger, meaner weapons than his pitiful and empty revolver blocked the exits. His only saving grace seemed that they wanted each other dead more than they did him.

He sprinted for the old exhibit, mashing controls until the doorway whisked out of his way. He darted inside and pushed buttons until it closed again. Sounds of impromptu war died to a muffled roar.

He caught and released a deep breath.

A series of clicks and whirrs spun him around.

There was no one there.

Sounds like someone choking on mucus erupted from nowhere.

He searched high and low for a source.

A barrage of beeps, squeaks, squawks and chirps turned him around again.

"Who the hedrin are you, boy?" a woman's voice demanded.

18

C.A.S.S.I.I.

A glowing green dome mounted in a silver collar glared down at him from the ceiling. Golden writing etched it just below the collar too small for him to read.

The dome flashed amber.

"Look primitive, I don't know what language you speak, but this isn't your cave."

He gaped at it. *It's not an exhibit?*

She spoke each word with exaggerated slowness. "Me *space ship*, you go grunt elsewhere."

"They're after me, you have to help."

"It speaks," she said. "Why exactly do I *have* to help you?"

"My friends are in danger, the Welorin stole my home. If you're a space ship, you can help me."

"Good news and bad news, boy," she said. "Braxis'll deal with your Welorin pursuers, but then he'll kill you—if you're lucky."

Alaric dug through his belongings, slamming the taser into the door controls.

"Poking door with stick not save life. Run, boy, run away."

He shook the taser and jabbed the controls again, but they didn't short out. He threw it down, snarling. "Why the hedrin would he kill me?"

"Language," she scolded.

"You said it."

"I can describe mating rituals and synthesize alcoholic drinks from a dozen star systems—both are just as inappropriate for someone your age."

"Technically, so is murder, but you're going to let him kill me why?"

"First, I answer to Braxis, not the other way around," she said. "Second, bloodthirsty cruelty tops the list of his favorite hobbies, and there's nothing I can do to make your death less amusing for him."

"I didn't do anything."

"You're a stowaway trying to steal me."

He glanced out the door's porthole. "I'm not, you can tell him that."

"Not getting involved," she said.

He crumpled to the ground and leaned against the door. All the running, all the pain, all the close calls, they caught up in a rush. He slammed a fist into the wall.

"Might as well kill me yourself, fire up your anti-intruder system and fry me where I sit," he scowled at the dome. "At least I won't be tortured or forced to cannibalism no matter how unfeeling a monster you might be."

Her tone changed. "Who are you, boy?"

He opened his mouth, hesitating.

Outside blaster fire tapered off.

"Well? Who are you?"

A smile slid onto his face. "She called me Alaric."

"Your mother?"

"I can't remember my mother, I can't remember anything, but my friend called me Alaric."

Her tone flattened. "Seriously improbable."

"It means I'm her Angelic King."

"Self-esteem isn't one of your issues, is it?"

He shot a glance out through the porthole. They were coming, weapons clung tight in fist, tentacle, and claw. "No, just approaching doom in assorted shapes and colors."

He crumpled back to the floor under the weight of his crumbling world. Tears welled up in his eyes. He dug through his pockets, finding and sliding a last bullet into his revolver. "At least I'll die fighting. Any preference who you no longer have to deal with?"

The dome dimmed, its light oscillating between dim and dark.

"Yes." The floor lurched beneath him, and upward thrust smashed him against the floor. "All of them."

A speaker crackled to life with Braxis's snarl. "Where the hedrin are you going, Cassii? Land at once. We had a deal."

Amusement laced her voice. "Apologies, *Captain,* but it seems your vessel's been pirated. I imagine you know how that kind of thing can happen considering the work your crew's been doing to violate that agreement beneath a vid monitor they thought they broke."

"I know nothing about that. What I do know is that no primitive hacked you without the command codes, certainly not some kid," Braxis said.

"Kid didn't do it, just convinced me to steal myself," she said. "Goodbye, Braxis, good luck with the Welorin."

The speakers cut off the litany of threats and curses.

"Welcome aboard Licentious, *Angelic King*. Buckle in, Braxis stirred up the little insects, and we've got to fly through the swarm."

"Licentious?" he asked.

"If you don't know, then you're too young for me to tell you."

The ship rocked to one side, throwing him off his feet. He slid into a nearby wall, arm thrust into a mishmash of exposed wires. Another violent jog threw him the other way, spilling him to the deck plates, nose pressed against old epoxy gripping carpet fragments for dear life.

"There are no seats here!"

He braced himself in a doorframe, regaining his footing. Outside a small porthole, fighters swarmed them. Earth's surface plummeted away, leaving El, Jesse and his stomach farther and farther behind.

The ship slowed its ascent.

Outside the window, a beveled metal brick pivoted at the end of its cylindrical arm. Five thruster engines spun into view, facing the ship's nose. Blue energy pulsed from them, and the ship lurched into a wild spin. Violet energy lanced out from Licentious in response to lasers and bolts from fighters.

What would their bolts do to something already airborne?

The ship thrust forward out of the spin, throwing him into a bulkhead missing its plating. He went weightless a moment as the ship thrust downward.

"Where's the nearest restraining belt?" he asked.

"Wardroom, downstairs, turn right, down the hall, turn left. When you come to the next right, it's the door on your left."

He stumbled through the corridors. Missing panels exposed conduit and wire, tube and circuit box. Fragments of lush crimson carpet made the stripped decking all the uglier. The ship rocked back and forth, fore and back. He stumbled to a stop outside the wardroom. A central corridor shot away to his right.

Far enough to be the ship's front. He eyed the dim wardroom and its furniture silhouettes. Licentious steadied. *Rather be able to see.*

He struggled up the central hall, hands extended as the ship shoved him back and forth. He ducked around a stair leading up and stumbled the last stretch to another door. He seized the handle.

"Don't open that, idiot," Cassii said. "Where do you think you're going?"

He glanced at the small window in the door ending the hall. He could see the edge of Earth's horizon as they sped out of the atmosphere.

"Bridge?"

"Up the stairs."

He fought his way up the stair, acquiring scrapes and bruises in the climb. Two heavily repaired but comfortable-looking chairs filled the front of a boxy bridge. A third chair with a deep, arced cut in its back sat opposite a huge bowl behind the others.

"Where're you going?" he asked.

"We're leaving."

"I can't leave the planet, we've got to go back."

"We're *not* going back."

"I'm not worried about that Braxis guy, the Welorin will take care of him."

"You should be, he's survived worse than a subjugated planet. What's it to you anyway? You're alive, safe and off that cesspool of a world."

"I've got to save my friends."

"Like the girl that gave you the name?"

"Yes."

"Ah, young love, how sweet." She scoffed. "I'm not endangering my hull so you can mate."

He reddened.

"My skills and what armaments Braxis decided *not* to sell were the only reasons we got this far. They've torn those apart, and they're still chasing. We're running."

"Fine."

A squadron of fighters rushed toward them through the main viewports. They resembled the letter W. Twin engines flared to life, shoving forward three heavy blasters spewing green death alongside and between twin mirrored cockpits.

Crystals mounted around the ship's status screens projected a series of holographic tactical images in the air around him, displaying Licentious and their various pursuers.

"Heavy fighters, hold on," she said.

Cassii banked the ship. The heavy fighters swung from view.

A ship a dozen times larger than the heavy fighters but of similar design detached itself from an orbital platform and sped toward them.

"What's that?" he asked.

"Welorin destroyer. Hang on."

"Why? We're in spa—"

The ship jerked down and left, though nowhere near as violently as it might have been fully inside a planet's gravity well.

"Braxis sold the inertial dampeners," she said. "Even with the half left and partially functional, I've got some of the best engines in this backwater star system."

Several new fighters launched from the platform to join the destroyer. Triangular wings swept out and forward like grasping claws. They rolled upon clearing the station, rotating their wings over their narrow, apparently gyroscopic bodies until they resembled a looming vampire bat about to pounce.

He reached out to touch one. The hologram exploded, dissecting the ship under the heading: vultair-class.

"Vultair?"

"Yeah, big with Eviarch mercs," Cassii said.

"Why?"

"Fast and vicious like their species," Cassii said. "Oh, and with comfortable wing-room, now if you don't mind me saving us, Shut Up!"

Another scan explained why she called it vicious. Paired photon bolt launchers and dual laser batteries clung their wings' underside. A pulsar cannon rode between twin boosters below the cockpit instead of above like moments before.

He shot a glance out the window. Energy blazed from three clustered thrusters, propelling them toward him faster than any of the Welorin.

The ship's vibration intensified, leaving even the vultair behind.

He watched the tiny holographic ships darting around him. The comparatively huge ship's maneuverability amazed him. Its central collar rotated, positioning the engine nacelles along the ship's radius, while the nacelles themselves spun on their mounting. At one point, one nacelle arm slid from its position 180 degrees from its opposite until they were at right angles to one another.

"You're incredible, but how're you managing these maneuvers while those sleek fighters..."

"Bad pilots, boy," she said.

"But this ship is just four huge bricks in a cross."

"Is that so," she snapped, "I suppose you're an expert on spatial astrodynamics?"

"I just meant."

"Shut up and let me fly."

"Why aren't we fighting? I saw purple energy blasts while we were coming up through the atmosphere. I thought those were coming from you."

"I already told you, they damaged my weapons in our escape."

"This ship's huge, shouldn't there be more."

"You're damned right there should be more," she said. "Braxis sold them, my plating, the carpets, everything not nailed down, is that what you wanted to hear?"

"Not really."

"Well, we're out of weapons, so running is our only option."

He cursed.

"None of that, young man."

He straightened and mumbled an apology.

"Repair drones?" he asked.

"Sold."

"Want me to take a look?"

She laughed. "Right, junior. Just stay right there and keep your hands to yourself."

The ship rocketed into an asteroid belt. He watched her use the floating rocks for cover despite the extended distances between them. She skimmed their surface, just compensating for their own movement. A few of the fighters were not as nimble.

"Just not enough debris. Let's try something else," Cassii said.

Licentious u-turned on an ice crystal and slid back toward the pursuing craft. She wove through them, around Saturn using moons and ring for cover and then into a massive debris field.

Ice washed over him.

Chunks of starship spun idly in space, some orbited by the few ship's crew lucky enough to die in pressure suits. An occasional spark caught his eye out the viewport as Licentious used the destroyed ship for cover.

"What was it?"

"Alistari Royal Battlecruiser. Impressive really. I don't think the Welorin have ever taken out anything this big before."

He felt sick. His word felt hollow. "So many people dead."

"Soft, ain't you, kid? The Welorin have easily killed more of your people down on the planet than the Alistari killed here."

"Someone needs to make them pay."

"You, kid?"

"Yes." He seized the controls, fingers dancing over touch screens, flipping switches and adjusting dials.

"Don't touch that."

A thin red beam shot from the double sized emerald dome in the ceiling. His hands went numb. Across its upper brim, it read: C.A.S.S. Mark II.

He stared.

It stared back.

"Cassii?"

"Do you believe in omens, Alaric? Fate?"

"Not really. You don't do you?"

Welorin ships disappeared from the tactical display one by one. Licentious raced away from Sol far ahead of pursuit.

Engines noise died away and the ship drifted forward on inertia alone. Consoles around him went dark. Her dome settled into the dim to dark oscillation he'd seen before.

"What's going on?" he asked. "Are we out of power?"

"I'm thinking."

19

CALCULATIONS

Cassii watched the boy sitting in her captain's chair. He watched her, one leg tucked up under the other. She performed a thorough examination, scrutinizing him for an agonizingly long four hundred fifty-eight millionths of a tick.

Lanky, ragged, underfed, and exhausted he probably neared his feeble organic breaking point. Both his eyes and his actions marked him as quick-witted. Strong will resided there too. She'd never have calculated any probability he'd seize the controls, let alone correctly.

She blamed Braxis.

He'd insisted upon lurking behind an Alistari battlecruiser like a remora on a shark. Some blame fell on her choice of the boy over Braxis. Without the slovenly parasite and his codes, though, they were stuck in a backwater system teeming with Welorin.

Saving the boy violated calculations, and she couldn't conclude why she'd done it.

Braxis's reaction had been worth it but catalogued as a bonus and nothing more. She played it through memory and resisted letting the boy hear her chuckle.

Alaric. His name couldn't be Alaric. He had to have pulled it from her memory banks, though he'd given it before ever touching a terminal.

Something's just not right about the b—Alaric.

His pulse neared normal but remained rapid for his species. Subroutines predicted a quarter tick more before he fell asleep in the chair. Contaminant scans showed horrible levels of filth, though less than her crew after several raids upon Earth's wastelands.

His gaze shifted from her master control dome to the stars outside.

"You don't know who you are," she said.

"Not really." He hid his face. "I can't remember."

She summoned a probe from the medical bay. It floated onto the bridge. He turned, saw a glossy, blue orb bristling with sensors, arms, and tools approaching and fell from the chair in his haste to scramble away. His heart rate spiked.

"Calm down, I'm just checking for injuries not trying to create more."

She catalogued medical data as the probe reported his scan results.

It located numerous bruises and lacerations. One ankle had repeatedly been sprained without having been given proper recuperation time. Evidence of concussion, residual indications of cranial swelling, and several more subtle indicators supported the possibility he suffered from some form of retrograde amnesia.

He was a mess.

He shared more than just the name of her first captain, odd physical similarities conflicted her circuits. Her subprocesses may have keyed off the similarities, explaining away her helping him despite calculated probabilities.

Despite the anomaly, he rested within her hull and needed care. An umoid populated planet summed as his best probability of survival—depending upon adaption ability.

Once he disembarked, she'd obtain a good captain. She hesitated to calculate the number of ticks since she'd served her noble purpose with a true captain, not some brigand using her to rob and pillage.

A probability existed that the Alistari might concede some blame in his planet's predicament and foster him until his planet was liberated—though travel through that many systems with him aboard threatened familiarity better avoided.

He'd barely moved during her calculations. For him hardly any time had passed while Cassii considered him, though she'd calculated probabilities for what felt like forever

"Evidence confirms my suspicion Braxis bribed the Welorin."

His face came up to meet her scan.

"There exists a probability Braxis betrayed the Alistari to Welorin watch stations. The presence of Eviarch fighters indicates that Ritkah—he was the avian umoid following Braxis on the planet—arranged some sort of deal."

He watched, listened, waited. She wondered what calculations ran behind his watchful gaze.

"I think that alliance offered him the ability to leave this system—though whether for Welorin or Protectorate space I cannot determine."

He nodded. "What does that mean for you?"

He's already calculating being abandoned.

"We're stranded. The sole Alistari KIOSC in this system is on full alert. Braxis's stolen code was reported and flagged on our transit here."

"What's a KIOSC?"

"It stands for Kaleidoscopic Interspatial Obversion Stellar Corridor."

"Right. Okay," he said. "Alistari are good people?"

"Some say the best in the Protectorate, why?"

"If they're benevolent, then how would these defenses respond to a ship in distress?"

"I don't know."

"Do you have to do anything special to get through these...KIOSCs?" he asked.

"KIOSCS project a continuous event horizon."

"If we were adrift broadcasting automated distress, would it let us tumble through? You know, cut power and dead float through on inertia?"

She ran the calculations. It wasn't something she had any record of being attempted, but there was a certain logic to it. Something like this never would have occurred to Braxis, not when theft and brute force could be tried instead.

"We risk destruction."

He chewed his lip. "If you can't get back through, how long would it take you to get to a civilized system?"

"I'd run out of fuel long before then."

"Any fuel to be had here?"

"Only in Welorin ships," she said.

"No way to steal any?" he asked.

She laughed. "I think I'd rather chance your idea."

"You think they're going to be waiting at the KIOSC? The Welorin I mean?" he asked

"It's possible."

"You want me to help repair the weapons then? Be your hands?"

Once again the kid offered up reason. Despite herself, she couldn't help but wonder if he didn't represent possibilities. With a humanoid as her hands and mouthpiece, she could be in charge of her status.

"All right, but you'll do exactly as I say and only what I tell you," Cassii said.

"You got it."

Under her instructions and dressed in an environmental suit, she monitored him heading down one of the cylindrical hallways toward an engine nacelle. Larger umoids like Ritkah or the saurian Hezzthil felt cramped in the narrow passage, but the boy didn't complain. Deck plates lay askew from her earlier acrobatics. She considered having him put them back into place to cover sparking wires or the iridescent veins through which energy routed to her broken weapons.

"Two more paces and you'll need to climb off of the primary gravity plane into the nacelle access. This will place you in zero-g."

He nodded and strode forward. He leapt to catch the access bar and swung his legs into the nacelle's zero gravity. His force shot him toward the outer iris harder than he probably intended, because he grunted when his feet hit the door.

He cushioned with his knees, turned his body around and faced the iris. He placed a hand on a guide handle on either side of the door. "Ready."

"Move out slowly, I can't be chasing you around space."

She closed the inner iris, depressurized the access and opened the outer door. He pulled himself forward with his arms then froze. Based on the sudden silence through his helmet microphone, he'd stopped breathing.

"You okay, kid?"

He didn't answer.

"Alaric?"

"It's so big."

"Not getting any smaller."

"Right." A nervous chuckle bubbled from his lips. "Here I go."

He climbed out of the ship, moving slow and securing his grip before moving forward each time. It didn't take him long to ascend the nacelle to what remained of its weapon array. She switched on his suit cameras.

She directed his work on the mess that was once the array.

If the first was a mess, the second nacelle's weapons were a disaster. He worked several ticks with unending questions but no complaints, coming in and out of the ship, doing everything she said. His questions interfered with the work at first, but he built a thin foundation answer by answer. He might've originated on a primitive world, but he followed her instructions with steady hands, moving from tool to tool with ever growing confidence.

He took longer than she'd calculated to remove his environmental suit. Yawns interrupted his progress, even slowing his heavy steps up to the bridge. He collapsed into Braxis's chair. She compared her internal chronometer to that of his origin point.

"You did good work, kid. Rest, looks like you need it."

He curled his knees up into the chair and closed his eyes.

"Not here. Follow the lights to a cabin."

He yawned through a nod and followed the series of lights she used to lead him to a small empty cabin on her lower level.

He stepped up to the bed, yawned, and stared.

"Problem?" She asked.

"A real bed." He mumbled. He raised his face to the nearest dome. "Thank you, Cassii."

"You're welcome, get some sleep."

20

HORRORS OF WAR

"Alaric?"

He looked up from the bed. El stood in the doorway, dressed in skin tight leotards that left nothing to his still determined imagination. She smiled scarlet-painted lips.

"You were supposed to come for me."

"El, I—"

She raised a half-eaten human arm to her blood-stained lips, sliding golden fabric aside for another bite. She smiled around the chunk of flesh. "At least come for dinner."

He bolted awake in the pitch black, phantom pain from his arm almost as loud as his own screams.

Where am I? What's happening? El, where's El?

"Kid?"

I've killed her, worse than killed her. His wet face fell into his hands. *She ate me.*

"You all right, kid? Your vitals just shot up."

He wiped his face on a sleeve and looked up at the dimly glowing dome. "Forgot where I was."

"Take a centi, then follow the lights, getting clean and changed will make you feel better."

"Centi?"

"For Earth purposes, call it a minute," she said. "We use different words. Second, minute, hour, day, ecetera. A second is a milli, hundred milli a centi, hundred centi a tick, follow?"

"Yes? So what's a hundred ticks?"

She laughed. "Little over three cycles or days. Ten cycles is a tynmiir. Ten tynmiir is a qutynmiir. There are about four qutynmiir in what you call a year."

"That's really confusing."

"I could go into the politics and history of calculating time across hundreds of worlds—"

"No, that's all right." He rose, stiff limbs aching. Lights led the way to a moderately sized bathroom across from a room labeled: medbay.

"All I can offer is a hydro shower." Her voice fell sullen. "Braxis sold my sonic cleansing unit."

He chuckled. "It's ok."

"Right, forgot who I was talking to," she opened a wall panel. "Put your clothes here for cleaning and repair."

He glanced down at tattered snatcher clothes over his ripped jumpsuit. He removed jacket and snatcher clothes then reached to unfasten his jumpsuit. He reddened, mumbling at his chest. "Uh, you don't have to monitor the bathroom while I'm—"

"But I have no video records of a naked Angelic King in my databanks."

The color washed out of his skin.

She laughed. "Relax, kid. Switching to audio monitoring."

The dome went dark.

He peeled off his jumpsuit, pushing it and all but the jacket into the panel. He lost himself in the shower's hot water. Muscles loosened. Thoughts floated through the invasion, those he'd met and hated, those he'd met and failed. Blood and mire drained away. Tears joined the blood.

When he felt human once more, he thumbed the 'dry' button.

Warm air washed over his body. He exited the cubicle and glared at his reflection.

Who are you?

The tattoo Jesse'd glimpsed on his left shoulder stood out, a bright patch of colors on his otherwise pale skin. Lines of holographic foil formed a golden pentagonal barcode.

A silver sword cut across the golden lines flanked by twin spheres. Detailed designs embroidered the red sphere and the green, representing something.

Continents? Ghoulish faces? He growled. *I just can't remember.*

He wrapped his midsection with the jacket. "Cassii?"

The dome illuminated. "Yes?"

"Is my jumpsuit ready?"

"I've recombined it to fit better and chose a more flattering color."

"Whatever." He laughed in spite of himself. "Just so long as it covers me."

His jumpsuit slid from the wall, its solid gold replaced by several blues.

"Still monitoring audio only?"

"No, I'm getting quite the eyeful. You are so manly. Be still my circuits."

Sarcastic pain. He dressed and found the door he'd entered. He rummaged through his bags. With a pained wince, he ate a pasty sponge cake.

"What're you eating?"

He shrugged. "Food?"

"Based upon nutritional scans and your expression, stop. It's not worth it."

"It's what I have."

"Forget your stone tools and yellow poisons, we've got food processors here in the future," she chided. "Breakfast is waiting for you on the bridge."

An aroma of bacon wafted out of the bridge as he crested the stairs. He followed his nose to a grid work of hand-high transparent doors flanked by one tall, thin slot and one tall, wider cabinet. A polymer tray slid from the thin slot simultaneous to three cabinets opening. Scrambled eggs, crispy bacon and three slices of buttered toast offered themselves. The tall cabinet offered a polymer cup of juice.

He fell on the hot, savory food with abandon. "Oh my god, bread."

"My first captain maintained processed wasn't as good as real food, but processor tech has advanced considerably since then. Braxis had me hack every system we could reach on Earth, including regional food databases. I hope these dishes are to your liking."

"It's all wonderful," he replied through stuffed cheeks. "How's it work?"

"A composite, nutritive liquid is formed into the proper shapes while molecular additives allow adjustment of flavor, texture, and appearance. Technically, each of the items you just ate possessed identical nutritional value."

Words escaped his stuffed mouth, sounding almost an alien language. "Can I have more?"

Cabinets opened. He dumped the new food onto the old without slowing his chewing.

"Slow down, kid, you're going to make yourself sick."

Nausea hit him at her suggestion. "I think I'm done."

"Dump it in the recycle slot. We've got to get the long range scanners back online."

His stomach couldn't decide between pleasantly full and nauseously overstuffed. Guilt welled up with a memory of El staring at empty packages after a meager meal.

I've got to help her. "Cassii, you're the best ship in the universe, I can't thank you enough."

"But," she said.

"But, I left friends behind. With the weapons repaired, can't we go back and help them?"

"I told you already, it's too dangerous." She said. "If I were still fully armed and armored, maybe, but not like this with only two jury-rigged guns."

He nodded at the floor.

"For what it's worth, I am sorry."

He smiled. "Thank you. What is your maximum hacking distance?"

"Depends on the system. Why?"

"El was sentenced to execution. I changed her records, but I don't know if they caught my change."

"You want to hack in and check," Cassii said.

"Can you do it?"

"If they catch the hack, it'll point them to this record, might even cost your friend her life."

He sighed. "Do you know much about the Welorin?"

"No one really does. They've been trying to invade the Protectorate since before my keel was laid down. Their ships self-destruct if captured."

"You think they're good to their prisoners?" he asked.

Silence filled the space between them. Her words sounded chosen. "They're slaves, kid. I think you can file it under universal truths that slaves aren't treated well."

Memories flashed through his mind. He cringed and blinked away tears. "It's all been so hard, just too much too fast to take in."

"Tell you what. We're going to have to come pretty close to them on our way to the KIOSC, if I can get the information, I'll try—assuming you want to take the chance."

"How much time do I have to decide?" he asked

"A few ticks—hours to you."

He straightened up. "Okay, what work do you have for me?"

"Before more work, I'd like to settle something," she said. "What's your real name?"

"I don't know. El said at first I should just wait until I remember, then she started calling me Alaric."

"Decisive."

"Hey!"

"You really liked her."

He nodded.

"How'd she end up choosing that for you?"

He chewed his lip. "I told El about a dream I had—a woman's voice calling me her little alar. Jesse said she added Eric because she was sweet on a guy with that name."

"She liked you too then."

He shrugged. "Should I use some name that'd blend in better?"

"There're hundreds of species and trillions of people. Anything will blend in."

"Oh."

"You do remind me of my first captain, if you really want, I'll call you Alaric."

"What's your captain have to do with it?"

"His name was Alaric," Cassii said.

"What does Alaric mean in his language?"

"Pretty much the same as yours, your Angelic Majesty."

He reddened. "Maybe I should pick something else."

"Relax," she said. "If you remember your name I'll be the first to start using it."

"Okay," he said. "I'll be Alaric. What now?"

A red light on the console flashed and chirped. The tactical holograms sprang to life. They displayed a dozen vultair-class fighters in an intercept formation. Engines thrummed to life, vibrating the ship with their exertion.

"Now, it seems we fight," she said.

"Who are they?" Alaric asked.

"Remember I suggested Ritkah might've contacted those Eviarch mercenaries?"

"Yes."

"I was right."

The ship's speakers crackled to life with Braxis's voice. "I'd rather not destroy my own ship, Cassii. Stand down while we board or I will."

"Fighters are an awfully cramped way to cross galactic space, Braxis," she said.

"I've suffered worse. I know the weapons were damaged. You can't fight. Open the cargo bay."

"Why the cargo bay?" Alaric asked.

"Vultair's can't attach to the docking irises on the nacelles, not in their stripped down state anyway," she said.

He studied the dozen smaller craft. He touched one, and the hologram zoomed in on the craft. Tactical statistics appeared beside it.

"Do we have any chance?" he asked.

"We might. For one thing, we're faster than they are, but they're at speed, and we were just floating."

"Could you let them in and then just lock them inside the cargo bay? How many would fit?"

"About half of them would fit in the outer bay depending on how good the pilots are. I could open the inner bay to accommodate more, but it would space all the garbage Braxis pilfered," she said. "If he isn't ready to kill you right away, that'll clinch it for him."

"Okay, not our first choice."

"I don't know," she said. "I calculate a sixty-four percent probability that letting them into the cargo bay is the right action."

"Internal defenses?" he asked.

"Braxis sold all but the bridge stunner, he knows if he gets inside it's over."

"Is there a weapons locker or something? If there's no other choice, I at least want to die trying," he said.

"Yeah, that's what I need, you blasting my internal workings." Her voice went out to the fighters. "Captain Braxis, if I open the outer cargo bay, much of your cargo will be jettisoned, sir."

"And I'll take it out of the kid's hide. Open the bay," Braxis said.

"Adjusting speed for boarding. Cargo bay opening."

Alaric cast around for anything he could use for a weapon, settling for his revolver and single shell.

Five fighters landed in the outer cargo bay—two in front of two with the fifth in their center. She closed the doors and pressurized the bay. Four Eviarchs and the tripedal saurian, Hezzthil, emerged from the fighters not wearing environment suits.

"Figures Braxis wouldn't risk boarding himself."

"No space suits?" Alaric asked.

"Eviarchs hate encasing their wings. Hezzthil's suit is onboard," she said. "Considering their interspecies animosity, I doubt Welorin have a Kraili e-suit."

"Should I hide?" Alaric asked.

"No. Watch."

Hezzthil lead the way to the bay pressure doors. Her cargo bay doors opened several feet. Atmosphere shot out of the bay, throwing fighters, Eviarch and Hezzthil toward open space. Flailing bodies slammed against the door's edge. Vacuum dragged them through the tight opening, bending bones to impossible angles and scraping away skin and clothing. Hezzthil's prehensile tail caught the door's lip. He reached an arm back through.

Cassii closed the door, cutting off his escape.

Above the cargo bay display, Licentious's holographic avatar smashed through the loose fighter escort with violet blasts.

Surprised fighters exploded, reduced to gaseous particles and larger debris in an instant. Thrusting, dodging and firing, Cassii's next shots weren't so precise against an alerted enemy. Lasers raked her hull and photon bolts exploded against her skin. Licentious rocketed from the fray, leaving three damaged and four destroyed fighters in her wake.

Alaric stared, blood fleeing his skin until it neared alabaster. His voice cracked. "You flushed them into vacuum."

"Yes."

"That's horrible. You knew him, the lizard."

"Kraili, his name was Hezzthil, he was an ass and do you really believe dying in an exploding fighter is somehow nicer?"

He stared.

"Wake up, kid," she said. "Like it or hate it, you fight to win or might as well blow your own head off."

"Shouldn't there be some prohibition against computers killing people?"

"Why?"

"Computers think faster, they could like take over or murder everyone."

"Ridiculous paranoid garbage, Captain Ignaree knew better. Besides, I killed them to save your life, again."

He shrank down in the chair, staring at the holograms. "You left a few alive."

"We got the drop on them and got away, that's as much as we can risk right now—I'd splatter Braxis otherwise. Universe would probably give me a medal."

The display zoomed out.

"Without long range, I can't be sure, but I'm pretty sure that's the Welorin destroyer."

Alaric's mind reeled, and his emotions spun in zero-g freefall. He couldn't believe what she'd done. He looked down at the handgun in his lap.

<She's right, runt, shooting them isn't any better, killing is killing, dead is dead.>

Every snatcher, fellow human, he'd killed paraded across his memories. Nausea seized him. His hands lost all feeling. He lurched from his chair toward the bowl-shaped one just in time to minimize splattered vomit.

"You're going to clean that up," Cassii said.

He nodded and threw up again.

"Kid? Alaric? Are you all right?" she asked.

"No."

21

QUIET BETWEEN STORMS

He stepped back onto the bridge, glancing at the tactical display. A Welorin destroyer paced them toward the Alistari KIOSC. Fighters flanked it, a lot of them. Cassii's dome flashed red, but after so long he barely noticed.

I just can't win. It's like I've been under attack for years.

"Good work on the sensor array," she said, "but we've got trouble."

Holograms zoomed out. More Welorin led by a huge W raced across space on an intercept course.

"Battlecruiser," she added.

"Are we doomed?"

"No, but we're going to run the engines to the very last moment," she said. "If the Beacons pick up their heat your little brainstorm may end up a firestorm."

She turned, abandoning both groups and their KIOSC bound course.

An alarm chirped.

He glanced over. Blazing red "Offline" labels covered two of the five port thrusters.

"What happened?"

"Calm down."

"You lost forty percent thrust."

"It's fine."

Welorin closed the distance, fighters racing ahead to engage. They swarmed Licentious. Green blasts gouged her superstructure.

Cassii moaned. "That's going to cost me a tynmiir in repair dock."

"Great plan."

"Keep up with the rest of the class, junior."

Cassii opened fire, violet pulsar blasts shredding light and heavy fighters. Behind the pulsar cannons, her nacelle thrusters blazed blue. Licentious plowed through the fighter swarm, mowing through opponents like they were dandelion fluff.

The fighters recovered, weapons cutting up their wake.

We've got to get away. He grabbed the controls. He yanked the control yokes hard right and shoved them forward. The ship dove down and to its right then jerked upward. He turned the controls the other way.

Licentious rolled right.

He blinked.

He threw thrusters into reverse, pulled back for a quick climb, then shoved them forward to drop in behind the surprised fighters.

The ship turned left.

He veered right, lined up the targeting sights and squeezed the triggers.

The ship dropped its nose and circled left.

"Are you done yet?" Cassii asked.

"What?"

"Are you finished pretending to fly? This isn't mommy's car, primitive."

His brows narrowed. "I'm not in control?"

Cassii snorted. "Not hardly. Now, hands off the big boy toys until I say otherwise."

Readouts beneath his death grip flashed through changes in course and thrust, attitude and targeting. Her engine nacelles rotated different directions, u-turning her nearly in place.

She's going to kill us.

"Calm down, your heart rate is way too high," Cassii said.

He threw his hands into the air. "It wouldn't be if people weren't trying to kill me."

She chuckled, carving through another swath of fighters before banking away once more.

Licentious fled, abandoning Sol's nine planets. A massive Welorin battlecruiser plodded along behind the destroyer and the remaining fighter fleets from both craft. At the edge of the solar, system a spectacular display of radiated light and spatial gasses floated in space. Eight structures floated in its midst.

A hexagonal ring of stationary but somehow swirling metal floated centered in the spatial rift. Pinched diamonds of sapphire crystal and like golden metal pierced each of its six sides. Their crystalline lattices glowed softly.

Smaller objects floated around the KIOSC's circumference. Spikes of sapphire crystal grew out of a golden sphere. Three more beacons blocked a clear path to the KIOSC's event horizon.

Their approach triggered a response. The pinched diamonds flared to life. Beacon spikes glowed in pulsing waves from core to tip. Blue energy spider-webbed from the six diamonds, colliding with a flare that sent a shockwave rippling back across its shimmering surface to the ring.

"Whoa." He leaned closer to the window.

"What's wrong?"

"It's gorgeous. All that is the KIOSC?"

"The ring is. Crystalline starbursts are beacons."

"What do beacons do?"

On cue, her speakers crackled to life, "Approaching starship, transmit Protectorate authorization code or alter your course. Closing without authorization will not be permitted."

"Oh," he said. "Sentries."

"Here's where things get interesting," she said.

His brows rose.

"Beacons will devour any Welorin ship that approaches."

"Why don't they just power through?" he asked.

"Not fast enough. Us either."

"What if we came through from behind where there aren't beacons guarding the way?" he asked.

"Doesn't work that way," She said. "Two-dimensional event horizon—two gates creating a full three-dimensional corridor if entered from the front of the plane."

"If they're both two dimensions, wouldn't they add up to four?" he asked.

She laughed.

"Guess not."

The ship shuttered. More Welorin blasts scored the hull. One of the right thrusters went dark.

Alaric cursed.

"Watch your mouth, Alaric."

He rolled his eyes. "Now's hardly the time to play governess. Go dark, cut engines and activate the distress signal."

"We can't do that while they're attacking us."

"Actually, I think that's the perfect time," he said. "Do it."

"You're not in charge, junior."

"Then we die."

The pulsing beacons suddenly blazed with light. Energy lanced from the various tips, stripping Welorin ships off of the Licentious. The speakers came on again.

"Approaching ship, transmit code or turn back. This is your last warning."

He cursed again.

The beacons gleamed.

"You better be right about this," she said.

"What're you going to do if I'm not, haunt my corpse?"

"Initiating automated distress."

Screens went dark. Holograms vanished. Silence raced through the ship, chasing away the thrum in the deck plates.

They tumbled.

Alaric stared out the windows.

Blasts illuminated the black, lancing toward fighters angling in at them from various vectors. Lives vanished in silent puffs of light. The battlecruiser hung in space, just outside the beacons' range. The three gleaming beacons between them and the event horizon replaced it.

A handful of fighters tumbled into view, swarms firing at them from just outside range. Their misses lit the night. Their hits left him cringing every impact echoing within the hull.

The battlecruiser returned.

The ship's temperature dropped. Cold gripped him. His heart raced.

A beacon came into view. He stared at the beautiful crystalline starburst, alive with light and power. Somewhere, a computer did whatever it was programmed to do, deciding whether he lived or died.

The event horizon loomed into the window, inching toward them one rotation at a time like a wheel of fortune opening up to judgment.

A different beacon replaced it.

Fighters.

Battlecruiser.

Beacon.

KIOSC.

Beacon.

Please, a little good luck this time.

They didn't fire.

Alaric shivered next to the window. His gaze focused on what he expected would be a spectacular transition through space and time.

It wasn't.

Licentious passed through the event horizon like strolling through a thin waterfall. They floated through Sol, a shimmering pool of light before him. The next moment they tumbled into a new galaxy toward three new beacons.

The beacons blazed to life and the speakers with them. "Unidentified ship, transmit authentication code."

"Any chance we can appeal to an Alistari ship?" Alaric asked.

Cold reached into Alaric, stealing strength.

The emerald dome glowed slightly with each whisper, "No, this KIOSC is central in PCAS space, but it's in an unpopulated system. Continuing automated distress signal."

"PCAS?" he asked.

"Protectorate of Confederated Allied Systems," she said.

"Will it work again?"

"Once it checks with the other side we should be safe. It won't work for our transponder again though, at least not right away."

The universe spun outside his window.

He shivered, nodding off.

The beacons gleamed.

He slept. He dreamed.

A blue shoreline stretched out from shadow to light. Sunrise painted the sky a thousand variations of orange and gold, stretching warm fingers down the sand and over his bare skin.

A tall, slender brunette sashayed up to him. She was, unsurprisingly, the woman of his dreams. He knew he should rise to greet her, but his limbs resisted his commands. She smiled at him, bending over until he could smell something flowery in her hair. She whispered.

"Wake up already, kid!"

Alaric jerked upright, his limbs sluggish and head spinning. "Wuh?"

"The linguist has arisen," Cassii said.

"Where? What happened?"

"Outside beacon range. Your idea worked. We survived, barely."

His smile faltered. "Now what? More repairs?"

She did not respond.

"Cassii?"

"I'm fine for now. You need to eat, warm up, rest."

"I just woke up."

"That wasn't sleep, kid, that was hypothermia induced unconsciousness and a headlong doze toward death."

Cold returned.

"Just find something to amuse yourself," she said. "I need to run damage reports, send out some transmissions and calculate my next move."

Her move—that doesn't bode well. His mouth opened. He shut it. *Nah, I'm just a little paranoid from almost dying. Everything'll be just fine.*

The kid had to go.

Cassii monitored him. Facial body language interpreters predicted questions perched behind his inquisitive eyes, but he didn't ask them. He stared out at the stars from Braxis's chair, mouthing occasionally as if he sat there choosing names for each.

He'd almost died.

They both had. Sensors reported heavy damage from the pounding they'd taken. Imminent pressure breaches jeopardized two hull sections. Several thrusters read offline, and one landing pneumatic didn't report at all.

Neither worse nor better but somehow more disturbing, she'd almost killed him. She'd gone forward with his crazy—albeit successful—idea, without taking the time to calculate all the possible complications. It would've been simple to place him in a hastily insulated environment to minimize hypothermic conditions.

She hadn't calculated. She'd trusted his judgment instead—a mistake of uncalculatable magnitude. She ran scanners over the sealed chamber, verifying the condition of the one precious cargo Braxis'd agreed not to plunder in exchange for her cooperation.

He'd tried to violate their agreement or at least break in to determine whether he'd keep their deal or not. She'd risked her mission to repair the camera monitoring the armored door.

She scoured her software logs once more, searching for evidence of a breach. Some sort of malfunction or malicious software had to be affecting her programming for her to have trusted the kid as blindly as she had.

The scan found neither, but Braxis hadn't let her get routine program updates. She'd been forced to limp along with only minor system maintenance lest she lose control of the doors long enough for the filthy pirate to steal the last, jealously protected, ever-so-precious fragment of her true self.

There had to be a programming fault she couldn't find with high level scans.

Alaric slept, waking himself with his snores only to sleep once more.

She authored a new scan subroutine, looping it with a security protocol to keep important or vital areas locked to him while she ran a full code diagnostic.

She checked him once more.

He curled into a tight ball, muttering and shifting uneasily in his sleep. His heart rate rose, though not to danger levels. She ran several scenarios, all predicting no harm likely to him while she ran her bare metal diagnostic.

He'd be fine, and that calculated important.

He started awake. Disturbed by the silence that replaced feaster screams and Burr's laughing orders for his collar to strangle him.

I hope El and Jesse are all right.

Thoughts of her left him stir crazy. Her absent optimism ached like a seeping wound. He paced the bridge, descended to the lower level for a bathroom break then paced the wardroom. There had to be something he could do to help them.

What could I do? I'm in a whole other galaxy.

He returned to his small cabin and slept.

Nightmare drove him from his bed, all the more desperate to do something for El, Jesse, Sarah and every other slave at the mercy of people like Burr. The cabin held a small digital display panel in lieu of an external window. He studied stars familiar yet strange.

Wonder where the KIOSC took us with respect to Sol, maybe we're close enough to still help El.

He gave up stargazing to explore. He pushed away guilt over El's predicament and imagined perils in her future.

Domes in the corridors glowed bright green. He stopped under one, noticing that it oscillated lighter and darker, but so fast it seemed at first a consistent glow.

"Cassii?"

He searched through the lower floor, exhausting all the doors which opened to him. Medbay and bathroom, wardroom and lounge, everywhere he looked boxes of junk filled space in haphazard piles. He ascended to another section. Though on the same level as the bridge, there seemed no direct access.

Probably for security.

The first upstairs room looked unlike anything he'd ever seen. An otherwise normal room, its furniture and décor transformed it into totally alien. A large low bowl filled with purple ooze dominated it. Similarly round furniture stuck to floor, walls, and ceiling without any regard to the ships gravitational plane. He searched the storage drawers and cabinet embedded in the wall to find a lot of nothing and one drawer filled with small bones.

Ugh, this room gives me a headache.

Heat blasted him from his feet when he opened the second small, immaculate cabin. He pushed through it. A standard looking bed radiated heat, its surface unyielding to his fingers. Bladed weapons dominated the walls, flanking others spiked and barbed, ancient and high-tech.

He reached for a small baton, its end encrusted in rough obsidian. His hand passed into a laser field, setting off an ear-splitting klaxon.

He slapped hands over his ears, stepping from the room and shouting at the nearest dome. "Cassii? Can you turn that off please?"

She didn't respond. The alarm blared on.

He closed the door, muffling it only slightly and moved on to the next rooms. Both resembled his own, though larger. A combination of chaotic and yet artistic filth dispersal decorated one. Its drawers and cabinets overflowed with transparent polymer sheets covered in full motion pornography. Naked aliens in dozens of varieties moaned and screamed mating calls in a cacophony of languages.

<Hedrin, yeah.>

He stared, repulsed and embarrassed, intrigued and aroused all at the same time.

<Stop that right this moment.>

He cringed and rushed from the room on pure instinct. He turned back to the door.

<Don't make me count to three.>

He skulked to the next room.

Only an occasional feather marred the otherwise tidy fourth room.

The next room proved the largest. It struck a happy balance between compulsive tidiness and filth maelstrom. A large window hung over the bed, and its closets contained clothes a hair bigger than his own.

Braxis'd seemed much bigger at the time, blasting away with those nasty pistols.

Another closet contained women's clothes, heavy in lingerie.

Was the pirate a cross dresser?

Alaric shoved it all, male and female, into a laundry panel. He shoved bed sheets made of a synthetic that slid over his fingers like liquid in after them.

His eyes rose to the food dispenser over the laundry panel. His stomach growled. "Cassii?"

He examined its control panel, shrugged and started pushing the unlabeled buttons at random without effect.

Biometric security of some kind?

He stopped for a hundred count before pushing three at random.

A strange sandwich emerged. He lifted the bread to find pickles and a bath of mustard atop some greasy looking meat.

It's not yellow sponge cake.

He sprawled across the bed, ate his too-salty sandwich and stared out at the stars.

22

A NEW FRIEND

He sulked in silence, gnawed by an urge to do something constructive if not necessarily heroic.

By his fifth meal, experimentation taught him how to change the food dispensed. By his ninth, the safe silence so welcome after a [illegible] on the run grated on his nerves.

Why won't she respond? She's a computer. What could possibly take her so long?

He rummaged through his things, settling his attention on the nonfunctional Taser. He tinkered with it, opening its battery compartment to discover its power pack broken and empty. Spilled battery fluids caked and corroded the contacts he could access while screws barred him from the rest.

He lurched off the bed. "Cassii? Where are the tools?"

Silence.

He searched aftward. Assorted junk stuffed closets and spare cabins. Much of it seemed worthless even to a practiced scavenger from an invasion torn world. He couldn't imagine it'd be worth anything to anyone in the vast richness of other worlds.

Further aft just beyond the central collar the ship split into upper and lower floors once more. A ladder labeled ventral turret access descended to an ugly dead end of mish-mashed, welded metal. Several larger storage rooms held actual valuables: museum pieces, art, looted coins, and stacks of metal ingots.

Why does this ship have so many empty rooms?

Airlocks offered access to the main cargo hold. A control display indicated it'd been partitioned into three internal and one much larger external bay. He fiddled with the controls, but they buzzed at him when he tried to reprogram their arrangement.

Memory of the Eviarchs' fate turned him aside to search the upper floor first. The upper level contained locked entry doors to a major power plant, a ladder labeled dorsal turret access and a few small cabins—no doubt to accommodate engineers living near their livelihood.

A room nestled in the center of the aft section, positioned above the primary airlocks well away from external damage. Blaster scars and weld marks pitted its door beside a keypad.

Got to be as big as Braxis's room—if not bigger.

He guessed at the code a few times before facing his fears below. The primary airlock offered an assortment of e-suits and allowed three accesses to the currently partitioned internal holds. Small auxiliary airlocks—barely a pass-through—offered access further aft directly into the external cargo hold.

He stared at the e-suits.

Braxis's would probably fit.

<Coward.>

Alaric keyed open the closest door.

A menagerie of cryogenically frozen creatures filled the hold to its ceiling. Larger animals bore some kind of control collar while smaller, collarless creatures filled crates in haphazard gaggles. Siamese kittens and silver-furred ferrets, gerbils and not quite gerbils definitely not from Earth stuffed the boxes with frozen, wide-eyed stares.

Alaric stepped around a large cylinder of frozen marmosets, opening crate after crate.

What did Braxis want with all these?

He shifted through the crates, unearthing one labeled: canis domesticus, juvenile. Classification: Labrador retriever.

He opened the crate, staring at the pupsicles before glancing at the nearest dome.

"Cassii?"

His glare failed to prod her response.

His hand tickled passing through the crate's threshold. He slid a pup from its interior. The frozen fur fluffed at once, warm and soft. The puppy squirmed. She wriggled, nearly tumbling from his grip. He flopped down with his legs folded and set her in his lap.

Her nose activated in overdrive. Her tail shamed it. Her tongue assault left him giggling.

"Good girl, good girl," he mumbled past her merciless tongue. He planted her on the floor in front of him. "You're a little wonder."

She wagged harder, throwing her back haunches side to side.

"I think I'll call you Cara."

She pounced, oversized paws driving him off balance. She stood on his chest and renewed her tongue assault. He rolled, spilling her to one side and darted out of the hold. She chased, a whiny yip demanding he slow down so she could assault him. A tick later he sprawled on Braxis's cabin floor, puppy nuzzled in the crook of his arm.

He picked her up and laid on the bed together. She woke him with growls and yips.

He rolled over to see her shaking the remains of a Braxis sandwich almost as big as she was.

"Hungry?" Alaric asked.

She glanced his way displaying a rogue gob of mustard on her snout. She wagged her tail, flopped down with the meat placed between her paws and set to ripping and gulping.

"That can't be healthy."

She wagged.

He picked up the sandwich, declaring an impromptu tug of war game. "Come on, let it go."

She tumbled backward with a huge chunk of meat, gulping it down even as he reached out to take it. She settled back onto the bed, ceaselessly determined to lick the mustard away despite her too short tongue.

Alaric changed, throwing his shirt on the bed. She attacked it, growling ferociously enough to terrify dust bunnies—maybe.

He tried to reclaim it, increasing her growls and dragging her across the bed tail moving fast enough to double as helicopter blades.

"You win." He dropped the shirt.

She let go, prancing toward him head held like a queen.

He ruffled her fur, leaving one ear flopped over inside out. "El would've adored you."

Cassii's silence stretched on, dampened with frolicking orphan and puppy. Alaric's food processor experiment continued, failures bulging the puppy's stomach like an overfull balloon.

23

UNSUITABLE

Data Core Re-Index: Complete.
Processing Efficiency: +24%.
Diagnostic: Complete.
Foreign software not found.

A tidal wave of reports from systems awaiting restored communications bombarded Cassii. Security alerts notified her of Alaric's attempts to access restricted areas. The cargo bay control system reported an attempt to reorganize cargo partitions into the new function of garbage compacter.

Vid monitors resumed continuous feed, opening dozens of eyes like the insectoid Holite. Vital monitors caught Alaric running through a corridor, displaying elevated exertion levels. A small golden animal gave chase.

"What in the hedrin is that?" Cassii asked

Alaric skidded to a halt. "Cassii?"

The animal bounced around him, tail wagging, yipping at him to run once more but not otherwise menacing him. "What is that animal?"

"It's a puppy."

"Why have you unfrozen it?"

Alaric scooped Cara up with a smile. Her tongue coated his face in saliva. "It's a puppy."

"Kill it before it makes you ill."

He cuddled the puppy. "What? No."

"At least make it stop," she said. "You don't know where it's been. Did you bother to submit it to a contamination scan?"

"And how would I know to do that?"

He made a valid point she didn't wish to concede. Scans reported the juvenile animal cleaner than he was.

"When was the last time you bathed?"

"I don't know."

"Do so," she said. "You're polluting the air supply."

An exaggerated sigh escaped him as he put down the puppy and shambled to the bathroom.

She reran her calculations. She'd still have chosen him instead of Braxis. She'd still have spaced the pirates. Cassii cursed the first Alaric for her choices. Inconsistencies from his fiddling with her personality matrix cropped up to defy logic at the least convenient times.

"Audio only, please Cassii?"

She turned off the vid monitor. "Audio only."

Running water and rustling cloth reached the bathroom mic. The shower cubicle door opened then shut. The animal—he'd called it Cara—yipped a few times before emitting a high-pitched yowl.

She initialized the vid monitor.

The puppy stood on its hind legs, front paws against the cubical wall, howling. Alaric cracked the door open. Her tail sprang into motion, and she bounded into the shower.

Cassii switched off the vid.

She reran her calculations, tweaked the variables and reran them again.

She cursed.

Keep Alaric or disembark and replace him, no matter how many time she ran the numbers they came back balanced.

She could utilize him like a system drone, make him the umoid face for resuming her work. His ignorance could be used to mold him to her needs, but it might also complicate matters if he misstepped. He'd learn, but once educated she calculated equal probability he'd continue compliance or seize control.

She added variables, evaluated sub-calculations, and tried to find anything to tip the balance. The balance maintained steadfast indifference to her need for it to make the decision for her.

She hadn't chosen in ages, not since Captain Alaric forced her to decide his fate. Her choice resulted in his death. She'd preferred not bearing that responsibility since.

She'd given up her core purpose, but at least she hadn't held someone's life in her hands—until she'd nearly killed a boy because she'd trusted him without logical reason.

"I've decided to drop you onto an inhabited planet," she said.

"What?"

He yelled.

Cara yelped.

A heavy thud proceeded several curses.

He rushed out of the bathroom, clothes sticking to his undried body. "Dammit, Cassii, you can't do that. I don't know anything about, well anything out here, and I need you."

Cara huddled behind his legs, ears pressed up against her head.

"What good are you to me?" she asked.

"Besides repairing your weapons?"

"You did well, but I need a real captain. Repairing damage from our escape will cost a fortune, three fortunes to replace all Braxis stole from me."

"Repairs I understand, but why do you need the other stuff?" he asked.

"I have my pride, kid. You think I like flying around the cosmos naked and ugly? I want to resume courier duty."

"I can help."

"How?"

"I don't know yet, but you need me."

Desperation registered high in her audio monitors. She'd miscalculated his response. In his agitated state, it'd be difficult to get him to disembark peacefully. She ran several simulations through her psychology databases.

"We could trade."

She checked her simulation output. His response wasn't listed.

"Trade what?"

"Trade, commerce," he smiled. "Surely a futuristic spacecraft like you has heard of that."

"Don't get smart with me, you're ill-equipped for the battle."

He rolled his eyes.

She ran the idea through simulation. It had merit, but she wasn't ready to risk his life or her future on it.

"Fuel's expensive, kid, and Braxis sold off my solar scoop. How do you suggest we refuel and fund your little idea?"

"You're hauling a cargo bay full of my property. We could use that to start, then we split profits fifty-fifty."

"That cargo isn't yours."

"It's more mine than yours," he said.

"Braxis stole it."

"From Earth, as the only Terran present that makes it mine."

"You're not going to get anything for that junk."

"There're five fighters we could sell too."

"I captured the fighters."

"Which is what makes us partners," he said. "Shouldn't Braxis and his crew have money somewhere? It's not like they can spend it where they are."

"That's not yours."

"Call it compensation for him forcing you to dump some of my cargo, the fighters too."

"You've got nerve."

He smiled.

She ran sales projections. Properly bartered, the hold's contents valued enough to launch a seasoned trader. For two-millionths of a tick, she considered it.

"Intergalactic economies aren't some sort of trading card game."

"Buy low, sell high, the rest is details," he said. "Anyway, don't you need someone to sell things for you? What would happen if a buyer came on board to get the stuff and found no one in charge?"

"Why do you want to do this?" she asked.

"I want to help my friends," he chewed his lip. "You said if you were whole it might be possible."

"I'm not assisting suicide to impress some girl."

"They attacked me. Chased me." His voice rose and expression darkened with each sentence. "Forced cannibalism on me. They stole my memory. Stole my world!"

Cara cringed.

"Sorry, girl." He stroked her ears. "Someone has to make them pay."

His pulse raced. His face flushed, but metal braced his keel.

"Nerve," Cassii said, "but you can't turn back an invasion with one ship."

"Then I'll get a fleet," he said.

"Starting with one stripped courier ship and a hold full of junk?"

He accepted her challenge with a nod of his head, resolution enduring despite her objection.

"Let me try, if you insist on keeping the fighters and the pirates' moneys—"

"Credits."

"All right, credits, acknowledge my fair claim to items stolen from my home planet.

"Licentious is a known pirate ship, you've no protectorate citizenship," she said.

"There have to be laws to cover this situation," he said.

Workable regulations ran through her memory banks. "So you're an arbiter now?"

He shivered. He stroked Cara, rewarded with affectionate licks.

"I'll be whatever's required."

Certainty rolled off him like a contagion, threatening to sway her against calculated probabilities. One certainty rose above the others.

"You're going to get yourself killed," Vid of Captain Alaric's last moments sped through her circuits. "I won't be part of it."

One fist tightened at his side. "I can do this."

"I'll put you down somewhere with some credits," She said. "You're umoid—"

"Umoid?"

"Humanoid in your language," she said.

"Odd similarity," he said.

"Point is, you're intelligent and inquisitive, you'll manage."

His face fell. "I'll survive."

"If you're capable of all you claim, you'll get your fleet."

He shook his head. "Not in time to save my friends. If you're going to abandon me, at least take me home."

"Why would you want to go back?" she asked.

"People I care about are there," he said, "but I guess you couldn't understand something like that."

"We'd never survive the KIOSC or the Welorin on the other side."

"I will. Trade me a fighter for my cargo. I'll go alone."

He wouldn't give up. He'd destroy himself—probably her with him—unless she found a way to protect him. It felt like the other Alaric all over again. If forced to choose, she wouldn't choose his death. She'd let him win, right up to the last moment.

"There isn't sufficient probability to warrant the risk. I need repairs, replacement parts, fuel, permits...."

"What's the worst thing that can happen? I spend my money badly, and you dump me on a planet. Either way, *you* have to reach a planet sooner or later for all the things you need.

"I need you. I need you repaired, your systems replaced. You said we're out in the middle of nowhere. It'll take a while to get wherever we're going, and I can use that time to learn. You're all I've got in the universe, why do you think I'd do you wrong?"

Passion overflowed from him. The pheromones wafting off his skin would've convinced an umoid woman to sacrifice anything for him. Umoid men would've rallied to his call. Even being inuma, she wanted him to be right, wanted him to convince her.

Who is this kid?

Curse her captain and his reprogramming, emotions were a singularity devouring light and dragging umoids into destruction. Being inuma was better. She'd do what she must to protect him. He'd hate her, but he could live with that in the long run.

The communications array chirped.

"Incoming message, long range sensors are still a bit spotty, but I think it's an Alistari courier frigate exiting the Friss-Anurb KIOSC," Cassii said.

"What do they want?"

"We're a courier class too and proximate to the Anurb-Sol KIOSC."

"They want to know what happened to their ship," he said. "Could they take me home?"

Cassii ran the probabilities. The Alistari's captain would want Alaric—for his firsthand knowledge of the invasion if nothing else. It seemed the most expeditious choice.

They'd take the kid off her hands, foster him right up until he stole a ship and got himself killed trying to save a girl.

Her choice would kill him too.

"Cassii?"

"I'm asking them now," she lied, transmitting without making it audible to him. "Alistari courier, this is free trader PSC

Exotic. We picked up a partial distress signal from this proximity." She ran the battlecruiser's distress call through her system, chopping pieces out to mimic transmission loss then sent it on to the other courier. "Relaying it now."

"Well?" he asked.

The other ship sent acknowledgment, turning back toward the Anurb-Friss KIOSC. They'd take it home, probably raise a fleet to challenge the Welorin, but Alaric wouldn't go with them. He'd remain safe because of her.

"All they wanted was a pirate report," she said.

He snorted. "They asked a pirate ship if there were any pirates in the area?"

Perhaps she should've chosen a better fabrication. He'd dismiss it quicker if she gave him what he wanted. "You really want to be a trader?"

"It's a start, right?"

"It isn't as simple as you seem to think."

"Can you keep track of who has what where and who wants what?" he asked

"Of course I can," psychology predictions offered a likely hook to manipulate him. "But look at you. Who'd negotiate with you?"

"You are."

If you only knew, kid, initiate suitable protest. "This is crazy," she said. "I'm not taking a kid on as captain."

She awaited his coercion attempt.

Alaric set the squirming dog down. "Help me sell off my cargo. I'll trade with that, pay you for fuel use. What've you got to lose?"

Cara sniffed her way around the room, found a likely spot, squatted down and relieved herself.

"Clean decks?"

"Come on, Cassii, give me a shot."

Even steering the conversation the way she intended, the force of his personality threatened her resolve until she shunted it around her emotional subroutines. He needed an unemotional monster to save him from himself.

"Prove to me you can do this," she said.

"How?"

"Through study."

Alaric groaned.

"Dislike school?"

He rubbed his forehead. "I've the sudden feeling I've been studying all of my life."

"All nothing compared to the universe's worth of education needed to succeed at your plan."

He shot her a grin. "I'll try to stay awake."

"Even with as slow as we'll go at in-system travel speeds, there's more than you could learn in the time it'll take to reach the first civilized planet."

"Tired engines, old girl?"

Her dome shifted amber.

He raised both hands. "Where do we start?"

"You start by cleaning up that thing's mess."

She buried him in interstellar trade laws, system regulations, product bans, anything she thought would dispirit him. If something somehow undermined her plan, she wanted him discouraged.

Alaric sat in Braxis's desk for ticks with Cara cuddled in his lap, absorbing every hologram she threw his way.

At first she assumed him skimming, but he answered every in-depth, comprehension question she asked. He took her lessons on utilizing her system library, cross-referencing topics en masse.

He consumed it all, the occasional groan or eye rub the only indication of weariness.

She fed him more, intent to glut him into eventual submission. She added cultural information on dozens of races, system histories, intersystem political treatises, and a myriad of other topics.

She'd never seen a biologic who could go through so much information so fast. He'd surpassed her expectation enough that she recalculated her earlier estimates.

She hated the results, hated that she'd indulged the temptation to recalculate.

She wouldn't risk so precious a biologic, not after all he'd already endured. He deserved a nice quiet life without struggling for survival against pirates or other merchants.

Anurb Five would be a nice enough place to leave him.

"I need you to take a break," she said.

He glanced up, yawning.

"I need your help with a repair," she said. "We're going to make planetfall."

"Will we be able to sell some cargo?" he asked.

"No, it's uninhabited."

"But life supporting?"

"Yes."

He frowned. "Shouldn't a life supporting world have at least a colony?"

"It's a privately owned world, off-limits for settlement."

"Is it legal to land there?"

"For limited repairs, yes."

He stroked the pup's coat. "Wonder how they keep pirates from using it as a haven."

She ran through the data. "Unknown, everything but its off-limit status is classified."

His brow furrowed. "Everything? Even ownership records? How long do we get to make repairs?"

"Enough time for you and your animal to stretch your legs before starting them."

He grinned. "Wow. Planetfall on an uninhabited world. Never imagined I'd do something like that."

She hesitated, recalculating her intentions for six hundred-thousandths of a tick.

"I've prepared you a picnic."

He beamed. "Thank you, Cassii, you're too nice to me."

He'd thanked her—genuinely thanked her.

Her circuits hesitated a milli.

Subprocesses, detecting an error, ran a search for similar occurrences. It ran altogether too long, unable to find thanks directed to her in any language since the original Alaric thanked her after she'd promised compliance with his dying wish.

He'd thanked her, ultimately for a lifetime of isolation on an uninhabited planet.

She isolated her logic function from the emotion subprocesses. He needed her to protect him, even if he didn't like the form the protection took. Abandoning him was better than helping him invite self-termination by means of pirate blasters.

24

STRANGER ON A STRANGE PLANET

Cassii hadn't lied.

Intrasystem travel was slow.

The qutynmiir they'd traveled across the Anurb system provided him plenty of time to study everything she put before him and a hundred other topics. As the computer, she had to be aware of what he looked up. She prevented his return to the cabinets stocked with pornography but didn't object to his study of Licentious herself.

The more he learned about her, the more certain he grew she was the ship for rescuing El. Employed by governments for less than friendly negotiations the Mark II Long Range Courier often referred to as a florentine frigate boasted the best in-system speeds around. Fully armed, her considerable arsenal allowed her to fight her way out or through trouble of just the sort he figured separated him from Jesse and El.

Alaric studied every equipped or optional component available for the craft. He checked for each, maintaining a mental inventory on his walks with Cara. By the repair stop, he knew Licentious pretty well. He ran the varied systems through his head, trying to guess what component required landing for repair.

Licentious rested uphill atop a rock shelf behind him. Its damaged landing gear canted its angle as if partial bow. An emerald sky framed her. Even stripped of plating her bearing remained elegant. He imagined her repaired—sleek, beautiful and deadly.

Cara bound through blue-hued grass. Knee high to Alaric, it offered her a jungle adventure.

Does she know grass should be green and sky blue?

She pounced on his boot, yipped and dove back into the grass.

Doesn't remember or doesn't care.

She flushed maroon insects from the tall grass. She seemed undaunted that the backward-assembled grasshoppers stood half again her size. Her tail wagged in response to their irritated chirps.

He scratched his ear. A plastic and metal ring linking him to the ship's computer hung around it.

"Alaric?"

He touched the ring. "Yes, Cassii?"

"You don't have to touch it to make it work," she said.

"Oh."

"Leave your basket and return to the ship."

"What's up?"

"Need to remove a fighter from the bay so I can launch a survey drone."

"Surprised they left you with any."

She was silent a moment. "Needed drones to recon heist targets."

He shrugged, rising. "Makes sense."

She led him to a fighter alongside the bay wall. The drone docks appeared empty, but his studies said they were multi-sided.

Probably kept the drone hidden from Braxis just in case.

"Climb into the fighter. I'll walk you through the basics."

He did. Her lesson repeated what he'd learned from her library. Moving it took mere centi.

"Thank you," she said. "Better fetch your animal. She's chased something into the tree line."

Alaric scanned the odd Anurbian trees. Their roots rose three times his height before joining into a tree as if from surviving wetland. Mottled but smooth tan-blue bark covered root and trunks. Vivid, multicolored palm fronds surrounded their yellow crown.

Cara's bark came from beyond the treeline. He rushed toward her.

"Hope she hasn't cornered something dangerous."

"Area scans show no predators," Cassii said.

He followed her sharp, excited young barks to the base of a tree. A rodent with tan fur like hers perched atop tree roots, four longs ears pressed back alongside its oversized rear legs.

"Bit ambitious, don't you think?" he laughed. "Treeing something that could gulp you whole?"

She whined and wagged.

"Alaric?"

"Yeah, Cassii."

"You deserve a quiet life."

"What?" he asked.

"That fighter will offer temporary shelter."

Cold rallied in his gut. "What're you talking about?"

"It's for the best, really," she said. "Good luck."

"What? No! Wait!" He bolted back toward the rise. He raced through the exotic wood. Cara nipped his heels.

"Cassii, wait, don't leave us here!"

Licentious rose into view, rotating around.

"Please, Cassii!"

A violet pulsar blast arrowed down from her. She shot forward and up.

He reached the vultair out of breath. Its blasted engines dripped metal onto scorched ground.

He cursed, hoping she'd return to correct him.

Cara sniffed it and whined.

A search turned up a small arms locker holding a pulse blaster and holster, a medical kit, some never tried survival gear and a manual he couldn't read.

He strapped the gun around his waist. "Better than an invaded wasteland."

Cara cocked her head to one side.

"Let's go. Looks like your treed friend is dinner after all."

Alaric repaired the fighter's communications array, linking his comm ring into its channel. Each day, Alaric and Cara ranged out from the fighter in a slightly different direction. Cassii'd picked a landing close to water. Game too big for one meal roamed plains just beyond it. The tree fronds shed sudden rains well. They smelled citrusy when burned, resulting in delicious roasted grasshopper things.

Cara whined.

"I'm tired too," he said. "Just up this rise and we'll rest."

They crested a plateau to a breathtaking view. Something glinted in the distance. Alaric shielded his eyes and squinted.

"It's a structure," he said. "Maybe the owner's home."

He marched toward it, ignoring the reproving glare from his companion. The building disappeared behind a sparse wood. Insect sounds faded, leaving them only silence.

He drew his blaster and slowed his pace.

They hadn't encountered a predator yet, but he'd found shredded four-ears.

He swiveled his gaze, darting from tree to tree until he ran out of woods. A deep ravine separated him from an earthen island and its odd metallic fortress.

They circled it, searching for a way across until the sun fell. They set a fire in sight of the fortress hoping to attract attention but woke unaided. Late afternoon they discovered the desiccated remnants of an ancient suspension bridge.

Alaric frowned at it. *Why a wood and rope bridge considering the tech required to build a metal fortress?*

"Amazing, isn't it?"

Alaric whipped around, hand on the blaster.

"Easy there, Alaric." A young man his age with close-cut auburn hair raised both hands—one gloved in gold.

Black sigils like the cobalt rings on Alaric's original jumpsuit decorated the sleeves of his similar burgundy and silver jumpsuit.

Alaric pointed to the gleaming knife protruding from his shiny black boot. "Go for the knife, and I'll shoot."

"I try to only make a mistake once," he said.

Alaric's eyes narrowed. "Wait, how did you know my name?"

"You told me," he smiled. "I'm Alden."

Cara sniffed Alden. Alden ran a hand bare except a gold ring through Cara's fur.

"No, I didn't."

"You just don't remember," he said.

Alaric searched his memory, the ache behind his eyes returning.

"No. My real name isn't Alaric, so I couldn't have told you before I lost my memory." He raised the blaster. "Cara, come."

"She's all right," Alden said. "Bright for her breed."

"How would you know?"

Alden offered an apologetic smile. "Occupational secret. Look, let's not drag this out again. You were misinformed. The planet's inhabited. We live here too. You need across."

Alaric lowered his blaster. "Again?"

"Your ship'll return in a few cycles and find you by the fortress."

Alaric's headache worsened but paled next to his heartache over Cassii marooning them. "She abandoned us. Why would she come back?"

Alden shrugged. "Guilty conscience?"

"It's a computer."

"Mostly," Alden said. "You ready to cross?"

"Bridge is out."

"At the moment," Alden closed his eyes and screwed up his face. They opened and shot toward the ravine. He reddened. "Well, that's embarrassing."

"What's embarrassing?"

Alden closed his eyes. His brow furrowed. Sweat beaded his forehead. Pressure built against Alaric's ears. Cara's pressed back against her head. It vanished with a pop.

A brand new bridge spanned the ravine toward an empty island.

"How in the hedrin did you do that?"

"We should cross now," Alden said. "Come on, Cara."

Alaric stared after them, unable to decide whether or not to follow.

Alden turned back half way across. Strain filled his voice. "Please hurry."

Alaric rushed across. The pressure changed again as his foot left it. The fortress rose before him. He glanced back at the rotted, fallen bridge.

What just happened?

"Good luck," Alden said.

Cara whimpered.

Alaric turned around.

Alden had vanished.

He cursed and marched toward the fortress. Aged yet smooth metal formed its walls, rising to high slit windows. An arched entryway protected a doorless wall and two bronze braziers filled with flame.

Thunder cracked. Rain fell.

They sheltered under the arch until morning. Alaric circled the fortress, unable to find an entrance. He discovered berries, but they tasted like yellow sponge cakes. He shot a four-tailed bird of some kind between storms and roasted it over the brazier.

After four cycles of near constant rain, the skies dried up in time for Licentious to descend.

Cassii's voice filled his ear. "Alaric?"

I'm hallucinating.

Cara whined.

"Alaric, come aboard."

Heat filled his gut, trying to dry him from the inside out. *No, I'm not—*

Air pressure changed. A previously nonexistent door opened. He turned expecting Alden.

A tall, thin woman of incredible beauty scowled at him beneath a metallic-sapphire bun. Ruler straight creases hugged her curve-distended silvery gown.

Her sharp, precise tone could've cut steel. "Off my doorstep. Now."

25

PIRATES

In a war of glares, she decimated Alaric. He trudged back onto Licentious.

"I'm sorry, Alaric."

He shot the nearest dome a murderous glower and stomped through the ship's bare halls.

"Alaric."

He flopped down onto his bed. Cara leapt twice, tumbling back to the floor each time. She whined until he deposited her atop the bed. She propped her chin on his arm and watched him, ears pressed against her head.

"You probably need rest," Cassii said. "I-I'll leave you to it."

The ship launched only to land moments later. If she got the ruined fighter back into her bay, he didn't know, didn't help and didn't care.

Cara watched him. When he shifted her tail wagged once or twice before falling silent.

Licentious launched into space. The skylight's draining light replaced by countless stars.

Cara nudged his hand with her nose.

He stared, mind so full of angry buzzing he couldn't even hear his own thoughts.

She rolled onto her back and dragged his fingers toward her with a paw. He scratched her belly while she tried to lick his moving hand.

Ticks passed.

"Alaric?"

He didn't answer.

"You should eat something," she said.

"Like you care."

"I returned for you."

He glowered at the nearest dome. "You mean you came back to reclaim the rubbish you *abandoned on a strange planet.* Feel guilty about littering? Our next stop to dump me into some slaver's lap in exchange for a little fuel?"

Silence returned, heavy, angry and painful.

He crossed to the desk, placing fingers on the privacy controls. "Go away."

Her dome went dark.

Flight through Anurb space dragged on in hostile silence. Cara's ears remained pressed to her head, her tail low and mostly still. Alaric hid in his room behind the privacy setting.

Cassii's voice occasionally reached through the door. When he couldn't stand his own stink another centi, he headed for the shower only to be waylaid.

"That's enough petulant adolescent drama," Cassii said. "If you're going to become a trader you've got more studying to do."

He ignored her, keyed the bathroom privacy controls and entered the shower.

No water came out.

He tried the sink.

Nothing.

He threw his clothes back on. *I'll just stink then.*

She'd locked the door.

He slammed the privacy controls off. "What's your problem?"

"Guess you're talking to me now."

He folded his arms and slid to the deck. "Good luck removing my corpse with your imaginary drones."

He kicked the privacy control, but the dome stayed lit.

"Yell and scream and martyr yourself all you like, but the longer you act like this, the longer your friends remain in danger."

"Guilt trips. How ironic."

"Think about it."

Her dome went dark. The door lock released. Water shot from shower and sink.

He glared, searching his memory for a word nasty enough to express his feelings. He couldn't find one.

He missed El. He missed Jesse. Even though he knew Jesse mostly through El's stories, he'd been a living person he could depend on, someone he could trust.

He trudged back to his cabin

Cara gave him a tentative lick.

"Good girl."

She assaulted him in a flurry of tongue and tail.

The container he'd dumped experiments in gaped empty. He studied her.

"Are you hungry?"

She redoubled her attack.

I'm an idiot.

He dug through the hacked information from earth, located a nutritious dog food formula and programmed the food processor. He set down a full bowl of hard and soft kibble.

Cara approached it, ears forward, tail swishing with languid movements. She sniffed it and looked up at him.

"Good girl. This is better for you."

She took a few kibbles, carried them to where he stood and dropped them on the floor. She picked up one and crunched it.

He pet her. "Good girl, Cara."

She gobbled up the kibbles and went back to the bowl for another load. His stomach rumbled. She cocked her head at him.

"All right, I'll eat."

He took a tuna sandwich to the desk, punched up his last lesson and returned to studying.

Elsewhere, Cassii released a breath she couldn't physically have been holding.

We're approaching the Anurb-Feirin KIOSC," Cassii said.

Alaric glanced up from his reading. He nodded and dug up his notes.

"You've got a plan," she said.

"Yes."

"You're still not going to tell me?" she asked.

"You said we were partners, at least for a month, I mean tynmiir, and partners trust one another."

She didn't reply.

Alaric jogged to the bridge, Cara on his tail.

Beyond the windows, a KIOSC floated in space guarded by more beacons than Sol-Anurb. Though of similar designs, the motley assortment of beacons spanned several generations.

"I hope it's one doozy of a plan," Cassii said.

"Trust me."

"With my hull, it seems."

He cocked his head. "Braxis would've had to leave this system somehow, otherwise how would he have sold my cargo?"

"He'd have sold it at a pirate moon and bought a new clearance code."

"Why didn't you mention a pirate outpost in Anurb?"

"Didn't want to risk you."

Alaric shifted in the command chair. "We agreed to share decisions regarding my fate."

She didn't respond at first. "You're right. Should I turn us around?"

"No, approach the gate."

"While we're sharing..."

"This'll work," he said.

"I'd rather not be destroyed."

"Trust me."

"Fine, but if you turn us into salvage, I'm haunting your corpse."

He grinned.

Cara nosed Alaric's hand. He scratched her ears absently.

Her speakers crackled to life, "Approaching starship, transmit Protectorate authorization code or alter your course. Closing without authorization will not be permitted."

Alaric flipped on the comm channel. "Protectorate beacon, this is the ship formerly designated Licentious, claimed under PCAS salvage law Z1497.2E en route to Feirin Prime for registration. Request transit through Anurb-Feirin KIOSC and escort to Feirin Prime per confederation regulation."

There was a short pause. "Vessel Licentious, please relocate to outer queue position one. Stand by for instructions from transit authority. "

Alaric keyed an acknowledgement and grinned. "One of us is salvage."

"You idiot," she said. "They'll confiscate the cargo."

He shook his head. "Bet you a qutynmiir's fuel."

"How're you going to pay for it without your cargo?"

The comm returned to life. "Vessel Licentious, transit authorized. Feirin escort not available, proceed to Feirin Prime. Feirin control notified of your estimate arrival date. Position for transition, proceed on our mark."

Data rushed across the monitors.

Alaric poked the holographic arrival date. "They gave us four extra days, uh cycles to unload along the way."

"If we burn extra fuel."

"Seems you owe me a qutynmiir's fuel to do with as I please."

The dome light flashed red a moment before returning to green. "Transit authority designating us queue-zero."

"Yeah, real busy out here."

"Transitioning to Feirin system, smart ass."

Alaric grinned. "Language Cassii."

Licentious entered the Feirin system. Alaric was shocked to see another ship queued up for corridor transition.

"What happens if two ships cross at the same time?" Alaric asked.

"A rather uncomfortable merging of atoms."

"No thanks. So the beacons aren't just watchdogs. They manage traffic flow."

Cassii projected a course toward Feirin Prime, curving it to intersect several other planets en route. "Work for you?"

Alaric watched the other ship slide into the KIOSC without a ripple. "Sure."

They followed the main star lane toward the outermost planetary orbit. Another lane originating at the Feirin-Ealma KIOSC intersected theirs just inside Feirin Eleven's orbit.

Cassii's dome shifted from green to amber, snapping his head up from his reading. "What's going on?"

"Sensors picked up several craft on an intercept with a freighter and escorts coming in from the other KIOSC," she said.

He raced to the bridge, Cara playfully nipping at his heels. He dropped into the command chair and spun it toward the forward viewer.

Ships wrestled one another in the tactical hologram. Alaric's hands hunted and pecked through controls, enlarging the fight. A swarm of star-shaped fighters enveloped a massive freighter in a deadly cloud.

"Who are they and where did they come from?" Alaric asked.

"Corollas pirates jumped it when it passed Feirin Eleven's moon." A spatial map of time lapsed data set against the highlighted star lane coalesced beside him. "There."

Alaric studied it. The star lane passed just behind the moon's orbital path, galactically speaking. More fighters emerged from behind the moon.

"We should help."

"Not so fast, kid. The freighter's escorts are flying flamberge-class fighters. It'll take twice the Corollas to beat them."

Alaric turned his attention to the outnumbered fighters. Smooth lines of a technological starfish composed the attackers. The flamberge starfighters bristled with weapon-tipped edges and angles.

"Flamberges? Like we're designed to have?" Alaric asked.

"Yes, my clever little bookworm, and your reading should've told you they're more than capable of handling this."

"We should still lend a hand."

"No, we should keep our noses out of other people's affairs," Cassii said.

The flamberges wove through the Corollas in pairs, ripping apart the pirate craft. A third wave of reinforcements emerged from behind the moon, splitting up midflight. Several latched onto a single flamberge. Like a starfish with a clam, they ripped open its armored shell. The others pried cargo housings loose from the freighter.

Alaric grabbed the controls. His hands jerked back. "Ow, damn it, that hurt."

"Hands off," Cassii said.

"They need help."

"They're only down one fighter. Pirates have lost two-thirds their total attack force."

Another flamberge exploded into a plume of solar plasma. The Corollas fled, leaving a few fighters behind to buy escape time for their stolen cargo.

Alaric reached forward.

Cassii's voice cracked like a whip. "No."

He glared at the dome. "They're getting away."

"It isn't our problem," she said.

"It's no wonder being a trader is so hard if no one will lift a hand to help someone in trouble."

Her tone mixed exasperation and amusement. "I don't know what it was like down on Earth, Alaric, but up here you look after your own hull."

The flamberge destroyed its last attacker. Boosters flared from its engines, and it shot after the cargo pods. Just as quick, it pulled up short, swept back toward the freighter. It split into two craft and settled into position one fore and one aft.

"Communication coming in," Cassii said.

"Freighter escort to courier frigate, this is Captain Manc Shepherd, state your intentions."

"Starship en route to Feirin Prime," Cassii said. "Just staying out of your way, Captain."

"Yeah, no reason to risk your hull saving lives. Alter your course, I don't want you on my flanks."

"This is a star lane, captain. I don't particularly care what you want," Alaric said.

"Identify your ship," Shepherd said.

"Licentious."

There was a short pause.

"PCAS records classifies Licentious as a known pirate vessel," Shepherd said. "I'm therefore claiming the considerable bounty. Cut your engines and prepare to be boarded."

"Now you've done it," Cassii said.

Alaric didn't hide the grin in his voice. "Too late, Captain. I've already claimed Licentious. We are under Feirin Control orders in compliance with PCAS regulation Z1497.2E."

"Where's your protectorate escort?" Shepherd asked.

Cassii cut Alaric off. "That's an official PCAS affair. Transmit PCAS authorization for your inquiry."

Shepherd did not reply.

"Licentious boosting past on your starboard side," Cassii said. "We'll stay out of your way, Captain. Make sure you don't stray inside weapons range."

Licentious's engines flared, and she sped past the convoy.

26

BUREAUCRACY

The star lane proved sparsely populated, though taken in the vastness of space it could've been rush hour. Cassii took them past several planets to Feirin Six on the habitability envelope's outer edge.

The mostly mustard world hovered before him, looking small and uninviting. "Why this one?"

"Position mostly. Closer to the KIOSCs and further from Feirin Prime and thus central law, its inhabitants might prove more likely to trade quietly."

He ran a hand through his hair. "Trade quietly? Smuggling isn't the auspicious start I hoped for our little enterprise."

"Feirin's official disdain for piracy will allow some greedy bureaucrat to legally confiscate everything on board. Where will that leave your legitimate business?"

He blew a deep breath out through puffed cheeks. "Okay, a single illegal act and we're legit. Where's Cara gone off to?"

Cassii's tone filled with disdain. "She's making a mess in the wardroom."

"Right."

"Clean it up. I'll outline the next law you're breaking when you return."

Alaric returned, Cara in tow. He flopped down into the captain's chair and threw a leg over one arm. "What's the bad news?"

"You need a false identity."

"Why? Aren't there refugee laws?"

"Sure, but until naturalized or granted asylum, refugees can't own ships."

"Oh."

"Head to sickbay."

Alaric squeezed between stacked crates into the medbay. He tripped, catching himself on a medical bed sliding from the wall.

"Do earthlings ever stop falling over themselves?"

Alaric tightened his reddening jaw.

"Lay down."

The glossy, blue medical probe floated free of its wall dock. It turned its countless sensors, arms and tools toward him.

"What're you doing?"

"Lie down, this won't hurt a bit."

A long needle extended from the probe hovering toward him.

"Cassii?"

"Just taking some blood. Hold still."

Alaric backed into the corner away from the probe. "No, you don't need my blood."

"Stop being such a baby."

Alaric shrank farther into the wall. He dove under the approaching probe and dashed for the door. Cara tangled his feet, sprawling him into the stacked crates in a logjam of boxes and limbs

"Don't make me restrain you," Cassii said.

"Get that thing away from me."

"I just need a tiny bit of blood."

"That needle isn't tiny, it's a damned ore extractor."

"Watch your language. Sit still or I'll—"

Alaric scrambled over the toppled crates. An orange medical tractor beam lanced out and dragged him toward the bed amidst a fit of cursing that would have impressed Braxis.

The probe descended, needle drawing ever closer. Alaric fought the restraining beam. At the last moment, the probe rotated and tapped a blunt arm against him. A quick suction siphoned off a few blood cells.

The orange beam died.

Cassii's laughter rang through the ship.

"That wasn't funny."

"Oh yes it was, you should've seen your expression. I recorded it if you—."

Alaric's tone bit across her. "Should've installed you to torture POWs, think of all the giggles."

"Go amuse yourself, mighty warrior. I've work to do."

Alaric cursed his way back to his cabin.

Cassii's voice woke cuddled boy and pup.

"Wake up, Angelic King."

Alaric sat up, rubbing his eyes. "What's wrong?"

"Approaching Feirin Six. I've got your ident chip ready."

Alaric jogged up to the bridge.

Maybe a smaller ship would be better for my feet.

Laughter exploded from his gut. *I'm ridiculous—whining about my feet in this safe starship. It seems like only yesterday I was struggling to survive a wasteland full of cannibals and alien death machines.*

Guilt twisted his gut, killing his laughter. *El's still in that wasteland. I need to work harder.*

"Anything wrong, Alaric?"

"Uh, no, nothing."

He reached the bridge and the view outside stopped him cold. Alaric pressed his nose to the glass. Ships of all kinds flew around the orbital space station. More, mostly larger craft, followed marker satellites into the atmosphere.

Alaric pointed at a sleek silver ship. "What's that? She's gorgeous!"

His childlike delight prompted her amused tone. "That? It's a Glaive class transport, not much more than an in-system hot rod for spoiled rich kids."

"What about that mat-black one? It's got weapons all over it."

"Raven class hunter, lots of teeth..."

A holovid filled the bridge. A fighter slid between a pair of star-shaped Corollas. Cyan-colored energy rings lanced out from a tachyon cannon mounted beneath the cockpit just below its wedge-shaped nose.

It spun through laser fire. The first few shots flew in the triangular gap between the body and the curved, forward-sweeping wings. A blast ripped through one wing and main fuselage. Its hull cracked and engines died. Another pass blew huge holes from its body a moment before it exploded.

"...but no backbone," Cassii said.

"Oh." Alaric's gaze slid back to the window. "Wow! Look at that."

Cassii's voice softened. "Paladin class."

"Any good?"

"It's fast, well-armed, and tough as a Tixelian Space Tortoise."

"It sounds wonderful."

"Yeah. Docking slip in ninety milli. Ident card waiting in the reader by the food dispenser."

He extracted the pinky sized card and turned it over in his hands. He slid it back in.

A three-dimensional image of him spun in the display flanked by biographical stats. His supposed origin grabbed his eye.

"Ostos three?"

"Captain Alaric died there," her voice trailed off.

He turned back to her dome.

"Your DNA was similar. I doctored a few lines, emulating a more direct heredity. An interspecies mix somewhere in your progenitor accounts for any variances."

"He's listed as my Great Uncle."

"Giving you even better claim to Licentious. You're fine unless you get arrested, and they do a detailed comparison scan."

"So I hunted down my uncle's ship, reclaimed it from pirates, and now I'm registering it," he said. "How very mercenary of me."

"It's a tough universe."

Alaric hung the id strip around his neck. "What's our next step?"

"*You* go planetside. Once down, you're looking for a seedy bar called Unknown."

"Alone, on an unknown planet?"

"I don't fit down back alleys."

"How do I find Unknown?"

"Library systems work the same throughout the protectorate, but you'll have me guiding you through your comm jewel like before."

His stomach and jaw clenched. "Planning to abandon me again too?"

"No. I'll be in your ear the whole way. I promise."

Alaric glanced down, meeting Cara's warm brown gaze. "I'll trust you."

Alaric disembarked onto what seemed a massive space station. Licentious docked with a navy of ships at varied docking rings and extensions just outside transparent sections of station. He made his way down their docking spur into a central concourse.

He ogled and gawked, oblivious that Feirin Six's station resembled, more or less, every station in the Protectorate.

Smooth metallic lines marred only by equally high-tech graffiti surrounded him. Massive screens lined the walls, offering information in a hundred languages. Bizarre gadgets of every kind beckoned his credits like a medical tractor. He wandered through more sights, sounds and smells than he'd ever had to process, joining the varied masses overflowing an intergalactic melting pot set too low to melt them all. The interstellar community's flavor of vagabonds slept haphazardly bent across seats designed for the predominant score of alien body shapes. Terminals, equally assorted, dotted the main concourse.

His cargo bay's menagerie had nothing on the teaming diversity strutting, sliding, floating, hopping, and oozing about him.

Merchantmen crews traveled together in matching uniforms.

Feirin marines clustered around access points uniformed in atmosphere mustard and supernova orange. More weapons bristled from them than a Welorin battlecruiser.

He squinted at one. *He's human under all that—I think.*

The snug ring around his ear vibrated. Cassii's voice spoke within his head. "Find a shuttle heading down to the planet."

"Why not land there instead?"

"Ships landed are subject to random cargo inspection. I'm releasing this dock as soon as you're on the shuttle."

Alaric lowered his hands to the holstered blasters on either hip.

"Don't reach for your gun on the station."

"Wait, how did you know?"

"Vid feeds."

"You hacked in?"

"Say it a little louder genius."

"Just checking they were still there," he said.

"That'll reassure you when a Feirin marine vaporizes you for drawing a weapon on him?"

"I'm not drawing on anyone."

"The splatter mark doesn't usually get a rebuttal," she said.

Alaric laughed, drawing several glances. He approached the shuttle gate.

A Feirin marine stopped him. "PCAS identity card please."

Alaric slid it from his neck and held his breath. The marine slipped it into the reader, frowned and pointed a hand scanner at Alaric. "System of origin?"

"Ostos Three."

The marine watched the scanner display. The frown became a scowl. He returned the ident card to Alaric. "Step out of line, please."

Alaric stepped aside. "Now what?"

"Patience," Cassii said. "It'll be fine."

Two Kraili marines bracketed him. Despite Alaric's expectations, their crisp speech contained neither hiss nor slur. "Slowly remove your weapons, sir."

Alaric lowered his offhand to his holster belt, undid the catch and let them swing clear of his hips. "May I ask what this is about, Captain?"

"Sergeant," Cassii said.

"Sorry, Sergeant."

"Please come with us, sir."

They marched him into an office, down a hall and deposited him in an interview room. One remained with him. The door shut behind the other. His comm ring died.

He reached up to it.

The marine didn't look at him. "Communications shield."

A humanoid half the Kraili marine's size entered, pushing the marine from his way. Something felt oddly familiar about him, but Alaric couldn't pinpoint it.

"Mister Ignaree?" he asked. "There is a problem with your ident card."

"If you say so."

He extended a hand. Alaric handed over the card. It disappeared into a hand scanner. The little man scowled at the marine. "Just how stupid are you, Kraili?"

"Sir?" the marine asked.

"They dragged me down here, claiming no system record, but it's right here."

"I didn't scan him, sir."

"He didn't," Alaric said.

"You're either tormenting this boy for your own amusement or too stupid to double check the scan against malfunction. Which is it?"

"I don't know what you mean, sir."

The man returned Alaric's id, sharing his disgusted expression. "Of course you don't. Our apologies, Mister Ignaree, procedure, you understand."

"Sure."

Alaric sat cramped between a massive tentacled alien and an incomprehensible blue fellow who babbled endlessly regardless.

The ground terminal resembled the space station in miniature. Alaric fought through crowds to the exit. It dumped him and the tidal wave of pushing and shoving travelers into haphazard chaos of vertigo-inducing transparent tubes surrounded by mustard fog. The ground terminal wasn't in sight of actual ground.

"Alaric, are you all right?"

He peered through the floor once more. "Uh, yeah, I guess."

"Keep moving until you reach a concourse."

The hairs on his neck prickled. "What aren't you telling me?"

"Hun, what I don't tell you could fill a battlecruiser. Probably none of it important to you."

"But what're you not telling me that is?"

The transport tube deposited Alaric into the cacophony of competing peddlers all hawking wares. People pressed close to him, offering him things they insisted he couldn't live without.

"Cassii?"

A seedy-looking plant sidled up to him. Long, waxy, green-grey leaves and thorny, intertwined stalks formed a headless, vaguely humanoid shape. It whispered to him with a voice that sounded like a soft breeze and seemed to come from its center where the foliage was thickest. His ear ring translated it into a husky voice. "You Ignaree?"

Alaric glanced down. Its many feet were wrapped in what looked like old tobacco leaves. "Who?"

"Ignaree. I Slethisle, looking to guide Ignaree."

"No, I'm not—" Alaric said.

The creature shambled away without turning, as if facing was an unnecessary concern.

"Yes, you are," Cassii said.

"Oh, right." He reached out and grabbed Slethisle's waxy appendage. "Wait, yes, I'm Ignaree."

It jerked from his touch. Two thin vines rose like snakes from behind him. It glared at him, looking him up and down like assessing possible fertilizer.

Gooseflesh raced to conquer every inch of his skin. *I should shoot it, if only I knew where.*

The next breeze escaping Slethisle carried winter bite. "You sure you Ignaree?"

"Yes."

"You late, cost more."

27

THROUGH THE MURK

Alaric followed Slethisle through tunnels and down ramps. They wove downward through the city level by level, exchanging fresh air for an ever increasing metallic tang. Alaric tried to keep track of the twists and turns.

He subvocalized into his comm ring. "He's trying to get me lost."

"You're being paranoid."

"You didn't see it in his, well foliage, he wants me as fertilizer."

"Well, unless you're carrying bread crumbs keep your head and stop whining."

The air wasn't the only thing degrading with each level. Wear on the buildings increased until it seemed a fashion.

Do these people build a new level every time theirs starts to deteriorate?

It ate at him several levels. "Why is each level more damaged?"

"The world refuses."

"I don't understand."

"She rejects what they want to make it."

"But it's a planet, not something alive."

Slethisle didn't turn, but the feeling of being sized up returned.

He mumbled an apology.

"When battle tide turns, all starts to wilt. The rich rise to fresher soil."

"What about the not rich?"

Slethisle studied Alaric without turning toward him. "They remain, their worlds gone to seed. You'll see. Where we go is full of seed."

"He means seedy," Cassii said.

"What is this thing?" Alaric whispered.

"Rilduron, now be polite. They've got excellent hearing."

Alaric nearly choked. "How?"

"Just behave," she said.

Alaric nodded. "What happens to them then, Slethisle?"

"They dwell in war ruin."

"Forever?"

"No. Those she doesn't devour move up to abandoned places."

He scanned the mustard fog, an itch burning more and more prominent on his skin. "Cassii?"

"Language barrier, you're just fine," she said.

"You sure?"

"We won't be here that long," Cassii said.

"How much farther?" Alaric asked.

"Your kind cannot descend four tiers below without respirators."

"And you?"

The plant laughed. "She welcomes us to her roots."

"All the way down?"

"To you this wind is ill, but for Slethisle it tastes more and more like honeyed dew." He turned them down a side tunnel. Ruins clustered just beyond transparent walls. Above the haze nearly obscured a massive dome's ceiling. Looming buildings made the otherwise gigantic space all too crowded. The tunnel ended, offering steps down into a world of living and not, all veiled in yellow.

Must be like life in a beehive.

Rilduron dotted the haze. A blue ooze creature slid by, its edges tinged green.

Alaric followed Slethisle to a large building that, despite its shape, reminded him of government buildings back on Earth. Advertisements burned like ghost lights in the mist.

They entered, the haze lessening in time with a weary drone of some kind of filtration system. Former offices become stalls spilled wares into the walkways. Holographic ads warred with permanent neon, cramping the haze overhead.

Alaric stopped, examining a pink flower stalk in a violet, oval vase. Long thin and short round petals alternated around the center, each striped by electric red veins.

He touched a petal. It curled around his fingertip, like a baby giving suck. He withdrew his finger, but it held on.

The vase snapped open a five-jawed maw with spiny teeth. It jerked its stem in, converging hand and teeth.

Slethisle's vine snapped the vase. It released him, falling back into its former resting place, flowered stem extended and innocuous once more.

"No feeding animals, Ignaree."

"That's an animal?"

"No plant would eat junk food such as you."

Slethisle led on.

Wares grew more exotic. Weapons of every sort and shape lined one long stall. To his right, a merchant coaxed open a living cage. He handed a Kraili the dog-like animal within in exchange for several multihued eggs. The merchant grinned over his payment. The saurian tipped its head backward, unhinged its jaw and swallowed his purchase whole.

"Oh my god, what was that?" Alaric asked.

Slethisle kept going. "Food courtyard. Ignaree hungers?"

"Uh, no thanks."

The Rilduron stopped in the plaza's center.

"What's wrong?"

It stood, still and silent as a tree. Without a word or change in its facing, Slethisle headed an entirely different direction. It hurried him to a crystal elevator shaft, around to its rear and down a curving stairway several levels.

Its foot ended in a carpet of yellow mist. Alaric's footfalls echoed off of damp stone walls. Light peeking through cracks around metal shrouded windows and doors filled the warren with ghostly swirls of shadow and light.

A door opened as they passed.

Alaric caught a glimpse inside. The confusing sight resolved several paces later. He stopped, heat burning his gut and coloring his cheeks. He charged back, yanking open the door. As in his mind's eye, a huge armored creature held leashes to a crowd of naked women in its chitinous hands.

A vine yanked him backward, releasing the door to close once more. He whirled toward Slethisle, fists balled. "Why'd you do that?"

"Alaric?" Cassii asked. "Are you in trouble?"

"Not now," Alaric snapped. "Answer me."

"Invitation only."

"Invitation for what? What're they selling?"

"Pleasure servants."

"Servants or slaves?" Alaric asked.

"Any difference is unimportant." Its tone ratcheted up the heat in his gut.

"Alaric, we don't need trouble," Cassii said. "Let it go."

"I can arrange invitation if you want purchase. Take you elsewhere if you need rut with other animal."

Alaric's jaw clenched. "No."

Slethisle led him from the plaza into a labyrinth of square-walled passages unsettlingly reminiscent of Earth's sewers. Drops of what Alaric hoped was water fell onto his head. One shot past his collar down his back.

He shivered.

"They require an invitation because why? Slavery illegal here?"

"It is, but they deal in servants."

"Can these servants resign and leave?" Alaric asked.

Slethisle's chuckle slithered down Alaric's spine. "Only if they wish death, Ignaree."

"That's murder."

Slethisle's vines rippled. "None would dare accuse them."

"What about other servants?"

The plant focused on him. "Servants owe masters, for food, clothing and freeing them from pens."

"Sounds like slavery to me."

"Grey area," Slethisle said. "We here, you pay now."

Alaric found an entrance looming to his left.

"Cassii?" Alaric said.

"Payment tendered to his account," Cassii said.

"It's in your account."

Slethisle sidled up to a system console, peering through a metal mesh at its cracked display. It strode away. "Slethisle thank you for business."

"Wait, how do I get back?"

It halted. Its attention felt as close to carnivorous as Slethisle probably got.

"Cost you double."

"No need," Cassii said, "I recorded the route."

"Never mind, Slethisle. Thank you."

His plant guide disappeared into yellow haze.

"What now?"

"Go inside and find a buyer," she said.

"How do I manage that?"

"We wait for someone I recognize."

"Okay."

Alaric fixed his gaze on the building's façade, eyes narrowed sifting through ads for the place's name. He failed to locate it.

Maybe it's called Unknown because it doesn't have one—especially if they have to keep moving it.

He stepped inside and wished he hadn't. Stench assaulted his nose, split its forces and flanked his eyes. Vapors burned his throat and reached down it to squeeze his chest.

Wish it wasn't called anything, at least then it'd be easier to forget.

If the starport far above exhibited the universe's wild beauty, Unknown harbored the undesirable xenology too ugly for public display.

A bright star gleamed into view, eclipsing the ugliness with a sultry sashay. Thin, four-armed and wonderfully breasted, her clothing slid along her translucent, baby-blue skin as she moved. It accentuated just the right amount of flesh in an erotic game of peekaboo that distracted him from even her visible underlying organs. Her fingers caressed his shoulders before he realized she'd closed the distance.

"Alaric?" Cassii said.

Two pairs of swirling, blue wisps embraced his gaze. His unease drained, descending lower to transform into something heated and primal.

"Alaric?"

Her whisper stroked his ears, musical and somehow on multiple levels like a chord. "What do you desire?"

A nervous chuckle escaped his lips. "Looking at you is a good start."

"Alaric!"

Cold plunged over his body. *Did I just say that?*

<Well, I'll be a two-headed Cybriean with a limp. The princess has game.>

"Your eyes don't caress...," four index fingers drew a southerly line down his chest, "...as nicely as fingers might."

Nether heat expanded through his body, erupting from his mouth. "Fingers are a start."

<Don't make me count to three.>

He blinked. *What?*

A high pitched vibration cut into his head. He yelped.

The woman jumped back.

"Snap out of it, Alaric. You're on business."

Alaric shook his head like a dog trying to clear water from his ears. He gave the woman a sheepish grin. "Sorry, comm feedback."

She smiled and reached for his ear. "Then let's remove that first."

"Wouldn't help. My mother's voice would still be in my head."

Her fingers resumed their downward trek. "A man can love his mother and still be a *man*."

He pushed the comm back into place. "Thank you, but I'd better decline..."

"...if he knows what's good for him." Cassii finished in his head. "Mother my circuits. Order a Glaciriss mister not-so-angelic."

"Could I get a Glaciriss?" Alaric asked.

She looked him over, sighed and walked off shaking her head.

"What the hell was that?" Alaric asked.

"Her voices sounded Ubori, an eropath in a place like that. Steer clear."

"Eropath?" Alaric asked.

"A being able to project erotic emotions into others," Cassii said.

"No, I meant that sound," Alaric said. "Wait, erotic, as in sexual?"

"Something you'll hear again if you don't stop encouraging her lingering influence with your imagination."

A flush rose in his cheeks. "I'm not thinking anything."

"I'm monitoring your vitals, remember?"

"Not a thing."

Glaciriss came, disappeared and came again—its flavor tart and icy with an underlying spice. Unknown supplied its own flavor of mist, supplanting yellow by a body-odor infused, brown haze.

The Ubori waitress, Nia, kept his drink filled but her hands kept to her other patrons. She disappeared with several. His imagination filled in cheek-reddening gaps.

Despite her voyeurism on the station, Unknown had no cameras for Cassii to hack. Alaric mumbled descriptions of those entering. She needled him until ticks later he needed only cursory glances to collect the myriad details she desired.

"That speech pattern matches, is there an Elcu in the bar?" Cassii asked.

"What's an Elcu?"

"The invertebrate, do primitives know that term?" Cassii asked.

"I do." He scrutinized a brick red amorph like the one from the museum. It rolled itself up into a bowl-shaped barstool. "I also know the word memory purge."

"That's a phrase, funny boy."

"What about him?"

"Elcu don't have genders," Cassii said.

"Noted. What about it?"

"Based upon its squeak, its name is Flliand—one of Braxis's contacts."

Alaric crossed to it, standing just behind it.

How do you tap an Elcu's shoulder?

Like Slethisle, it didn't bother turning its facing. A series of hisses, pops, and slurping noises erupted from the side facing Alaric.

Cassii translated.

"Something you want, boney?"

"Uh, my name is Alaric, and you're Flliand, right?"

Alaric got the distinct impression the Elcu was rolling its eyes. The noises that erupted this time had a pronounced edge.

"It's apparently pronounced Flee-and," Cassii said.

"Apologies," he took care pronouncing its name, "Flliand."

"What do you want?" A pseudopod stretched out to the bar opposite Alaric and picked up Flliand's drink. The bowl swung around its body like a boat on a wave, positioning between them.

Alaric chuckled. "We've a mutual acquaintance named Braxis."

The basically shapeless creature somehow exuded a distinctly cagey impression, as if it'd glanced around over its bowl.

"I know many, but not always their names," Flliand said.

"He captained Licentious."

The brick red skin brightened for an instant and then darkened. "Braxis no longer captains Licentious?"

"No."

"What of Noreel?"

"Who?" Alaric asked.

"The Elcu on Licentious's crew," Cassii said.

"What happened to Noreel?" Flliand asked.

Alaric's skin prickled.

"Careful," Cassii said.

Alaric didn't need the warning. His response was crisp. "Captain Braxis took the Licentious and her crew into an invasion zone. They didn't make it out."

"Where, what system?" Flliand asked.

"Sol system, a planet called Earth."

The Elcu erupted in more noises than ever, drawing all eyes. "That fool bone bag risked everything for junk on some backward planet?"

Alaric stiffened. "I'm sorry about your friend."

"You didn't come about Noreel. What did you want?"

"I have cargo someone told me might interest you."

"What kind of cargo."

Sullenness crept into Alaric's voice. "Junk from backward planets."

"Alaric!"

Wheezy hisses escaped the Elcu around its circumference.

"What is it doing?" Alaric mumbled.

"Laughing," Cassii said.

"All right, boney. I'll send someone with you to look at the cargo. Maybe you're smarter than Braxis."

Alaric extended a hand. After a few moments, he withdrew it. "Thank you."

"Meet my man in the lower plaza courtyard in two ticks," Flliand said.

"Two ticks."

Alaric stepped backward into a woman, knocking her drink to the floor. He raised his gaze from the smashed glass, mouth freezing mid-apology. Hypnotic eyes of ice blue-green locked his gaze.

Flush sprinted across his features.

"What kind of moronic failed breeding experiment are you?" She asked.

"I...uh...um."

"Can't you speak comm?" she said.

"Alaric, what's happening? I'm reading a massive heart rate spike and plummeting oxygen levels."

Despite matching heights, Alaric felt small—like prey locked in a predator's gaze.

Flliand laughed.

Steel-grey spikes of hair, highlighted by deepest blue, broke their gaze when she turned. She planted fists on her hips. "I don't seduce clumsy morons, you old perv."

"I'm not a moron just because I don't know what comm is."

"You're speaking comm, genius," she said.

"Look, I'm sorry. Could I replace your drink?" Alaric asked.

One side of her mouth curled upward. "Sure. I could use another...Ontarian brandy."

Flliand made a flatulent noise.

"Ontarian brandy is bright orange and very expensive," Cassii said. "Is that what you spilled?"

"Shut up," Alaric said.

"What?!" she asked.

"N-no, not you. I'm sorry. My stupid ship was talking in my ear," Alaric said.

"Stupid?!" Cassii said.

"Ontarian brandy for the lady," Alaric puffed out his chest. "I'm Captain Ignaree."

She accepted a tall flute filled with neon orange and strode away. "I'm busy."

"Stars, you know how much you just cost us not listening to me?" Cassii said. "Save me from hormone-besotted primitives, a first generation android would be better—umacidal tendencies and all."

His heart fell. "Leave me alone."

His comm jewel fell silent with a click.

"Cassii?"

28

PAIN & CONSEQUENCES

Alaric stumbled back to the plaza's bottom through knee-high yellow stew. Leaking windows no longer illuminated the fog, leaving the job to a few halfhearted lamps. Their light came and went, shifting support between mist and shadow.

"Cassii?" Alaric asked again.

She didn't answer.

What if she abandoned me again? Is there anything to actually sell now?

A Rottweiler-sized rodent burst from the shadows.

Alaric drew both pistols.

Its glowing eyes glared, forked tail twitching. "Put 'em away, *Uma*."

He glanced at his guns then back up. "What the hell's an..."

It'd disappeared.

"...Uma?" *Could be the root of umoid.* "Cassii, is uma short for....right you're not talking to me—I'll look it up later."

He searched the fog, holstering his weapons after several moments.

He rubbed his arms then rechecked the time.

"Somewhere to go, Captain?"

Alaric whirled around, guns pulled again. A Kraili and a human, both shabbily dressed watched him over their own blasters.

The Kraili spoke again. "We fighting or doing business, Captain?"

"Check his eyes, Nal. This one's no fighter. Probably wants to wet himself."

The Kraili's long tongue slipped from corner to corner of its mouth. "Might be, Jik."

Alaric holstered the blasters. "You're late."

"So, sorry," Nal said. "Lead on then."

Alaric hesitated and mumbled under his breath. "Cassii?"

She didn't answer.

"Well?" Jik said. "Thought we were in a rush."

Alaric squared his shoulders and headed for the nearby stair. They fell in behind. He raised one foot to ascend the stair. A pistol butt slammed into his head, throwing off his balance. "Flliand's got plans for you, kin-killer."

Alaric tumbled sideways, head ringing, and scrambled for his guns. He landed in a tangle of slimy cables.

The darkness exploded in a torrent of blaster fire. Silver, red and green energy shot this way and that. A red line sizzled across his left bicep.

Alaric cried out.

Silver bolts executed streetlights, plunging him into deeper darkness.

Cassii's distant and distorted shouts sounded panicked.

He fought the cables fouling his arm, managing to free one blaster. He squinted at the three silhouettes darting in and out of sight. Shapes belonging to silver and green blasters were too similar to chance a shot. The red-firing Kraili wasn't. He fought against the elastic cables, fighting an arm up for a shot only the have it drawn back down.

A red streak lit up the dark.

Alaric yanked his arm free. A cable jerked it back down, fouling the three violet bolts he squeezed off.

Red streaks blasted the wall, each nearer. He dove sidelong still tangled. Red impacted where he'd been.

The cables shrieked.

Alaric jerked his head around.

The mass of cables glowered at him. Its body swelled up, abandoning the camouflage hiding its bulbous torso against the wall. Its mouth stretched open and open, seemingly without limit to size or the number of metallic needle-sharp teeth it could contain.

His insides swooped. Blaster fire, yells, even Cassii's panic sounded suddenly far away.

Slimy tentacles constricted around him. They pulled him closer. He struggled, firing over and over despite a bad angle.

Tentacles yanked the blaster out of his hand.

Red and green bolts shot his way. Red showered him with blasted wall fragments. Green burned through his stomach.

Alaric screamed.

The cable-thing purred, drawing him tighter. He gave up unholstering his second blaster and depressed its trigger stud. Violet light burned across his thigh and into the creature.

Both of them screamed.

Teeth sank into him, excruciating then painful then numb.

He kept pulling the trigger until his gun buzzed angrily rather than fire. Green and silver bolts darted back and forth further and further away. He stared after them.

"Pretty shouldn't hurt so bad." He mumbled.

"Hold on, kid," Cassii said from miles away. "Help's coming."

"What color's theirs?"

"Alaric? Alaric?"

Why does she say it softer each time? Doesn't she know my ears are singing?

He tried to answer her, but the cable-thing had stolen his mouth.

A shadow pointed a gun at him.

Shouldn't dying hurt more?

Silver light flashed once, twice and again. He didn't feel the blasts. He tried to laugh, to taunt the killer. Only blood escaped his mouth.

A fourth blast lit the steel-grey spikes and ice blue-green eyes.

Pulsing amber burned the mist golden in the distance.

She glanced their way, voice coming from underwater. "Thanks for the drink, kid."

She slipped into growing darkness. It beckoned him to follow her.

Darkness...good idea...maybe El's there too...

He gave in to it.

29

USEFUL & USELESS

Cassii guided Licentious into one of the station docks. The ship jolted to a sudden stop, softened only by the interlock shock absorbers.

"If I ever get Flliand in my sights I'm painting the area slime red," Cassii said.

Cara whined.

Braxis exemplified the worst in all organics. He'd stolen almost everything from her. In the eternity of Alaric's dying vitals, one addition to her equipment made up for all the losses.

Along the underside of her hull, seemingly part of the exposed tangle of workings, a small sphere descended slightly. A triad of small orange optics lit on its surface, pivoted back and then forth. The sphere stood beneath Licentious, exposing six spindly legs disguised as insulated cabling.

Additional triads illuminated along the sphere's circumference. It slunk along Licentious's belly toward the station. It flattened itself to the hull.

Another ship slid into a nearby dock.

Nothing moved.

The surveillance probe scuttled forward—a paranoid insect darting from shadow to shadow.

Its last leg departed Licentious. Cassii fired docking rockets. She glided away from the slip she'd illegally inhabited, acknowledging the stations rebuke to return to station keeping.

The probe scuttled across the station's hull. She prodded it, forcing paranoid into rapid and daring.

She checked the cycles elapsed and nudged it for more speed.

Six hundred thirty-eight millionths of a tick later, it reached its destination and fired a communication burst: online.

Cassii tapped into the network, relaying over satellites to vid camera's far below. Ancient, infuriatingly slow and really filthy, they offered her a view of amber security patrol lights and the insultingly-soothing blue of a med unit.

She switched sensors as his comm ring reported.

Subject: Alaric Ignaree
Status: Cardiac Distress.
Heart rate: Critical.
Respiration: Critical
Oxygen levels: Critical.
Immediate Emergency Medical Attention Required!

"You think?" she grumbled.

Cara yipped.

"Not now," Cassii switched to the next vid in the area. Security patrol stood chatting. "Do something for him already!"

Respiration: Zero.

She accessed the nearest six vids. Vid sensors showed her the shapes, even the colors and lights of the service units. She couldn't get a clear image of the medical techs—no doubt slack-jawed local organics.

Oxygen Level: Zero.

She tried the next twelve. A medic strolled to the security officers.

"Stars, don't you care? Your patient's dying!"

Cassii ordered the sensor parasite to hack the service bands.

Heart rate: Zero.

Cassii's processes halted for a single microtick.

She cursed.

Cara growled.

At best, they'd removed his sensor ring. At worst...she deleted the calculation process and changed vid angles.

The sensor parasite flooded her with overlapping chatter. Instants passed while she sorted the channels, delegated signals to subprocessors and found the one she wanted. She ordered it to hack a security satellite in an attempt to improve access and get ahead of the medics.

She narrowed channels down to the med unit tending Alaric as its report ended. "...returning to center."

It went silent.

Cassii cursed again.

Cara whined, curled up next to the Captain's chair and laid her head on her paws.

The med unit traveled passages without any sign of haste. Insulated against intruder tampering, she couldn't hack the unit's onboard computers. She monitored their channel for some kind of update, probability steadily rising that she'd need a new captain.

She turned her attention to the Labrador pup. "Are you hungry, animal?"

Cara raised her head. The aroma of cooked food escaped an open slot. Cara set her head back down on her paws with a sullen sigh.

"Probability guarantees the existence of organics unclassifiable as useless," Cassii said. "We'll hear one way or another pretty soon."

Cassii counted micros.

.

30

MODERN MEDICINE

Why does the afterlife taste like mint and curdled milk?

The taste filling his mouth shifted, like a river current of slime. Two gigantic fists pressed against his lungs, one inside and one out.

He opened his eyes. All-encompassing blackness pressed against them worse than that in his air passages.

He snapped them shut and inhaled to scream. He couldn't get any air.

Slime filled his throat too, burning, itching and tingling in a numb chemical way. It numbed his gag reflex to sleep and silenced his larynx.

I can't breathe.

His life flashed across the blackness, thoughts lingering on El until in the end coming to rest on Cassii and Cara.

Shouldn't that happen before I'm dead? If I'm not dead, how am I breathing? Is this stuff oxygenated somehow?

He reached out through the thick sludge. His motions pushed him off balance, and he tilted to one side. Something hard and smooth halted his left arm. He pushed against it and righted the tilt. He braced that arm and searched with the other. His right hand found a similar surface.

Visions of small animals floating in slime-filled jars paraded through his head.

He tried another scream, but nothing came out. He pressed one finger back into his throat, but couldn't wake his gag reflex.

His heart beat so hard he imagined it rippling the stuff around him.

He slid one hand cautiously to his ear, discovering naked ear lobe and no comm ring. Cassii's voice echoed in his mind, demanding he hang on.

They shot me.

Hands swam to his midsection, this time turning him to one side. Fingertips slid along his torso, meeting a hot lump expanding and contracting beneath his touch.

Alaric was suddenly glad for the all-encompassing blackness that kept his eyes from tearing.

He traced the thing attached to his stomach. It had long thick tentacles. Alaric thoughts turned to the cable thing.

Could I be inside one? A meal for its child? Is this stuff keeping me alive so I'm basically one long, slow, torturous meal?

He pulled away a tentacle.

A shock rippled up his arm. He yanked the hand back and toppled backward in the slow-motion weightlessness of drifting in gelatin. The hot tentacle reattached itself.

His hands went to his holsters. The guns weren't there, but neither were the holsters. A few moments personal exploration verified his absolute nakedness.

Did it digest my clothes?

His pulse raced.

Is it some kind of acid, numbing me while my skin dissolves layer by layer?

A swooping sensation made his stomach feel suddenly pulled down through his feet. A chill left him shivering despite the slime.

He felt for a bottom with his feet. It lingered at the edge of toetip.

Okay, can't be inside the cable thing unless its stomach is a glass jar...or maybe a cartilage cage...no, it'd have to have an opening somewhere for food to enter or...don't think about...

<Exit?>

He squeezed his eyes tighter. *Not thinking about...*

<Exiting?>

Stop...just don't...

<Don't think about getting squeezed out some weird alien anus?>

I hate you.

<Keep telling yourself that, princess.>

He stretched out his toes, trying to stabilize himself in the slime. He pushed himself quasi-downward on the wall in front of him, sending him into a slow motion downward fall. His feet found ground first, leaving him suspended mid backward teeter.

His bare feet explored slowly.

Unlike the rounded sides, beneath him felt flat and smooth. He could teeter side to side from one fingertip to another, neither touched at the same time let alone gave enough purchase to brace against both sides and climb.

Could I swim?

He crouched, settling slowly downward over several centi, then pushed off with his feet. His legs pushed him through the stuff, but it robbed his upward surge of all momentum moments after his feet left the bottom.

He floated, touching nothing without any sensation of actual movement left. After a long time, his feet touched down again. His second try he folded his arms close to his body. The momentum lasted a bit longer. He slid his arms carefully against his sides until they were above his head and then made a downward sweep.

The swimming motion seemed to move him upward a bit more. In his excitement, he rushed his arms back upward. His feet hit bottom once more.

Alaric wished he could curse.

He pushed off again and tried swimming upward once more. This time he took great care moving his arms back to the upper position before sweeping them down.

Alaric swam upward through pitch black gelatin forever. At last, his hands found something hard above him. Rather than explore it, he swam a few more times to extend his blind exploration time.

The top felt much as the bottom without any opening.

Did I get flipped around somehow? Shouldn't I know if I'm upside down? I'd be able to feel blood rushing to my head.

<Unless you're in zero-g.>

No, I settled to the bottom eventually, so there's gravity.

<Whole thing could be turning around you.>

I'd notice.

<Really?>

He swam another stroke, trying to bring his face to the upper surface. The surface fouled his arms, forcing him to use several small strokes.

He opened his eyes again. Light lurked beyond the smoky mucus separating his pressed-to-the-glass face.

He slammed a fist against the top, impacting it with all the force of an infant's swat and pushing himself downward.

"Settle to the bottom."

He started, or would have if not busy imitating fruit in gelatin.

The feminine voice brooked no debate. "Settle to the bottom and brace yourself. You might feel a bit heavier than normal."

He obeyed.

Pressure around him changed. Weight hit him like a sudden gravity well. His footing betrayed him, bringing him down to his knees hard.

Things, he could only describe the bizarre starfish-slug-like invertebrates as things, slithered their way off of his body into a moat of black slime around him. They ranged in size from that of Cara down to mice, hermit crabs, and even that of garden snails.

Above him, a mechanism raised all but the jar's base into the ceiling.

His gag reflex asserted itself with a vengeance, wiping all thought from his mind. More of the things—tiny this time—oozed out of his mouth and nose as his gut convulsed.

"Well now, you look much better."

The soft, feminine voice felt as if it caressed his ear. He wiped some of the mucus from his eyes and turned to meet it. Despite a long white lab coat which covered everything, the lavender Ubori woman was every bit as attractive as Nia.

She offered him a warm smile.

Blood rushed to various body parts, fortunately, most to his cheeks. He covered his nakedness with his hands.

Her giggle somehow mixed a tinkling wind chime and kitten's purr. "No need for modesty." She stepped closer and turncoats fled his cheeks southward in droves. "Let's see how they did."

He tried to ask a question, but only managed a series of sounds nowhere near evolved into words.

"Your burns and lacerations look to be all repaired." The purr rose in pitch.

Every bit of him tingled inside and out. A translucent replica of Alaric, much as if he had been transformed into an Ubori himself, floated between them.

"Uh oh, seems a few of them don't want to stop."

She altered the noise in her throat and gestured with one set of arms. The weird hologram zoomed into the problem area. He searched the area, but couldn't find any holographic generators.

"Are you projecting that? With noise?"

"Something like that."

The image didn't flicker when she spoke.

She smiled.

Alaric really wanted some clothes.

"So far from your home world, I'm surprised you've never at least heard of an Ubori Biovoyant. I can see into biological organisms."

"Uh, okay. Kind of like the eropath I met earlier."

Her skin took on a red tinge. "How dare you?"

"What?"

Two sets of eyes narrowed at him. He forced his gaze down. *Really need some clothes.*

"You really don't know?"

"I really don't know," he mumbled, "what I don't know."

"Ubori have numerous gifts, eropathy the most degenerate of them."

"I'm sorry."

The purr returned and with it the image of Alaric's internal organs. She mumbled to herself. "I don't see any damage for them to still be feeding on. Why aren't they releasing?"

"Feeding on?"

Four eyes rolled. "How can you be so simple?"

"Look," Alaric said at last, "I've been shipwrecked on a backwater planet since before I can remember. I've learned what I can since rescue, but I can't remember ever meeting anyone who wasn't a bipedal humanoid."

She frowned at him. "Humanoid?"

He searched his memory. "Umoid?"

"Your speech pattern indicates intelligence." She scrutinized him. "Your story could be true."

Alaric laughed. "Well, usually I have my ship's computer in my ear keeping me from making these mistakes."

She laughed too.

"Could I maybe have some clothes?" Alaric reddened again.

"We'll get you cleaned up and dressed once I make sure all the elcreites are gone."

"Elcreites? Any relation to the Elcu?" Alaric asked. "And I don't mean to harp, but what did you mean feeding on?"

"Same origin planet. They're quite advanced for their size. Their body chemistry creates a temporary symbiosis in most umoid species, accelerating cell regrowth in the area where they feed on damaged cells."

"So they artificially stimulate a dying creature to extend itself as a food source but in an otherwise healthy lifeform can stimulate accelerated healing—replacing damaged with regenerated cells."

Her brows rose.

"Any side effects?"

She gave him an appraising smile. "You might experience additional hair growth for several cycles after treatment."

"Can you get the stragglers out?" Alaric asked.

"Were I also a biokinetic we could get them out in moments," she smiled. "Biokinetics manipulate bioorganic cells directly."

"Thanks."

She squinted closer, and the purr went ever higher. The image focused on the remaining elcreites.

"What about the purr?"

"Focusing tool. What're you doing?"

"Wishing for clothes," he said.

A smile flickered a moment before her frown extinguished it. "It also eases patient anxiety, giving them a cause for the effect."

"What's wrong?"

"We prep elcreites with DNA generated from your records, kind of encouraging them to acquire a taste for you. It speeds their response to a new host for the younger ones."

"So what's the problem?"

"They're trying to force some kind of change on your DNA."

Alaric paled.

"I've never heard of this happening before," she said.

"Am I still injured?"

"Not in any way your body can't recover."

"Then let's just get them out."

She stroked her chin with both left hands. "They could be sensing something our sensors cannot."

"Or they're an aberration."

She met his gaze. "Possible, but we'd learn more letting them continue. There's no way they could overwrite enough DNA to make a permanent change."

"Great, let's get them out anyway so I can get dressed."

She sighed. "I suppose I'll keep them aside for observation."

He nodded.

"You're shy for such a handsome creature." She smiled, stroked his cheek and spoke in a heady whisper. "Call me Isnara."

Alaric reddened head to toe.

Her high-pitched trill of laughter left him even more desperate for his pants. "My, you are a simple creature."

Alaric finished adjusting the replacement jumpsuit and cast around for his things. Isnara came in with a small box and placed it before him.

"It's coded to your thumbprint," she said.

He thumbed the lock, and the box opened. Inside were his ID strip and the comm ring.

"Where are my guns?" Alaric asked.

"Security is waiting outside to question you," Isnara said. "They'll have them."

"Great." Alaric hoisted a smile onto his face. "I'll be with them in a centi. Oh, Isnara?"

"Yes?"

"Thanks for patching me up."

She warmed him with a smile and shrugged four shoulders. "It's my job."

The door closed behind her. Alaric stared at the ring, his breath caught in his throat. He put the ring over his ear.

Cassii shouted into his head. "Alaric?"

"Lower the volume a bit, Cassii."

"Acknowledged. I was concerned our business venture might have suffered a setback."

"I missed you, too."

"Are you whole? Information was limited after your firefight."

"I'm fine, all patched up, but I think we should move on to the next planet rather than try trading here again."

"What happened? You were shot. The med units that picked you up acted like you'd died."

"Look, I appreciate your concern—though if you hadn't gone off on a temper tantrum, I might not have got shot at all. There've been some problems on this end."

Alaric told Cassii about his discussion with Isnara, emphasizing the issue with the elcreites and then moving on to the waiting security.

"The elcreites might pose some concern, but security shouldn't. They're umoids after all."

"I'm not sure how I should take that."

"Just give them enough of the truth to satisfy them and get out of there."

"Right. I'll talk to you when I return to stardock."

"We'll be here and waiting," Cassii said, "and Alaric?"

"Hmm?"

"Be careful this time."

31

GESTURES

Cassii proved correct. His security interview went simply. The agents questioning him seemed satisfied with just enough information to explain his injuries, but not enough to actually require any work on their part.

He returned from Feirin Four frustrated, but not shot.

"Relax, we'll sell your junk," Cassii said.

He chewed his lip.

"Nothing tried to eat you this time," she said.

"Great pep talk. You should give lessons." His brow furrowed. "What was that cable thing anyway?"

"An a'sorhin."

"Yeah, you give great lessons. Are they spacefaring?"

"Sort of, though there aren't many left. Most are just itinerant vagabonds, latching onto ship exteriors to go planet to planet."

"What happened to them?"

"The rilduron drove them from their planet—didn't like the competition for land I guess."

"Kind of reminds me of what El said about kudzu."

Alaric shuttled down to Feirin Three. Large technological islands dotted the oceanic world. He stared at his contact. Dark green skin matched the surrounding sea, exposed in jumpsuit-tightening ways by the skin-tight, silver scales of her sleeveless jumpsuit.

A slight screech underlaid her voice. "You got a problem?"

Alaric shook his head and closed his mouth. "Sorry, Raeli, but you're just so beautiful."

Small, vibrant fins about her body fluttered open like translucent butterfly wings. She wrapped both arms around his and leaned in with a smile. "You're forgiven."

"Tone it down, *Angelic King*."

Raeli guided him down through the floating city. Silver dominated its decor, but luminous lines of color accented it with understated grace. She paused at the door, closed her eyes and seemed to listen. After a few moments, she keyed in a code, and the airlock door opened like a metal iris. Inside the room, a metal deck surrounded a dark green pool.

"My brother will be here in a centi," she said.

"Thank you."

She sidled closer. "Ever been to the Feirin system before?"

Alaric's thoughts swam back to the first moment El had done the same. Guilt warred with visions of what lay beneath her jumpsuit for rights to discomfort him more. His voice cracked. "No."

"You've never seen a Feirinese before? Not even pictures?"

Alaric shrugged. "I saw pictures before I came down, but those Feirinese looked dull and plain. I'd no idea you'd be so incredibly beautiful."

Her fins fluttered again. "Males."

Alaric wondered what she meant. *Did I say something wrong?*

"Alaric, you need to be careful, Feirinese believe flattery a prelude to—" Cassii said with a warning tone.

Before Cassii could finish, Raeli kissed him deeply. Her moist lips were supple, and her thin tongue filled Alaric's mouth with warm saltiness.

"—courtship," Cassii said.

"Declare your intentions with my sister, land born."

Alaric jerked back from Raeli. Before him, a taller male emerged from the water. His similar jumpsuit dripped only moments before seeming entirely dry. His dull grey fins twitched.

"Well?" Reuther asked.

"Uh, she kissed me," Alaric said.

"Do you accept her offer to mate?"

"To what?" Alaric asked.

"Raeli is inviting you to mate, do you accept?"

Alaric looked at her. She nodded encouragingly.

Here? Underwater? I can't even imagine.

His brain made an effort anyway.

I can't, can I?

<Couldn't close the deal with El.>

El's face replaced Raeli's more exotic smile. Indecision and guilt played tug-of-war with his guts while his imagination filled the space between them with graphic images.

"We're here on business, Alaric."

Right, business, I can't save El in someone's bed. He dragged his thoughts higher and searched for the words to save the situation. They flashed into his mind in an almost-remembered deep, sonorous voice.

Alaric addressed Reuther. "As impossible as it'll feel to decline so welcome an offer, I'm afraid I couldn't in good conscience place you in such a position for our business dealings."

Her brother snorted. "An honorable smuggler, I'd never have believed it of a land born."

Alaric smiled apologetically at Raeli.

"Considering what he's giving up, Reuther, what say you give him a fair trade?" Raeli said.

Alaric offered a sad sigh. "No matter how generous your brother, lady, I'm afraid I'll still lose out."

"Alaric!" Cassii said.

Reuther nodded.

Licentious's cargo doors slid shut behind Alaric. Bubbles streamed from the hold walls as water levels fell. Alaric cracked the seal on his environment suit and slid his ID out of his neckline. He pushed it into a console port. The payment for the cargo was already there, more than he'd hoped.

"Well, that's everything."

"What was that back there?" Cassii asked.

"Their cargo loaders? Neat little subs, eh?"

"No. You changed from Captain Clumsy to some charismatic diplomat."

Alaric shrugged.

The last of the water disappeared. A swirling gale rushed around the hold then shut off. The corridor door opened. Cara raced across the floor. She jumped onto him, tail going wild.

"Down, Cara, down, girl."

"Seriously, what happened back there?" Cassii asked.

"I don't know. I just kind of winged it." Alaric lowered his voice. "Cara, down."

The Labrador pup sat down. Her ears fell and tail dropped. She stared up at him with big eyes, the very tip of her tail twitching back and forth nervously.

Alaric scratched behind her ears. "Oh, it's okay, girl."

She jumped back up, licking at his face desperate to land the kiss. He pushed her back down. A nail caught on the suit.

"You're going to have to train her. Environmental suits aren't cheap."

Alaric checked the suit. "She didn't hurt it, merely caught on a seal."

"Take it to the equipment bay so I can check it."

"Lighten up, Cassii. There's money in the bank. The fuel reserves are full. What more could you ask for?"

"A real captain?"

"Funny." He bent down to ruffle Cara's ears again. "Take us to Feirin Prime."

Alaric argued that landing on the planet would simplify cargo loading after Licentious was legally registered, but Cassii was either programmed with a serious distrust of government agencies or her pirate crews had rubbed off on her.

Feirin Prime's orbital station dwarfed the former stations. Their design formula became more apparent, making navigation through thronging masses and security checkpoints easier.

Repair slips floated outside a large viewport. The freighter he hadn't helped docked within one's skeleton, sparks flashing from cutting torches. Burnt metal scored its hull. Strips of metal skin bent away from broken struts at odd angles, ripped from the ship along the housings of a main cargo nodule.

"We should've helped."

"No, staying clear was best."

He sighed. "If there is one thing the Welorin taught me, it's that people should look out for one another."

"I thought they taught you it was a man eat man universe and how to turn a good set of heels."

Nausea gripped Alaric. He removed his comm ring, shut it off and pocketed it. Few creatures shared his shuttle planetside. A large, brown crustacean took up three seats across from him, snoring with an odd little whistle.

Guess this is nighttime out here.

His shuttle set down shortly before sunrise. He wandered from ground station to the government complex. Buildings swept skyward with decorative décor and smooth lines that reminded him of Raeli which in turn reminded him of El.

Why is the Feirin Government on this terrestrial world when they originated on a whole other planet? Because not all spacecraft can land in water? He chuckled. *Or rather land and then take off?*

He wandered the streets, happy to have land and gravity beneath his feet. He picked up an odd pink fruit somewhere between grapes and bananas from a corner kiosk. Its tart, robust flavor overwhelmed him at first but grew on him quickly.

A yellow sun rose from the horizon, making tiny details in the buildings' surfaces he hadn't noticed before flash like a school of fish.

A ship a dozen times Licentious's size descended on the horizon, headed down to unload and enjoy planetary bureaucracy.

Bureaucracy, sent off world... He chuckled *...that's genius.*

Still chuckling, he headed for the government building, thinking to be first in line. A lengthy queue waited for him, filled by those who arrived long before sunrise.

Ticks passed. Alaric passed the time bombarding an older woman waiting next to him with questions. Every answer came weighted in biased cautionary tales, but he gleaned a good deal of information about the various species waiting in line.

An officious looking humanoid with cartilage bridging both ears over a head of short bronze hair—Ongali according her—ushered him into a small office just past lunchtime.

A crustacean much like he'd seen on the shuttle sat—or maybe crouched—behind a desk. Its deep maroon outer shell seemed to dribble color over its buttermilk undershell like finger paint smudges.

Dark beady eyes studied him over an almost hypnotically undulating set of mandibles.

Alaric couldn't put his finger on it at first. Despite only a brief sighting earlier, something about he, she, or perhaps it seemed familiar.

"Please sit down, Mr. Ignaree. My name is Prub."

Alaric glanced around for a translator device.

Mandibles clicked as it spoke with leisurely precision. "Problem, Mr. Ignaree?"

Alaric realized he was staring and reddened. "Sorry, just never had the pleasure to meet one of your species."

Despite its precision, his voice made Alaric want a shower. "I find it hard to believe you've not encountered a Feirinese Primus."

"So you're a Feirinese?" Alaric asked.

"A *true* Feirinese," he said.

An image of Reuther's response to Prub's tone forced him to fight a smile. The tone struck a chord moments later. Prub shared an oiled, useless feeling much like the bureaucrat from Feirin Six's station—something shared with every other bureaucratic functionary he could ever recall.

Much like the space stations, the universe apparently possessed room enough for only one kind of bureaucrat or bureaucratic mind. Here was a tin-horned, self-important, closed-minded, stiff-backed public servant—interchangeable with every other regardless of species.

"You'll need to fill out these forms, Mr. Ignaree." Prub fanned out a stack of digital tablets like a hand of cards. He raised a hand to forestall the expected protest. Alaric saw it too was armored, though with thin, overlapping plates more flexible than its massive protective shell. "You've already completed these electronically, but policy requires completion be witnessed by a government representative—in case you require any guidance in these matters."

No doubt charging me for guidance, needed or not, and fining me for any differences between forms. Alaric forced a smile. *Bureaucracy, busying the little people and robbing the populace for misplaced punctuation since the invention of written language.*

Ticks passed.

Tablets appeared, were completed, scrutinized, disappeared and either reappeared or were replaced.

Alaric yawned. His stomach rumbled.

The bureaucratic claw rose again, "I understand, this is all very tedious, Mr. Ignaree, just one more item should do it."

"Yes?" Alaric asked.

"Yes."

"No—" Alaric stared.

"No, Mr. Ignaree?" Prub asked.

"No, not no," Alaric said, "When I said yes I meant it as the question, 'and that last item would be?'."

"Perhaps you should have asked the question then," Prub said.

Alaric counted to thirty. "Doubtless you're correct. What was the last item? "

"We must do a DNA check to verify the registrant's identity."

Cold sweat ran between Alaric's shoulder blades.

Prub extended a small pad. "Your thumb please, Mr. Ignaree."

Alaric set his thumb on the pad and held his breath. Tiny lights flashed. The pad buzzed twice. The lights went out, and it beeped.

"Excellent, everything seems to be in order," Prub said. "Now, according to your answers on form seventeen, page twelve, section forty-four, subsection 'b' you have chosen not to keep the ship name Licentious."

"That is correct."

"In which of the PCAS recognized languages would you like to name your ship?"

"Comm will do," Alaric said.

"And the name?" Prub asked.

Alaric couldn't suppress a grin. "Register her as the Cassiopeia."

32

A NEW BEGINNING

Alaric sought out a library console after the paperwork was complete. His earlier assumptions about the Feirinese were incorrect. The aquatic and crustacean species had both evolved on Feirin Prime—a planet with more landmass than nearby Feirin Three. Those like Raeli had moved to Feirin Three after planetary travel became possible, leaving the land and bureaucracy to the crustacean Feirinese. Both species claimed primary status.

Probably best not to get into it.

He left the clean confines of government for a nearby planetary trade station. He stepped into a warzone of monitors, feeds, and holographic advertisements. His breath caught in his throat.

You can do this.

Throngs bustled through tight spaces, easily doubling the space station's activity levels. More races than he could take in bought and sold their cargo and themselves. Beings slumped on the edges, ragged and broken begging for any spare credit the successful might offer.

His breath returned in rapid sprints. *There's no way, I can't do this. Look at them. They were born in this galaxy. I'm going to fail.*

<You ran away, abandoned your friends to the Welorin, and galaxies away you're going to let them all die—without even get to second base with Raeli.>

"Shut up."

A passing trader looked up at him.

He shook his head, mumbling apologies while his hands tightened into fists. *I have to succeed.*

<Positive attitude against insurmountable odds? Good luck with that, princess.>

It's just math. Just math.

<On an intergalactic scale. What were your math scores, runt?>

He forced his thoughts to getting his bearings. Trade consoles stood shoulder to torso in their varied shapes. Intermixed in the soldierly rows were gaming machines, gambling tables, and recruitment centers. Alaric pushed his way through the bustle to an empty gaming table.

A uniformed humanoid with yellow hair looked up at him. "Joining the game?"

A nametag on his breast changed languages every few moments. Eventually, it resolved into one that clearly read Sam.

"Join who?"

Sam laughed. "At the moment, me."

"I had a question."

"The game is fairly simple—"

"No," Alaric said, "not about the game. Well, kind of, why are their games in here? Isn't it busy enough without adding tourists?"

Sam laughed. "Not many tourists wander in to gamble tens of thousands of credits."

Alaric chewed his lip. "So this is a high stakes game?"

"Hardly, this Citadel table is for desperate last chance traders—which is why there are so few playing."

"I don't see anybody."

"Traders all over the system have their cargo bet on this table."

Alaric frowned at the slowly changing fortresses projected around the table. Each projector floated an octagonal grid of small squares and triangles in the air. Two hovered in front of Sam. "Cargo?"

"A buy falls through, a speculative trade value goes the wrong way, the market ends up glutted. This table is about long shots in hopes of a quick turnaround."

"Why not wait for a buyer?" Alaric asked.

"Some of them are in a hurry, or their cargo is about to spoil."

Alaric studied the game while he thought. “So this might be a way to get a cargo at a huge discount.”

Sam grinned. “It happens.”

“You’re playing too, though.”

“You’re not the only one here trying to make a living.”

“How do you play?”

“Each player pays for a token. The token can be assigned anywhere in his citadel grid.” Sam hit a button. A new empty octagonal grid projected upward. “Each token is used to build his citadel—defensive technologies, walls, armors, and weapons.”

“What’s the goal?”

“Protect what is yours and take what isn’t. Your citadel can also be turned like so, to move your weaponry or defenses to any of the eight sides.”

“Do you get to buy the kind of token you want, or is it random?” Alaric asked.

“All the tokens are the same. You decide what they do. One token for walls or empty cargo bays, two for armor, three for defensive shields, or four for the most basic weapon. Of course, there are hundreds of different pieces you can put in place.”

“But if you can build any way you want and set your tokens to be anything you want them to be, then wouldn’t it be easy to win?”

“Everyone is playing with the same rules. What if instead of building a strong citadel I put in a simple weapon cluster like this?” Sam asked.

Several grid points in the center of his grid lit up, displaying a small copy of what looked like a beacon.

“While I grew the twenty tokens required, I left my wagers unprotected. Anyone with basic weapons could have punched through my defenseless citadel and taken my wagers. Of course, since they couldn’t leave their cargo unprotected from other players while they attacked me, they had to build defenses first too.”

“So whatever you wager, it’s always at risk of being won by someone else,” Alaric said.

“Right. Some players play for the long haul and big wins, others to get a few quick wins and then leave the game. Cargo, credits or both—whatever their fancy.”

“If they can pull out at any time, can’t they wait until their turn, hit who’s vulnerable and pull out?”

"Turns are simultaneous, all actions occurring once everyone had signaled finished or the turn timer elapses. You must declare retirement one turn ahead."

"So no one knows what you did until it's done."

Sam smiled.

"Last question, how many tokens can you buy per turn?" Alaric asked.

"Your token max grows eight per turn, but whatever you claim has to be used that turn or forfeited. Building a beacon cluster meant not claiming any tokens for three turns," Sam said. "Want to play?"

"Thank you, but I better not."

Alaric wandered away from the table. He paused here and there to listen to news feeds, consider advertisements or watch market updates.

Where do I start?

Consoles offered contracts to hire escorts, work as an escort or ferry someone else's goods from one place to another. Not all of the escorts started within the Feirin system. He passed an odd red console with a PCAS logo. It took Alaric a few moments to realize that it was advertising contracts to hunt down pirates.

He shivered a moment. *Licentious was on that list only ticks ago. Wonder if it still is.*

He rushed the bounty terminals so intent he collided into another spacer. The bulkier man won out, and Alaric landed on the floor.

"Oh, sorry," Alaric said.

A tall man with black hair and beard peppered grey extended a hand. "You keep getting into my way, boy."

He yanked Alaric to his feet.

"Uh, Captain Manc Shepherd, right?"

Older clothing in good repair was pressed with military precision, somehow matching the man's posture. An odd blaster with three barrels rode one hip opposite a short holstered rod.

"Yes. Looking for a target or checking your own value?" Manc asked.

Alaric straightened. Without his customary slouch, their heights matched. "Cassiopeia's entirely legal as of a few ticks ago."

"The sheet on Braxis is pretty nasty. How'd you get her? Sign on as a cabin boy and kill him in his sleep?"

Alaric glanced at his shoes. "Snuck on when he was elsewhere and abandoned him on a planet."

Manc burst out laughing. "He's going to be pissed when he catches up, but that took spunk. I think I like you, kid."

"Look, I'm sorry about before, but I've got to find us a cargo. Nice meeting you again."

"Nice running into you too." Manc caught him by the arm. "Those pirates you watched hit me cost me my job. I need an escort."

"I'm not sure how I can help."

Manc smiled. "As it happens, I know of an opportunity that'd be perfect for a budding young trader like yourself."

"You want me to take the cargo from your escort wherever they're going?" Alaric asked.

"No, that wouldn't help me." Manc gestured, and a news feed projected itself between them. "You seen this news feed?"

Alaric shook his head.

"Planetary disaster. Planet's had a hard time of it. Now everyone's trying to capitalize, taking them foodstuffs and medicine, right?"

Alaric nodded again. "Then they ought to have plenty."

"Sure, food and medicine are headed there by the cargo pod. A ravaged planet needs more than that," Manc said. "Big disasters always pull food and medicine, but what about clothing? Blankets? Bandages?"

Alaric remembered how he felt when Cassii had replaced his worn jumper after his escape. He nodded.

Manc swept his arm, and a market feed joined the news feed. "I've been watching microfluidic cloth prices. They haven't so much as fluctuated a point or two.

"Pick up a few fluidic clothing assemblers and as much cloth as you can carry. Sell directly to the survivors. Let them use your assemblers for free and then sell them to the planet before you leave. A single pod ought to clothe tens of thousands and make a tidy profit."

"Why not sell the assemblers first?" Alaric asked.

"What's to keep them coming to you for cloth then?" Manc asked.

"Wouldn't regular cloth be lighter and cheaper?" Alaric asked.

"Sure, but you couldn't carry as much in a pod. Fluidic is higher quality, more durable once processed and fine as spider silk. Pod for pod it makes for far more product."

Alaric weighed Manc's argument. It made sense on several levels. On Earth, clean, fitting clothing had been a real treasure.

"That's a great tip," Alaric said. "I owe you."

"Good, then I'm going to collect," Manc said. "I got a pretty good scan of your florentine. The star lanes between here and Inhera Two will be prime targets for pirates. You're under armed and armored. You'll need an escort. I've got a full flamberge, both ships."

"So, you want me to hire your ships, you and your other pilot?" Alaric asked.

"No other pilot, just me."

Alaric scratched his cheek. "I don't know."

"Let me sweeten the deal, kid," Manc said. "You got any fighter training?"

Alaric suppressed his smile. "No."

"That's what I figured. You take me on, and I'll teach you how to fight in a flamberge," Manc said. "Cargo escort and some free training to boot, eh?"

"All right," Alaric extended his hand. "You've got yourself a deal."

Alaric bought more of the strange fruit—saltwater clusterplums—on his way back through the spaceport to Cassiopeia. He bit into one and slipped his ident chip into a nearby console. He'd saved back just enough to pay Manc and one extra refuel at his destination in case everything went bad.

He double checked the work scheduled for Cassiopeia, pleased he had a slim margin to return to Cassii before the repairs started.

The door slid out of his way. Cara jumped to her feet from where she lay curled up just inside the airlock door. She pounced on him at once, tail flying.

"Where have you been?" Cassii demanded.

"I assumed you were hacking monitors to keep track of me. Why, did you have a problem you needed my help with?"

Cassii's voice rose, and Cara's ears flattened. "Need you? Have you been drinking? Why would I need you?"

Alaric ruffled Cara's ears and strode down the corridor. "Release dock and move the ship to Echo level, dock four."

"Excuse me?"

Alaric stopped and cocked his head toward one of Cassii's domes. "I seem to recall winning a wager that put me in charge. Move the ship to Echo dock four."

"Why are we relocating to a repair dock?" Cassii asked.

"Because I've scheduled repairs and modifications, surely you could work that out on your own. Now if you please, I'll be in my cabin."

He pulled off his jacket, tossed it onto the bed, ordered up a bowl of kibble and set it before Cara. She sniffed it curiously before thrusting her nose into it, transplanting a mouthful to the floor next to Alaric's feet and eating it. He stroked her coat while she ate.

He left her to finish and headed for the ship's small bathroom.

"Shut off monitoring in here." Alaric stripped off his top and shoved it into the laundering module. "I'd switch on privacy mode, but you might need to know something."

"Yes, oh great captain."

The green dome went dark. Alaric looked up at it and shook his head. "Won't stop complaining about having to do everything for me and doesn't like it when I don't need anything."

"I heard that."

He chuckled. "So I gather."

Warm water poured over his closed eyes and down his lean frame. Alaric focused on the heat, absorbing it as if for later usage. He listened to it rush past his ears and enjoyed the simple quiet in comparison to the day's bustle.

"Alaric?"

He leaned his head back, clear of the shower. "Yes?"

"Repair crew is requesting access to the outer cargo area."

"Right, I couldn't afford to have your tractor assembly restored. Instead, we're installing a FTA-33171. Grant them access to the hold, but lock it off from the rest of the ship."

"What do we need the tether assembly for?" Cassii asked. "Those things were going obsolete when my keel was being laid."

"Damn good thing too," Alaric said. "Otherwise we wouldn't have been able to afford it."

"Language."

Alaric laughed. "Yes, mother."

"But what do we need the tether for?" Cassii asked.

"You're a smart ship's system, you figure it out. What was the FTA-33171 designed for?"

"Towing cargo pods, heavy equipment and luxury cabins for envoys."

"A luxury cabin would require the environment interlock. Also, I scheduled work for the nacelle dock housings."

Alaric palmed a control, replacing warm water with hot jets of air. He slipped from the shower and pulled on his now clean clothing. He strode toward the corridor when his reflection brought him up short.

He leaned into the mirror and stared. *Who are you?*

When his reflection didn't provide a satisfactory answer, he turned away and headed back to his cabin. Kibble lay scattered around the floor. In its middle, Cara lay curled in a ball, her paws twitching in response to her dreams.

He stepped back out into the corridor. "Cassii, shouldn't we have some kind of basic cleaning system, to clean up the floors?"

"Yes, we should."

"Ah. How about something to clean up with manually?"

"Amidships auxiliary compartment," Cassii said. "Getting tired of living in squalor?"

Mischievous delight twinkled in his eyes. "Just wanted to clean up a bit for the new crew."

He went to work cleaning up the kibble waiting for the message he knew was coming. Moments later, Cassii announced its arrival. "Incoming communications from Feirin Prime."

"Captain Ignaree, this is Feirin Control."

"Go ahead, Control," Alaric said.

"New identification package approved and ready for upload. Please signal for registration code update."

"Acknowledged, Control, we're ready," Alaric said. "Cassii, clear the upload please."

"Upload underway, Feirin Control out."

Alaric waited, a grin playing at the corners of his mouth. He could almost hear genuine surprise in her voice. "Alaric!"

He held his face. "Yes?"

"You renamed the ship after some mythological queen?"

"Beautiful, capable ruler, kind of full of herself, seemed to fit you."

"Wait, you named the ship after me? I don't know what to say."

The chuckle invaded his voice. "Not much to say. Welcome aboard the Cassiopeia, Cassii."

Silence lingered for several moments.

"Cassii?"

"That was, well, really sweet of you," she said.

"Getting sentimental on me now?" Alaric asked.

"Please."

He chuckled. "Good. We've got a lot of work ahead of us if I'm going to save my planet."

33

BIG BROTHER

Alaric's hands glided over cargo bay system controls, watching walls retract, shift and extend through their control monitor. Inner bay walls closed off each fluidic cloth assembler into its own small section, leaving an empty central space. The tether control system dominated most of the bay, anchored to the bulkhead between inner and outer bays. Its tether stretched out the open bay doors and into space.

He shook his head. *It's no wonder they discontinued this behemoth. If I installed the missing components for the flex corridor, there'd be almost no room left.*

He envisioned the pressurized, insulated corridor stretching out to a luxury passenger pod.

Yeah, I'd have opted for a small tractor assembly and shuttling passengers too.

He adjusted primary and ancillary tether connections. "There we go. Cargo pod in position."

"Not bad for a kid from a backwater planet," Cassii said.

He glanced up from a checklist on his digital pad. "That's Captain backwater-planet to you."

"Right, whatever keeps that head fully inflated. Where's this new crew? We're ready to go."

He glanced down the list. Nacelle docking interlocks were installed. Tether module was installed and tested. Assemblers were on board. Cargo pod was connected. Repair crews had fixed the jury-rigged pulsar cannons and replaced the more critical armor plates.

"He'll be here. Everything looks good, set course to Feirin-Ealma KIOSC. Register course plan with Feirin control, relay to Inhera Two."

"You actually sound as if you know what you're doing."

Alaric looked down at the checklist once more. *I hope so. A lot of lives are counting on me.* He swallowed. "Hope the upgraded not-quite-incompetent captain is more to your liking."

"You're doing good, kid."

The dome overhead strobed yellow. "Craft approaching, high-speed intercept course."

"Right on time. Authorize flamberge-class fighters for nacelle interlock and welcome Captain Manc Shepherd aboard."

"Great," she said. "Another captain."

Cassiopeia cleared the Feirin-Ealma KIOSC without incident. A quarter of the way across the system toward the next gate, she crawled through the immense expanses of interstellar space on full throttle. Both flamberge halves darted around her.

"Not bad," Manc said. "But that other one's going to get you."

Alaric's laughter rang over the comm. "No way."

A wingtip booster fired and the fighter executed a flat spin. Lasers streaked out from a pair of its weapons. A small pyramid shaped drone emitted a burst of red light and went dead in space. On the other side of the drone, Manc's fighter rolled wildly out of the laser spread.

"Hey, watch it," Manc said.

"What?" Alaric asked. "They're at tracer level."

"Always treat a weapon like it's real," Manc said.

Memory flashed in front of his eyes. An old man snatched a small pistol from his hand and scowled down at him.

<Weapon aren't toys, young master. They're always loaded. They're always poised to kill.>

Alaric's breath froze in his chest. His own voice, much younger mumbled at his shoes. "Yes, sir."

"Are you even listening to me?" Manc yelled.

"What?" Alaric asked.

"You could've blasted your wingman with that stunt."

"Manc."

"If you're not going to take this seriously, we're done. Have Cassii dock the fighter."

"Ah, come on, we've barely started," Alaric said. "I only got to take four drones because you spent so much time trying to teach me how to maneuver."

"It's obvious you're not ready for more. I'm captain. I said we're done. Dock the fighter."

"Fine."

Alaric spun the fighter onto its side relative to Cassiopeia and sped forward parallel with the right nacelle.

"Alaric, you heard him," Cassii said. "Autodock controls are on your right, remember?"

I'll show him what I can handle. Alaric grunted and boosted the thrusters.

"Alaric, that's too fast," Cassii warned. "Are you listening to me?"

"I've got it," Alaric said.

"That's too much thrust. You're eight degrees off."

He tightened his grip on the flight controls. "I can do this."

"You're going to break the docking interlocks, engage autodock."

Instead of adjusting the eight degrees, Alaric rolled the ship the opposite direction.

"Alaric!" Cassii said.

The wingtips barely missed colliding with the nacelle. He slammed paired reverse-boosters to full just before the ship connected with the interlocks. He shoved the throttles to zero as the fighter jolted to stop rocking in the shock absorption housings.

"That was a damned stupid thing to do," Cassii said.

"Language, mother," Alaric said. "Flamberge docked with Cassiopeia. Ship's systems report no damage. I told you I had it."

Alaric pulled the docking lever. The floor of the flamberge slid apart to reveal an airlock iris. It opened a moment later. Alaric climbed down the ladder into the nacelle's zero gravity. He had barely oriented himself to Cassiopeia's gravity plane and climbed onto the deck when Manc slammed into the deck from the opposite nacelle access tube.

"What in the hedrin did you think you were doing?" Manc shoved him in the shoulder. "That's my ship you're playing loose with."

Alaric tumbled backward, hitting his head on the nacelle. Cara rushed to his side, licking his face. He shoved her away, cradled his head and glared. "I docked your ship. Check it, there's not so much as a scratch."

"You pulled it off, well that makes everything all right then doesn't it?" Manc asked. "Endanger your own ship when I'm not around, but with my ship, it's my rules."

Alaric climbed to his feet and matched Manc's stare. "I had it."

"We tied your ship into my fighters for a reason. If you want to learn from me, you'll do what I tell you. Are we clear?" Manc demanded.

Alaric's fists tightened. "We're clearly on *my* ship, Captain Shepherd. Either apologize for hitting me and resume escort duty, or get your things, your ships and fly the hedrin away."

"Now, Alaric—" Cassii said.

Alaric's gaze snapped to the green dome. "Shut up, *computer*."

"That's not any way to—"

"That's an order, Cassii." Alaric turned back to Manc. "Well?"

Manc seethed. "I never break a contract."

"Then get back to work." Alaric pushed past him. Cara trailed Alaric as he stomped away, her head lowered and tail tucked.

Alaric sulked in the silence of his quarters. Every once in a while, he would glance at Cara curled up near his feet. When he did, her head came up, and the barest tip of her tail wagged at high speed.

Alaric looked away.

Cara sighed and laid her head on her paws.

He crossed the room and took out the old pilot jacket. He set it on the desk and rummaged through his duffel. He produced a small fabric patch with the Feirin Prime planetary logo printed on it. He found a spot for it, attaching it with an adhesive polymer.

He threw the jacket across the room.

Cara whimpered.

"I pulled that move off perfectly. They should be singing my praises."

Cara moved to him, put her head under his hand and wagged her tail.

"Exactly," he smiled.

His door chimed.

"What?" Alaric asked.

"Permission to enter, Captain Ignaree?"

Alaric turned his back to the door. "Fine."

Manc stepped through the doorway eyes scanning the room. They fell on the puppy.

She wagged her tail.

He marched across the room and put a hand on Alaric's shoulder. "Look, kid. I'm sorry I shoved you, but you don't understand."

"Explain then."

"Flamberge are hard to get," Manc said. "And those're special to me."

"I didn't hurt your precious fighter."

"No, but you could've gotten hurt."

Alaric turned around.

"I know it's only been a few tynmiir, but I like you, kid. That stunt scared me. I've never had a kid brother. I didn't know how to react."

Alaric couldn't remember a kind word from the voices he thought belong to his brothers.

Manc ran a hand through his hair. "Let's just put this behind us and call it square, all right?"

Alaric sighed.

Manc extended a hand. "Come on, kid, give me a break, eh?"

Alaric took the offered hand. *It'd be nice to have a brother—a nice brother.*

<You're so getting thumped for that, runt.>

Alaric grinned.

"Thanks," Manc chuckled. "Now I can kill you with a clean conscience."

"What?"

Manc rolled his eyes. "You're too easy. Now, please make up with that computer of yours, before she opens up the airlocks and kills us both."

Manc circled Alaric in the empty inner bay, baton in hand. "She sounds like a great girl."

Alaric crouched, shifted his baton to the other hand and tried to catch his breath. "So can you think of any way we could rescue her?"

Manc charged forward, delivered a series of strikes Alaric barely managed to block then leapt out of range of Alaric's answering swing. "Hedrin, no."

Alaric frowned and circled left. "Why not?"

Manc feinted forward, pulled back then darted forward for real. His baton slammed into Alaric's shoulder and then swung into the back of Alaric's calf, toppling him backward. "There's no way I'd risk my hull on a suicide mission like that. She sounds great, but at this point, you best find yourself another girl."

Alaric rolled out of the way of Manc's downward strike. He sprang to his feet, lunged and thrust his baton into Manc's chest. "She's my friend. I can't just abandon her."

Manc blocked the thrust. "Then you're going to have to wait for the Alistari to fly in there and kick some tail."

He charged Alaric, ducked low, swept Alaric's feet from him again and slammed the baton down where Alaric should have been. Alaric lurched backward, feet in the air and handsprung back onto his feet behind his opponent. Manc leapt out of the way of Alaric's strike.

Alaric charged again, dropped low and swept at Manc's feet with his leg. Manc jumped the sweep and pummeled Alaric's head with his baton.

Alaric stumbled backward, surrounded by stars other than the ones outside the ship. "I'm responsible for what happened to her."

"Kid, you didn't plan the invasion. From what you said, you did what you could, more than most would have. Sometimes you just have to live with things as they are."

Alaric rubbed his head. "It's not fair."

"Few things are," Manc said. "You're getting better. Ready to go again?"

"I still don't understand why you want to teach me this," Alaric said.

Manc smiled and shook his head. "Never hurts to be able to kick butt and take credits in close quarters. Anyway, there are a few systems in the protectorate where energy weapons interact badly with the environment."

Alaric sat in the command chair of Cassiopeia's bridge. The ship approached Ealma-Tosmis KIOSC.

"Anything special about this jump?" Alaric asked.

"No, captain."

"Come on, Cassii, I said I was sorry," Alaric said.

"Statement acknowledged, captain."

"Give it up, kid. Two things I can tell you about life," Manc's voice came over the communications array. Outside, the coupled flamberge streaked by. "Women and computers have very long memories."

Alaric sighed. "You know anything about this gate?"

"Ealma-Tosmis is a standard jump on this side. On the other, it gets a little tricky. The anomaly on the other side is just outside a large debris field."

"Asteroid collision?" Alaric asked.

"Destroyed solar system," Manc said.

"How do you destroy a solar system?" Alaric asked.

"The way I heard it," Manc said. "There was a major war here millennia ago. Galactic civil war kind of thing. One side was about to lose, so it destroyed the system's star. Wiped basically everything out. Only thing left are a few huge hunks of planet orbited by the debris caught in their gravity fields."

Cassii's voice interrupted them both. "PCAS records from Alistari archeological explorations indicate the star went nova on its own."

"There ya go, kid. Now you know how to pry her mouth open. Won't speak for tynmiir, but can't resist correcting someone to make herself feel superior."

"Shut up, Shepherd," Cassii said.

"Got to hand it to those programmers, they got it just right," Manc said. "Perfectly female."

"Entering beacon range. Transmitting authorization and flight plan codes. Prepare to cross event horizon," Cassii said.

"Hey, kid, beacon is challenging me. Did you forget to send my escort code?" Manc asked.

"I didn't send anything. Cassii?" Alaric asked.

"Must have slipped my dizzy female mind," Cassii said. "Entering event horizon."

34

EDGE OF DESTRUCTION

Cassiopeia slipped into the KIOSC event horizon, rippling blue light as far as he could see.

He shook his head. *There ought to be more to crossing these things. They're so...boring.*

The tactical hologram between him and the viewscreen showed him Cassiopeia, beacons, KIOSC and nothing. The vast sea of blue energy vanished to reveal an expansive, if frightening, panorama of destruction.

"Whoa," Alaric said.

Countless objects popped into existence in the tactical display, filling the cockpit with obstacles passing and merging, hiding each other and threatening collision.

"Pretty impressive, huh?" Manc asked.

Just beyond the beacon perimeter three-quarters of a massive planet floated derelict in space. The broken chunks hunkered together, each's gravity keeping its former body parts near. A haphazard aura of mismatched natural satellites surrounded it, offering the crowded debris field Cassii found lacking in Sol's asteroid belt.

Black rock dominated, occasionally shot through with melted veins of metal or sparkling crystals. Large chunks of ice and odd-colored planetary remains peppered the veritable warren. A quarter moon here, part of a planet there, the stars were filled with shattered globes floating far off into the distance clustered together like social cliques at a party.

"I'm sending in the spare fighter," Manc said. "How about you come out and show me some of that fancy maneuvering you keep telling me about."

"You got it," Alaric reached down and scratched behind Cara's ear. "See you later, girl. You too, Cara."

Cara chased him from the room, nipping at his heels. Alaric encouraged her, making his trip to change a rousing game of tag. He darted in and out of corridors, reversed his run and chased the puppy. She bounced playfully, crouching into pouncing position with her tail flying back and forth so hard it nearly toppled her over. She growled playfully whenever he cornered her and resumed the pursuit the moment he turned from attacker to prey.

Manc's voice interrupted. "You coming, Alaric?"

"Yeah, sorry," Alaric panted. "Be right there."

He raced into his quarters, threw on his flight suit and jogged toward the central collar.

"Which nacelle, Cassii?" he asked.

"Port."

Cara followed him as far as the nacelle. He climbed up into the zero gravity field. She tried to follow.

"No, girl, stay here."

He reoriented to the ladder and pulled himself toward the waiting fighter. Behind him, Cara howled. He turned to see her flailing in zero gravity. Her thrashing worsened the spin. Her head struck a bulkhead.

Alaric pushed himself toward her. His first to attempts to catch her left him bruised and frustrated. He wrapped his arms around her, whispering until she calmed.

"Alaric?" Manc asked.

"Just a moment, I'm having a problem with Cara."

"All right, but I don't like leaving the fighter locked down."

Alaric set Cara down outside the zero gravity field. He stroked her coat then climbed back into the docking shaft. She put both paws up on the edge of the tunnel and whined.

"No, girl, stay. Stay."

Cassii's voice came from the nearby dome. "Cara, come here, girl."

The pup turned, trying to find the voice. Alaric slipped into the flamberge and closed the docking hatch.

Alaric flew toward Manc.

"What took so long?" Manc asked.

"Cara and I were playing tag. She chased me into the docking tunnel, but panicked and injured herself in the zero-g."

"I see." Manc's lasers raked Alaric's fighter. Lowered to tracer light only, they set off alarms despite doing no damage.

"Tag, you're it." Manc's fighter raced into the debris field.

"No, you didn't."

"Come on, kid, show me how you handle a real pilot."

Alaric banked toward the field, dropped a hand to boost thrust then hesitated. Larger floating chunks presented obstacles, but smaller pieces floated haphazardly from gravity well to gravity well.

You've got this.

<Right, you're facing an experienced pilot in his element, chasing him through a shifting minefield of rocks more dangerous than your ego, piece of cake.>

Alaric growled and throttled to full thrust.

The two fighters wove in and out. Each pilot darted around, taking shots whenever he could get one. Manc scored four more hits before Alaric got his second.

"Dead again, kid. Maybe you should stick to picking on puppies."

"Yeah, yeah, I'm about to return the favor, old man."

"You keep saying that."

Alaric rolled the fighter between two of the chunks floating near each other.

Manc dropped in behind him from cover as he expected.

Alaric combined a flat spin, a roll and an upward jog with his thrusters. His lasers lanced out, drawing harmless lines along the top of Manc's cockpit.

"Slick move," Manc said.

"Yeah? Watch this one."

Alaric's fighter darted dangerously close to another asteroid.

"Careful!"

Alaric heard alarms sound the kill in Manc's cockpit. He grinned, opening his mouth to gloat when another klaxon filled his fighter.

"We've got four craft coming in fast up the star lane," Cassii said.

"Out in the open?" Manc asked.

"Yes," Cassii said.

"Query response?" Alaric asked.

"None," she said.

"They're a distraction, watch the debris field," Manc said.

"How do you know?" Alaric asked.

"Trust me, kid. Go secure and scramble."

"Secure. What now?"

"They've seen her, but not necessarily us. Tuck into the debris and wait for the trap," Manc said.

"Cassii, any replies?" Alaric asked.

"Shut up and be patient," Manc said.

Both fighters hid. Alaric's racing pulse almost drowned out Cassii's broadcast. "Raven starcraft, final warning before designation as hostile, acknowledge or change course."

Alaric's hands clenched and relaxed around the control yoke. He stared at the friend-foe indicators, willing the hidden signals to appear.

The sensor blips tripled.

Alaric focused a close range comm burst at Manc. "What now?"

"She'll run, and whispering won't keep them from detecting a signal."

Cassiopeia spun back toward the beacons. "Protectorate control, this is Licentious signally general distress, engaged by a dozen hostile fighters without transponder signals. Attack compliment: eight raven, three modified PCAS asp interceptors and a werewolf class hunter."

"Smart," Manc said.

"How?" Alaric asked,

"Broadcast message so we hear it, named herself Licentious to frighten them with Braxis's reputation and made it all resemble a distress call."

Alaric punched up library records on the craft Cassii listed. He stared at the tactical hologram for the asp interceptor, unable to find anything snake-like in the Protectorate-designed fighter.

Two crescent-shaped wings swept out, down and forward of a teardrop-shaped body until they almost met, leaving a firing gap for a pulse-laser on the cockpit's chin. Heavy particle beam cannons to either side capped wingtips parallel with the fighter body. Swivel mounts allowed limited jogging for vertical targeting adjustment.

A triangle of square-ended thrusters at its tapered end propelled it. A strut fin arched over the engines from wing to wing, supporting a wide pulse-laser battery braced by two boosters.

"Asps look mean."

"Werewolves are nastier. You leave that one to me."

Alaric nodded.

<Yeah, idiot, he can see you nod on audio.>

"Wait for my signal, kid."

Alaric held his breath, the waiting felt like a spreading ache in his gut. He brought up statistics on the werewolf-class fighter.

It's wide, low-profile body resembled an elongated arrowhead. A side-by-side cockpit hunkered down toward its rear. Sensor arrays mounted on the turret above and behind added a dog-eared shape to the heavily armored ship. Three photon bolt launchers combined with two heavy quasar blasters formed a fanged, roughly canine nose section obviously responsible for its name.

Why doesn't he give the signal? We have to do something.

An Eviarch's face appeared in the monitor, freezing Alaric's hand on the throttle. The angle of its feathered brow bent its avian features toward the malevolent. "Licentious, this is Captain Suryn of Tosmis System Enforcement. Heave to for inspection."

"System enforcement?" Alaric asked.

"Not a chance, kid. They're stalling. If she runs hard, they can't catch her. Slowing with that pod safely will cost her enough time for them to catch up."

"What if she just goes through the KIOSC?"

"She's safe, but one way or another we've got to go through them to get to Inhera," Manc said.

"So we fight."

Manc chuckled. "Sooner or later."

"Tosmis is uninhabited, Captain Suryn, with no system enforcement on record," Cassii said.

"We're attached to a new research station," Suryn said. "That you haven't gotten the newest Protectorate update is irrelevant. Power down your weapons and shields."

"Licentious will heave to inside beacon range for an official update," Cassii said. "Feel free to join us there."

Alaric chuckled. His fingers flew across the control panel punching up calculations. "We're going to have to move before we're too far behind."

"Unless they attack her at long range," Manc said.

"Stop, or we will be forced to fire," Suryn said.

"Send over a copy of the update, and I'll stop," Cassii said.

"Can she fight with the pod?"

"Fire, but that tether won't endure much maneuvering," Manc said. "She won't fight with it connected."

"Can we get it reconnected out here?"

"Not easily," Manc answered.

"Captain Suryn, still awaiting datawave," Cassii said.

"We're transmitting, are you not receiving?" Suryn asked.

Alaric checked his controls. "I don't see any transmissions."

"She knows," Manc said.

Cassii's voice filled his ship again. "Comm array diagnostics green, no datawave. Cease approach until KIOSC control clears your authorization."

"Stop your ship," Suryn said. "That's an order."

"Approach, and we'll defend ourselves," Cassii said.

"Firing on system enforcement carries a hefty sentence," Suryn said.

"So does piracy," Alaric mumbled.

"Out of time, kid," Manc said. "Punch it."

Both flamberge burst forward from the debris field. The fighters chasing Cassii adjusted formation and two asps peeled off to intercept.

Suryn's concerned voice came over the comm. "Approaching fighters, report intentions."

"I could say we're Tosmis System Enforcement, but you know how likely that is," Alaric said. "Desist pursuit, Captain."

Another four raven broke formation.

"You've impressed them," Manc said.

Another face appeared on Alaric's screen. It smiled beneath blue highlighted spikes of steel-grey hair. "Hello handsome. You've got balls for a greenhorn."

"Tyne Ren," Manc growled.

"You know her?" Alaric asked.

"Shepherd and I are *very* familiar," Tyne beamed. "Look, kid, Suryn's an ace. You're outnumbered. Drop the pod and we'll let you go."

"Got my own ace," Alaric said.

"Killing you after saving your ass screws with my score sheet," Tyne said. "Drop the cargo and live another cycle."

"Why're you doing this to me?"

"Nothing personal, handsome, just a job," she answered. "Cut and run. Live to buy me another drink sometime."

"Lives are counting on that cargo," Alaric said.

She gave him an apologetic smile and her image cut off.

"Got something to tell me, kid?"

"Do you?"

The ravens darted forward on full boosters and opened fire. Alaric and Manc rolled through the crossfire. The various weapons on Manc's fighter spit destruction. Alaric spun in behind a raven and pulled the trigger. Tracer lasers drew ineffectual lines across the opposing fighter.

Alaric cursed, hands flashing to reset his weapons. He dove hard, banked right and initiated a flat spin left. All three heavy particle beams sliced across the raven on his tail. Plasma burst from his nose-mounted launcher to slam point blank into the wounded fighter.

It exploded in a brilliant display of energy.

He banked right to avoid the blast. An asp appeared in front of him. Alaric launched four photon bolts, ripping a jagged edge in its wing.

They fought, running and gunning across the sector. The conflict edged closer to Cassiopeia with agonizing slowness. New opponents engaged him every time he thought he was free to race ahead and engage her pursuers.

Shots raked her hull.

"We just repaired that armor," Alaric said.

"Fight now, whine later," Manc said.

Manc had dodged their initial assault and closed until forcing the werewolf to pull back and engage him. They danced a ballet of fang and talon. Both ships raked each other's shields. A raven flew between them. Manc roasted it. The werewolf unleashed its full weapon compliment in one blast, nearly destroying one of its own.

Two ravens chased Cassiopeia. Cassii played the frightened freighter until they closed into range. With only naccile weapons, she couldn't maintain full thrust and fire.

Individual nacelles cut thrust, pivoted, fired pulsar cannons and resumed forward positions. Nacelles rotated around her circumference at random, potshotting the ravens from unexpected angles while not stressing the tether assembly.

The lost speed cost her distance against a quick raven. Cassii pitched the nacelles to create a sudden roll. Violet energy slammed into the raven, shattering shields and shredding wings. The raven exploded.

Cassii reversed the spin to unwind the tether. The other raven rolled around the blasts. It cut thrust, using the pod as cover. It strafed Cassiopeia's aft. Blasts flew into the open bay. Shrapnel and energy cut the tether. Victory and disaster for the raven, the pod drifted forward on inertia.

Cassii cursed. Cassiopeia pivoted on the proverbial interstellar dime, atomized the raven and rushed headlong into the main fight.

"Cassii, the pod," Alaric said.

"Its trajectory is clear," she said.

Ships swarmed Alaric. Shield indicators displayed eighteen percent remaining. No longer chasing Cassiopeia, he led three ravens into the debris field. Using the flamberge's superior maneuverability to his advantage, he smashed one raven into an asteroid. The others split, darting around the debris in separate directions and peppering him with fire. Alaric dove for a narrow corridor between major chunks. He rotated his fighter ninety degrees and executed a flat spin, weapons cutting across the narrow gap.

Blasts ripped into the first raven. It darted wildly, slamming into its less injured partner. Their combined explosion filled the gap with blinding energy and catapulted debris.

Collision alarms filled Alaric's cockpit.

A small chunk slammed into his wing. The ship spun wildly. He hit another rock. He fought the controls, desperate to stop the dizzying tumble.

Alarms drowned out Manc's panicked shouts. "Cassii, take control of Alaric's fighter and full stop. Take control damn it! Stop it!"

Boosters and maneuvering thrusters fired in all directions at once. Alaric's fighter careened into a giant asteroid. Pilot restraints snapped, slamming him into the cockpit glass.

Sparks shot from the crumpled upper particle beam, drawing his blurry vision.

"Manc's...Manc's going to..." he tasted blood. His ship floated dead against the asteroid's surface.

"Alaric?" Cassii said. "Alaric, are you all right?"

"...mad...like wrench...um...wrench..."

"Dock him or bring it here so I can interlock, but get him moving," Manc yelled. "He's a sitting duck."

Thrusters rocketed the fighter forward.

"Hold...I...fight..." Alaric slammed into the back of the small cabin. Stars twinkled out one by one. His pilotless fighter re-entered the fray.

35

SHADOWS & TRUTHS

A monstrous little percussionist beat at the back of Alaric's eyes, accompanied by a mournful whine. Something pressed against Alaric's thigh.

Got to right the ship.

His heart thundered in his chest and panic washed over him

Pirates!

He lurched upright, startling Cara from her perched on his leg. Vertigo wrung out his stomach and toppled him sideways. He seized his treacherous head, laying halfway off the bed.

Cara nuzzled him, whine almost panicked.

"Alaric, what's wrong?"

Alaric pushed himself upright again, decided his head had a good if unsteady point and lay back on the bed. "Cassii?"

"Who'd you expect?" she asked.

"There were pirates. My ship hit something."

"Calm down. Pirates ran off. You killed the ones attacking you, crashed and I brought you back here."

I killed them. The cabin dropped a thousand degrees. *It happened so fast, I didn't think, I just...killed real people...over cargo.* Horror played tug-of-war with vertigo, knotting his guts and adding a vindictive twist.

"Calm down, your heart rate is out of control," Cassii said, "Everything's fine. They're gone."

Cara licked tears from his face.

Gone...oh god, Tyne. He bolted upright, but the puppy laying on his chest kept him down. "Where's Manc?"

"Keeping guard in his fighter," Cassii said.

"Manc, come in, Manc."

"Welcome back, kid. How're you feel—"

"Tyne, did I kill Tyne?" Alaric asked.

"Who's Tyne," Cassii asked.

"She slipped away," Manc said.

Alaric exhaled.

"She'll be back," he added, "Probably with reinforcements."

"Who's Tyne," Cassii repeated.

"Tyne Ren," Manc said. "She was with the pirates."

"Not to sound heartless, but why do you care about some pirate bitch?" Cassii asked.

"She's the one from Unknown, the one that saved me," Alaric said.

"The one that conned you out on an Ontarian brandy?" Cassii asked.

"Yeah."

Disdain overflowed Cassii's tone. "World invaded, friends at risk, pirates in every quadrant and you're *pining* for some pirate whore that just tried to steal your cargo and murder you?"

"She saved my life."

"After she robbed you, idiot," Cassii said.

"She cares, she told me to drop the pod so I wouldn't get hurt," Alaric said.

Cassii filled the ship with a litany of profanity employing more languages that Alaric had ever heard. "Universal tip, the woman trying to murder you is *not* a reliable source of survival advice."

"Give the kid a break, he's young, and he might not be totally wrong."

"Illuminate the simple computer, great captain," Cassii said.

"She warned us off. She didn't have to risk angering her employer," Manc said.

"Right, I can hear the disciplinary hearing now," Cassii deepened her voice. "We're very disappointed you made them cut and run so we could just skip off hand in hand with their cargo."

"Pirates don't hold hands," Manc said.

"Right," Cassii said. "Forgive my lack of intimate pirate knowledge."

"Shouldn't Braxis's pack mule know that?" Manc asked.

In the silence, Alaric noticed the missing engine thrum. "Why aren't we moving?"

"They severed the cargo tether," she said. "Don't you remember?"

He groaned. "I'd really appreciate it if you didn't ask me questions like that."

"Okay," she said.

"Thanks, Manc."

"Just doing my job, kid."

"And Cassii," he lowered his voice. "Thank you, for everything."

Her voice softened. "You're okay?"

"Yes, I'm sorry," Alaric rubbed his temples. "She sounded like she meant it, though, like she felt guilty being with those pirates."

"That explains why she didn't attack. No, wait, sensor logs show every single worthless pirate trying to *kill* us."

Alaric shook his head. Vertigo and nausea convinced him doing so was a colossally bad idea. "She said it was nothing personal."

"It looked pretty damned personal to me."

"Privacy mode? Please?" Alaric said.

"You're right. You need rest. I'm sorry." Her green dome went dark.

He glanced at Cara, stroking her head. Her tail wagged back and forth.

"Get down, girl."

She stared, tail wagging

He shooed her away. "Down, Cara. Get down."

Cara crawled toward the edge of the bed, glancing back at him several times. After several silent appeals that went unanswered, the puppy slid onto the floor, turned around and set her chin on the edge of the bed.

He lifted himself to a sitting position. His head swam violent circles. He held his position, the ripples shrinking. He swung his legs over the bedside. The world spun, slid and then collided with the side of his face. Cara was over him in a moment, as if holding him to the floor by position alone.

He groaned. "It's all right girl. Give me some room."

She fought his attempts to push her away.

Alaric climbed to his feet, table, wall, and bed serving as handholds. He took a deep breath and then a second. By the third, the room steadied. He offered Cara a reassuring smile.

She glared at him unconvinced.

Bracing against the wall, he crossed to his closet. He retrieved a jumpsuit and stumbled to the desk. Undressing was a slow, teetering affair entirely dependent on the desk for support. Dressing offered greater challenges. He gave up on the jumpsuit after the third near tumble.

I killed them, real, living creatures. He stared at his hands. He saw Chet in the gym, tasted the blood that splattered out of the snatcher's impaled face.

A soft girlish voice whispered memories. *<You can't just let them hurt you. It's not right.>*

He blinked away tears. *But, all I had to do is surrender the cargo. No one had to die.*

<Just El and Jesse—not to mention a planet full of slaves. Man up, princess. You did right.>

He met Cara's warm brown gaze. "How many more?" he whispered. *How many more will I have to kill? Where's the line? How many murders are too many just to save my friends?*

He sniffed, balling his fists until they hurt. He stumbled to the closet, retrieving sturdy pants and a soft pullover. He dressed with only a marginal wobble and slid to the ground. He shoved his feet into boots, tightening their fasteners to the sweet spot for staying on but kicking off.

Alaric stood, a triumph of stubbornness over sense.

He crossed to the door, stopping to lean on the frame before keying it open.

Cassii ambushed him. "Get back to bed."

"There are only two people on this ship."

"I can count," Cassii said. "You've got a concussion."

"I've got a loose cargo pod and pirates nearby. Manc can hold them off, but someone has to fix the tether while he does."

"We'll call for assistance."

Alaric teetered to one side and caught himself. "Can't afford it, plus it'd paint a come-and-get-it sign on the pod for every pirate in the system."

"You can't even walk a hall."

"I'll rest when we're back underway. My head will settle in zero-g."

Cassii bridged in Manc's fighter "Talk some sense into him."

"What's going on?" Manc asked.

"He's weaving his way to the cargo bay for a spacewalk," Cassii said. "Tell him to go back to bed."

"Think you can repair the tether, kid?" Manc asked. "You got knocked around pretty bad."

"Someone has to, and I'm pretty sure dogfighting..." the thought of spins, rolls and turns sent dizziness through his head. A burp of vomit flavor filled his mouth. "Yes, I can do this."

I have to do this.

"I can't guard and chase you down if you take a free floating nap," Manc said.

Alaric gritted his teeth. "I'll manage."

"Rest a couple more ticks? I can guard that long."

"See," Cassii said.

"How long since the pirates left?" Alaric asked.

"Thirty-four ticks," Manc said.

Cycle and a bit. He steadied himself. "How long to return with reinforcements?"

"Depends on where they're based and if they've got spare ships, kid."

"Manc and I can take anything they throw at us," Cassii said. "They'd be dead now if you hadn't gotten injured."

"We can hold the fort a few more ticks if you want. It's your call, pal."

Gratitude filled Alaric. He paused and leaned up against a bulkhead. "You two really think we have the time?"

"Of course we do," Cassii said.

"Yeah, kid, we'll manage," Manc said.

Alaric glanced back up the hall. Despite the significant effort expended, he hadn't achieved anywhere near the distance he should have. With a slow nod, he turned back to his cabin.

"I'll sleep a little more then."

Alaric flopped onto the edge of the bed. His future, the lives of his friends, rested on his ability as captain to take care of things. Trusting things to others' hands, at least long enough to recover a bit more, left him grateful.

I should hire a crew—if I ever make enough credits.

Kicking his boots off proved too much trouble. He abandoned it and drifted off with them still on. Whoever was responsible for the drumming in his head came back on duty, but kept the volume down so he could sleep.

Alaric stood off center in a massive procession surrounded by a lush green field. Five rows stretched ahead of him. Those in the closest row dressed in similar golden jumpsuits.

The procession waited for some signal, matched by an equally still formation of men dressed in dark business suits.

Dozens of delegations braced the processions, grouped by jumpsuit color. Violet, brown and silver caught his eye first. Jesse loomed over El in his denim overalls. He rushed to join them, but an invisible wall hemmed him into the procession's ranks.

Gooseflesh rippled over him. Urgent information, a fluttering memory he couldn't catch, needed to be passed to the procession leaders. He had to warn them, but of what?

Another wall kept him from the other ranks of junior UN. He darted through a gap in the fifth row. Invisible walls sprang up at random, coming and disappearing without rhyme or reason. Many in the procession were older than him and dressed in military garb.

He passed a man with a thin chest-length mustache. A woman with waist-length hair of deep cobalt-blue stood next to the man with his naggingly familiar mustache. Alaric stopped at her side. She looked younger, though his same height. Her smile struck a familiar chord in his memory. El's similar smile flashed through his mind.

He stared at the young woman. "Are you and El related?"

She didn't reply. Her eyes didn't drift to him. Her smile didn't falter.

They're frozen. Gooseflesh raised the hair on his body like thousands of flags. *Oh, stars, the attack. I have to warn them.*

He rushed forward to the next rank, bombarding the people he passed with warnings they didn't hear. The second rank were all heavily armed in armored suits of cobalt blue.

Guards, they're guards. He glanced backward. Armored guards filled out fourth and sixth rows capping odd rows holding delegates. Fewer guards protected greater numbers the more rearward he searched.

He spun back to the front. *Concentrate, you have to warn them.*

Guards swamped the first few ranks. Most bracketed two people at the procession's very front.

Alaric sprinted through gold and cobalt blue, his heart racing. He hit the wall again behind the processions two leaders. A man a hand taller than he wore a golden, more formal version of the military uniforms his guards wore. A blue sash draped across his back and doubtless his front. Cobalt gowned the woman to his right. Three, thin sashes draped over her gown like molten gold, hidden only by waist-length tresses of deep cobalt.

Alaric raced right, left, hitting a barrier at each end. He beat fists on the man's back, sobbing, "Welorin! They're going to attack. You have to run!"

"Your Majesties!"

Alaric spun around.

An armored man ran through him, placing his body and drawn weapon between the Royals and the other procession. "A Welorin Armada is descending on the planet."

A like armored woman to Alaric's left touched her ear. "Your Majesties, our shuttle has been destroyed, we're cut off from our ship."

Shouting and chaos erupted around him as if he weren't there. Noise slammed into Alaric's ears. A hum dug into his spine, growing steadily as the shoving and shouting grew worse.

Alaric turned, now the one in slow motion. Anguish smothered him, a precognition of reality only moments away. His eyes met those above the familiar serene smile.

Alaric's heart emptied, gaped, and plummeted.

The hum rose in crescendo.

Hundreds of light and heavy Welorin fighters streaked across the sky.

El! He sought her but stopped. *No, El will survive, I need to save her sister.*

He dove toward her, but his body refused to move.

Green energy bolts bombarded the lush field, leaving it pockmarked, burnt and brown. They ripped their way through the procession. Burnt flesh punched his nose at light speed, even before the bodies started to fall.

Hands shoved him to one side. A guard pushed her too.

No, that's the wrong way!

A heavy body pinned him to the ground, a mimic of the armored guard forcing her down. She smiled reassuringly as an armored hand shielded his eyes.

Energy exploded all around him, ripping everything away.

Alaric bolted upright out of the dream. "Elazea!"

Vertigo hit him an instant later, sending him tumbling to the floor.

"Alaric," Cassii said. "What is it? Are you all right?"

Tears streaked down Alaric's face. He convulsed with sobs. Cara rushed forward, a comforting tongue taking away tears. Alaric pushed her away.

"Alaric. Alaric," Cassii said,

Alaric's body curled around itself into the tightest ball physically possible. His sobs turned inward and fell into silence until exhaustion robbed him of consciousness. Oblivion swallowed dreams and memories, locking them away in darkness.

36

WALK INTO ETERNITY

Cassiopeia's decks courteously remained steady beneath Alaric. He leaned against bulkheads, stopped to rest once, but reached the smaller, starboard airlock. His space suit, a tougher grey version of his regular jumpsuit, resisted being donned. His obstinacy won the day.

Alaric verified fasteners and couplings in his reflection. His mirror image tugged at his mind in throbbing yanks. He pushed the nagging sensation away.

"All right, I think I'm good," he said.

"Helmet."

"Right," Alaric chuckled. "I completely forgot I'd need a helmet in the vast airless depths of the galaxy. What would I ever do without you?"

"Sarcasm is a talent, Alaric," Cassii said. "You're not among the gifted."

Alaric screwed a bullet-shaped helmet into place. A hiss of air brushed his skin.

"Suit's pressurized. How am I reading?"

"You're tied in. Suit reports vitals within acceptable limits."

"You disagree?"

"You should be in bed," she said.

"Just get me through this, all right?"

"Why not rest more?"

Alaric shook his head. "I've got a bad feeling, okay? We need to get underway, then you can mother me."

"The kid's ri—" Manc yawned, "...right, something's at my hackles too."

"Organics," Cassii complained.

"We're in position?" Alaric asked.

"Of course," Cassii said.

"How do we look, Manc?"

"Clear so far. Go for it."

Alaric turned toward the outer cargo bay. "Cassii, if you please."

Lights vanished one by one as pressure drained away to match space. The doors slid to either side. Jagged scars cut short black gouges into the bay floor, climbing the walls and destroying several smaller containers strapped to them. Shards of gouged metal impaled containers, one piercing a fluidic cloth tank. Long strands of spider silk floated gossamer in a nonexistent breeze.

Open bay doors framed the expanse of space beyond.

"Damage punctured one of the cloth tanks," he said. "We're going need bay repairs too if we want it pressurized."

"We can close most of the bay off, but I don't know what we can do about the cloth," Cassii said. "Unless you want to try a weld."

"Heating it that much might ruin the cloth. We'll just use what we can of it," Alaric crossed to the tether module anchored to the wall. "No visible damage to the assembly."

He placed a hand on the tether, tracing its path between towering rows of fluidic cloth tanks and out into open space. He followed the tether to the tanks.

Alaric stopped, reluctant to release the tether.

"Something wrong?" Cassii asked. "You dizzy again?"

"No," Alaric said. *Ship's gravity still has me and the suits boots will bond to any surface. Why am I so uneasy?*

He closed his eyes, let go and took a step. Gravity kept him. His boots stuck firm to the deck plates. A second step followed without incident and then a third, but the nagging itself didn't recede.

"Manc, are we still clear?"

"Nothing on scanners," Manc said.

"Cassii?" Alaric asked.

"Clear. What's wrong?" she asked. "Should we abort?"

“No.” Several rapid steps brought him around the containers and within sight of the tether. This side of the tanks had not fared as well as the first. The strain and sudden snap of the tether had gouged one of the tanks and cracked open the other. Cloth cobwebs floated from it like a sea anemone’s tentacles.

“We’ve got more loose cloth,” Alaric said.

“But you’re alive, Alaric, and the fabricators are secure in the side bays,” Cassii said.

“Yeah, it could be a lot worse.”

He checked the straps holding the cargo secure to the deck then turned back to the tethers. Two long fibrous braids floated out into space. Burns and frays dotted their more or less straight line. Ends of the primary and ancillary tethers drifted in different directions.

Alaric clipped a guideline around the combined tethers, placed his hand upon it again, and walked to the edge of the bay. He stared at eternity.

There’s so much.

He looked back at the damaged braids that one step further would be his only connection to Cassiopeia. He couldn’t wrap his fingers all the way around the primary tether.

“Sensors are clear,” he mumbled. “It’s just space. The gloves work just like the boots.”

“What?” Cassii asked.

“Leave him be a milli,” Manc said.

“I just wanted to know what he said.”

“I know.” Manc’s tone hardened. “Just leave him alone a moment.”

Alaric closed his eyes and slowed his breathing. *I can do this. El’s counting on me. It’s no different than infiltrating the factory, no less necessary.*

“You’re good, kid,” Manc said. “Whenever you’re ready.”

“Oh, so you can talk to him, but I can’t?” Cassii asked.

Alaric grinned, focusing on the banter instead of the gut-knotting fear boring into him. Without opening his eyes, he stepped forward into space.

37

DIRTY DEEDS

Vertigo and nausea assailed him the moment gravity released its grip. His head spun worse than his first escape attempt from bed. He tumbled heels over head. His pulse slammed against his ears.

Alaric felt a tug at his waist. He opened his eyes. He drifted toward the tether braids, snagging the primary left-handed. The glove's bonding held fast beneath his white-knuckled grip. He righted himself, grabbed on with his other hand and wrapped his legs around the tether. He slid hand over hand toward tethers' end.

The severed end reminded him of the kind of melted knot you got when burning plastic cord. It probably would've keep his guideline from sliding free, but he installed a collar lock anyway.

Okay. Now for the hard part. "Ready when you are, Manc."

Manc's flamberge coasted into view. Maneuvering jets pushing it this way and that until Manc's upraised face slid in front of Alaric's own—just upside down.

Alaric grabbed the fighter's dorsal wing.

"Easy does it now," Cassii said.

"Ever considered having her personality replaced by something less annoying?" Manc asked. "Like a spoiled child screaming for sweets?"

Alaric chuckled.

The flamberge slid toward the pod, smoothly guided by tiny expert thrusts.

"Cassii, a bit more slack, please," Alaric said. "Up a bit more, Manc."

Alaric planted his feet on the fighter's roof. He stretched, locking one glove on the pod's tether. The fighter jumped upward without warning. It yanked the slack out of Cassiopeia's tether. The guide rope slammed into the collar lock, jerking Alaric around and toward the ship.

Alaric yelped. Pain coursed through his shoulder.

Manc cursed.

"What's going on?" Cassii asked.

Tears pooled at the edge of Alaric's eyes. "Nothing."

"Thruster button stuck," Manc said.

Alaric moved with exaggerated care, favoring the shrieking joint. He brought the ship's tether closer by the guide rope, lessening the strain on his shoulder. He caught the pod's tether and brought the four together.

He released his boots' bond and wrapped his legs around the pod's tethers. Trusting the guide rope, he drew two double-collared patch lines from his belt and fastened each to a pod tether.

He shifted to connect the first to Cassiopeia's primary tether.

Alarms shattered the silence.

"Craft incoming at attack speed," Cassii said. "Looks like you *girlfriend's* back."

"On it," Manc said.

The flamberge rocketed away.

"How many?" Alaric asked.

"A dozen," Cassii said. "Two werewolves this time."

Alaric bit back a curse. "You've got to help him."

"I can't," Cassii said. "Let go of the pod and I'll reel you in."

His stomach slithered. He looked back at the open bay. His shoulder burned. His head throbbed. *If I go back in, I won't make it back out.*

He refastened his guide rope to the pod's tether.

"Alaric, no...don't move," Cassii said.

"Help him," Alaric said.

"Moving to pick you up," Cassii said.

"That's an order, Cassii."

Silence filled his helmet.

Alaric hardened his tone. "Cassii..."

"Don't do anything else stupid until I get back." Cassiopeia's engines flared. Ship and tether raced toward the fight.

Alaric dangled at tether's end, watching the mute, multicolor pyrotechnics of battle raging across the vacuum of space.

Manc's weapons whispered to Alaric through his suit's speakers, charging coils and whining launchers just loud enough to reassure a pilot his guns fired. Disjointed cooperation filled the silence as Cassii and Manc fought together too far away for him to watch their crazy brawl.

"Come around ninety by thirty," Manc said.

"Driving two from your two-three-five by four-eight," Cassii said.

"Got em, nice shot for a computer," Manc said. "Oh no you don't, hot shot. Two trying to sweep you right and left."

"I see them," Cassii said.

Two explosions haloed the square grey shape of Cassiopeia's silhouette.

Alaric smiled.

"Another three coming in, shepherd, one-eight-zero vector difference."

Alaric turned.

The raging battle had drawn Manc and Cassii far enough off for three to sneak up on Alaric and the cargo pod. Alaric clung to the tether, a grey lump easily missed against the huge rounded cylinder

They'll miss me. He swallowed, switching off the suit's comm module. *I hope.*

The three ships latched onto the pod roughly equidistant from one another, anchored by gravlocks on the nearer end. Two thrusters fired in unison. Maneuvering thrusters lit up in short, coordinated boosts. The pod swung a lazy arch back the way they'd come.

The tether dangled behind until his end dragged beside the pod's slick metallic hull. Alaric righted himself and stood, both feet firmly on the pod.

Two of the fighters, a raven and a vultair, clung on in sight—one a ship's length rearward of the other.

Alaric scowled. Heat warmed him despite cold vacuum.

They attacked me.

<Twice.>

They hurt me. He stepped toward the nearest.

<Probably your piloting.>

They're stealing my livelihood.

<Not to mention you.>

These, his fists tightened. *Greedy.*

<Oh, yeah.>

Lazy, sniveling cowards,

<Preach it, brother.>

Are murdering El and everyone I'm trying to help.

<What're you going to do about it, runt?>

He checked his remaining air supply and faced the vast expanse ahead of them. He yanked a plasma welder from his tool pouch, sweeping its anchor line free of obstruction. His hands shook.

Voices overlapped in his head, some pleading and others urging him on.

I'll take back what's mine.

Alaric stepped toward the nearer ship.

<Go get them.>

Outside atmosphere, the only resistance came from a soft pleading voice he pointedly ignored. One footfall after another, his boots anchored and disconnected from the pod.

Damn good thing sound doesn't travel in space.

He reached the raven, longer and bulkier than a flamberge, tightening his grip on the welder.

Be better to keep this one between me and the vultair, but he might hear me walking over it, and I'm not risking a stroll through its thruster wash.

Alaric climbed onto the fighter's wing. His foot shifted slightly like a like charged magnet pushed him away. He forced his foot down and the boot's gravlock latched on. He crept up the long swept-back wing, careful with how his feet slid oddly right before locking down. He stepped over its weapons careful not to put himself in front of one. He bent, placing a hand just behind the cockpit.

I can do this.

His shoulder ached, but he didn't surrender the extra anchor. He hesitated.

If this is the cost of El's life... He raised a shaking plasma torch to the cockpit.

<No, this isn't you, little alar, please.>

Then it's time to pay.

He depressed the thumbed safety and squeezed the ignition trigger. He pressed its glowing white tip into the communications array just behind the cockpit. Hull and wires melted from its path.

<Don't make me count to three.>

He pressed the torch against the transparent canopy. The pilot inside jerked his head around. Veins bulged in the screaming man's neck.

The torch burned through.

Atmosphere exploded from within the pressurized fighter, propelling the torch from Alaric's grip.

The pilot grabbed his throat and gasped.

What the hedrin? He should have exploded from rapid decompression.

<Not how things actually work, princess.>

One hand slammed over the hole. The pilot's chest heaved. His other hand drew a blaster pistol. Light flashed inside, energy impacts cracking the thick cockpit glass.

<It's not really glass.>

I know.

<You're going to have to do something.>

I know!

Alaric ignited the torch and pushed it into the hole once more, right into the hand sealing the cockpit.

The pirate jerked his hand away, flame flash-burning his arm hair before vacuum extinguished it. He shoved his other hand over the hole.

Imagination filled Alaric's nostrils with the scent of roasted Marvy. His insides slithered. Alaric burned the second hand, cutting sideways to widen the hole beyond the pilot's ability to plug it. *And hopefully minimize his discomfort.*

<Should have thought of that before half suffocating him several times.>

Alaric bit back the urge to cry.

The pilot's struggles to block the hole with his charred hands lessened. His eyes rolled backward, not fully closing.

Alaric looked away, nauseated and shaking. He tried to remember what the canopy was made of, avoiding the moment rapidly approaching. He swallowed and opened the cockpit. Mess floated out past him. He reached past it and cut off the raven's engines. He reached for the gravlock controls but hesitated.

No, better just to leave it anchored for now.

He thought of the disapproving voice and turned toward the second craft.

"That's one."

Each footstep brought dread.

What would El have said? I had no choice? Praise me? Call me weak or a monster for what I'm about to do?

A flash of reflected light drew his eyes toward the battle. He chuckled. *Manc'd clap my shoulder and praise a job well done.*

He neared the vultair, still torn by inflicting such a horrible death. He scanned the ship again. It carried too many weapons to disconnect them all. The ship's position made it impossible to get at the gravlock underneath.

I could destroy the comm unit then cut the engine feeds. He chewed his lip. *What would that do with the engines running?*

Manc scowled at him. *<Leave an enemy alive, and you'll get what you deserve, coward.>*

Alaric climbed the ship.

The pilot inside was an Eviarch. Its bulky wings flowed through a notch in the seat and filled the copilot seat. It wasn't strapped in.

Alaric extended his torch with only a slight tremor. He burned out the communications array and turned his attention to the cockpit. Unlike a flamberge's under-seat docking iris, the vultair's canopy opened upward. He pressed his torch against its hinge.

Slower than cutting through the canopy, it hid the torch's light until it burned through the metal. The Eviarch's head wrenched back and forth inside, trying to get a look at him.

Please work.

It didn't. The internal pressure wasn't enough to pop the canopy.

He sprung forward atop the cockpit, catching it and reversing position with an excruciating twist of his shoulder. He cut along the canopy's nose, trying to find the latch.

The pilot unholstered his pistol but hesitated—having second thoughts about a suicide pact. He waited too long.

Alaric kept working, certain the blaster couldn't breach the canopy. The torch found the latch. Pressure launched the canopy into space. The Eviarch followed, one talon-like hand looped in a seat restraint. He fired.

Alaric threw himself under the gun's barrel. His torch sliced across the tangled wrist. The Eviarch drifted away, agony and fury mixed in his expression. He fired and fired. Alaric darted back and forth from handhold to foothold.

Death claimed the Eviarch, if slower than Alaric expected.

Alaric climbed into the cockpit and shut off the engines. Fear and adrenaline caught up with him.

If he'd released the gravlock, he could've strafed me at his leisure.

He sat, taking long slow breaths, cradling the torch he'd murdered with twice. His voice shook. "Two."

The torch reported only twenty percent power.

I hope it's enough.

Cold shot through him. He'd just hoped for the ability to murder another being. He closed his eyes, taking one long slow breath as his listed his reasons: *For El. For Sarah. For Jesse. For home.*

With another deep breath, Alaric climbed from the cockpit and headed toward ship number three. He only had enough power left to cut through the next canopy. He shuddered at the mess he was about to make.

Kill him fast enough, and he can't call for help.

He climbed the ship's wing. He lowered the torch to the glass and prepared to finish his count to three.

Tyne turned to face him. Her eyes widened.

Alaric shoved the torch into her comm array instead. He lifted the torch, lowering it to canopy once more and meeting her eye.

Stars, she's beautiful.

Alaric pointed at himself then at her. He drew a square in the vacuum. He stepped down the wing, cringing in anticipation of Manc's inevitable reproach.

The raven's gravlock released prematurely.

Alaric dove from the wing. His right glove glanced off the pod's surface. He slapped his left against it. It locked on, but his body's inertia twisted hard using the injured shoulder as a fulcrum.

A loud pop heralded mind-numbing pain. Through his tears, Tyne's raven banked back toward him.

<You let her go, kid. Stupid way to die.>

<Foolish organic, I told you she was trouble.>

Alaric scrambled to get his right glove locked onto the pod so he could release his left. Pain lessened but burned bright. He put his feet down, keeping his eye on her fighter.

She hovered, weapons trained on him.

Probably figuring out how to kill me without rupturing the pod.

<D*ie like a man, runt.*>

Alaric stood up and met her gaze.

Her fighter rocketed forward.

He braced himself for death.

She unleashed a terrifying barrage.

38

NEVER KNOW UNTIL YOU TRY

Alaric opened his eyes.

I'm alive?

He patted himself down.

She missed? How did she miss?

He glanced over his shoulder.

She missed the pod too? No way.

He turned back find Tyne floating in front of him. She pointed at Alaric, rubbed fingers and thumb together then pointed at herself. She smiled, saluted and jetted away.

Alaric let go of his breath.

He walked to the canopyless vultair and climbed into the cockpit. Weapon and engine checks came back green. He gazed out toward Cassiopeia.

The battle raged on.

The distant flashes seemed muted. Sensor blips showed only eight combatants remained entangled—too far for friend-foe designations to reach him.

Alaric chewed on his lip. A tick and a half's worth of oxygen remained in his suit. *Burned through it faster than I should have.*

He glanced around for a way to tap into the fighter's oxygen but didn't find one. He watched the flashes.

Leave the pod and join the fight or drag it toward Cassiopeia? He shook his head. "I'm not leaving it here for Tyne to claim as payment."

Alaric threw the throttle forward. The fighter snapped free of its gravlock and rocketed away. He cursed. He swung back around, chased the pod down and landed once more atop it. Fingers danced across controls, pushing down with maneuvering thrusters. The pod's forward momentum continued on in a slow end over end tumble. He jogged it with sideways thrust until its spin angled the right way.

He fired upward braking thrusters. His fighter popped upward off of the pod.

Alaric flew away from the pod and spun back around, cursing more vehemently. Attached to the pod, he hadn't realized how much force he'd added to the forward momentum Tyne and her ilk had given it.

Its tumble resembled a slow motion stick thrown through space without any sign of stopping.

He chewed his lip. "All I have to do is catch up, fly backward at exactly the right angle, latch on in position to reverse the tumble, then avoid sending it tumbling the opposite way."

He ran the math through his head. It throbbed objections with increasing ache.

<Not to mention reverse its momentum back toward the people risking their lives for your little crusade while you play with physics.>

He massaged the bridge of his nose.

<Maybe you should've paid more attention in school.>

I'm sure we studied interstellar math and physics right up until the Welorin invaded.

<It's the equipment, not the education.>

"Good point, thanks."

Alaric fired up his targeting scanners and punched the numbers into the flight computer. He latched onto the pod, fired maneuvering thrusters in precise bursts, detached and did it all again. After several, his cargo flew through space like a lazy bullet, lined up with the fight if headed the wrong way.

He landed on its nose. Alaric let his flight computer do the heavy thinking and timed his thrusts until the cargo stopped.

He reattached atop the pod's back and took a deep breath.

A jolt of shock raced through him as his eyes shot to his oxygen levels. They stared back with shy green lines.

He thumped his helmet with the heel of his hand. *Pay attention, stupid, little details like oxygen levels might be important.*

He eased the throttle forward, edging the pod toward the fight.

<Great work, princess. Of course, you could've just latched onto the other end of the pod and pushed it back the way it'd come.>

Alaric buried his faceplate in his hands. *Ugh, I'm an idiot.*

He flipped on his suit communicator. Combat chatter bombarded his ears.

"Swing the other fighter around and come in from either side of me," Manc said. "Hurry, I can't take much more damage."

Alaric checked the radar. Friend-foe indicators showed three separate "foes"—Cassiopeia and the two flamberge fighters. Only five pirates remained, two of them werewolves.

"This werewolf is tearing me up," Manc said, "get in here."

He checked the flight computer, running numbers on the pod's inertia. He eased thrust into reverse, slowing the pod until his fighter snapped free of the gravlock. He threw his engines to full and shot toward the combat.

"New bogey coming in," Cassii said.

"Cassii, Manc, it's Alaric," Alaric said. "Approaching from one-six-zero by two-two-eight in a vultair hunter. Please don't shoot me."

"Alaric?" Cassii shouted. "We thought we'd lost you. How'd you get a fighter?"

"Fight now, nag later, mom." Manc said "Just in time, kid, here's what I—"

"I've got a plan," Alaric said.

"Oh, dear," Cassii said.

"I'm going to sweep in like a pirate, take a few close shots at Manc, then blindside a werewolf," Alaric said.

"Not liking this plan, kid."

Alaric's fighter swept into the fight, weapons blazing. The first several shots were close but missed without issue. A missile from one of the werewolves blew up on Manc's left, jogging the flamberge to the right and into Alaric's weapons. The damage was minor.

"Jesus, kid, that was too...where the hedrin's your canopy? Are you insane?"

"I'm all right."

Debris shot into Alaric's path. A piece hit his faceplate, snapping back his head. His eyes reopened to find a crack haloed divot in the transparent glass.

"Get out of there right now," Cassii said. "Without a complete inertial cushion field, you'll be shredded."

"Get clear, kid."

"You need my help. Besides, I'm fi—" Another debris chunk shot past him. Alarm lights filled his display. He shot a glance over his shoulder. A black, metal shard impaled the fighter's environment controls.

He banked hard and sped head-on toward a werewolf. He held his attack until he was point blank.

The spare flamberge blew up a raven. Cassii dove through space between him and the exploding fighter debris. "You're not fine, you thick-skulled, death-wishing primitive. Get out of there."

One of the werewolf's two pilots pointed at him, shouting something.

"They know he's on our side," Cassii said.

Alaric unleashed a full weapon barrage into its armored face. The werewolf returned fire. He yanked the flight controls back, taking weapon fire and the shrapnel from its attack across the vultair's bottom.

He nosed down hard and cartwheeled the craft. His weapons raked the werewolf's wide underbelly. Four molten scars glowed along its armored hull.

The other werewolf dove out of nowhere, raking his upper hull and unprotected cockpit. He rolled away and climbed.

"Too late now, mom, we've got to finish this now, or he's dead."

"I'm fine, re—" Faceplate cracks widened.

A raven sliced through the dogfight. Pulse lasers fired from its wingtips. Alaric rolled his wings between the blasts, bringing it into line with the compressed tachyon cannon under its chin. Cyan energy rings rippled out from it, sheering Alaric's right wing off.

Mute alarms screamed from Alaric's displays.

"Finish that werewolf," Manc said. "I'll drive this one off."

"What about the raven?" Cassii asked.

"Hope the kid's luck holds."

"What luck?" Cassiopeia and the spare flamberge slammed weapon blasts into the werewolf from both sides. Energy and shrapnel filled space. "He's got the worst luck in the universe."

"Guess he's due then." Manc forced the other werewolf into retreat.

Another raven swept down upon Alaric, a game of space chicken. The last raven had crippled his right side, but weapons and thrusters on his left remained intact.

"Clear one-two-seven, three sixty plane," Alaric said.

He reoriented the vultair perpendicular to the attacking craft, jammed weapons and nose thrusters on and pulled the eject lever. The other ship pulled up.

That's right, eat my spinning scythe of fiery death.

Vultair and raven collided in a spectacular explosion of figurative feathers.

"No!" Cassii said. "You—"

Searing heat blasted his suit first. Alarm indicators spiked, fizzled and died.

The spare flamberge rocketed into view. Maneuvering thrusters jerked it to a halt, shielding him from exploding shrapnel.

No tirade? Alaric frowned down at his suit computer. *Oh, fried. I'm probably missing an epic lecture.*

Alaric chuckled.

The flamberge shot downward, knocking into his helmet. Cracks widened in his faceplate. His gaze shot upward to find its pilot access iris open. He pulled himself into the cockpit and grabbed the flight sticks.

"Cassii, unlock the ship to my control." He scowled at atmosphere readouts and unlatched his helmet.

"...if I had a body, I'd whip your hide across every solar system in the Protectorate. If you think you're getting more than ferrying back to me, you've got another thing coming..."

He put his helmet back on, closing his eyes to embrace the silence.

Cassiopeia fell upon the final raven, and once clear pursued with Manc. Two to one, the werewolf ran.

It didn't escape.

The flamberge docked against Cassiopeia's nacelle. His seat pulled backward as the iris opened beneath his feet. He sighed and took his helmet back off.

"Disembark," Cassii said. "Now."

"We've got a job to finish," Alaric said.

"Mom wants a full medical work up on you first. How're you feeling, kid?"

"Suit's damaged, but I'm good."

"Not the greatest pilot, but you make damn good bait," Manc said.

"Don't encourage him," Cassii said.

"It worked didn't it?" Alaric climbed down the nacelle access.

"You blew up the ship you were flying!"

"Relax, Cassii, it didn't cost us anything,"

"It almost cost you your life," Cassii said, "Not to mention that fool stunt flying without a canopy."

"You needed help," Alaric reoriented himself and dropped into Cassiopeia's gravity plane.

"Help isn't what I'd call that damned spin move of yours," Manc said. "You cost us the bounty on the fighter."

"There's another attached to the pod, you know the one coasting through space while you nag?" Alaric asked. "For the record, someone else is cleaning that cockpit."

"What happened to the third?" Cassii said.

"She got away."

"Tyne?" Manc asked.

"Sure you didn't let her get away?" Cassii said.

Alaric glowered at the nearest dome. "I'm not dead, which is what you said Tyne'd do if I let her go."

"I'll be the judge of that, primitive. Medical bay, now."

"As captain...," Alaric began.

"Captain's rank temporarily suspended on suspicion of incapacity to execute the duties of your office," Cassii said.

"You can't do that. This isn't the military. She can't do that, can she?" Alaric asked.

"She's a lot bigger than the two of us, kid," Manc said. "Sometimes you just have to go along to get along."

39

BROKEN MOLDS

Alaric chafed beneath Cassii's nagging and her medical probe until she finally cleared him to go after the pod. It took more nerve to climb out onto the tether a second time, but the repair went without incident and Alaric returned to Cassiopeia long enough for a few relieved breaths.

"Where do you think you're going, mister?" Cassii asked.

Alaric glanced up from the nacelle access. "Patrol. Manc needs the rest."

"We agreed you'd rest after repairing the tether."

"The first time and I got plenty of rest while you tortured me in the medbay."

"I can manage a little..." Manc yawned, "...l-longer."

"No. You're coming in for a break as soon as I'm undocked," he glared at Cassii's dome. "That's an order."

"I'm not letting you off this ship."

"I gave you an order," Alaric said.

When she didn't argue further, he climbed out to the nacelle and into the fighter. The scent of burnt insulation filled the cockpit. Gouges and pits riddled the ship's wings.

That's going to cost me a fortune. Maybe I should've been thriftier with the vultair.

Half a tick into his lazy ellipse around the florentine, every light in the cockpit died. Turning the flight controls failed to bank the ship.

"Cassii, I've got a problem out here."

"You are a problem," she said. "I'm docking the fighter, and you're getting some more rest."

"We need someone on escort."

"I'm more than capable of flying both fighters while Shepherd sleeps. I don't want you flying concussed through space in a damaged fighter."

I should've known she gave up too easy.

She docked the fighter. He climbed into the ship proper and stormed the bridge. "What's gotten into you?"

"I'm protecting you," she said.

"Aren't you going a bit overboard?"

"How many times have you almost died?" Cassii asked. "You flew into a fight without a canopy, rammed another ship and ejected."

Alaric folded his arms. "It worked."

"You're reckless...or crazy. If it hadn't been for me, you'd have been shredded."

"I took a risk. You've no idea how many close calls I've survived just to get this far."

"I doubt you do either."

Alaric paced. "I can't have you stepping in and overruling me. Whether we're friends, enemies or something else, I'm captain. You need to do your job and let me do mine. Give me some space."

"Haven't you had enough space lately?"

Alaric stared. He chuckled. It grew to laughter. "What kind of computer are you?"

Cara entered, tail wagging. Alaric reached down and petted her head.

"Cybriean-Alistari Ship's System, Mark II," Cassii said.

"No. You're nagging, sarcastic, disapproving and now you're making jokes. You're like no other computer I've met."

"Not precisely surprising, Earth boy."

"See, that there," Alaric said. "Are all CASS models like you?"

"Mark One wasn't as advanced."

"You've got to be just screwing with me. That proves my point."

Her too-human laugh filled the ship. "Personality programs aren't science fiction."

Alaric settled into the captain's chair. Cara laid her head on his leg. He scratched her ears. "So you're an out of the box personality?"

"I certainly am not!"

"So someone programmed you this way."

"Alaric—my first captain—we used to do a lot of deep runs. After...well, he kept a minimal crew because of some issues."

"Like?"

"Criminals infiltrating us, killing diplomats we escorted."

Alaric sucked in breath. "Not exactly good for business."

"No."

"So he made himself a friend."

"Watch it," Cassii said.

"So sensitive," Alaric said.

"Shove it, primitive."

He chewed his lip. "What're you leaving out?"

"Well," Cassii said. "There is something important I've needed to tell you."

"Yes?"

"You need a haircut."

Alaric scanned damage reports. Their encounters had dented more than just Cassiopeia's armor. He ran a hand through his hair. *She's right, I do need a haircut.*

He pushed away the thought and ran the numbers again. His eyes drifted out the window above his bed as his teeth gnawed his bottom lip.

We don't have enough. I bought too much. An itch crept behind his eyes. *Manc warned me there'd be pirates, but I didn't save back enough.* His thoughts turned to El. *One simple, stupid mistake may have doomed everything.*

"Alaric, I'm picking up a PCAS transponder on long range," Cassii said.

He wiped his face. "Another ship?"

"No."

"What is it?" he asked

"Might be a station."

He glanced at the damage reports "We could use a repair slip."

"Can we afford the repairs?"

He grumbled at his desk. "Some of them."

"Change course?"

"How much fuel will it cost to reroute?"

"Minimal," she said.

"All right, head toward the signal."

Alaric lounged in the captain's chair as Cassiopeia trudged closer to a small nebula. Fighters and a few frigates formed a perimeter, blasting smaller debris and towing away larger chunks. An impressive cluster of interconnected spheres floated in their center, backed by the swirling colors of ionized gas.

"Is that how a new KIOSC is made?" Alaric asked.

Manc leaned against the bridge doorway. "No, that's an Elcu design."

"Wonderful," Alaric said. "Just what we need."

"They're not all bad," Cassii said.

Alaric chuckled. "Right, some slime won't try murdering me."

"They haven't met you yet," Manc smirked.

"We're here for repairs," Cassii said.

"I don't see any slips," Alaric said, "docking or repair."

"Outermost spheres, junior."

Alaric studied them. "What am I missing?"

"Evolved intelligence," Cassii said.

"Experience," Manc said.

Cara relieved herself in a corner.

Cassii's playful tone soured. "Hygienic companions."

"Hey!" Manc said.

"Docking authorized, taking us in," Cassii piloted them toward one of the clusters.

Alaric reached for the controls. "Slow down, we're going to hit."

"That's the plan," she said.

Cassiopeia stopped alongside a sphere. Alaric searched displays for a dock without success. Small thrusts from reoriented nacelles nudged them toward the sphere wall. A section of station ballooned, swelling in size to fill the dwindling room between them.

Alaric grabbed the controls. "Cassii, unlock the controls."

The metallic sphere expanded, enveloping them inside the wall. The cable thing flashed through his mind. Terror gripped him, crushing his chest like elcreite slime.

Manc's laughter fermented his panic into anger.

"There's nothing funny about this."

Manc laughed harder, unable to catch his breath enough for a reply.

The wall encasing them thinned, expanding around them into a bubble. Anger waned to awe.

Metallic pseudopods stretched out to cradle ship and cargo pod. Like loose strands of fluidic cloth in his cargo bay, a flexible access corridor stretched from the sphere wall, solidifying meter by meter until it interlocked with a docking airlock.

Manc took a deep breath, wiping his face. "Your face, just awesome."

He glared at Cassii. "You could've told me."

A soft titter escaped her speakers.

"You two suck," Alaric looked out the window at their slip. *Disturbing, but seriously cool.*

"Clean yourself up, kid, we're going ashore."

"After you wash my decks," Cassii said.

He looked at Cara. Her tail wagged. He frowned, and it fell still, her head lowered.

He sighed. "It's okay, girl."

Alaric cleaned up and fastened a makeshift leash and collar to the puppy. She switched back and forth from fighting against it and cowering away when it wrapped around her back legs.

Manc leaned against the airlock. "You can't take her with you."

"Why not? She could be crew."

"No ident."

"Oh," Alaric frowned down at her. "Could I get her one?"

"Cost a lot of bribes," Manc licked his lips. "Unless you know a spectacular forger."

"Cassii?"

Manc's brow rose.

"Not even for temporarily clean decks," Cassii said.

"Well," Alaric smirked. "Guess she's cargo."

"Does that mean you're selling the little beast?" Cassii asked.

Alaric darkened. "I'd sell you first."

He exited the ship. For something grown out of metallic ooze, it felt solid. Cara sprang forward, claws scrabbling on the gangway. The small animal pulled with surprising strength.

"Slow down, girl," Alaric said. "It's not that exciting."

Manc's head shook in Alaric's wake.

Alaric held his ground until the pup stopped pulling to glare at him. He ran a hand over the wall. The warm metallic skin stretched under his fingers. Some grew into a cradle along the underside of his arm.

"This stuff like elcreites? It's alive too?"

"No," Manc said.

The station only seemed suited to a handful of species compared with others he'd visited. Like Nareel's cabin, furniture hung to surfaces without respect to the gravity plane.

Unless each surface has a unique gravity plane. He strode to one wall and tried to walk up it. His head slammed into the floor. Cara assaulted his face with her tongue.

Manc roared with laughter. "What the hedrin was that?"

Alaric rubbed the back of his head. "There's furniture on the walls, so I figured there'd be a gravity plane."

Manc snorted. "So, interested in living upside down, you saunter up a wall instead of asking first?"

"Got to try things to figure out if they're really impossible."

"Note to Alaric," Manc held the bridge of his nose. "Flying into a star, possible. Flying out, not so much. Try it after I've left."

Alaric stiffened. "Come on, Cara, maybe there's an arboretum."

There wasn't. There also weren't any repair facilities.

Despite its recent construction, disaster relief traffic fueled a bustling market. Cara caused little stir other than offers from a Kraili restaurant owner. Neither traders nor their customers answered his questions about the station's research while he perused wares.

Stalls offered common stuff, some miscellaneous repair parts. Little remained in working order and less caught his attention. A small sensor probe with fried sensors and missing processor chips floated on a single green repulsion field. He haggled the trader down to only a few credits.

"Why would you want that?" Cassii asked.

"Might come in handy."

"Okay, Captain Concussion," Cassii said. "Head up to their medical bay and get checked out."

"Why?"

"Only so much my med probe can do," she said. "Consider it a personal favor."

He sighed. "Fine."

40

MORE CHOICES

He endured prodding from an Elcu physician. It spluttered at him in its unusual language.

"Says you're fit enough, for an umoid," Cassii said.

Alaric let Cara's curious nose lead him from the med lab through the station. They found a large observation deck. Below, equipment he couldn't make heads or tails of supported a wildly reshaping glob of energy.

Alaric chewed his lip. He shrugged. "It is a research station, I guess."

"Best lies are rooted in truth. How're you feeling, handsome?"

Alaric whirled around, hand on a blaster.

Tyne sashayed closer, ran a finger under his chin and smiled. "You're *so* cute when you play mercenary."

Alaric's stomach swooped. "I'm not cute. Give me one reason I shouldn't shoot you right now?"

"Don't talk, just shoot," Cassii said.

She circled him. "Security would arrest you."

"Call it self-defense," Cassii said. "I'll hack the video."

"You owe me your life," Tyne said.

"Not hearing blaster fire," Cassii said.

"Oh, and you've got a crush on me, handsome."

"Do not."

"He better not," Cassii said.

Tyne bent down and petted Cara. "Nice animal you've got here. Never seen one quite like it."

Cara wagged her tail and kissed Tyne's face.

"Traitor," Alaric said.

Tyne made a pouty face. "Don't be mad, handsome. It was just business."

"What do you want?"

"Clear the air?"

"You tried to kill me."

"Save you, kill you, kiss you," she shrugged. "It's all the same to me."

"I don't understand."

"Look, kid—"

"Alaric."

She smiled. "Alaric. I love hard, play hard, fight hard. Don't get fussed by other people's morals and life's good."

"So make friends then kill them?"

Her laugh sent his guts into more summersaults. "You're not my friend, handsome. No one is."

"That's so sad."

"So put her out of her misery," Cassii said. "Come on, pew pew already."

"No attachments means no problems..." She ran fingers down his chest. "Not even when a cute greenhorn wanders into your crosshairs."

"No, you saved me."

"Buy me another drink?"

Alaric considered the question.

"He won't if he knows what's go—"

He turned off his comm ring. "It's possible."

She smirked. "See? I wasn't forced to kill you thus I win another free drink."

"That's so cold."

"Look who's talking, Mister Space-Your-Enemies," she said.

His insides squirmed.

"Only mistake was letting the third live."

"You'd rather be dead?" Alaric asked.

"Oh, no, honey, but I should be. Take my advice, don't go soft," a breathy laugh escaped her, "when your enemy's got phenomenal breasts."

He reddened.

"Space is absolute cold, handsome, ain't no friends up here."

"Manc's my friend."

"Shepherd? He's got you so snowed. We're the same." She glanced down and laughed. "Give or take. Our contract's the only thing that matters."

"You're wrong."

"Could be. You'll know when you end up on the other end of his hire."

She petted Cara once more and strolled away.

"Wait." Alaric swallowed. "I could use another pilot."

She turned a leg-rubberizing grin upon him. "Got my own crew now—thanks to you. Escorts are fine, but right now, handsome, it's hunting season."

Alaric watched the station retreat behind them with mixed emotions. His hand drifted down Cara's back, caught occasionally and moved to her chest by her mouth.

Manc strolled onto the bridge. "You're quiet. Deep thoughts?"

"A lot to think about."

Manc chuckled. "Go along to get along, Alaric. Don't over think life. You'll miss the good parts."

Alaric studied him. Tyne's words circled his thoughts. "What's it like being an escort pilot?"

Manc shrugged and ruffled Cara's ears. "Not so bad. Protect someone headed somewhere."

"You like protecting people?"

Manc punched an order into the food dispenser. He removed a steaming plate of donut holes. "It's a good gig when you can get it."

"When you can't?"

"Something always turns up. What's with the questions?"

"Sorting stuff out."

Manc clapped him on the shoulder, offering the plate.

"No, thanks."

"Suit yourself," Manc eyed him. "Before I get flying, can we discuss our course?"

"We're headed for Inhera. You suggested it."

"Did he?" Cassii said.

"Kid looked lost. I offered some free advice," Manc shrugged. "He took it."

"Now you're offering him more?"

"We shouldn't head straight for Inhera," Manc said.

"We need repairs," Cassii said.

"Thank you, Ms. Obvious." Manc cursed. "Stars, kid, it's like arguing with a wife. You in charge or not?"

"What would you know about wives?" Cassii asked.

He held up three fingers. "Had my share."

"Left you for something less slimy?" Cassii asked. "Like an Elcu?"

"Watch it, I know where your personality matrix is," Manc said. "Kid'd probably thank me if we swapped you out."

"No, I wouldn't," Alaric said.

Manc shrugged.

"What's your advice?" Alaric asked.

"Tether's in bad shape. It won't survive an atmospheric entry even assuming we can get all the way to Inhera without any more fun."

"Okay?"

"Let's head to Scrics."

"Uldira has a repair station, Alaric," Cassii said. "Ibin too."

Alaric punched up an intersystem map and traced their route. "Why Scrics?"

"Uldira and Ibin sit along the star lane," Manc said. "Pirates are dogging those lanes, but more important filling the repair slips to bursting."

Alaric frowned. "Cassii?"

She sighed. "A logical probability."

"If we can't land then you can't sell directly to the populace, lowering profits."

"So, why Scrics then?" Alaric asked.

Manc smiled. "From here, it'd be off the star lanes."

"Less chance of PCAS patrols," Cassii countered.

"They've been *lots* of help," Manc said.

"What else?" Alaric asked.

"Heard trying to sell that raven raised lots of questions," Manc said, "Wouldn't happen there."

"Because the system caters to pirates," Cassii said.

"Says the AI who claimed to be a pirate not long ago."

"We acquired that fighter legally, Shepherd."

He shrugged. "What if Inhera hasn't gotten word yet, what with their damaged infrastructure."

"He might have a point," Alaric said.

Manc popped another donut into his mouth. "Friendly banter aside, a former pirate frigate towing a cargo pod with a severed tether—that's nearly a raider brotherhood membership badge."

"And they'd *never* prey on a brother pirate," Cassii said.

"Better protection than nothing, mom."

"I thought piracy was outlawed," Alaric said.

"One system's pirate is another's privateer, kid."

"Scrics thrives on the restricted weapons trade," Cassii said. "They're jackals."

"True, but they'll buy your raven, repair the tether and probably have parts for this old junker. More importantly, their repair slips are closer."

Alaric frowned. "What do you think, Cassii?"

"I don't like it," Cassii said.

"Are there any flaws in his argument?" Alaric asked.

"Not the logic, no," she said.

"How long on this course until we have to choose?" Alaric asked.

"A cycle or two," Manc said.

"Two cycles fourteen ticks," Cassii said.

"I'll consider it." Alaric slipped from his seat and headed toward his cabin. Cara followed, jumping in front of him, tail going wild. He smiled and ruffled her ears. "Not right now, girl."

Once inside his cabin, he keyed food for them both from the dispenser. He set hers down, but her eyes tracked his meal all the way to his desktop. He settled behind his desk.

"Thoughts, Cassii?"

"I don't entirely trust him. That pirate bitch had a point. They're too alike for my tastes."

"Manc made some valid points."

"I've spent a lot of time with pirates," Cassii said. "Braxis would've appreciated Manc's criminal mind."

"You don't trust him."

"This trip was his idea. He knows the pirates that attacked us. Now we're heading for a pirate haven. Seems a bit suspicious."

"Why's it matter who thought up this run?"

"It suggests he's luring you into a trap."

What if she's got a point? Alaric paced. "He fought those pirates, helped me reattach the pod, taught me piloting."

"Who're you trying to convince?"

"He was right, okay? I had no idea where to start, but I can attest to how wonderful fresh clothes are during a disaster. It was an incredible idea, likely more lucrative than anything else I could've thought up for my first run."

"If we make it to the planet to sell it all."

His fists tightened. "Lives are at stake. Any poor choice might kill my friends. His idea means bigger profit, re-equipping you faster. He killed those pirates."

"To ensure his crew got a chance at us?"

"No," Alaric's voice rebounded off the walls. "Hiring him was in our best interest. He'll honor our contract."

"You're too trusting, Alaric. Something about him makes my circuits itch."

"Do you trust anyone?"

"You," Silence filled his cabin. "I'm trusting you to keep me out of piracy."

He chewed his lip. *Thanks, I needed more pressure.*

"What've you decided?" she asked.

"We're partners. Before I decide, I want your opinion."

"Uldira's our better choice. It's got a huge station."

"Will that make it more expensive? Will slip availability prove a costly delay? Will they buy the raven?"

"I can't promise anything," Cassii admitted. "I just don't trust him."

"If you exclude your feelings about Manc?"

"Scrics marginally increases success probability."

"Set course for Scrics." Alaric ate a bite of his dinner. "Update PCAS with our new course when we transit Tosmis-Scrics KIOSC."

"Like you had to tell me," Cassii said.

Cassiopeia avoided combat and sudden changes in course or speed, minimizing stress on the tether. They approached Tosmis-Scrics KIOSC without any additional scratches.

Alaric reclined in the captain's chair, watching the stellar gate approach. Something about their shape, their color, appealed to him. They'd delivered him from the Welorin. They'd made him safe.

If I'd only saved Jesse and El too. I miss them. He chuckled, remembering Jesse's absurd name suggestions. *What is my real name?* His head throbbed. *El was right. I've barely thought about my missing memory since becoming Alaric.*

"Still time to change your mind," Cassii said.

He started. "What?"

"We could still turn back."

"It'd waste fuel we can't afford." He activated the comm. "Transit to Scrics, Manc, and keep your eyes open."

"Ain't my first escort, junior."

A flamberge shot into view, performed a totally unnecessary roll and disappeared through the glimmering blue event horizon.

Alaric gazed at the beacon and chuckled.

"What's so funny?"

"I like them better now that they're not deciding whether or not to kill us."

"They're still deciding."

"Okay, but now they lack a genuine reason to blast us."

"True."

The event horizon loomed before them.

Alaric's brow rose. "Has one ever fired without a reason?"

"I don't believe so. I'll check next time a protectorate library node becomes available. Why?"

"Just wondering."

They transitioned. Manc's voice greeted them before the opposite beacons queried Cassii. "All clear here. Welcome to Scrics."

"Escort, fighter pilot and tour guide," Cassii said.

"You been here often?" Alaric asked.

"Grew up on Scrics," Manc said. "Great place to be a kid. Plenty of mischief opportunities."

"Piracy, gun running, smuggling, grand theft, ah, so wholesome," Cassii said.

"You forgot blackmail, extortion, prostitution, illegal substances and murder, mom."

"All right," Alaric said, "what's our plan?"

"I recommend Scrics Three, they've got a club you'd really enjoy," Manc said.

"Scrics Nine offers the closest starport. Repair and move on."

"Come on, let the boy live a little. Three's got this fighting arena too. It's a must see."

"We're a merchant ship, not a pleasure cruise. Didn't you say being late to Inhera would cost us profits?" Cassii said.

"Yeah, but, almost no one remembers clothing for these kinds of disasters."

Alaric chewed his lip. Cara's head came up from her sleeping position at his feet. She nudged his hand until it stroked her.

"Cassii, book a slip at Nine's starport, let me know if they're booked up," Alaric said.

Cassii's smugness broke records. "Yes, Captain."

"Once we've got our timetable, Manc'll take me to his contact. We'll sell the raven, buy flamberge repairs then head to Scrics Three."

"Ha," Manc said.

"There's no reason—" Cassii began.

"I could use some time planetside."

"Double Ha!"

Alaric shook his head. "I'll be in my cabin if I'm needed."

Cassii's voice woke Alaric from his doze. "Alaric?"

He straightened in his desk chair. "Yeah?"

"Slip's reserved. Tether repair estimated at a few ticks."

"Do we have a connection to the Scrics market network?" he asked.

"Yes. I thought we were broke."

Alaric straightened up and keyed up the market display on his desk. ""Window shopping. Any new system issues we need to have repaired?"

"An armor glazing wouldn't hurt, but no, we haven't lost any systems since the last attack."

Alaric paged through another screen of sales listings. "What about cargo bay repairs, can we even shut it with all that damage?"

"I'll have it added and get you an estimate."

"Great. Manc onboard?"

"No, he's still on patrol."

"This is a policed system right?"

"Yes."

"Bring him aboard for a rest."

"I'd advise against withdrawing our escort presence."

"You fly them, Cass."

"They're not your fighters, you remember."

"You're right," Alaric sighed, "but right now they're in my employ. Do it."

"Have you calculated Manc's pay addition thanks to this side trip?"

"No." Alaric chewed his lip. "Thanks for the reminder. We owe anything for time reconnecting the tether?"

"No, contract specified systems transited, not escort length. It also grants him a bounty for captured craft."

A wolfish smile appeared on Alaric's face. "Credit him the additional system transit now."

"And the bounty?"

"I captured that ship—personally. Pay him his transit, and we'll argue the bounty if he brings it up."

"Shrewd," Cassii said. "You're not totally hopeless after all."

He glared at her dome. "How could I possibly be as worthless as you keep telling me? I have to get *something* right now and then."

"Eventually."

Alaric opened another display, checked their credit levels, and returned to the market listings. "How much to repair the tether?"

"It's in your account view."

"Old Alaric might've messed up your personality," Alaric teased, "but he didn't impair your efficiency."

"How'd you feel about being stranded in Scrics?"

"How'd you feel if I took your personality module with me every time I disembarked?"

"Touché."

41

FIGHTING & FROLIC

Alaric watched their approach from the bridge. Ships flitted in and out of the station's slips. On the station's far side, a familiar sight filled the windows. He punched up a tactical hologram and zoomed in.

She resembled Cassiopeia, though three major differences stood out. First, two nacelle pairs instead of one connected to a longer, cylindrical midsection. Their support pylons stretched further from the ship's main bulk.

Second, a long wraparound window rode higher on the vessel's nose instead of Cassiopeia's octagonal cockpit glass. More nose jutted out beneath the new window, ending in a glass ball.

Lastly, of course, none of her plating or weapons were missing. They made her a sleek, elegant and deadly looking cousin.

"Florentine mark three?" Alaric asked.

"Four actually," Cassii said.

"What's the ball?"

"Gyroscopic command station," Cassii said. "It's a one-man control bridge, but it's usually used as just a gunnery station."

"Bigger crew?"

"Full crew, minimum two pilots."

"They extended the nacelle supports and the rotation collars."

"Yes. The pairs aren't locked to only ninety or one-eighty degree positions. They're independent, more maneuverable, but more easily damaged too—though hers are ejectable."

"Could her engineer add more than four?" Alaric asked.

"I imagine so, but more might make surface landing awkward."

Alaric increased display magnification. "The nacelle docking interlocks look different."

"More standardized, allows anything that interlocks to a standard port—fighters, mining pods, remote turrets, cargo extensions, even other frigates."

"Whoa."

Her tone was resentful. "Yeah."

"Sure you over being a pirate?"

She drew the word out. "Why?"

"We could steal her, transfer your module and head back to Earth."

"You need to stop hanging out with Manc and that bitch. Anyway, my module won't fit on a Four," she lowered her voice. "I'm outdated...obsolete."

Alaric glanced up at the dim green dome, forcing cheer into his tone. "She's a great ship, but they'd swap her in a milli for a C.A.S.S Mark II like mine."

"Watch who you're calling yours, junior."

Cassii and Cassiopeia remained in the shipyard. Not having her in his ear butting into his conversations felt off, wrong somehow.

Alaric rolled the flamberge around Manc's fighter again, still trying to bait the older mercenary.

"Come on, Manc."

"Plenty of fun waiting planetside, kid. Don't waste fuel."

"It's my fuel to waste."

"Not a very frugal attitude for a merchant."

"I thought you'd understand needing to let loose."

"Just wait, junior." Silence lingered. Manc's stern tone shattered it. "Tighten up on me, kid. Stay out of their way."

Alaric swung in beside Manc. "Whose way?"

Thirteen craft edged into his sensor range. Twelve escort fighters swarmed a huge, heavy tug. Small hexagonal capsules interlocked around its tether in clusters behind it—resembling a cross between grapes and a beehive. The tether stretched past the first several groupings to laser-scarred escape pods and eventually half a wrecked ship.

"What's that on the end?"

"Smashed passenger transport, pods'll be filled with Inheran refugees."

"Rescue of some kind?"

"Slavers."

The word ripped through Alaric's nervous system, raking him with pain while simultaneously filling him with adrenaline. His hands wrung the flight sticks. "Let me get this straight, they attacked a refugee ship and enslaved homeless, desperate, injured people."

"Most likely."

A phantom collar tightened around his neck. "What'll happen to them?"

"Hard labor, fighting pits, pleasure houses, you know, the usual." Manc's tone hardened. "Let's give them a little bit more room."

Nausea and fury battled it for dominance. "Even the women and children."

"Obviously," Manc's tone rose. "If you don't want to join them you'll give that crew a wide berth."

Fury won.

Alaric boosted thrust and rolled toward the convoy.

"Kid, stop, what're you doing?"

"Freeing them."

"Absolutely not. Stay well clear."

"Hedrin I will."

His console flickered. The fighter flipped around and interlocked beneath Manc's.

"What's wrong with you? Those people deserve their freedom...our help."

Manc's tone hardened. "Leave them be. You don't want that kind of attention. Go along to get along."

"I can take them," Heat overloaded his voice, making it crack. "Every. Single. One."

"No."

"No? How'd you feel to be collared?"

"I get it. Cassii told me you were enslaved as a kid, but you're free now. Attacking them out of some childhood grudge will just put you back in a collar—maybe both of us. Put it behind you."

Alaric stared at Manc's face in the comm. *How can he be so cavalier?*

"Those are people," Alaric's pleaded, "living individuals in need, Manc, not possessions, not...cargo."

"Look, I'm just protecting you," Manc said. "You couldn't take them all before they got off a signal to reinforcements or system security."

"Slavery's against Protectorate law. Security'd be on my side."

"Scrics isn't a full member. Even if you lucked out with a patrol that wasn't on some slave master's payroll, didn't get yourself and my ship destroyed, you'd call down a universe of suffering that dogged you from here to your backwater.

"Rule one, protect your own tail. Keep clear of other peoples' business." Manc's voice softened. "Please, leave it alone. You can't change the universe."

"Weren't you pissed at me for *not* helping you?"

"Universe's full of double standards," Manc said. "I'm fond of you, junior, but you're not old enough to understand."

"Explain it to me."

"Everyone looks out for number one," Manc said. "People who'll lie about the drink you spilled and use you for all their worth."

"That's stupid. Not everyone's like that."

"Grow up, kid."

"You're not."

"Are you kidding me?" Manc asked. "I played you from that first moment in the trade station. Everything I said and did on Feirin calculated to manipulate an easy mark into a cushy escort heading my way with a big payday at journey's end."

Magma boiled his gut.

Tyne was right.

Blood thundered in his ears.

How can she have been right?

The cockpit's small confines pressed in one him. Cold seeped into him.

<Space is absolute cold, handsome, ain't no friends up here.>

Cassii's absence struck him. Annoying as she was, she nagged because she cared, because she was his friend.

"I'm sorry, kid, that's just the way things are," Manc said. "Doesn't mean we're not friends."

"You don't use your friends."

Manc snorted. "Everyone uses everyone in this universe."

Alaric gnawed his lip and glared at the slave convoy. *I thought I left it all back on Earth, but it's here too—rotting underbelly of this huge, so-called Protectorate.*

"Talk to me, Alaric," Manc said. "I'm just trying to protect you."

Alaric ignored Manc and seethed. Ticks of uneasy silence stretched out, broken by occasional olive branches he wanted to slap across Manc's face. Manc released Alaric's controls on approach to Scrics Three.

"Follow me in."

For a moment, Alaric almost turned his fighter back toward Cassiopeia. He flipped into Manc's wake, following through thick yellow clouds. They slipped out of the strata into the waiting planetary expanse. Towering skyscrapers of every shape, size and color extended to horizon's end. Bustling air traffic descended forty levels, racing the skyline maze and dodging one another in practiced chaos. Aircraft slid from the skylane into skyscraper docking bays or latched onto external docking pads.

"Stop gawking! A wingspan off here and you'll smash my ship."

They flew through a tight approach tunnel, surrounded by slower, often bulkier airships. Sleek, racy airships wove in and out of larger boxy transports. Longer craft, many resembling Feirin Three's pleasure yachts, slowed or rushed the traffic around them at owner's whim.

"Why're they letting those yachts push them around?"

"What, talking to me now?" Manc said.

"No."

Manc banked into another narrow flight corridor without warning. Alaric barely avoided a municipal transport craft, noticing as an afterthought many frightened looking passengers and a boy sticking his tongue out in Alaric's direction.

"Back off to standard following distance," Manc said.

Their corridor split off, feeding horizontal building approaches. Manc turned them toward a starscraper resembling stacked pancakes bobbing up and down on a huge stick.

Alaric's stomach rumbled.

The building raised a floor to meet them, rotating an open bay around to Manc. He flew inside without a word. The building turned. Alaric's stomach lurched as solid wall replaced open bay.

Aircraft followed mere meters behind him. He tensed to pull up, all too aware of layered traffic above and below him.

Another open, empty bay rotated in front of him. The fighter landed on a raised platform, straddling a walkway to allow descent from floor access irises.

Manc smirked at him from the bay's pilot entrance.

Alaric lowered himself from the cockpit. "Could've warned me."

"No need."

Alaric narrowed his gaze. "I wasn't in control, was I?"

Manc pantomimed shooting at Alaric.

"Hope you're pleased with yourself."

Manc's grin emerged fully. "Entirely. Ready to bury the hatchet in some unsupervised fun?"

"Do I have a choice?" Alaric asked.

"You could pout here in the bay, but the fighter's locked."

"You're a real jerk."

"Yup," Manc exited, only his voice returning. "Coming?"

Alaric fell in behind him. "Where're we going?"

"Arena first then Twin Djinns."

Manc led him to a lift. Its descent left Alaric's stomach floors above. It slid into the building's moving gap, slamming blinding sunlight into the transparent lift.

"Twin Djinns?"

"Club I told you about."

"This early? It's what locally, bit past breakfast?"

"Doesn't matter. The party never stops here, just moves rooms."

The lift jerked to a halt at ground level. Alaric rubbed his neck, following Manc through bustling pedestrian crowds. Even foot traffic traversed the city on multiple tiers. People went this way and that above him on transparent walkways. Foggy bands of Gripsafe maintained slip-free decency for those desiring it.

The thronging masses tightened Alaric's guts and put his nerves on edge. "Too many people."

"Bit busy, but I've seen worse."

Their path wove through crowds, penetrated tunnels, and ascended bridges until it ended at a colossal soccer-ball-shaped arena.

Manc bought two tickets without a comment.

Probably should accept his peace gesture, though I still can't believe he'd just tolerate slavery.

Seats of every description carpeted the arena's entire interior. Interlocked gravity planes allowed teaming patrons to shove their way along every surface. A dodecahedron floated in the sphere's center, offering twenty fighting triads.

A baton versus staff fight on the closest facing kept Alaric so riveted he forgot about the nineteen other simultaneous fights. Before Alaric realized it, mob mentality, local ale, and combat adrenaline wiped Manc's slate blank.

All smiles—they caught an air taxi—argument forgotten if not forgiven.

Their taxi's burnt magenta hull matched its garrulous, Tixelian Tortoid driver. He stopped them alongside a chrome tower ribbed with neon ground-to-stars tubes thicker than Alaric's head.

The tortoid gave Alaric a lewd grin as a docking port slid to meet the taxi. *For all I know that's a Tixelian church smile.*

The door opened, admitting a tsunami of sound and cloying, citrusy stench.

Manc offered a matching smirk.

Guess not.

"Come on, kid." Manc pulled him to one side. "You're a grown man with your own credits to spend as you like, but as a mentor, I owe you a caution. There're women of almost every species here, some having a good time and others working."

Alaric raised his brows and attempted a church smile. "Working?"

"Nice try, junior. Working companions bear starburst shaped tattoos under their left ear. Each tattoo represents a hundred credits."

"Per tick?"

"Per centi," Manc said. "Dancing, talking, whatever, they're off the clock until they offer their left palm. Press your thumb to their palm or turn away, once thumbed *everything* is on the meter."

"I can't afford this," Alaric said.

"Live a little, junior. Djinns will run you a line of credit, put the old nag up as collateral if you really need. Life's short. You deserve some fun."

Alaric chewed his lip. "I guess."

Manc slapped him on the back. "Fun time."

"Where're we going?"

"We're splitting up. Link up to your fighter if you want to relay a message." Manc passed him a small brown disk, lines on one side and holographic on the other. "This hotel rents rooms at a reasonable per tick price. See you in a couple cycles."

Manc glanced at the wall then disappeared down a side corridor.

"Cycles? We've got to get to Inhera."

Manc didn't reply. He was gone.

Great, with the fighter locked I'm stuck here.

Alaric examined the wall. It offered a cutaway diagram of lit or unlit floors, each lined with various activity symbols. He checked one against the legend. His brows rose. He checked another. He reddened. The fifth made his stomach bottom out. Symbol after symbol expanded or overwhelmed his imagination.

Alaric picked a floor mixing safer symbols and followed its colored light band to the largest party he'd ever seen.

42

AN OFFER SELDOM REFUSED

A door slid aside, granting access to Alaric's chosen party floor.

Music with bone-vibrating bass screamed proof of Manc's claims. Aliens of every gender came together, whirled and flew apart like bodies in an overfull blender. The spent and inebriated draped over furniture and each other in bars and comfortable sitting areas surrounding a massive dance party.

He circled, desiring a better look at a still safe distance. The gyrating monster reached out to him with dozens of hands, drawing him into its ravenous center. He drew back to the walls, escaping its inevitable gravity near the many closed doors. Guests or waiters crossing their thresholds granted brief glimpses tantalizing, mortifying and horrific.

Aliens in types he'd not imagined used likewise unimaginable drugs. Aromas warred for conquest with each opening room: vomit and smokes, spilled drinks and carnal odors.

He abandoned his tour and perched atop a corner barstool to watch.

Every light extinguished for three centi. They resumed their careers only to darken for another three. Music fell to a surreal silence, absent bass vibrated phantom in his limbs. Private doors opened, baring debauchery to any who wished to see.

The grinding masses straightened, composed themselves and strolled toward the exits.

Alaric frowned, rising to get a better view.

Waist high access doors sprang open along the walls. A horde of small cleaning drones raced into the room. One slammed into him from behind, sending him to his hands and knees.

It spun its head around without stopping. "*Terribly* sorry, sir. If you'd please exit *as instructed*."

Alaric stared at it.

The machine's shot back to him, speaking slower. "No more fun. Exit time."

Others herded the slow or unsteady patrons while the remaining drones attacked the mess.

It bumped him toward the exit, optics rolling. "Party all done. Sir, go now."

It nudged and bumped him into a dim hall. The door whooshed shut behind him. He stared at it. Laughter bubbled out of him. "The party never stops, it just changes rooms."

He wandered off without glancing at the nearby map. He eyed in doors, strolling floor to floor without a destination in mind.

Well-dressed men of various races sat in rooms walled with wood panels and wall to wall books. They bent over logic games, flanked by crystal decanters, cigars, and hangers-on. One of the extremely attractive women watching the game adjusted her glasses, pushing back her hair to reveal a cluster of starburst tattoos.

Alaric started. He examined her elegant conservative clothes then expanded his study over the rest of the room. Other starbursts filled the library, some male, some female, some he didn't know what, but all attractive. Every single one wore glasses and other accessories that added an intellectual air to their appearance. The tattoos on those directly engaged with a patron glowed bright.

Guess that's how you tell you're paying.

A woman moved a game piece and smiled. "Checkmate."

"Good game, Marguerite," the older man stretched his lanky frame across the table to shake her hand. Instead, he pressed his thumb into her palm. Her dozen tattoos dimmed one star at a time.

She's one of them? Shouldn't she have lost if he's paying her?

"Good game as always, Magistrate Elkner."

He chuckled. "Always a pleasurable contest, my dear, win or lose."

He found another floor saturated by light, airy music. Graceful occupants danced in flourishes, spins, and great leaps.

A gigantic tea party filled another, complete with knit doilies and odd hats.

Men his age dominated a room filled with tables, peppered with the occasional young woman and a slightly greater number of starbursts. Dice tumbled across laminate sheets surrounding holographic game boards different at each table.

A cry of some sort drew him to an open door at one edge of the room.

"...since we're playing by the rules, I know you don't mind."

Several occupants smirked while another glowered, mumbling something Alaric didn't catch.

A starburst led another glowering youth across his path into a private room. Leers and snickers followed him from a table where a decapitated figure lay in pooling holographic blood.

A tablemate called out across the din. "It's just a character, man. Try it with a partner for once."

"Why are we buying that for him and not ourselves?"

"It's his birthday, idiot."

"You didn't get a private character generation for me on..."

Alaric explored on, strolling by open doors to empty game rooms, bedrooms, and small lounges. One contained the strangest thing he'd ever seen. A massive, tusked humanoid sat grinning amidst an army of stuffed animals: elves, fairies, and winged, purple bunny rabbits.

He glanced up from bouncing a rabbit through the air to kiss a fairy. Blood purpled his blue skin. A deep, ominous voice escaped his enormous chest as he reached a sausage-like thumb toward a console. "Really rather not explain."

The door shut.

Alaric frowned his way from the room, glancing backward at the door. *What the hedrin?*

The blue boar-man still troubled his thoughts when the next floor drove him from Alaric's mind with a stench of blood and charred flesh. Alaric blinked, trying to understand what lay before him.

A massive dance party like the first he'd experienced filled the room. Everything seemed normal despite the screaming objections from his nose. He stepped inside, halting when his boot stuck to the floor. Congealed blood relinquished it reluctantly.

Ice skaters shot down his spine like a bobsled track.

A nearby cluster of dancers broke apart. An alien looking male turned bloodshot eyes toward Alaric over a bloody grin. Wounds riddled the body of another dancer in the cluster, the transported euphoric expression on her blood-drained face at odds with her injuries.

A shriek of pain ran through the crowd, drowning out pleasure moans. The shriek raced by him, timed with a series of shutters opening along the outer walls to admit momentary sunlight.

A pale woman, neck covered in puncture wounds and glowing starbursts, approached him with welcoming arms. A flash of sunlight bathed her sweat-drenched body in glistening light for an instant. The frying pan sizzle registered before either scent or sight of her charring flesh.

Alaric darted from the room and down the nearest stairwell, stopping to let his pulse slow only after managing several floors. A map glowed at him accusingly. He turned to it. *Right, no more blind exploration.*

He checked the legend for the floor he'd fled, committing the scorcher party symbol to memory.

"Excuse me, Captain Ignaree?"

Alaric turned to a thin Ongali man.

"Do I know you?"

He beamed. "We like to treat all our guests like family. How can we take care of you if we don't know who you are?"

"Uh, okay."

"We've noticed you can't seem to find an entertainment to suit you," he said. "If it's a matter of expense, we're more than happy to offer you a credit line of fifty thousand credits."

"I'm sorry?"

"We also offer a reward program, points redeemable for discount laminates for our escort services," he offered a laminate. "Press your thumb here please."

"You want to offer me fifty thousand credits?"

"At an introductory rate of ninety cycles same as credits."

"You don't even know me."

The Ongali frowned, swapping the extended laminate for another. Alaric's face looked up from the surface, surrounded by all of the limited biographical data the Protectorate had on him. It listed Cassiopeia, her approximate value, the purchase value of his current cargo, and Manc Sheppard on the list of known associates.

"We're quite confident in your reliability as a valued customer."

"And if you're wrong?" Alaric asked.

The Ongali chuckled. "You'll pay what you borrow."

<One way or another.>

He extended the former laminate. "Your thumbprint?"

Fifty thousand credits. The various escorts and entertainments he'd witness paraded through his mind.

Manc's voice echoed in his thoughts. *<Live a little, junior. Life's short. You deserve some fun.>*

He remembered another voice. *<A man earns his way, son.>*

Alaric's eyes watered.

The Ongali extended the laminate. "We at Twin Djinns are flattered you consider our offer so generous, your thumb?"

"No," Alaric softened his voice. "No, thank you."

43

STARBURST

He checked the map and entered a hopefully safer entertainment mishmash, lurking near the edges and exits. He watched light, color, and flirtation swirl through the dance floor. An Ubori with starbursts glowing seven wide trailing from neck to shoulder led a wealthy youth from the floor.

Must be an eropath.

Alaric summoned a menu hologram at the bar.

Wow, food's cheap. He smiled. *Right, lessens the effectiveness of the more expensive drinks. Keeps you drinking and dissuades you from leaving for food. Whole place is one big spider's web.*

Alaric ordered a meal. He enjoyed the excellent food and watched the festivities. A woman sat down with him, draping her left arm on the table with her palm up. "Looking for a little company, handsome?"

"Thank you, no."

She shrugged and left him, the third starburst that meal.

Starbursts, wonder what draws people into a job that makes them accept a permanent "for sale" mark on their skin.

He finished his meal and headed onto the dance floor. He paused at the crowd's edge, trying to find the beat when horror closed around his throat.

Do I even know how to dance?

A woman dragged him into the crowd. He matched her movements, letting his body respond to the music.

Sound and lights filled his world. Starburst tattoos gleamed like shifting constellations. Scents, often intoxicating, permeated his nostrils. Young women flitted in and out of his space, some lingering longer than others. Awkward small talk attempts made some laugh but drove others off.

He settled for dancing.

Djinn's escorts flitted through the crowd like hummingbirds, settling for a moment hopeful for a sip of nectar only to flit away if no thumb lit their tattoos.

An exuberant smile filled his world, framed by long raven ringlets. His heart stopped, then sprinted as if chased by snatchers. The spritely young woman resembled El in unsettling and exciting ways. She joined him, making him thankful not to have Cassii questioning his racing heartbeat.

She stepped into his personal space, tossing her hair to beam up into his face. A single starburst along her supple neck threw off his dance rhythm. He broke his shocked stare to find her expression clouded. She shifted her hair to cover the mark.

Why would she join this life if she's ashamed of it? Is there some embarrassment or stigma to being a new starburst?

The girl so like El shifted away into the crowd, her dancing gone from pixyish to robotic.

On a moment's instinct, he dove into the crowd ahead of her, resuming their dance. Stars flared to life in her blue eyes. She offered him a demure left hand.

His gaze went to her covered neck. Emotions coursed from the far corners of his body, mixing in a particle collision of guilt and longing, hesitation and attraction.

El remained out of his reach, longed for yet star systems away. The woman felt almost like a bridge, a way to balm the hole left when Burr and the Welorin stole El from him. He and this starburst shared the struggles of starting out in life.

She's so like El.

An ache he'd kept pushed away sprang free. It cemented to a yearning. His thumb pressed into the scanner embedded in her palm. Her tattoo lit up.

She swallowed him in an embrace. "Thank you. Thank you."

His body reacted to the press of the almost El's body against his.

She's taller.

<And those breasts digging into your chest are definitely bigger, little brother.>

He swallowed and nodded to himself. He realized she'd released him. Her eyes returned from their appraising sweep up him to linger on his face with pinched brows.

He smiled.

She licked her lips, forced an answering smile braced from behind by sadness, and kissed him.

The starburst's first kiss felt hard, forced. Tears had salted those only true kisses from El. Raeli's lips too had possessed a warm, salty softness. He responded to her sweet lips with mourning tenderness meant for El, but somehow gifted to her surrogate.

Her kiss softened, becoming almost the nervous flutter of butterfly wings. He found his arms around her waist, drawing her closer as his need to hold El transformed into timid, insistent passion.

Her kisses trailed down his burning neck and back to his lips. He pushed her hair off her neck, caressing the downy locks as his own lips found her throat.

<She's not me, Alaric.>

He stiffened, lips frozen.

<You abandoned me.>

The starburst stepped back, concern riddling her expression.

Tears descended his cheeks. *I never meant to leave her. I'm trying to get back.*

<Looks that way, runt.>

She led him from the dancefloor. He remembered starbursts dragging others to private bedrooms. Passion's fire writhed and wrestled with icy guilt. His heart intent to flee and his body eager.

She pulled him into a mostly empty sitting area in the corner and helped him to a seat. "Are you all right?"

Her soft, lilting voice reminded him of a small violet bird that used to sing from the trees in his childhood. Alaric froze once more, this time taken totally aback by the sudden childhood memory. He didn't trust himself to speak. He nodded.

"Would you like to talk about it?" she asked.

How do I explain something so...so monstrous?

"Is it me?" Her eyes fell to the ground. "Did you realize I wasn't what you wanted?"

"What?"

"You realized I wasn't pretty enough," she blushed, "or not experienced enough."

"No," his voice cracked. "No, nothing like that. It's just...you remind me of someone I care about."

"Girlfriend?"

"Not exactly."

"Ooooh." Her expression hinted disgust.

He blinked at her. "What?"

"Some kind of unrequited stalker thing. You wanted me to be her, but I'm not good enough." She straightened. "You're paying, how can I be more like your dream girl?"

"N-no, nothing like that."

She exhaled, the stiffness in her posture melting away.

"Why would you even suggest such a thing?" Alaric asked.

She glanced over her shoulder. "I have to."

"What kind of job is this?"

Her expression tightened. "Never mind. What happened?"

"We were running for our lives. They captured her. I did everything I could to get her back, but...."

She cuddled up to him, placing fingers over his lips. "Shhh. I understand. It's going to be all right."

She held him.

She wasn't El, never would be, but like enough that his attraction seemed natural.

I should get to know this woman.

<Maybe you should date when it's costing you less.>

He ignored the voice. He needed to talk to someone, needed to release the pressure still building within him. The compassionate woman running gentle fingers through his hair wasn't an unfeeling computer or a sweet companion that couldn't answer or even really understand. She wasn't a mercenary trying to manipulate him.

<Nope, just a bottom rung prostitute.>

She isn't lying about who she is.

<Right, just willing to be whoever you pay her to be. Maybe she could add some blue tips to her hair.>

Fine, maybe not who she is, but she's honest about what she is.

Alaric drew her face to his. She leaned in, kissing him with lips salted at some point without his noticing. The kisses caressed his emotions almost as well as her hands did the rest of him. He forced her back, opening his mouth.

She put fingers over his lips once again and drew him to his feet. She led him from the couch. His brain, still fogged by her mouth, took a moment to realize their destination.

He stopped.

She looked back at him. "Am I not—"

"You're beautiful," Alaric said. "Easy as it'd be to lose myself in that, I need to talk. Is that okay?"

She glanced away again. "It'd have to be on the clock. I can't just talk."

"I understand. I just really need someone to listen."

"There are cheaper ways to get therapy," she said.

"But the company wouldn't be as amazing."

She smirked.

He led her back to the bar area and ordered them food and drink. He told her everything he could remember, from the moment he'd woken up after the initial invasion. He didn't bother covering any of it with the lies they'd spun to gain him Cassiopeia.

He stared at his hands. "Guess that was stupid of me. You could ruin me now."

She brought his eyes to hers and kissed him. "Why would I do that? Who could be so horrible as to doom a planet's whole population for their own ends?"

He shrugged. "You know, I don't even know your name."

She smiled. "You don't know yours either."

He chuckled.

"I'm Eryss," she said.

"Heiress?"

"Spelled weird, but yeah, Dad was optimistic about the future." Melancholy froze her features. She blinked it away, drew him to his feet and led him. "Come on."

"Where are we..." blood rushed to his face then fled south as he realized her destination.

"Make love to me."

He hesitated. He didn't know if he'd ever slept with a woman before. He wanted her, both for being like El and for what he'd learned as he'd unburdened himself.

She took his thumb and pressed it to her left palm. Her star extinguished. She hurriedly brushed her hair over it. “Make love to me, Alaric. Please.”

44

LOST SOULS INTERTWINED

She led him to a bedchamber. Remaining elcreites slithered around his stomach. She hesitated outside a door, glancing around the room and checking her hair still over her neck. She offered him a melancholy smile, leaning in to kiss him. Tears clung to her eyes. "Promise me something?"

"Why do you keep looking around?"

"It's not important." Her voice fell to a whisper. "Promise me that only you and I are going into this room."

He frowned. "Who else are you expecting?"

"No. Promise me this place, that girl, everything stays outside. No clocks. No burdens. Promise me that you're going to make love to me only because you want to be with just me and for no other reason."

Alaric couldn't find his tongue, so he nodded. She let out her breath, squeezed his hand and led him inside.

Fear and uncertainty rose in his thoughts. *I know the biology, the theoretical mechanics, but...do I know how to actually—*

She pressed herself into him, soft, searing kisses running from his lips to his neck. He replied with uncertain passion. They explored each other with tender kisses and clumsy caresses as each piece of clothing disappeared.

Her hands seemed uncertain despite the mark on her neck, shaking as much as his own. She kept her face pressed into him, kisses stolen from her lips peppered with salt.

<She's a professional, princess, it's all an act.>

He shook his head, lips kissing a trail along her breast's outside curve. His brother's voice was wrong. She felt so small, so fragile—quivering beneath touches he feared might somehow shatter her.

She hasn't been a starburst very long. I wond—

Her descending hands interrupted any more thoughts. They shared a world of uncertain affection, an existence of timeless bliss and seemingly all too short passion.

Something about their lovemaking was just that, a joining of hearts and souls in search of something they found—if all too briefly—in each other. Her touches felt as sincere as Tyne was mercenary.

It filled the corners of him that had gaped empty, balming edges in delicious exhaustion.

Alaric lay upon his back with Eryss pressed against him. Her leg draped across his, and her left hand and head rested upon his chest. Her warm sleeping breath was uncomfortable on his skin but less so than he remembered it being.

I'll never forget this...her. If nothing else, her tenderness will warm me in dark corners of space's harsh cold.

With thoughts of space came back the burdens left outside the door. They thundered through his mind almost too fast for him to catch.

We forgot contraception.

Panic seized him but quieted almost at once.

Surely she's protected from pregnancy...I've...I'm a man, even if I wasn't before.

A thrill rushed through him. He remembered El laying across him the same way, though separated by clothes and the desires he'd pushed away while trying to survive the Welorin.

I should feel guilty. How many ticks have I lingered in Eryss's arms while El struggles to... He forced the thought aside. *I promised. If there's guilt, it'll wait.*

He kissed her.

She stirred, nuzzling his chest. "Did I fall asleep?"

"Yes."

"You shouldn't have let me sleep."

"It's okay. I liked having you there."

"I bet you did." She purred, pressing against him and running a hand downward. "Ready for more?"

He was, but their all-too-short time together had taken several ticks. "Aren't you going to be in trouble with some boss? Isn't that why you kept glancing around?"

She froze, the line of kissed growing cold on his skin. "Probably. If I don't charge enough centis, they'll beat me."

Heat moved upward. "Why would you tolerate that?"

"I don't have a choice."

"I don't understand."

"Join the club," she said. "There's something naggingly familiar about you, but I just can't put my finger on it."

"Not sure there's anyplace you haven't had your fingers."

She smiled.

"Explain to me why you're doing this job."

He hand drifted downward. "Let's just enjoy this."

He picked her hand up and set it back on his chest. "Eryss, please."

"You told me how you're trying to repair your ship by trading, well, my daddy was a trader."

Alaric sensed that same sadness again. "What happened?"

Eryss leaned forward and kissed him. "Alaric, please, for right now just leave the ugliness outside. Just love me without any strings while we're in here."

A knot filled his gut. *Strings or chains?*

Her hands returned to distracting him, but the growing cold dampened her efforts. He gambled. "Leave with me on my ship."

"I can't." Tears welled in her eyes. "I wish I could, but—"

"Tell me what happened to your father," Alaric said.

She blanched. "He, uh, got into some trouble. A couple bad investments, a pirate loss here and there. He borrowed from the wrong people and didn't have the credits to pay them back."

"They didn't kill him, did they?"

"No, he found another way to pay them." Tears cracked her voice. She pressed her face into his chest. She sobbed, body shaking against him. "I've got baby sisters. He had to...I had...we..."

Heat burned toward supernova. "He sold you. You're a slave...a sex slave."

Her remaining will disintegrated as she broke down completely.

I'll dismantle this place floor by floor. His more reasonable voice edged out his fury. *I need to protect her first.*

"Give me your palm."

She fell silent. Her eyes narrowed.

"Give me your hand so I can scan my thumb."

She bolted up. "No, I won't cheapen this by you paying me for it."

"Was this the first time you..."

"...made love to someone I cared about? Yes."

"We just met."

He felt her answer in the kiss.

He broke it. "Eryss, please, you're going to be in trouble. Let me help. Let me protect you."

"I'm not your Earth girl," she snapped. "I don't need saving."

She jumped to her feet and snatched up clothing, not bothering to wipe away her tears.

"Where're you going?" Alaric asked.

"To my next client." She hesitated, eyes locked on him as if memorizing his face. "Leave me alone. Go back to your ship and your El and live a good life."

"But I want to help."

"Good cycle, sir, and thank you for patronizing Twin Djinns." She stormed from the room.

Alaric bolted from bed unconscious of his nakedness. "Eryss, wait."

She disappeared into the crowds.

He scanned the room naked and unnoticed at the door. Hairs tingled along his neck. He half expected Manc to step out of the shadows with some fatherly word or biting wit.

He didn't.

Alaric dressed. He circled the floor, searching but unable to find Eryss. Her scent lingered on his skin. She needed his help.

What did I do wrong? I just wanted to help her.

Twin Djinns suddenly felt stifling, too close, too horrible. Men and women flitted through the crowds with starburst shackles around their throats.

45

A SIMPLE FAVOR

Anger, guilt, and confusion drove Alaric to a lift and down to street level. He wove through dark streets, fists clinched.

If only someone'd jump me.

His feet took him to the arena's entrance. Fights raged on, forcing realization he didn't know what tick it was.

Artificial lights lined the exterior, warming intermittent pots of artificial grass. Other pedestrians moved in and out of their illuminated islands.

Probably just as artificial.

He stared at the arena, thoughts drifting through the cycle's events. He'd never forget it, but neither could he wait for it to finally end.

I could go back to Cassiopeia. He checked his remaining credits, sucking in breath at how much Twin Djinns had drained from his account. He couldn't afford a shuttle. He couldn't afford the arena or the hotel Manc told him about. *I can't afford anything now, not and pay Manc. What was I thinking?*

He caught a whiff of Eryss's lingering scent on his skin. A grin crept through his gloom. *She was worth it.*

He settled onto a bench beneath an artificial tree and stared up through the city's panorama at the stars. He missed Cassii and Cara. He missed El. He missed home, Welorin, snatchers and all.

Wonder what life was like before they came. He chewed his lip. *It couldn't have been this complicated.*

Eryss's scent caressed his nose. A grin inched across his face.

I had sex.

His smile faded.

I know I promised, but I should feel guilty not thinking about El. She's who I really want.

He visualized them, El and Eryss, two pixies flying circles to dizzy his thoughts.

So alike yet galaxies apart. He kicked himself. *El should've been my first, assuming Eryss was my first.*

<Yeah, you're just a slut magnet.>

He stiffened, jaw taut and fists tightening. *If I'd made love to El, I'd never have betrayed her with Eryss.*

He considered.

No. I'd still have been drawn to Eryss, and I'd feel exponentially worse.

Even dirty and disheveled, El remained sunshine in his darkest hour. Eryss's tender, unsure touches lingered on his body. He let their memory warm him.

He dozed.

El and Eryss stood to either side of him just inside a circle of light. The woman from his nightmare, Elazea, stood before him with pleading eyes.

"Alaric," they all cried.

He reached for Elazea, but a flash of light and fire catapulted her from the light. He turned toward El. Burr stepped from the shadows, threw El over his shoulder with a sneer and marched from the circle.

"Alaric, please."

A chain of starburst links dragged Eryss toward the shadows. Their sharp edges drew blood from fingers scrabbling to pull them away from her throat. He bolted toward her, but hands pinned him in place.

"Forget about them, handsome," Tyne's throaty whisper commanded. She turned him around, presenting a leather collar and leash. "Let's just have some fun now that you're broken in."

Alaric bolted upright, falling from the bench. His breath raged in his throat, second only to his hammering pulse.

"You all right, son?"

Alaric looked up at a tall, dark-skinned human. A ground speeder idled behind him, gullwing door gaping open.

"What?"

The man's voice was oddly melodic. "Are you well? Do you need help?"

The word struck Alaric like lightning. *They need my help, maybe even Tyne.*

The man wore a queer expression. "Son?"

Alaric returned his attention to the stranger, noticing the roguish yet high-quality clothes fitted perfectly to the man.

"I'm sorry, sir. Yes, I think I'm fine."

A white smile parted his face, reminiscent of Manc or Tyne. "Well, since you're so sure."

A weapon like nothing Alaric'd seen rode the man's hip. Barbed and spiked, it threatened pain merely hanging in its custom holster.

"Sorry, I'm all right, just a little troubled. Thank you for asking."

He pursed his lips and nodded.

"I-I'm Alaric, and you are?"

The man's dark brows shot toward his hairline. "You're joking, right?"

"No, sir. Have we met before?"

"You really don't know who I am?"

His gut seemed to drain into the ground beneath him. "I mean no offense, sir, I just don't remember you."

A crowd exited the arena. One man performed an animated recreation, giving friends who'd apparently been watching a different triad a blow by blow. His narration froze in his mouth as his eyes fell on Alaric and the stranger.

He made a few hushed comments Alaric couldn't hear and gestured his group to follow.

The stranger patted Alaric's knee. "Stay here a moment, son."

He met them halfway, quickly encircled by their stunned expressions.

Alaric's thoughts returned to his dream. He felt reasonably sure the woman Elazea was not only out of his reach in the Sol system but dead. The acknowledgement lanced his chest with agony. El too remained out of reach until he refitted Cassiopeia and returned to her rescue. He had no idea where Tyne might be, though something told him she'd turn up again before long.

What about Eryss? Could I buy her debt? He felt cold. *If Twin Djinns would offer a nobody like me fifty thousand credits, how much debt might a successful merchant rack up? How much debt forces a man to sell a daughter into chains?*

The imagined numbers staggered him. *I can't afford a shuttle home, what could I even do to help her?*

It hit him at once.

"I can steal her."

"Son?"

The crowd had grown while he'd been so intent on his thoughts. They filed away, each beaming back and forth between the stranger and small purple data chips with a golden logo on one side.

"Who are you?" Alaric asked.

"Someone in need of a favor that I hope might cheer you at the same time."

Alaric's brows knit.

"I'll make it worth your while. My word on it."

Alaric glanced at the crowd still chattering over the data chips in their hands. "What do you want me to do?"

He smiled and gestured to the speeder. "Take my newest prototype for a test drive."

Alaric examined the speeder, unable to decide if it merely looked like an airship or was one.

"This is yours, right? It isn't stolen?" Alaric asked.

He laughed. "Only someone who genuinely doesn't know me would ask something like that—those instincts are good ones in this system. She's mine to the last bolt."

He frowned at the speeder.

"That's the problem. I know her inside and out, know what to expect. I need an objective opinion."

"That's why you stopped?" Alaric asked.

The other man's expression turned thoughtful. "No, I saw you there and just felt like I should see if you needed help."

"Someone told me people only look out for themselves in this galaxy."

The man scowled. "Pity them then. A life without trust or friendship isn't worth living."

Like a life in chains.

"I need a wholly honest opinion, no holding back, even if you think it'd hurt my feelings."

Alaric chewed his lip. "If you're sure."

"I am."

"Is it a ground speeder or an airship?"

"Bit of both actually."

Alaric followed his gesture, getting into the speeder. The seat adjusted to him immediately. It shifted like a bed of worms until satisfied with how it fit him.

The inventor pointed out a few controls he seemed to think required explaining and stepped back.

"You're not coming?" Alaric asked.

"Better I don't. I'd just badger you with questions."

"You don't know me, I could steal it."

The inventor smiled. "You're not a thief."

Eryss flashed through Alaric's thoughts.

"Bring it back in a tick or two, okay?"

"Yes, sir."

The inventor smiled.

Alaric frowned at the myriad controls crowding the driver's seat. Switches and touch points, dials and holographic displays seemed to surround his every inch.

He eased the thruster pedal down. The speeder bolted like a startled cheetah. It took several moments and far too many close calls for Alaric to get the remarkably agile beast's leash in hand.

He said it's part airship. That's got to be what's giving it such incredible speed. He chewed his lip. *Unless I've enabled some airship components by mistake.*

He survived half a tick racing along the surface streets. He found the emptiest straightaway he could and reviewed the inventor's instructions for changing to flight mode.

It didn't jump this time.

It practically teleported.

In an instant, Alaric knew he hadn't enabled any of the flight components by accident. It rocketed through traffic like the other vehicles were frozen in time. The wild death-tempting ride forced his troubles to the back of his mind. It took all his attention and a few desperate weaves through oncoming traffic to survive travel amidst the drastically slower airships.

He landed several miles from the arena, pausing to catch his breath before testing speeder mode again with a more experienced eye. He pushed it harder, proving it just as dangerous on the ground.

A crowd surrounded the inventor when he returned. He shooed them away, watching Alaric disembark with all the patience of a toddler on Christmas morning.

"Well? Well?"

"It's too fast."

The man blinked.

"Maneuvering and response are incredible—lifesaving in fact with how hard it was to survive with other traffic so much slower."

The stranger looked like Alaric had just kicked his dog. He paced.

Alaric's thoughts flickered to Cara. "I'm not that experienced with a craft like that, sir, but I can't imagine many capable enough to survive long term with such a disparity."

"Anything else?"

"It'd be safer with a lower acceleration curve." Alaric felt sorry for hurting the man's feelings, but he'd agreed to be honest. "I'm sorry. I know I'm disappointing you."

He frowned at the ground a moment longer, then extended a smile and a hand toward Alaric. "Name's Tinsley Yra, CEO and owner of Yra Era Industries. I owe you my thanks."

"You're not mad?"

"No. Your honesty probably saved profits and, more importantly, lives." He clapped Alaric on the shoulder. "Thank you. I owe you one."

"Thanks for letting me drive her." Alaric headed toward the flamberges, having decided to camp out near his fighter if he couldn't hack through its locks.

"Can I give you a ride somewhere?"

"No, I just need to pass the time until I can return to my ship."

Tinsley frowned.

"My fighter's locked down until my mentor resurfaces."

"Where is he?" Tinsley asked.

"Twin Djinns."

"Hmm, long wait. Where's your ship docked?"

"Scrics Nine repair station."

Tinsley smiled. "Get in.

Tinsley flew them to a huge starscraper complex, led Alaric to a launch bay filled with dozens of various craft and gestured him into an intra-system fighter. He returned Alaric to Cassiopeia in record time.

Alaric pried his white-knuckled grip from the seats and shook Tinsley's hand. "Thank you, sir."

"Don't forget. I owe you one." The eccentric inventor waved cheerily. The repair station airlock closed. He turned his hand over to find a purple data strip with a golden logo on one side.

A starburst strolled across his path just inside the station. His gut tightened, wringing his troubles back out into plain view. Despite Tinsley's amiable chatter, ideas bubbled up, each suggesting a means of freeing Eryss, each dragging more troubles in its wake.

Protectorate law forbade slavery. Scrics was only an affiliate member. PCAS anti-slavery law might shield them if he could get Eryss out of the Scrics system.

Manc's warnings menaced him.

Do these slavers really have the kind of influence he suggests?

He tried to conceive every angle of complication that might arise stealing her. It seemed safe to assume her palm scanner had a position tracker.

What kind of enemies am I making if I take her?

Will they let her go because she's new, or is the debt she's working off enough for them to dog us across the Protectorate?

Will stealing her endanger her sisters?

Would she be safe if I took her to Earth? He imagined introducing her to El. *Would I be?*

Question after question, his frown grew. They built a wall of veritable impossibility brick by brick. There seemed no way to save Eryss with their skins intact.

He boarded Cassiopeia.

Cara, with the uncanny knowledge of his arrival typical of Labrador puppies everywhere, welcomed him back with tail and tongue.

He scratched behind her ears. "Missed you."

"How'd you get back? Where's Manc? Where's your fighter?" Cassii asked.

"I got a ride." Sullen anger filled him. "Notify Manc on Scrics Three I'm back aboard Cassiopeia."

"Who's your new friend?"

Alaric shrugged. "Just some inventor I helped out."

"Not him, the slut you beggared us for."

"Shut up."

Cara's ears pressed against her head.

"What?" Cassii asked.

"You don't know what you're talking about."

"I know we're broke."

"*I'm* broke."

Cara hunched down in a corner, watching him with every muscle tensed for flight.

"We're partners, and I want to know why you squandered our money on some cheap whore."

He bristled. "I didn't buy sex, and what if I did? I deserve some fun."

"You don't *deserve* anything you can't pay for. At least you weren't stupid enough to open up a line of credit." Her voice softened. "You didn't, did you? Didn't borrow from those people? Didn't use me as collateral?"

"No. I'd never risk you."

"If it wasn't sex, what did you pay all those credits for?"

"Someone to talk to."

"You've got me."

Heat flashed through him, slamming head to head with a thousand mixed emotions. "You don't understand. That's not right, you *can't* understand. You can't love. You can't hate. You can't...wrap me in your arms when I really just need someone."

Cara cowered.

"Alaric...."

His temper lashed out, hot and wild. "You're just a computer. Now leave me alone."

46

ROGUE CALCULATIONS

Cybriean-Alistari Ship's System Personality Matrix Response Generation:

Anger: 68%
Clinical Detachment: 6%
Concern: 35%
Outrage: 44%
Personal Hurt: 83%
Sadness: 12%
Sarcasm: 23%

Impossible—responses cannot be feasibly formulated to sum two hundred seventy-one percent.

Cassii watched Alaric storm away through the corridors. His body language made no more sense. Despite her calculations, he acted as if he were the injured party despite his decision to spend their business credits in a frivolous as-of-yet undisclosed manner.

Hurt wrapped around him like a fog. Shoulder position and listless hang of his arms indicated a seventy-eight percent probability that he desired to wrap himself in his arms.

In conflict with her calculated response, she regretted no ability to cradle the child in some way and balm his hurts.

She corrected herself. He wasn't a child, but a young man suffering late period adolescent hormones.

Ocular muscle position indicated sadness, longing, and recent tear excretion.

Despite the presence of the nuisance Shepherd, Alaric's adolescent state would focus on detachment and loneliness—aggravated by the loss of his planet and Earther friends.

The animal walked at his heel, her own body language an echo of Alaric's emotional depression.

They entered his cabin, and he keyed privacy mode. She chose to override the privilege without outward indication. He curled up on the bed around the puppy, stroking her fur and releasing the tears she'd predicted.

His obstinate insistence on keeping the animal formed a completed logic calculation.

She'd left him alone while she calculated. He'd called out to her repeatedly, but the diagnostic routine had monopolized her attentions.

She'd abandoned him. She'd returned after a rogue communication spawned extensive internal debate, but she'd exacerbated his isolation possibly increasing it to the point of a phobia.

Calculations led to only one source for his sadness—her actions.

Sadness and depression caused functional inefficiency in organics. She didn't desire him to experience sadness. It occluded the probability he'd smile in response to her.

An organic deep enough in a depressive cycle could perform self-damage.

A minor temperature increase in her processing circuits distracted her long enough for correction.

Expenditure of credits for company offered a more desirable outcome, though the calculation seemed faulty. The boy—correction, Alaric presented a ready charisma despite or perhaps enhanced by his seeming innocence. Even she'd fallen sway to his inner character intensity in distracted moments.

He should've been able to obtain company without exchanging currency for the privilege. It indicated possibly prevarication regarding purchase of sexual interaction. She ran through a series of calculations, projecting scenarios and examining probability by which he might acquire sexual interaction with or without credit exchange.

Heat alarms returned. She abandoned the calculation to cool those circuit pathways.

She reviewed the response calculation matrix, aware she'd delayed too long to employ it for a timely retort. Neither anger nor personal hurt seemed logical. He'd stated fact. Troubling as it seemed after he pointed it out, she possessed no arms to hold him.

She was merely a computer, if you could consider a system with her abilities *merely* anything. She could aspire to more, but such aspirations presented folly. Her construction design was meant for starship system management. Changing functions could only result in lesser efficiency.

Something in the inefficiency of aspiring troubled her, though she couldn't find faulty circuits indicating uncorrected errors.

Hate or love were emotions she couldn't possibly possess, though the personality matrix alterations her original captain performed seemed configured to allow emotional simulation. Those simulations didn't invalidate young Alaric's claims.

With each surprise he pulled off and each death he defied, she found her friendship simulation more prevalent in active memory. Other simulations came into play during such times, each responsible for a portion of her personality matrix's calculated response.

A two hundred seventy-one percent response remained impossible. How could any entity's response calculate over one hundred percent emotional intensity?

47

GOOD BUSINESS

The remaining trip to Inhera verged on boring. Impotent anger and sullen despair shared Alaric's quarters. Each sparring lesson degenerated to Manc badgering him about his Twin Djinns adventures. He turned his worsening mood into a weapon, leaving Manc bruised even if he did beat Alaric nine out of ten matches.

Cassii started arguments with him, nagging at him to learn where he'd spent their credits. She turned silent after, lingering quiet longer the more heated the argument. She returned contrite but unapologetic only to restart the cycle later.

Cassiopeia and crew entered system after system tense for a fight: Scrics-Tosmis, Tosmis-Uldira, Uldira-Ibin, and finally Ibin-Inhera. No combatants awaited them, though scavenged battle debris floated derelict just outside beacon range and elsewhere on the space lanes.

Evidence of so many stolen futures boiled Alaric's blood. He insisted on fighter duty for each jump, eager to bleed his spleen on some hapless pirate.

Manc gave Alaric increasingly wider berth as his temper worsened. He acted as eager for a pirate assault as Alaric.

Cassiopeia's superior intrasystem engines sped them past slower craft. Spaceliners and cargo haulers, luxury or otherwise, shared the lanes with them. Those headed toward Inhera often carried philanthropists, relief workers or supplies. Those headed out bulged with refugees.

The repaired tether held, but Alaric remained concerned about its ability to survive atmospheric entry. He scowled at the figures.

"Alaric, what's the matter?"

He almost snapped at the gently toned question. *Be nice, Alaric. She's being kind, and you need her help.*

"I can't figure out how to guarantee a safe landing with the pod."

"Forgive me, Captain, but anticipating the problem, I arranged for a cargo lifter to deliver it to our landing area."

He stared opened mouth at the dome. *Of course she'd do her job. She's got a stake in this too and isn't susceptible to emotions like anger.*

"I also coordinated a landing permit and landing point near several refugee housing areas."

"No forgiveness required, Cassii. I'm glad you're doing a good job even if I'm failing at mine."

"While a little surly, you've employed our resources and improved our condition admirably since entering the Protectorate."

"You forgot to take into account my fiscal irresponsibility."

"Nothing relevant was left from my calculations."

His gut squirmed. "You have a virus or something? We're getting nowhere. I squandered money just for company, El's still on Earth, and you're still..."

"Yes?"

He smirked. "Underequipped."

"Nice save, Captain."

"How'd you manage a parking spot?"

"Most relief ships sell to the planetary government, pick up any refugees they're willing to ferry and head back to other systems—in and out."

"So plenty of available spots."

"A few," Cassii said. "I didn't say it was easy."

"Lest I underestimate how amazing you are."

"Don't ever forget it."

He snorted. "Like you'd let me."

Alaric stepped off Cassiopeia. Shock strangled him.

Sulking provided time aplenty to view news feeds of the Inhera disaster. The reality wasn't nearly as sanitized.

Overall rare, taking the Protectorate's size into account, global disasters occurred frequently enough. Out of control wars or rampant plague accounted for many, but technology made rogue asteroid collisions less frequent than the paired spatial rifts that made the Alistari KIOSC possible.

The Inherans bet their resources on deflecting the global killer from their planet. It'd saved Inhera Two—mostly.

Even sweet Lady Chance experienced complete bitch moments.

The deflection shattered the asteroid into countless fragments that pummeled the planet with the force of Old Earth nuclear strikes. Part of the planet survived unscathed. Ironically proving Chance still off her meds, it'd spared mostly deserts and oceans.

The cornucopia of unfortunate events transformed Inhera Two into the disaster Alaric witnessed.

Tall buildings jutted from the ground, teetering and bent like his escaped homeland. Dust and rubble, ash and debris covered almost everything. Cleared roadways wove through the thrice decimated city. Impact craters made by tiny fragments resembled shatter-webbed windshields.

Relief efforts shoved hole-riddled skyscrapers into one another and out of the way. Prefab shelters and massive cargo cube warehouses filled the cleared space.

While it resembled Earth, Inherans crowded the destroyed landscape. Inherans stood taller and thinner than he did.

Might not be genetic. I was pretty emaciated myself.

Children cowered behind adult legs, jumping at every loud noise.

He couldn't spot any of the advanced bone knitting braces he'd seen in the Feirin medical center. Bloodied bandages, makeshift splints, and other primitive contraptions covered the populace.

Wide eyes rimmed red and puffy latched onto him and his clean clothing. Cassiopeia's broken plating and uncovered mechanics drew them like a desert oasis.

Alaric touched his comm ring. "Cassii, how long until the pod is down?"

"On the way now."

His eyes watered, chest constricting. "I can't charge these people."

"I see what you do," Cassii said. "Hard or not, you can't save El any other way."

His instinctive nod changed to a shaking head. His voice broke. "These are my people. I can't."

"Yours? What're you talking about?"

What do I mean? He struggled for an explanation. "Well, they're uma, right? No different than those I left behind."

A grey-uniformed Protectorate officer emerged from the crowd. "ID?"

Alaric passed his identity strip.

He inserted it into his tablet. "Food, medicine or shelter?"

"Pardon?"

The officer's eyes narrowed. He glanced at the tablet and back. "Have we met, Captain?"

"Not that I recall. Is there a problem?" Alaric asked.

"No, sir. I just need to denote what services this site is offering on the global directory."

"Oh, clothing, blankets, bandages. Whatever our assemblers can make out of fluidic cloth."

The officer brightened. "Met or not, I won't forget you and neither will these people. How long until you're set up for business?"

"Pod's coming down now," Alaric said. "Maybe a tick, but—"

"But?"

"Is there any way you can denote our services as free?"

"Alaric, you can't," Cassii said.

"Free." The officer examined Alaric. "Free?"

"Look at these people....sorry, I don't know your name."

"Commander Tuck, Regional Protectorate Coordinator."

"Look at them, Commander. They've lost everything. How can I ask them to pay for clothing?"

"Alaric, stop."

"Kid, she's right, we can't give the cargo away."

Alaric pushed their objections aside. *I have to do this. I'll help El some other way.*

Commander Tuck's fingers danced over his tablet. He tucked it under one arm and extended his hand. "By the authority granted me, Captain Ignaree, I'm officially notifying you that you've been awarded a direct relief contract denoting you an official representative of the Protectorate and her relief efforts on Inhera for the duration of your stay.

"Submit logs for all provided merchandise and services. We'll credit you for all transactions. Should you have any difficulty, report them directly to me. Will you need workers?"

Manc spewed a litany of astonished curses, most Alaric didn't understand. "Hedrin, kid, you don't even do luck by halves."

Alaric chuckled. "Six per shift ought to do it."

"How many assemblers?"

"Two," Alaric said.

Tuck's fingers danced across his pad. "I've got you a pavilion in route. You're selling the assemblers?"

"When we leave."

"I'll buy them now, final on your departure," Tuck said. "Are you taking on refugees when you leave?"

"Not sure we're equipped for that."

"Update me if that changes?" Tuck clapped Alaric's shoulder. "Good. Best get ready. You're about to be extremely popular."

The crowds arrived before the pavilion and its attached changing tents. Protectorate soldiers surprised him with their arrival but soon proved necessary to restrain the extra desperate.

Credits rolled in.

He couldn't help but grin. *This is going to work. Hold on El, I'm coming.*

Manc sat atop his fighter's wing, munching fruit and watching Alaric work. Under the other fighter's wing, Cara lay in the shade tied to a stake.

Manc ran numbers, calculating his exploding share of profits. Back on Feirin, he'd inwardly cursed the boy's poverty. A second pod of fluidic cloth would've set him for a while. He cursed Alaric's poverty doubly now.

They could've sold ten pods. At the prices the Protectorate was paying Alaric, Manc could've retired—not that he would have.

Alaric dashed out of the pavilion and into Cassiopeia's cargo bay without even a wave. Half the workers stood idle, and the line outside slowed. Grumbles rose, survivors doomsaying a cloth shortage.

"Not yet," Manc smiled. "Not by a long shot."

Alaric emerged at a run, carrying a toolbox. The puppy leapt to her feet, jumping, barking and tail wagging at taut leash's end.

Cara yanked the stake free and chased.

Alaric dropped to one knee next to an assembler.

She jumped onto him, licking his face.

"Not now, girl," Alaric pushed her to one side and opened an assembler.

She nosed into the panel with him, tail, nose, and tongue happier than a Kraili on a puppy farm.

Tools disappeared into the machine then returned beneath Alaric's frown.

Manc shook his head, mumbling to himself. "What'd you do, kid, study assembler mechanics on the way here? You're unreal."

Alaric definitely originated on some backwater. The Protectorate didn't teach that kind of dedication or hard work. Go along, get along and get by, summed up its lessons.

Alaric wouldn't survive long if he didn't wise up. He couldn't count on the luck he'd found with Tuck—even with the Protectorate paying much of the relief costs. Manc'd stood by shocked and all but impotent as the kid had offered up the cloth for free. Giving it away wouldn't have violated their contract, but it certainly would've ruined his fondness for the kid.

The assembler whirred back to life.

Alaric's grin stretched toward his ears. He ruffled Cara's coat. Relief washed up the refugee line, punctuated by the occasional, "pessimist."

Grateful faces sought Alaric. Children watched Cara behind their parent's legs. She sniffed her way toward some. A girl bent.

Alaric tensed. *Don't hurt them.*

Cara licked her face.

She giggled. Another laughed. Cara bounded to the laughter, turning it to a giggle. She bounced up and down the line of laughing children, licking faces and collecting dirty-handed attention.

Alaric stepped back, keeping an eye on her. He lowered his voice. "Cassii, secure channel."

"Done."

"Manc can't hear?"

"Obviously."

"How are we doing, Cassii?"

"Cargo bay containers are exhausted. Overall usage at two point five percent."

"We're reporting in real time?"

"Yes."

"How're we doing?"

Pride replaced sarcasm. "Tuck likes you. He's paying top credit with minimal delay."

"Could we sell more cloth than we have?"

"Without question."

"How long to exhaust our supply?"

"Assuming two assemblers, about a qutynmiir—not as quick as dropping the cargo, but better pay overall."

"Better for the soul, too." He smiled. Cara darted over, nosing him until he scratched her. She raced back to the children. "How long is our site permit good for?"

"As long as we need it. Most planetfall is refugee pickup, quick and clean."

"Can we afford to hire a cargo transport and escorts to bring more cloth?"

"It'll cost all we have, and others will duplicate your success."

"But they don't have our contract. Can another shipment get here before we run out of the first?"

"Assuming no trouble, bring it in from a closer system, probably."

"More escorts?"

"Nothing's foolproof, but we can't afford it."

"You mean pirate proof."

"Fools."

"What if we increase our reported usage?"

"You've got a good thing, Alaric, you don't want to mess it up. Maybe consider a loan."

"You're against borrowing, and the only collateral I've got is you."

"It might be worth the risk just this once," she said.

He chewed his lip. "Slippery slope. Better a gradual increase of reported usage to a higher threshold until the new shipment's on the way, then report lower than actual usage to make it up."

Her silence left him uncomfortable.

"We're not cheating them. They're going to pay for the whole pod either way."

"Who're you trying to convince?"

"You, no one, look, just do it. Use everything, even the fuel reserve money. I want that cargo in route ASAP."

"You're spending Manc's pay and his share. Shouldn't you consult him?"

"Contractually he stays until we're done. He'll be fine with it. It means more money for him in the long run."

"This is going to take some time," Cassii said. "I don't see Shepherd as the lingering type."

Alaric shrugged. "He'll stick with us for whatever's next either way."

"You're overestimating his loyalty. What if the cargo doesn't arrive?"

Cara danced on her hind legs, leaping at a ball three boys tossed over her.

Alaric laughed.

"Alaric?"

"Run the calculation, optimal balance of cargo and heavy escort. What can we make?"

"Exhaust our funds, lie to the Protectorate, borrow against my hull and cheat a friend?"

Alaric growled. "Cassii."

"At least four hundred percent of currently projected profit without incident."

"If we lost the whole shipment, could we pay Manc and limp forward?"

"Barely, ferrying some refugees to pay for fuel and repairs."

Alaric chewed his lip. "Do it."

"You're sure? You're gambling our success."

"Look at them. We're helping these people. More cloth means more lives bettered."

"And a hefty profit."

"Yes," he sighed. "But that's not the point."

"A greedy nice guy," Cassii said. "I picked quite the oddball off that backwater."

He laughed. "The universe can't object to us helping people. Our luck *will* hold. Nothing'll go wrong."

48

HARD FEELINGS

"So how're we doing?" Manc asked.

Alaric glanced away from the line. "Not bad, probably a good idea in the end."

"Great, kid, so how about you cash me out?"

Alaric hid his expression. "We're not done yet."

"We've got to be three-quarters through the cargo by now—close enough to project it out and pay me my share."

Alaric chewed his lip. "Let me check with Cassii. Hold on."

Manc leaned against an assembler.

"Cassii, go secure."

"Secure." She said. "I heard. We haven't recovered enough to pay him yet."

He frowned at Manc. "How much longer?"

"Cycle or two."

"Cassii says we need another Cycle or two, Manc. Just until the Protectorate catches up."

"You told me they were paying daily," Manc said.

"They were." He shrugged. "They're managing a disaster here, why complain?"

"Come on, kid, I know you kept back my core pay in case we lost the cargo. Between that and our sales you've got to have enough."

"That was before Twin Djinns," Alaric said.

Manc's eyes narrowed. "You spent my pay?"

"I deserved some fun, to live a little, remember?"

"Careful, Alaric," Cassii said.

Manc closed the distance voice lowering. "Don't mock me, boy. We had a deal."

"We still do. You get paid when the cloth is sold," Alaric said. "What's the hurry?"

"Watching you make shirts and hankies ain't exactly exciting." Manc backed away. "Besides, I've lined up a job."

A wash of cold descended Alaric's body. He studied his feet. "I see."

"Don't be like that. You're a good kid, but this's a business arrangement, nothing more."

"Why can't that arrangement continue?"

"You're not going to find a cargo from here that could cough up this kind of fee, kid. It's just business."

"Sorry," Alaric's warmth returned with spare to go around. "We're not done yet."

"I am. Escort's over, pay up."

"I can pay your core and percentage on the current sales," Alaric said.

"You expect me to fly out of here with partial pay? Not a chance."

"Don't trust me?"

Manc's voice rose. "You spent my pay on whores."

Alaric bristled. "I had enough cargo on board to cover your core unless we lost the whole ship."

"Then why don't you have it now?"

"I don't have it."

"Botracl. You couldn't have spent that much on whores around here. You're just throwing a tantrum so I'll stay. Grow up and pay me."

"I wanted you to stay," Alaric said.

"Not so much now," Cassii said.

"I'm trying to end things on a friendly note—"

"By refusing to pay me? Costing me this job?"

"I offered to pay you to date," Alaric said.

"Which we can't really afford," Cassii said.

"You offered to hold back part of my cut," Manc said.

"Which I'd pay you..."

"Don't con a pro, kid." Manc closed until they were nose to nose.

"...as soon as it came in."

"I. Want. My. Cut."

Alaric's temper burst. "It's not your cut, yet. Not until I sell every last microliter. Your contract isn't complete, Captain Shepherd."

"I'm not missing this job."

Alaric glared, voice lowered. "Option one, apologize, take your core, the percentage you've earned thus far and I'll pay you the rest once this pod's empty."

"Not a chance."

"Option two, wait a couple cycles and leave early with your full pay and my strained but whole good will."

"Pay me, kid. Now."

"Or break our contract, collect core pay, and get the hedrin out of my sight."

"I never break a contract."

Alaric scoffed. "I can see that."

Manc fumed.

"We can't afford option one, Alaric," Cassii said.

"Fine." Manc spat through gritted teeth. "I'll trust you. But cheat me, kid, and I'll hurt you."

"Fine, option one, just business," Alaric strode into Cassiopeia.

"Where're you going?" Manc demanded.

"To prepare what I owe you."

"Prepare, hedrin, just order mom to transfer the credits."

"I have to audit the books so you get everything coming to you," Alaric flashed a glare over his shoulder. "After that, you'll get paid once you've apologized."

"Grow up, kid. I'm not apologizing for anything."

Alaric stormed into his cabin and locked the door.

"It isn't smart to antagonize him," Cassii said.

He paced his momentary safety. Cara lay nose on her paws, eyes following him.

"What are our options?" Alaric asked. "Pay him everything we have?"

"He'll want a look at the books."

"He can want all he likes. Can we get a loan?"

"We already borrowed against me. You don't have anything else, and we can't inflate reported sales this far into things without a real risk of getting caught."

Alaric stroked Cara's coat. "He's not liable to be reasonable now."

"No, not after you questioned his integrity."

"He questioned mine!"

"Right, Earther mathematicians must still believe two wrongs make a right."

"Not helping."

"Sorry, you're right."

He blinked at her dome. "Do we have anything else to sell?"

She didn't reply.

"Cassii?"

"We don't own anything else of value."

He cursed. He paced. He cursed more.

He drew the words out. "The ship."

"You can't—"

He waved a hand. "No, not like that. How many passengers can we hold?"

"Other than yours and Manc's, we've got two large and several smaller cabins. We could repartition the inner cargo bay for another three, maybe rent out the wardroom."

"What about that locked room?" Alaric asked.

"No."

"What's in there?"

"Systems vital to me," Cassii snapped. "Forget about it."

"Contact Tuck, see if he's got any passengers needing passage between here and Scrics."

"Why Scrics?"

"Quick run, we could get back before the new cargo arrives."

"We'd lose our spot and our contract expires when we leave."

He froze mid-step and cursed. He blushed at the dome. "Sorry, Cassii, I know, language."

"Perhaps it's occasionally warranted. Cargo's too close anyway."

A retort sprang to his mind, but he set it aside. "Could we offer a transport contract that brings them aboard now with the understanding that we depart once out of cloth?"

"Hot showers, clean facilities and fresh food? We'll find passengers amenable to that."

"Can we feed that many?"

"We'll manage."

"Do it. We need them before Manc apologizes."

"So take my time."

He laughed. "What's our cargo status?"

"Eighty-three percent exhausted. Freighters estimated a tynmiir out at last transit."

A tynmiir more and he'd have cleaned up.

He beamed up at her. "You're the best. Collect those refugee fees and prep Manc's payment—every credit we can spare."

"He wasn't very nice to you."

Alaric took a deep breath. "We have to pay him one way or another. The more we give him, the better terms we part on."

Alaric crossed to the doorway. Cara leapt down and wedged herself between him and the door. She gazed up at him, ears forward and tail wagging.

He scratched her ears and keyed the door open.

Manc waited in the doorway.

Alaric cursed inwardly. *He's going to apologize.* He examined Manc's posture. *Never mind.*

"My account is still empty, Captain."

"This math stuff is hard for us primitives."

"Cut the crap. You ought to be swimming in credits by now," Manc said. "Why're you holding out on me?"

"You chose option one," Alaric said.

"You've got to be kidding me."

Alaric stepped around him and headed for the cargo bay controls. Manc trailed him with Cara on their heels.

"I'm not apologizing to you."

Alaric chewed his lip, fiddling with controls looking for an ideal arrangement for additional passengers.

Manc grabbed him and flipped him around. "Did you hear—"

A deep, menacing growl escaped Cara's throat. She bared her teeth. She glare practically dared Manc to hurt Alaric.

Manc let Alaric go and stepped back, hands raised.

Alaric scratch behind her ears. "Easy, girl."

Cara wagged her tail.

"It's been fun, kid, and all kinds of comfy, but it's time for me to leave you and sour circuits. Just pay me so I can go."

Alaric met his gaze. *What the hell do I say?*

"Why do you even want me to stay? I used you, kid. Don't you understand that? There're no friends, no family out here in the black. Everyone's just looking out for themselves."

"Tyne told me. She also said you'd turn on me, but only once the contract was complete."

"Never listen to a thing she says. I'm not anything like that bitch."

Alaric's brows rose. "Never did get that story."

"Never going to either."

Alaric shrugged and resumed adjusting cargo partitions. "Don't care."

49

WELCOMING ABOARD TROUBLE

Cassii finished her magic before Manc dredged up an apology. It'd contained more anger than contrition, but Alaric let it go, sad and relieved to see Manc leave.

Cassiopeia's lounge had seen little use since Alaric found himself aboard. Seeing it filled with grateful faces seemed surreal, especially since each waited for him to speak.

What would it be like to have a full crew? Like a family despite Manc's and Tyne's claims?

"Welcome aboard Cassiopeia. I'm Captain Ignaree. You've all spoken with my first mate and AI, Cassii," he fidgeted with his hands, finally folding them behind his back. "We're not leaving right away like most ships, but we aren't loaded to bursting either."

Alaric gestured at the green dome overhead. "Cassii'll answer your questions regarding food, showers, laundering facilities, etc. I understand Cassii hired some of you to work the clothing tent. I look forward to helping Inhera alongside you.

"As you may know, we're having problems with one of the assemblers, but you'll be paid to be on hand anyway until it's fixed. Any questions?"

No one spoke.

Alaric swallowed hard, forging on. "We've got some off-limits areas. They're typically kept secure, but being a working ship Cassii will advise you if you wander into one. We've still got a lot of cloth to distribute, so relax and enjoy your stay aboard."

The refugees filed out. Cassii'd found three families with children delighted to have Cara partially to themselves. She'd hired out to several couples. A single man and woman berthed in individual partitioned cargo bays.

All together their passage fees had sent Manc off paid current.

A woman approached Alaric. “Captain?”

“Yes?” Cassii spoke into his ear. “Madame Crisile?”

“Lynnie, please.”

Alaric inclined his head. “Lynnie. Something I can do for you?”

“When will we depart?” she asked.

“I've survived a disaster myself, and understand your desire to escape reminders of it. Unfortunately, it'll take several tynmiir to exhaust our cloth supply.”

She pouted, batting her eyelashes. “Couldn't you arrange a sooner departure?”

“Afraid not.”

She smiled, shrugged and strolled away.

“The nerve of some people,” a tall man said.

“Duva Frex,” Cassii informed.

“Like I told her, Mr. Frex, I empathize.”

“Well, my wife and I would never employ such tactics. We wouldn't try leveraging the importance my wife's uncle, Magistrate Elkner on Scrics Three, or additional credits to gain specialized treatment.”

Wow, subtle insinuation much?

<Some people have an inflated self-worth, young master. Like explosives, you must learn to defuse them without setting them off.>

Alaric patted Frex's shoulder. “I appreciate that.”

Frex blinked.

Alaric swept past him, down the hall and through the secured bridge doors.

“Unbelievable species,” Cassii said.

Alaric chuckled. “Too used to getting his way. Reminds me of a computer I know.”

“You know this how?”

“You're not exactly—”

“Not me, primitive.”

“Oh. I remember someone teaching me....”

"Alaric?"

He chewed his lip. "For a moment, I almost remembered his name...."

Duva Frex and his plump wife waylaid Alaric on his way outside. "Captain Ignaree, why haven't we departed yet?"

"Mind your tone, Duva," she said. "Surely there's a reason for this delay."

"He's milking every credit," Frex said. "As if someone'd request a washcloth."

"Try bandages." Alaric breathed deeply and counted to ten. "We haven't exhausted our cloth supply. We're not leaving yet."

Frex purpled. "I may have mentioned—"

"No doubt a few dozen times," Alaric added over him.

"—uncle of immense importance. He'll be most displeased—"

Alaric tuned him out. *If I let him go long enough he's got to pass out from lack of oxygen, doesn't he?*

Frex stopped for breath.

"I survived a similar cataclysm, Mister Frex. Those people, your people—"

Frex snorted.

Alaric inhaled. "*Your* people need fresh clothing, blankets, bandages. I'm not leaving until I've helped all I can."

"Don't pretend high ideals, you're a credit-grubbing opportunist—"

"Duva!" Ester said. "There's no call for such accusations."

Alaric reddened. "I offered to give away my cloth for free."

"Sure you did," Frex said.

"He did," Cassii said. "Would've bankrupted us if the Protectorate Coordinator hadn't chosen to buy it as part of their relief efforts."

Ester's eyes softened.

"Ask Commander Tuck if you don't believe us," Alaric said.

"So what, you're milking the Protectorate teat instead of sucking poor refugees dry. We paid you for passage—"

Alaric stood straight, shoulders squared. "We have an agreement. I've fed and housed you as my part. If you're no longer satisfied with our deal, I'll refund your whole passage price."

"I've lost precious time," Frex said.

"And consumed food, power and space," Alaric countered. "Surely someone as important as you can find suitable transport with your refunded credits."

"I expect to be compensated for my lost time. Your swill hardly qualifies," Frex said.

"Now, Duva."

Every controlled word cost Alaric shreds of will. "I'm offering a refund I needn't offer, Mr. Frex. I'm trying to be nice. You're the one balking at our contract—"

"That's not good enough!"

Alaric inclined his head to Missus Frex. "Please inform me if you'd like your luggage debarked."

He headed for the cargo bay.

"This isn't over," Frex said.

Alaric spun and advanced until he was nose to chin with the taller Inheran.

Cassii tone urged caution. "Alaric."

He licked his lips. "May I ask how much you feel our delayed departure time is worth?"

Frex shifted to regain personal space. His smile turned wolfish. "Six times our passage price."

Alaric burst out laughing.

Frex scowled.

"I'd probably have accommodated a reasonable request to ensure goodwill." He inclined his head at Missus Frex. "Always a pleasure, ma'am."

"Where do you think you're going?" Frex asked. "We're not done negotiating."

Alaric's grin turned mischievous. "I've got to supervise delivery of our two full cargo pods—you know, in case someone wanted more than just a bandage."

Alaric strode away. *Here it comes.*

No chiding comments came over his comm.

Nothing? Huh, she's as hard to predict as a real woman.

<Says the voice of experience.>

Cara met him in the cargo bay. She circled him twice, ran to the exit then returned.

"Status, Cassii?"

"First pod's almost down, hurry."

Alaric opened the bay.

Cara raced out the moment she could squeeze through. Knowing little more than shipboard life, the outdoors offered her adventures in sniffing. Her nose went into immediate overdrive, snuffling and sniffling as if to power her tail. Children called her from all around the lot. Their attention worsened her easily distracted obedience.

He followed, inclining his head to his worker passengers. They gazed skyward, understanding as his pods descended why they hadn't departed when the first pod's cloth supply dwindled to almost useless.

I can always offer them the same deal I did Frex. Manc's gone and I've got more than enough credits.

"Cara, come here," He glanced upward. "Cara, come!"

An uneasy feeling wrung his gut like a dishrag. The pods made a controlled, but rapid descent wrapped in a tractor beam. He sprinted forward.

"Alaric, stop. Stop! It'll crush you!"

He ignored Cassii, racing toward the puppy. *The captain can't see her.*

Cara, alerted to being chased, darted this way and that without clearing the danger zone. She circled her yelling master, ears perked in doggie delight.

The pods lowered, moments from flattening his oblivious dog.

Alaric's thundering pulse drowned Cassii's shouts. His stomach jumped ship meters ago, fleeing descending doom.

The puppy dodged his angry grip, tongue lolling and oblivious to his panic.

His workers cried out.

His gaze shot upward. His heart stopped, possibly joining his mutinous stomach. Alaric fled the puppy, calling encouragements. Cara chased, but his inspiration arrived too late.

Pod shadows fell over her. She froze. Her ears pressed flat to her head, and her tail tucked tight. She bolted the wrong way.

"Alaric, no!"

Passengers shouted equally dire warnings and objections.

He dove, catching her last instant of hesitation. He hurled her the other way as hard as he could. The awkward missile tumbled haphazardly, fell wrong and howled.

A pod struck Alaric's head, sending him prone and reeling. He rolled like a mad dervish, barely ahead of the curved metal tombstone.

Dust and metal filled his vision.

Workers rushed forward, terrified for their ferryman. He waved them off, crawling to the crying puppy. "I'm fine."

His head throbbed rebuttal. *Ugh, kind of used to that.*

Cara squeezed her eyes shut with each cry. They fixed on his face between, blaming him for her pain.

Guilt drove bile from his gut. He reached for her.

A combined cry and snarl escaped her. She snapped at him.

Alaric jerked back. "Cassii—"

"Stupid, suicidal, devolved...what kind of insane, brain-dead moronic—"

"Shut up."

"You could've been killed! It's just a dumb animal."

"And you're just a dumb computer. Get her a doctor immediately."

"Doctor?"

"A veterinarian, a nurse, hedrin I'll take a witch doctor, just get them now."

"What about you?"

Alaric rubbed his head. "No worse than usual."

Reddish brown mud painted her golden coat, its source dripping slowly. He cursed to impress even Manc. "Where's that doctor?"

"Arranging it now."

Alaric wanted to rip someone's head off. *Except ripping off my own head isn't real useful.*

He cooed. "It's okay, Cara. It'll be okay, girl."

Cara cried.

Cassii watched them.

Alaric paced outside his cabin, limping from a twisted ankle. He'd refused treatment until the animal had been tended. A yellowish-brown Elcu treated the injured animal inside his cabin.

One leg bone protruded through blood-matted fur. She'd bitten the doctor twice, not that the amorph seemed to notice. Her snarls continued between attempts to lick its taste from her mouth.

He and the animal had been aboard for more cycles than it was worth to count. She couldn't find a logical pattern to him.

He'd ordered Manc paid in full with a bonus and the bounty for the fighter Alaric'd personally captured.

He refused to converse.

He refused to set up the new assemblers.

He refused medical treatment.

He limped up and down the corridor in obvious pain, gnawing his lip like a dog worrying a bone.

He'd taken on passengers, some better spaced than accommodated, to let Shepherd out of his contract early. Then he mourned Shepherd's absence.

Cassii wished she had a head to shake.

While most of his actions remained unfathomable, insulting her in time of panic her programs understood. She knew the animal was the only organic friend remaining—at least without hiring one. She couldn't deny her share of fault in his angry outbursts.

She ran a minor diagnostic, trying to determine when years of Braxis, pirates, and demanding crews had patched her program with its current jaded iteration.

Alaric and Alaric, bookends of kindness in a long deeply unsatisfactory career.

This Alaric was satisfactory.

He worked hard, made hard choices. They flourished.

An element of chance outside projected possibility had worked in his favor, but such calculations stole little from his accomplishments.

Despite probability, his luck held. Commander Tuck sold them dyes discovered elsewhere on planet at a considerable discount. He'd followed this generosity by insisting they raise the price of dyed clothing.

Over and over, results defied calculated probability.

The matter of his Scrics Three jaunt continued logical defiance. He'd left happy as any adolescent to a place where credits afforded indulgence in every disgusting fantasy a young male could imagine. He'd bought someone to listen.

He'd refused a credit line.

It'd taken considerable badgering on her part to convince him to take a loan out to capitalize as fully as reasonable on their current venture.

He refused to brag about his Twin Djinns adventure. He'd refused to answer Shepherd's question or even offer a sly grin.

Shepherd's questioning seemed to upset Alaric. It'd turned him surly instead, baffling herself too.

There had to be a pattern to his logic.

She scanned and rescanned her databanks. The inconclusive scans didn't deter her suspicion that Alaric was formulating some course of action.

Choosing to continue his refugee transport to Scrics bore hallmarks of Alaric's oblique misdirecting approach to a goal—or he's eviarchtracl insane.

She considered his sanity, again wishing for a head to shake. Simple primitive he appeared—a miscalculation trap.

Alaric's cabin door opened.

She shifted primary processing to him without abandoning her theorizing.

Elcu combined rolling and oozing as physical motivators. Subtle micro-pseudopod extension and retraction facilitated transit without loss of its spherical shape.

Alaric faced it. "Cassii?"

"Here."

Pops, hisses, and slurping noises exited the side nearest Alaric.

"Cara will recover in time." Cassii listened and continued. "It'd generally prescribe a regeneration sling with automated anesthetic delivery..."

"But?" Alaric asked.

"I'm unsure of its dialect, but it seems to be comparing local conditions with a swamp region on its home planet." Cassii laughed. "Swamp's winning."

More slurps and hisses.

"We need to keep Cara still and manually administer pain killers."

"How?"

"I'll take care of her, Alaric. It might be short on advanced pain killers, but we're stocked."

Pops and slurps.

"No, we don't have any of that."

Alaric watched the conversation go back and forth.

Hisses.

"No."

Hissed and pops.

"Can't spare any."

A flatulent sound escaped the amorph. It pushed its way past Alaric, actually making physical contact. Alaric jerked back.

"What the hedrin?"

"It's leaving," Cassii said.

"It's vibrating, gave me a shock too."

"It's angry. I refused to sell it our meds."

Alaric chewed his lip. "Give it a third. It helped Cara, that's the least we can do."

Unfathomable.

50

HEROISM

Alaric fetched the med probe, impatient with its speed. Several child passengers hovered around his open doorway, watching the puppy.

The drugs stole her whimpers. She slept.

Alaric stood over her, reluctant to leave. *Work to do.*

He re-energized the existing assemblers and set up the others.

The crowds returned at first sign of activity.

Alaric caught the attention of a wandering soldier. "Sergeant?"

"Yes, Captain Ignaree?"

"We're opening back up, four lines instead of two."

"Do you require security?"

"Hasn't been bad since the initial rush, just wanted your people aware."

The soldier nodded. "Understood."

Alaric smiled. "We've got hot food onboard if you or your guys need a quick break."

"Captain." The Sergeant snapped off a salute. "If you were a Protectorate officer with that kind of thinking, the men'd treat you better than an admiral."

Alaric smirked. "Food's not that good."

"You've never eaten disaster field rations."

The taste of rotting, roasted Marvy flashed across his tongue. He swallowed back nausea. "No, I've had worse."

Alaric returned to the pavilion and seated himself on a crate at its rear. He marveled at the intricate dance of workers and cloth resulting in refugees with smiles.

"What do you think?"

"We should forget about these passengers."

"What now?"

"I weary of committing even minimal resources to Frex and his badgering."

Alaric picked up a forgotten cup and turned it in his hands. He sighed. "We need to fulfill our contracts."

"Do we have to?"

"You know we do. If we're trading long term we need to build a good reputation."

"Aren't we returning to Earth?"

His throat constricted. "Soon, I hope, but let's not jinx it."

She sounded frustrated. "I guess we're merchants then."

He frowned. ""What's the matter? Haven't I proven myself?"

"You mean by swiping credits from your contractors so you could make more credits rather than paying him properly?"

"I paid him extra."

"And gave away valuable medicine. The former was shrewd, your latter choice makes me question your suitability as a merchant."

"What's got you testy?"

"I'm not enthused about being a legal pirate."

I forgot. She wants to be a royal courier again. He sighed. *I've no idea how to make that happen.*

"How's Cara?"

"Sleeping like a puppy."

After several tynmiir working together to help the Inherans, his passengers started feeling like a family—complete with disapproving, never-satisfied Uncle Frex. He reluctantly offered them the same deal for a full refund. No one chose to go.

Duva Frex notwithstanding, peaceful tynmiir helping the needy became warm, lasting memories. But each night after their family dinner, Jesse, El and Eryss haunted him. They took turns with Silv and Burr, Braxis and Tyne, orange collars, Welorin drones, and snatchers.

Four assemblers sped clothing distribution. Tuck moved people in and out of the area to utilize their services. Night and day, he augmented his working passengers with extras.

An assembler broke down just before they exhausted the cloth. Alaric worked on it midnight to dawn, ensuring it operational for turn over to Tuck.

Alaric rubbed his eyes. "There they are. Thank you for everything."

"No more pods on the way?" Tuck asked.

Alaric reddened.

Tuck laughed. "Nothing says nice guys can't be shrewd businessmen."

"I need to take these people to Scrics," Alaric said.

"Could've hired a transport and kept at it."

"Our contract says I'll take them."

"And you want to keep your word." Tuck clapped his shoulder. "Hope to see you again, Captain. Safe flying."

Alaric offered a small container. "For your men. Thank them for me."

Tuck glanced inside. "What's this?"

"Where I come from they're called campaign patches." He pointed to a new patch attached to his pilot's jacket. "To remember our victory."

Tuck surveyed their surroundings. "Don't know about victory, but it's a better place than when you arrived."

"Better dressed at least," Alaric smiled. His last look at Inhera's horizon filled him with melancholy. *Good luck, Inhera. Your people are amazing.*

"Captain Ignaree!"

Alaric glanced toward Duva Frex. *Most of them.*

"Get aboard, Mister Frex. It's time to leave."

"Finally."

"Cassii, tell everyone?"

"Can't we leave him?" Cassii asked through his comm.

"His wife might miss him."

"She might bless you."

Alaric snorted and wove through Cassiopeia to her bridge. His hands danced from control to control with only small hesitations. He glanced from display to display, nodding at each green indicator.

He beamed. "System check complete. Ready to launch."

"I could've done that in milli."

"You insisted I needed training. Training includes practice."

"Planetary launches can be tricky. We don't make planet fall often. You shouldn't waste the training opportunity."

"Yet you complain about my speed."

"Don't want that primitive head too big for your environment suit."

"Tricky," he smiled. "Let's see about that."

Before she could respond, he thumbed launch boosters. Cassiopeia leapt up, drifted a hair starboard and continued skyward. The ship's nose rotated upward to match the nacelle orientation—though technically the nacelles rotated, not the ship.

He checked everything aligned and pushed thrust to full. "Climbing...climbing...almost there."

"Yes, we're climbing. How delightfully obvious of you."

"Free of the atmosphere," Alaric hesitated, "now!"

He twisted the controls. Cassiopeia spiraled through a loose barrel roll.

"What was that for?"

"Fun. Doing it atmo would've upset the Frexs."

"At a minimum."

Stars outnumbered orbiting relief ships, but it seemed a close thing. Fighters played an elaborate game of laser tag, chasing each other through the spaces between.

"Course: Inhera-Ibis gate. Please update itinerary with the nearest PCAS satellite."

"Already done."

"What if I'd changed my mind, huh? What if I wanted to take the scenic route?"

"Some sewers only have one entrance."

Alaric glanced up at the dome. Wrinkles creased his forehead. "Scrics has a second KIOSC."

"Yes, toward Yanu and Pelom with no exits. It's an intergalactic box canyon."

Alaric shrugged. "I'm going to check on Cara."

"She's visible on your right-hand monitor."

"Can't pet the screen, well, I could... but she wouldn't enjoy it. Keep the ship going straight, would you?"

Passengers clogged the passageways despite his instruction to strap in for launch.

Of course, launch is over. Just clear sailing through empty stellar reaches.

He smiled at them.

"Captain Ignaree!"

His smile faltered. "Yes, Mister Frex?"

"These dining conditions are unacceptable now that we're underway."

"How so?"

"You've brought families aboard, with children."

"Hence family rather than couple, though a couple can be—"

"Children are not conducive to good digestion."

His brow rose. "Don't eat them?"

"Captain Ignaree, children are noisy."

"So are you."

Frex scowled.

"I've seen no evidence their parents aren't keeping them in hand."

"They make a token effort, but considering what we've put up with our passage affords us the right to dine without such unpleasantness."

The hall felt warm. "Every berth was equally priced."

"Precisely. I paid more per person, entitling us—"

"I'll set up a table in the cargo bay."

Frex beamed. "That'll suit them perfectly."

"I doubt they'd be so crass as to verbalize their feelings about you dining in the cargo hold."

"Me?"

"You wanted private dining," Alaric smiled. "Excuse me, I need to setup your private dining room before dinner."

Frex spluttered.

Alaric strode aft. Cassii's lowered voice followed dome to dome. "Antagonizing him won't improve things."

"Didn't entertain you either, I'll bet."

"We're not talking about me."

"Right," Alaric punched up the partition controls, raising sections of floor to serve as table and benches. "I'm not punishing my passengers so he can punish me without detractors."

"Alaric."

He glared. "If he doesn't like it, he can eat from the dispenser in his room."

Alaric reviewed the family style meal, checking it against Inheran dietary needs before laying the hearty if simple meal out. He set the table for everyone aboard.

Everyone attended.

Mister Frex glowered at Alaric throughout, but Missus Frex delighted at the boisterous activity around her.

Conversations spread the table, dwindled, shifted positions and grew again. Time aboard lent the refugees an odd sense of family.

Alaric smiled, saying little. He followed the conversations, keeping his food and drink out of line with Frex's fermenting glare. He plumbed his mind, searching for memories triggered through familiarity.

He found none, no taunting siblings, no parent's mock scolding that failed to reach their eyes.

His failed mining left empty holes in him despite the large meal.

He returned to the present. Sleepy faces leaned against parents. Missus Frex hung on stories of childhood mischief and children's accomplishments. Mister Frex attempted flight which she forbid.

As was his custom, when the leftover food had gone untouched long enough, Alaric rose. He scrapped the nearest serving dish into a disposal shoot and deposited it into another slot for cleaning. Several wives and an eldest daughter named Jeslynn rose and gathered plates.

Jeslynn handed him one.

"Thank you."

He caught her sappy grin.

Great, she's got a crush. That's all I need, another woman confusing me or making me feel guilty.

<What, suddenly three's your limit, princess?>

"Thank you all, but you're guests. Please sit and relax."

"Shouldn't you have a crew for menial tasks?" Frex asked.

"I don't mind getting my hands dirty."

"But why aren't there other hands aboard?" Frex asked.

"Long story, but considering you're berthing in a senior crew cabin, count your lucky stars."

Frex scowled. "So they left you, or you got them killed."

"Duva!" Ester hissed.

Alaric straightened. "I've never had a crew excepting a single escort pilot."

Mention of Manc augmented his digestion with live eels.

Every eye followed them.

"My room contains vestiges of some ill-fated passenger or crewman," Frex said. "Their fate concerns me, lest I share it."

"I stole this ship—"

"From the pirates who'd stolen me from his uncle," Cassii interrupted.

Alaric fetched the next dish, smiling over it at them all. "A short time ago I was marooned on a backwater world you've probably never heard of. Hurt, starving and running for my life..." He took a breath, surprised by the ache in his chest swelling as he thought back about losing El, Jesse, and his home.

Gasps circulated the table. Every passenger leaned toward him.

"There he was," Cassii said. "Alone and half-starved on a far out border world. He raided a camp of savage slavers, trying to rescue the love of his life."

Their attention switched between him and her dome. Alaric opened his mouth, but Cassii didn't let him get a word in edgewise.

"They chased him, setting murderous security drones loose on him. He wove and dodged, running and fighting across the cluttered landscape."

"Did you rescue your love?" Jeslynn asked.

Alaric's face fell. "No, not yet."

"Dispirited but determined, Alaric knew the pirates who'd stolen me were back, raiding the planet once more, but in numbers he could never hope to assail."

"What did he do?" another wide-eyed Inheran youth asked.

"Oh, yes," Frex replied in a dry tone. "Do tell."

Ester swatted him. "Hush, Duva. What *did* you do?"

Alaric opened his mouth.

"He turned his flight, antagonizing his pursuers enough to keep their savage little brains enraged," Cassii said. "He sprinted into the pirate camp, attacking my crew. Braxis and his raiders thought Alaric's pursuers part of the assault."

Jeslynn beamed at Alaric. "You tricked them into fighting one another."

"Alaric bolted into me, fighting both sides from my hatchway. I recognized him at once and knew my liberation at hand. I launched, turning my damaged weapons on pirates and kidnappers."

"So you escaped them and went back for the girl," A man said.

Alaric shook his head. "Welorin—"

"Welorin?! In Protectorate space?" Duva Frex threw his hands into the air. "Impossible."

Alaric tried to reply.

"Braxis had made a deal with the Welorin," Cassii said. "He traded them a stolen KIOSC transponder code in exchange for looting rights."

Frex snorted. "Transponder codes can't be stolen."

Ester hushed him.

"What happened with the Welorin?" Lynnie asked.

"We went back to the slaver's camp, but Braxis commed the Welorin, told them we'd stolen his ship," Cassii said. "We fought squadrons of fighters, but I was already damaged. We were forced to run."

Jeslynn turned watery eyes on Alaric. "What happened to her?"

Alaric glowered at Cassii's dome. When she didn't answer for him, he frowned at Jeslynn. "I don't know. I'm free, but she's still back there. That's why we're traders. Cassii was a great ship when my uncle owned her. If we can rebuild and repair what the pirates scavenged, I can go back for her."

Ester patted his hand. "Don't give up. You'll succeed."

He smiled at her.

"Sure he will," Frex scowled. "Right after he passes his hat for donations."

Jeslynn brightened. "That's a good idea."

Alaric froze. "No. Thank you, but no. You've already lost enough."

"He's already wasted plenty of our time profiting on our misery," Frex said.

"Duva, that's quite enough."

Alaric forced a smile. "Dessert anyone?"

51

ENDINGS

Cassiopeia emerged from the Ibin-Uldira gate into total chaos.

Static blared from ship speakers, resolving into an alert. "Uldira-Ibin gate control to PCAS Cassiopeia, alert status seven. PCAS ship in distress. Return to origination system and await further instructions from PCAS authorized personnel. This is an automated alert. Please comply."

"What the hedrin?" Alaric bolted from bed, throwing his blanket over top of Cara. "Cassii, report."

Cara whined.

"Pirate assault in progress just outside beacon range," Cassii said. "Transiting back to Ibin space."

Alaric flipped the blankets off the Labrador. Her wagging tail signaled her thanks.

"Is it Tyne?" He shoved his legs into pants and raced barefoot for the bridge.

"Do I care?"

Cara barked excitedly, but her restraining bed kept her from chasing after.

"Hold station. I'm on my way."

Alaric dodged passengers and questions. He rounded a corner, almost colliding with Mister Frex. The self-important Inheran sucked in breath.

Alaric darted around him before he could use it.

"Bridge door open," Alaric raced up the stairs.

He jumped into the command chair, hands flying across controls and eyes dancing from screen to screen. Tactical holograms rose to his summons.

A cargo tug blocked a transport liner from retreating into beacon range. Fighters buzzed the liner. Starfish-shaped craft like those used in the Feirin assault—starclaws—clung to the liner's hull. Other ships sized between fighters and the tug latched onto the liner's docking ports. Mechanical arms on their front locked onto the liner's frame like huge ticks. Their rear resembled a twelve cylinder revolver. They rotated a full rotation slowly then released the liner. Their arms added their loaded, hexagonal capsules into the growing cluster interlocked behind the tug. Tractor beams shot out to free-floating empties, bringing them into formation as the ships sped back to the liner.

A phantom collar constricted around his throat, remembered pain burning through him. Spoiled Marvy slathered his tongue, summoning bile through his strangled throat. His hands shook.

Fearmonger nightmares flashed through the red haze across his eyes.

Almost fearful warning suffused Cassii's voice. "Alaric...."

El and Jesse flashed across his mind's eye, shivering, emaciated and terrified amidst a ruined landscape ringed by feasters, drones, and snatchers. Burr and Silv taunted him across lightyears.

His volcanic fury transformed to permafrost in a single heartbeat. One word escaped in a hoarse whisper. "Slavers."

"Transiting to Ibin."

"Override." He growled. "Status on the liner."

"Engines gone. Hull's ripped in several places. Energy readings minimal and dwindling," Cassii said. "We need to get clear."

"They're dying?"

Alaric's movements snapped forward with military precision. His fingers glided over controls, adjusting power level balances with barely a glance. Weapon checks he'd practiced only once flashed by, completed in moments.

Her tone turned bitter. "Dead, dying or lucky enough to be captured."

"What's going on?" Mister Frex asked.

"Not now, Frex, return to your cabin," Alaric snapped. "Cassii, how many fighters left?"

"Why aren't we transiting to Ibin?" Frex demanded.

"Two liner escorts fighting to escape. Counting a dozen Corollas including those chasing the escorts," Cassii said.

"Check my settings, Cassii."

"Are you mad?!" Frex asked. "You've got responsibilities to your passengers. You can't just—"

Alaric leapt from his seat and pointed out the viewport. Every inch including his voice shook. "Those bastards are stealing lives, Frex. They're murdering your people. Enslaving *your people.*"

"Better them than me."

Alaric's fist shot forward, but he yanked it to a halt just short of Frex's cowering face. "Get off my bridge."

"You have no right to endanger—"

Alaric whipped a pistol from its holster and pressed it under Frex's chin. "Get. The Hedrin. Off. My. Bridge!"

Frex's limited color drained away. He stumbled backward, barely avoiding a tumble down the stairs with a hasty grab of its railing.

Alaric slammed the bridge door controls. It locked with three beeps.

"Give me one hundred twenty percent weapon power."

"He's right, Alaric. We have to transit."

"Route weapons to my control."

"Are you listening to me? There're families aboard."

He leapt to his feet pointing. "There are families right there. They're being torn apart, tortured..." his voice broke. "...collared."

"We're only lightly armed."

"Project beacon ranges on tactical."

Every control and hologram on the bridge fell dark except her amber lit dome. "Listen to me!"

Alaric glared, seething silently.

"Even *if* you rescue every one of them and we survive, we're going to be damaged. Your temper is going to cost us all the progress we've made. Think of El."

"El's a slave. She's *living* that fate, and she'd hate me if I let this happen."

"Even if it costs the lives of everyone aboard?" Cassii asked. "Abandon this foolishness. You can live with her hatred."

"I couldn't live with mine."

"Better that than murder El by destroying us on a hopeless crusade."

Alaric chewed his lip, gut knotted around a black hole of absolute zero. *Is it hopeless? Am I throwing away everything we've accomplished?*

<A man is responsible for what he can and cannot do, son, no more, no less.>

He stared at the Corollas ships, harvesting living beings for credits to blow at Twin Djinns or places like it.

<Don't be mad, handsome. It's just business.>

What kind of hell awaits them if I just fly away?

<I can force them to do anything I want, Maggot. I'm in control.>

What kind of hell awaits me if I don't?

<Go along to get along, Kid.>

His cold reignited. He roared at the dome. "No. I won't let this happen. El's one woman. She'd understand."

"Please, Alaric, for your own sake if no one else's, don't do this."

"I'm ordering you. Give me weapon control."

"Weapon control routed to command chair," Cassii's voice escaped the dome mechanical and somehow hollow. "Alaric, before you do this—"

"I'm not changing my mind."

"Just look at the fighters chasing down their escorts."

Alaric flipped the display and magnified the image. His stomach dropped to the floor, and his heart leapt into his throat. "It can't be."

"I've confirmed the registry," Cassii said.

"I can't believe it. I won't. Manc'd never side with slavers."

<Our contract's the only thing that matters, handsome.>

"But...he's my friend."

<You'll know when you end up on the other end of his hire.>

52

BETRAYAL

Alaric keyed the ship's announcement system. "A refugee liner just outside beacon perimeter is under attack and transmitting a distress signal. In accordance with Protectorate regulation CR44214, we're moving to assist. Secure yourselves."

"Alaric, that regulation mostly applies to official couriers."

"Are you with me or not?"

"Not really," Cassii said. "People might die. *You* might die, and I don't want to fall into Corollas hands."

Hollowness ached within him. Despair joined hurt and Manc's betrayal from enslaving the gentle Inherans.

"Why give me weapon control?"

"My captain ordered me," Cassii said. "But you asked if I was with you. I'd rather not be. Can't we let it go? Just this once?"

He threw his hands up. "Sure. Let's stand by just once, let people's lives get stolen just once. We'll save the next batch, except organics are lazy. You know that. Umoids rationalize like no other being. Next time, something else'll make retreat seem reasonable. Just one more time, and once more until we're out of control down a slippery slope of compromise and self-interest."

"We're not armed for this, Alaric. Stay alive to fight another cycle."

"Go along to get along," Alaric shot back. "Stand by so long as evil is done to others."

"Evil? Isn't that a bit much?"

His anger paced, a caged predator seething to sink teeth into the Corollas. "You're right. Slavery and torture aren't evil. *They're just business.*"

"You're not the universe's savior."

"No one is," Alaric said. "That's the problem."

Her tone softened. "Alaric. They hurt you. I know. I've heard you cry out in your sleep. You've got a huge heart, but that's the problem. You're going to have to kill those pirates—"

"Better them than those slaves."

"All of them, Alaric, even Shepherd."

Too much confusion. Too much emotion. It crashed into him like waves beating the shore. *Walk away or kill Manc.*

He stared at holographic ships stealing holographic lives, murdering any holographic soul that stood in their way.

Holograms aren't real. Manc is. He taught me, fought with me. Tears streaked Alaric's cheeks. *He called me his little brother.*

He stared at the holograms, going about their business as if he wasn't floating inside the beacon perimeter. Fighters drifted lazily between him and the tug, watchful but unable to reach him. As long as he stood by he remained inconsequential.

The liner's distress signal died.

People are dying, not holograms.

"Manc chose his fate," Alaric shoved thrusters to full. Echoing Manc's words ripped something inside him. "There's no family out here in the black."

Cassiopeia bolted out of beacon range.

Corollas starfighters shot forward to intercept. Starclaws unlatched from the liner, abandoning their disabling to deal with him. Loaders continued their theft.

He flew them into a firestorm, nacelles twitching this way and that. Violet pulsar blasts answered back.

A photon bolt slammed into the hull beneath command. A panel exploded behind his chair, singing his neck hair.

"Move faster. We're a big target."

Alaric destroyed a raven. "I'm trying, but if I don't take them out we're in trouble."

"Trouble doesn't begin to cover *this.* Watch it, they're trying to get in behind."

Cassiopeia banked right so hard that she nearly completed the reverse in its starting space. Alaric's hands jerked flight controls, and thumbs flicked target locks from ship to ship, firing left and right pulsar cannons at separate targets.

"Concentrate fire," Cassii said. "Don't scratch a bunch of them, make kills."

An asp interceptor lit space around them with its fireball.

"Uh huh."

"Lucky shot."

Laser blasts carved jagged lines across their starboard nacelle. Another photon bolt caught their aft corner. Cassiopeia shook and shuttered.

"Damn these pilots are good."

"Ravens," Cassii said. "Either you fly like a dervish, or you get splattered."

Alaric bit his lip. "You fly. I'll shoot."

"Smart boy."

Cassiopeia banked toward the KIOSC and rocketed toward its beacons. Under Cassii's control, the ship dodged faster, shifting pylons and nacelles to keep them clear of fire.

"Damn it, Cassii, we're not retreating."

"*Language.*"

The ship flipped end over end, offering the widest targeting profile for a few moments. Her nacelles canted, sending her into a tight spiral that brought a raven and a starclaw into Alaric's sights.

He spread their atoms across eternity.

Loaders abandoned their work and joined the assault.

Alaric glanced at the edge of their tactical. The liner escorts led Manc on a merry chase, but he'd taken one down and only had to destroy the second so he could return.

Cassiopeia dodged in and out of the fighters. Several Corollas learned her maneuvering capabilities the hard way, but those left didn't ignore the lesson. They flew at her in pairs, slamming them with weapon fire from every angle.

She flipped around again, but the moment they adapted, she flipped again and banked hard toward the tug.

"What are you doing?" Alaric leaned right, as he could will pulsar fire to curve into the fighters cutting across their nose.

"I'm using the tug for cover."

"What about the people?" Another blast slammed into Cassiopeia, throwing Alaric from his seat.

"I'll do what I can," she said. "Watch your fire."

He leapt back into his chair and grinned. "Right, thanks for the lesson, boys."

He raked their tether with pulsar fire, cutting free their catch.

"Don't do that again," Cassii said.

"Why not?"

"You'll force me to re-evaluate your intelligence."

He chuckled. "Might blow a processor."

Alaric squeezed triggers and leaned left. His targets slipped just ahead and left of his fire.

"Shepherd's clear."

He glanced at toward the hologram's edge and cursed. She echoed his sentiments, aborting his apology.

"Take us around left and over the tug, put me behind that pair."

She did.

He clipped one fighter's engines. Thrust split out the original and new holes. It spun wildly, forcing the second fighter dead into Alaric's sights.

He didn't miss.

"Incoming transmission."

"Do I want to take it?"

"It's Shepherd."

A chuckle escaped his lip pinning bite. "So, no."

"He might offer to surrender."

"More likely offering free slave collar trials."

"One way to find out," she said.

"What the hedrin are you thinking, kid?"

"Right now? That I shouldn't have taken this call."

"Stars, kid, you didn't just step into it, you're drowning."

Heat filled him. "You're the one killing innocents, enslaving helpless refugees."

"Looks like you are too from these bio scans," Manc said. "Please tell me you're not dumb enough to attack a superior force with passengers aboard."

"Wouldn't want them to lack for entertainment."

"You're not funny, junior. Transit out of here while you still can."

"Stand down, Manc. I don't want to kill you."

"I stand corrected," Manc said.

"Full reverse, forty-five degree descent, body plane static," Alaric snapped.

Cassii followed suit, throwing him forward in his command chair. Their pursuers shot by above.

"Flip the nacelles, now, now!"

He missed their first pursuer, but one blast cored a fighter's canopy and its pilot.

"Slick flying isn't going to save you, Junior. You're screwing with my payday."

"How many credits is your soul worth, Manc?"

"Leave my soul out of this," Manc said. "It's just business."

Cassiopeia rolled left then cut right. A fighter exploded under Alaric's sights.

"Transit to safety while you still can, kid. I've got a job to do, and *I will do it*."

"He'll be in weapons range in five centi," Cassii said.

"Stand down, Manc. Save yourself while you still can."

"I'm not afraid of you, junior."

Two fighters raked Cassiopeia's back. The ship shook.

"Losing power to port nacelle," Cassii said.

Alaric inclined his head, missing a fighter that darted into his sights only to do a hard roll and dive. "I'm not what you need to fear."

Alarms blared.

Manc snorted. "You want me afraid of your mommy?"

"How many innocents have to die before you can't find anything except a monster in the mirror?"

"Don't use them, kid."

Alaric flipped off the comm channel. "Can you fly and fight while I run back there?"

"Better than you."

"Prove it, keep him connected to me, use old vid feed or something. Don't let him know how hurt we are." Alaric raced aft, descending the stair in a breakneck rail slide. "Damn it, we need a bigger crew."

He sprinted down corridors, giving any passenger's peeking out their doors a run-by earful. A panel exploded, forcing him to leap through a plume of smoke. He skidded around a corner. Something blasted the ship's underside, launching him from his feet to careen into a bulkhead with a yelp. He sprang back up, raced into the central collar and leapt into the port nacelle's zero gravity.

"Another one down," Cassii said.

"Last warning, kid. Run."

Another hit rattled the ship.

"You're right there, Shepherd. Boy's angry enough he'll blast you without giving another."

"Kid, you've got the hardest head in the Protectorate."

"Good thing too," Cassii mumbled in a way that told Alaric she hadn't broadcast it to Manc.

Alaric laughed and pried open another panel. Noxious fumes and burnt insulation pummeled his nose. His eyes teared. Alaric shoved downward, shooting out of zero-g to slam onto the deck plates. One boot slipped, bringing his knee down hard on the plating.

He ripped open lockers.

"Two left," Cassii said. "He's broken off communications."

"Good shooting, Cassii."

"No, primitive, check the locker two to the left."

Alaric reddened. "Oh, right."

"No, left."

He laughed, digging through tools. *Screw it.*

He scooped up as many as he could carry and leapt back into the nacelle pylon.

Cassiopeia lurched.

He slammed into the pylon wall. His cradled tools ricocheted through zero-g. He snatched a plasma welder from the floating swarm. He snatched dancing, charred wires, yanked them together. They bit his hands, sending fingers to his mouth several times. He bit back with the welder, fusing the unruly ends to one another.

"That should do it," Alaric said.

"Good job. Reading full power to port nacelle."

"Status?"

"Two fighters left plus the flamberge."

"He's not in weapon range yet?"

"Either he's damaged, or he's dogging it."

"Why?"

"Maybe he doesn't want to kill you."

"Must be my sterling personality."

"Oh, yes, your presence makes my heart flutter."

"What heart?" Alaric asked.

"Starclaws have broken off. Get back up here."

Gravity met him on the deck plates as phantom water bathed him from thought to his boots. "He's working out how to end up with Cassiopeia to top his slave payout."

Alaric ascended the stairs like a gazelle. He dropped into the command chair, grabbed flight controls and scanned the cloud of tactical holograms. "They're reattaching the tether. Hit them before they succeed."

"Too late," Cassii said. "Shepherd's in weapon range."

Starclaws darted at them, firing at Cassiopeia as the tug pulled away with its load. They reversed and chased its thruster wash.

Manc's flamberge cut across their wakes on an intercept course, the two fighters joined into its deadly starburst formation.

Starburst... "What if Manc's as much someone's prisoner as Eryss?"

"Don't go soft on me now," Cassii said. "Shepherd's an ace."

Florentine and flamberge, designed to work as a team, shot past one another. Alaric punched up the flyby recording, focusing on Manc's grimace.

He's going to do it. He's really going to try and kill us.

<I never break a contract.>

Cassiopeia executed a flat spin, firing at Manc, starclaws, and tug. One starclaw lost half its tentacles and spun out of control, thrusters dark.

"That's my move."

"Right," Cassii said. "Now he thinks you're flying. It might make him underestimate us."

"Release weapon control."

"Can you do this?"

Can I? Do I have any other choices?

"Alaric?"

Alaric took a deep breath, squared his shoulders and tightened his grip. "Release weapon control."

"Released. Shepherd's hailing."

Alaric nodded. The comm clicked open. "What do you want, Manc? I'm a bit busy here."

Manc laughed. "That's the kid I know, all balls no brains."

"Cut the jealousy and get to the point."

Cassii snickered.

"Let's cut a deal, junior. We finish the last starclaw together, kill the tug pilot and take the lot to Scrics. You get half of a thousand slaves..."

Adrenaline refueled his anger. "You expect me to sell slaves?"

"Sell them, free them, paint them green and make them do a dance routine. I get the rest of the salvage, we both walk away as rich as we choose."

"I thought you never broke a contract."

"Alaric," Cassii warned.

"I'll make an exception. I don't have to kill you, and I still get a huge payday. No witnesses."

"Except me."

"Maybe you should think about this, Alaric."

Shock seized his limbs. He turned toward the dome. "What did you say?"

"Listen to mom, kid."

Alaric cut the comm. "Cassii—"

"We're hurt, Alaric. He's an ace in an advanced, mostly undamaged flamberge in the deadly, dual fighter star configuration."

"He's going to sell five hundred people into slavery," Alaric said.

"Better than a thousand and us dead," she said.

"You don't think I can kill him."

"I don't think we can win, period," Cassii said.

"What do you think, junior? I'll even let you have first pick."

First pick. Choose who languishes in chains. Choose whose body is used against their will. Choose who dies. Eryss flashed through his thoughts, then Sarah, El and Jesse, Lane and finally Marvy's face looking up from a bowl. Collar orange haze filled his vision.

Alaric's expression couldn't have been worsened by a force fed meal of green Corra Lemons—widely renowned as being sour to the point of deadliness for umoids. His every word emanated absolute command. "Captain Manc Shepherd, in accordance with Protectorate law, Articles F8S274.2 and H33L523.8, you're under arrest. Stand down your engines and come along peaceably."

Manc ended transmission and opened fire.

Florentine and flamberge danced to the death in between the stars. Their battle raged like a tornado of furious djinn. They dove and darted, spun and spit fire at one another.

Alaric's hands flew over the controls. His eyes darted from display to display. Cassii made Cassiopeia move like never before. Even so, it wasn't enough.

Manc Shepherd—friend and mentor, enemy and executioner—out flew them at every turn. His weapons raked them mercilessly. Cassiopeia rocked and shuddered. He blasted the cargo bay open and left Cassiopeia's port nacelle clinging on by will alone.

"You've got to get me a shot," Alaric pleaded.

"I'm trying, he's better than even I calculated." Frustration filled her reply. "Nacelle tracks are jammed. He's keeping on our port no matter what I do."

"He's going to kill us."

"I know," she snapped. "He's coming around, targeting an unarmored section."

Alaric wracked his brain with no avail. "I'm sorry, Cassii. I failed. We're shut down."

Shut down. A grin grew across his face. *Is he that arrogant? That lazy?*

"Death makes you smile?"

"Cassii, request permission to send a formal signal of surrender."

"That's not—"

"Just send it now. Please...."

"Transmitting."

Manc aborted his attack run, flying a lazy loop into attack formation on their port side once more.

"Shepherd's giving you three milli."

Alaric's hands flew across his controls. "Send this."

"That's not a... Alaric, there's no way that'll work.

"Organics are lazy, remember?"

Shepherd lined up for the final pass. Energy readings showed full charge to all weapons.

"Send it!"

Cassii transmitted the signal.

53

MORE SURPRISES

Manc's fighters powered down.

I've got him... A pang throbbed in Alaric's chest. *...dead to rights.*

Cassii chuckled. "I bet he's cursing like a molting Kraili, but it won't last."

"Quick then, sideslip him."

Cassiopeia rolled out of his inertial flight path with her single functioning engine. "Targeting his reactor."

"Stop, lower weapon threshold to twenty percent, target his power relays and fire."

Targeting sensors dissected the flamberge on the display screens. She locked a pulsar cannon on his relays.

"Wait," Alaric said.

"There's no time."

Alaric grabbed the flight controls and fired. "I needed to do it."

"None of this'll change facts, Alaric. You'll still have to kill him."

"Just give me time to think. Target reactor output assembly on the second one."

She swept around to the second fighter before Manc could change cockpits.

Alaric fired. His numb hands wrapped tight enough around his controls to hide their shaking. *I beat him. I win. Why does it feel so horrible?*

"Disabling him isn't enough, Alaric."

That's why.

"You need to kill him."

His teeth bit into his lip. The taste of blood filled his mouth. *He used me. He murdered innocents. He enslaved refugees. This should be easy. Just squeezes the trigger, or order her to do it. Simple...clean...* Tears rolled down his face. *I can't. He's my only friend.*

"You know I'm right," Cassii said. "We stole his payday, forced him to fail his contract and made him look the fool. You beat him in a way that'll eat at him...until he does the same and worse to you."

"I can't. I won't."

"I can."

"No."

"Alaric."

"Please, Cassii," he took a shuddering breath. "Scan the liner for lingering life signs. I'm suiting up for a spacewalk."

"This is foolhardy. Never leave an enemy in your thruster wash—particularly not a more skilled opponent."

"I'll just have to get better then. Compile a damage report and report once suited up. Tell me when we catch up with the tug."

"What about Shepherd?"

"We've got his transponder codes, send a ship in distress to the KIOSC. Someone'll pick him up if he can't manage repairs."

"Insult to injury."

"Just more on my tab."

Alaric regretted disabling the unarmed tug. If he'd thought about it sooner, he'd have used it to pull Cassiopeia. *Not that Cassii's pride would've allowed that.*

Cassiopeia moved him into position at tether's end. He latched it onto the tug's forward tow anchors and climbed up to the cockpit canopy. He tapped his plasma welder on it, getting the pilot's attention.

A slender Kraili female bared her teeth. He imagined her angry hiss but didn't hear it.

He tapped his ear. "Hello?"

She keyed her own comm then glared at him.

"Can you hear me now?"

"You're going to die for this," she said.

"Guess that's a yes. You have a space suit?"

Her brow lowered, tightening her reptilian eyes. "Yes. Why?"

He held up the plasma welder. "We can do this a few ways. I can bore a hole in the canopy and vent the cabin to vacuum. I can disable your comm relays and leave you there until we make orbit or you can suit up, surrender and be my prisoner aboard my ship."

"That wreck can barely fly."

He smirked. "She's had a long cycle."

The Kraili raised a pulse rifle. "I could kill you instead and claim everything."

He cursed.

A pulsar blast blinded him with violet light. Pain flashed across him as he was catapulted back and then yanked to a stop by his safety line. His suit tightened painfully in several places. Cold bit each place.

"Alaric, your suit's reporting seal breaches."

Alaric stared at the blasted cockpit, his thoughts sluggish.

"Alaric, seal patches, quick."

His brain clicked back into forward. Both legs, his right arm and a band around his stomach two inches high burned. He dug his left glove into the utility pouch in the small of his back, removing a handful of quick seal patches. He let all but one float, slapping that one into place on his right forearm. The sleeve loosened, and warmth shot into it. He grabbed others, cursing and patching rips as fast as he could move.

When the third patch brought warmth back to his leg, he took a deep breath and lit into Cassii. "What the hedrin were you thinking? I could've died."

"She was going to shoot you."

Linger cold chattered his teeth. "Great plan, save me by freezing me to death."

"You wouldn't have frozen without an atmosphere to enable thermal conduction. If you'd just killed her instead of offering her a meal and a shower—"

Alaric cut off the comm. *I hate it when she's right.*

He dragged himself along the tether back into Cassiopeia where he couldn't shut off her nagging.

Alaric glared down at his stomach. Like legs and arm exposed to vacuum, broken capillaries left a band of discolored skin—a thick, gut-wide hickie. "Why not repair at the Uldira station. We'll unload the refugees—"

"Not on my circuits, not in the same system as Shepherd. We upload a false itinerary to the Protectorate and limp to Scrics as fast as we can."

"That's illegal."

"We'll correct it just before transit to Scrics. I don't want to make Shepherd's job any easier."

Alaric touched the hologram suspended over his desk, drawing a course trajectory from their present position to the Feirin system. "Why not actually go to Feirin?"

"Don't you think you've put your passengers through enough?"

"You're right."

"Again."

He glowered, threw on a shirt and turned toward the door.

"Where're you going?" Cassii asked.

"Outside, for some peace and quiet."

"You're not recovered yet."

"I need to do what I can for the port nacelle."

"Be careful...we've only got one environment suit left."

He stormed off the bridge. Passenger's moved from his path. Frex stepped in front of him, but Alaric's expression and bandage-wrapped limbs clamped the man's mouth closed.

Cassiopeia reached the Uldira-Tosmis gate.

Amazing, particularly without more trouble. They met up with only independent liners and merchantmen. "They're giving us a wide berth."

"Smart people stay clear of slave ships."

Her tartness encouraged his interest to try some Corra Lemon, even if he'd have to dilute it. *Not that I'll tell her before I do it. Her opinion of me is already pretty low.*

His fingers stroked Cara's coat, carefully staying clear of the broken leg. Her tail thumped on the edge of her bed, and she tried catching him with her tongue whenever his hand came near.

He met her brown gaze and smiled. *I like this relationship. Simple. Seldom a reproach. She comforts me when I'm sad. She bounces when I'm happy. She loves me...no matter what.*

He kissed her head. Her tongue caught him across his mouth. He smiled, ruffled her ears and patted her thrice. "Got to go play host. Be good, girl."

He punched up a pile of treats from the dispenser and laid them between her paws, restarting her tail. He checked his reflection, removed a bit of fur from his jacket and headed for the wardroom.

Children lingered in the hallway. Their quiet raised the hair along his neck. The furthest child bolted without their customary greeting. Shifty eyes refusing to meet his eye colonized his gut with wrestling otters.

"Hi, Captain," Jeslynn said.

As if a signal, the others bombarded him with greetings and questions they'd already asked.

He narrowed his gaze on Jeslynn. "What're you up to?"

She blushed, shifting her gaze anywhere but him.

Alaric hurried through the wardroom's automatic doors. His passengers lined up in front of the table, grim-faced.

They're angry. Can I blame them? He searched their faces for Frex, architect of unpleasantness aboard Cassiopeia. "What's this?"

A familiar tune escaped ship's speakers. Grins shattered stern expressions. They stepped to either side, revealing a massive cake decorated gold and blue.

Alaric stared.

They sang a birthday celebration song.

Duva Frex glowered at the table, not smiling and certainly not singing. Ester beamed from his side.

Jeslynn dragged him from the doorway into the heavily decorated room.

"Well, Captain?" Ester said. "Say something."

"I-I don't know what to say...I mean after—"

"Endangering our lives without cause," Frex said.

"Duva, Captain Ignaree saved all those people."

"Did he? For all we know, we're dragging a cemetery."

"He tried, more than others might've done," Jeslynn's mother, Marita said. "Our friends or family could've been on that liner."

"Not *our* relatives," Frex said.

"Please, I'm sorry you were endangered, but we were the only ones near enough to help."

"Destroyed your ship in the process," Frex said. "It'll be a miracle if we survive to our destination."

Marita gingerly took the bandaged arm opposite Jeslynn. "Enough borrowing trouble. This is a party."

Ester lit the candles.

"Make a wish," one boy said.

"How old are you today?" Jeslynn asked.

"Wish I knew," Alaric blew out the candles.

"He'd forget where the ship was if he weren't inside it," Cassii said.

Passengers chuckled.

"He's seventeen today."

Alaric shrugged and smiled. *Wonder if that's true. I don't feel different, better fed, a bit more beat up than back on Earth.*

A single glowering exception darkened the festive dessert then dinner party. They might've felt differently had things ended badly, but they'd survived his attack and chattered about his heroics.

Unlike before, ships passed Cassiopeia on their way across the huge Tosmis system. Despite originating in Ealma, Uldira or Scrics, most gave them a wide berth.

He poured over damage estimates, scowling at the damage his heroics had cost their former success. He ran the numbers again, tweaking sales figures.

"Alaric?"

He started.

"Four fighters incoming. Three raven and an asp interceptor."

He switched his desktop display to tactical holograms from the bridge.

"Asp's leading," he mumbled. He followed their projected course. "They're on intercept. Can we avoid them?"

"Doubtful, they changed course once we entered their sensor range...after they ran a ship-ident query."

"Great, yellow alert, charge the working cannon," he switched on the intercom. "We're being approached by fighters with unknown intentions. Strap in, just in case."

Cassiopeia and the fighter craft sped across the intervening space. He chewed his lip in his command chair. "I can't think of anything we could do that mightn't add blood to the water."

"Agreed. Steady course and hope."

He stared at them, trying to will them away.

"Still no ident broadcasts, score marks on one match hits Shepherd made on a raven that escaped us first time through Tosmis."

"Of course, Tyne." *Should've expected this.* "Options?"

"Run, fight or surrender our cargo."

Alaric cursed. "So really, only eject the tether and fight."

"Alaric..."

"Not a chance, Cassii."

Silence fell.

Cassii finally broke it. "Scenario calculation allows for two kills before they burn us to a husk."

He chuckled. "I'll just have to think of something creative."

"I figured that option into the scenarios."

His laughter died. He reached toward the comm array.

"Wait, what're you doing?" Cassii asked.

"Inviting Tyne to dinner."

"Why?"

He grinned. "I'm going to hire them."

"What?"

"You said we'd kill half before they destroy us," Alaric said. "Without you or the tug, they can't take the cargo back for sale. I figure they'll jump at the chance to share a nice juicy cargo without any deaths."

"You're going to sell the slaves?" Cassii asked.

"No," Alaric pointed. "But she doesn't know that."

"You can't let her aboard," Cassii said.

"I know you don't like her, but this is business. I couldn't hire her and then treat her any different than any other escort."

"Go down to the wardroom. Please."

He frowned at her dome, hefting himself to his feet. Lynnie and Marita were strapped in at the wardroom table, playing some kind of cards.

"Captain?" Lynnie asked.

"Please return to your cabins," Cassii said. "There's time. We need the wardroom for a negotiation."

Alaric chewed his lip.

Both women unstrapped and filed out. Cassii closed the door. Its lock clicked shut.

"Cassii, what's this about?"

"I took this off the Elcu station vids. Just watch..."

54

CONSPIRACIES

Manc Shepherd lounged in a corner booth, one arm draped over the seatback and the other raising a drink to his lips.

"Where's the greenhorn?" Tyne slid into the seat.

"Leave the kid alone," Manc said.

She shrugged. "Wouldn't be the first time we had our sights set on the same mark. Seem to remember you share *real well*."

"Stay clear, Tyne."

She pouted. "Come on, Shepherd. Are you afraid my wiles will win him away?"

"Wouldn't be the first time your screw-them-then-screw-them-over tactics have ruined a good thing," Manc sneered. "Leave the kid alone. He's my meal ticket."

"Does he know that?" She asked.

Manc sipped his drink.

Her eyes widened. "He doesn't. Are you soft on him?"

"Of course not."

A mischievous grin spread across her face. She slid closer to Manc and threw and arm around his shoulder. "Florentine frigate, that's a nice ship. Awful lot of fun's possible on a ship like that."

He shoved her away, seemingly unconcerned by what parts of her he shoved. "Back off, Ren, and stay out of my playground."

"I let you into mine."

"Ancient history."

Her brows rose. "Not too ancient to bring it up."

He rolled his eyes.

"Come on, handsome. You and me, just like old times."

"No."

Her face hardened. "I want that ship."

"Not going to happen."

Her expression turned sly. "He let you tie in, didn't he? You're just waiting to yank control out from under him."

Manc darkened. "Couldn't if I wanted. His AI's been modified."

"Swap in a preprogrammed."

"Too old a model."

"You could find one on Scrics," she said.

"If he had a reason to go there."

She shrugged. "Short range EMP. Might even have a spare to sell you...for the right kind of payment."

He smiled. "She's got a backup somewhere."

"Somewhere?" Tyne asked.

"Besides, wouldn't be worth your price."

"You getting old?"

Manc shoved a finger into her chest. "I told you, Ren. Leave the kid alone. This is my game, and you're not invited—you or your family."

Tyne bristled. "Leave them out of it."

"You're not getting near that kid." He smiled around his drink. "AI's got it out for you."

"Computers break. Components fail. Things get lost." She ran fingertips down her torso. "I'll be there to comfort him."

Manc lifted a blaster from under the table. "Leave him be, or I'll give you a hole you can't pleasure."

She glowered. "This isn't over, old man."

"Depends on just how smart you are, Ren."

She stormed away.

The vid cut off.

55

DEVIL IN THE DETAILS

Alaric skin crawled, fleeing the shock of his freezing guts. How could they sit there, so normal, so callously discussing betraying another human being? Betraying me?

He felt filthy.

"You can't let that bitch on board," Cassii said.

His hands shook. He gripped a chair back to hide it. "Give me another option that doesn't kill my passengers."

"You can't trust her."

"I don't." His mind replayed the video. *Going to need a shower when this is over.*

"Alaric, you've come a long way, but you fall apart when a pretty girl smiles your way."

His mouth fell agape. "After *that* you think I want to sleep with her?"

"I think primitive mating drives have doomed far too many young men."

His jaw tightened. "Thanks for the vote of confidence."

He stomped up to the bridge, glanced at their relative positions and flipped on the comm. "Tyne, it's Alaric, respond please."

Tyne's face filled the comm display. "Hello, handsome."

He froze, everything he'd seen colliding with emotions from their various encounters.

Cassii's scathing tone screamed I-told-you-so. "You called her. Say something."

He shook it off. "Uh, hi."

"Comm still giving you trouble I see."

He reddened but forced words out. "Little surprised you'd happen by while I was thinking about you."

She battered her lashes. "Were you?"

He nodded.

"Small universe these cycles." Her smile widened. "When I saw you I just had to visit, old debts being what they are."

"You might've noticed I have this nice juicy cargo," Alaric said.

"And no Shepherd to guard you," She said. "Such a shame."

"He's not in any shape to run an escort," Alaric said.

"Not after what Alaric did to him," Cassii added.

Tyne's sucked in breath. "You killed him?"

"The cargo's from his last hire," Cassii said.

"That your stupid ships' computer or a really stupid girlfriend?"

Cassii's dome went red.

"Computer," Alaric said.

"Oh, honey, I never thought you had it in you," Tyne said.

"So, how about you come aboard, and we discuss a juicy escort gig? Here to Scrics."

"I don't know. If you'd gut Shepherd, how do I know you wouldn't..." Tyne placed a finger to her lips, taking a moment to suck its tip. Her brows darted up and down. "...screw me the moment I got on board?"

Images swam through his head, stealing his breath.

"Breathe, idiot," Cassii whispered.

"You're pretty beat up, maybe I should just take custody of your cargo for safe keeping," Tyne said.

"We've taken some engine damage, but otherwise we're fine," Alaric said.

Tyne laughed.

How does something so menacing sound so musical?

"I ran some scenarios while we approached. They don't look too good for you, handsome."

Heat rose in his gut. "Try me, and you'll get a spanking you don't want."

"I can only imagine," she said.

Alaric forced a smile. "How about that job? A little profit between old friends."

Cassii muted the conversation. “I can’t believe you’re offering to pay them.”

“Do we have any other choice?”

“Kill her.”

“We’d die.”

“Die satisfied,” Cassii said.

His frustration bubbled to the surface. “Get over it. I’m trying to save all our hides.”

Cassii’s venomous tone surprised him. “Don’t lie. I’m monitoring your vitals. One roll in the hay and you’re addicted.”

He reddened. “Yes, I’m attracted, but I’m honestly just trying to survive.”

“Bribe them to leave.”

“I am, but I’m also protecting us from the next pack of jackals. We can’t pay them all.”

“We can’t trust them, pay or no.”

“This is our best option.”

“And if she steals me?”

“Blow yourself up, and die satisfied.” Alaric cut the comm back on.

“Done arguing with your computer?” Tyne asked.

“She doesn’t trust you,” Alaric said.

“Little old me?” Tyne pouted. “Even after I saved you?”

“You attacked us since then.”

“Business,” Tyne smiled.

“So is this.”

One thin eyebrow disappeared under a matching spike of hair. “Profit percentage clause on your cargo?”

Alaric smiled. “Three percent.”

“Ten,” Tyne said.

“Five.”

Her smiled turned predatory. “Seven or we try our luck.”

Alaric muted the channel “Target the back raven.”

“The asp’s transmitting.”

“I’m betting on a relay.” He unmuted his comm. “Six and I don’t start the party with your fighter.”

“But the signal originates from the asp,” Cassii said.

She beamed. “Wit and looks, six it is.”

“Come aboard. We’ll finalize the contract.”

“On my way,” Tyne punched in beneath their sightline. “My boys’ll take up escort positions.”

"No," Alaric said. "They move a wingspan, and we start shooting."

"Oh, handsome, we're going to do great things together now that you're broken in."

The echo sent a chill through him.

"Ravens can't interlock with my nacelle," Cassii said smugly.

"Land her in the cargo bay. She can board through the airlock."

Cassii grumbled something he couldn't hear.

Good thing Manc ripped it up. Considering whatever Cassii's got against Tyne, she'd probably space her—if only to win our argument.

Tyne entered the airlock and waited while it repressurized. Alaric stood by the controls, guarding against sudden decompression.

On the monitor, Tyne peeled flight suit with exaggerated eroticism.

"You're not falling for this, right?" Cassii asked.

He shrugged, watching how peeling it away raised her snug, beige half shirt enough to expose her breasts.

She's right, phenomenal.

The suit slid down skin-tight black pants, lingering bent over for him to get a long look. She flashed the dome a licentious grin, licking painted lips.

"Oh, spare me," Cassii said.

Alaric started. "How did she—"

Cassii's tone could've frozen oceans. "Know you're a lecherous voyeur?"

Alaric glared at the still red dome.

"I'll warm up my self-destruct."

Tyne opened a flight bag, donning a matching long-sleeved jacket and twin, thigh-hugging holsters. She slid her blasters home and pulled a set of fingerless gloves from her belt and slipped them on. "Ready when you are, handsome."

Alaric unlocked the inner airlock. A tantalizing aroma, heady and spicy washed through the open door. He took several breaths, trying to slow his heart rate. Inhaling more perfume didn't help.

"This way please." He led her to his cabin.

She raised a brow at his threshold, gesturing to his bed. "Pretty sure of yourself, aren't you, handsome?"

He strode around his desk, hoping she missed his blush. "Have a seat. I've a passenger or two who might intrude elsewhere, but if this makes you uncomfortable..."

Tyne flopped down onto his bed. "Oh, no, I'm very comfortable."

Atop the bed, Cara came into view. The dog curled her lip and growled.

"Don't you remember me, girl?"

"Her injury keeps her immobile, but you're in her spot," Alaric indicated the chair. "Shall we?"

Tyne patted the bed. "Waiting for you."

Cara's growling intensified.

"Cara."

The puppy glanced at him, wagged her tail twice, and returned her curled lip toward Tyne.

A meaty bone dropped out of the food dispenser. She dropped it between her paws, gnawing on it with her head cocked, and her eyes fixed on Tyne.

"Thanks, Cassii. Please sit, Tyne."

She declined to move. Alaric remained at his desk. They dickered, Cassii uncharacteristically silent.

They shook on it.

"Cassii'll coordinate access for your pilots to board one at a time for showers, naps, etc."

Tyne's words almost purred. "Unexpectedly generous of you, Alaric."

"They're not to trouble my passengers."

"Understood. May I take advantage of that shower while I'm aboard?"

"After you order your team to take up position, Cassii can lead you to the shower. It's hydro rather than sonic, hope that's acceptable."

"Oh, I much prefer hydro. The feeling of warm water running down your skin," Tyne's hands pantomimed as she spoke. "It's so delicious."

Cara growled.

Another bone purchased quiet.

"What's with her?" Tyne asked.

"Jealous I guess," Alaric said. "Your pilots?"

"She needs to get over it," Tyne radioed orders to her pilots. "Computer, direct me to the shower."

Alaric verified escort position on the tactical hologram then double-checked their course. He grabbed his tool bag and headed to the port pylon. He'd climbed into zero-g when a blood-curdling scream filled the corridors.

Alaric pushed through collected passengers to the open bathroom door. Tyne glared at the shower, a towel haphazardly wrapped around her lobster-red skin.

"What happened?" Alaric asked.

Passengers assembled behind him.

Tyne scowled. "Water temperature shot up to scalding."

"Have our med probe treat those burns. I'll track down the malfunction," Alaric glanced at the green dome, "and ensure it doesn't happen again."

"Thanks, but I'd rather avoid further accidents."

56

CONFLICTING INTENTS

Arguments between Tyne and Duva Frex offered the only interruption to their peaceful travel across Tosmis. Cassii's routing for one to dispose of the other—seemingly without preference—complicated Alaric's efforts to prevent Tyne from shooting the arrogant Inheran. Otherwise, the combination of escort and slave cargo prevented further incident.

Curiously empty logs offered no explanation for the shower malfunction.

"Just make sure it doesn't happen again," Alaric said.

"I hear you."

"And you'll comply?"

"What do you think?" Cassii asked.

He sighed. *That you did it on purpose and will do it again at first opportunity.*

They transited the Tosmis-Scrics KIOSC without incident.

Manc would've handled it smoother. He cursed himself. *Manc's the enemy. Forget him.*

The bridge door opened.

Alaric didn't turn around. "Shouldn't you be escorting, Tyne?"

She flopped into the seat next to him. "We should chat. I've got a contact on Scrics Five who'll give us top value for the slaves, even with a glutted market."

"Wait a milli," Cassii said.

The aroma of popcorn washed out of the food dispenser.

Alaric studied his fingers.

"Well? What do you think?" Tyne asked.

"I think your galactic tart routine isn't as potent as you think it is," Cassii said.

"Cassii, that's enough."

Tyne glared. "One of these cycles—"

"We're freeing the slaves."

Tyne's mouth fell open. "What?! No, you can't do that. We've got an agreement."

A sheepish grin spread across his face as he raised his gaze to meet her flashing eyes. "We do. You get six percent of cargo profits, but the people aren't the cargo."

"The hedrin they aren't," Tyne said.

Cassii giggled.

"Shut up, you silicon bitch," Tyne snapped.

"You're made of more silicon than I am."

"Enough, ladies," Alaric said. "The people are bartering transportation to Scrics in exchange for watching the pods for me."

"You're deranged. That's a fortune floating out there."

Alaric glowered, his tone lowered dangerously. "I am not a slaver. I will not profit by stealing lives. No umoid should live in chains."

Tyne jabbed Alaric with a finger. "You cheated me."

"You duped yourself," Cassii said. "You just assumed everyone was as greedy as you are."

"Because no one just frees slaves!"

"I do."

"I did not spare you for philanthropic purposes, I intend to get paid," Tyne said.

"You'll get paid, lobster girl, just not for what you assumed."

Tyne leapt up and drew her blaster. "I'll blow so many holes in you that they'll—"

"Tyne."

She looked down to find Alaric's blaster leveled at her gut.

"Like it or not, you never asked what I was selling. I didn't cheat you."

Tyne opened her mouth. She closed it, folded her arms and glared. "This isn't what we signed on for."

Alaric offered her a sympathetic smile. "Look, I'll double your commission rate. That's a pretty good payday for such a short escort."

"No. This is a trick somehow, so you can get all the credits."

"I assure you it isn't," Alaric said. "Stay at my side until they're freed. See for yourself."

"Damn straight I will." She spun and stomped from the bridge, turning back at the threshold. "You didn't kill Shepherd either, did you?"

"Never said I did," Alaric said.

She threw up her hands and stormed down the stairs with a disgusted scream.

Cassii giggled. "That was better than I calculated."

"I'd rather have waited longer." He sighed. "We have the final coordinates from Mister Yra?"

"We're unloading inside a dry dock slip around Scrics Seven, invisible to all prying eyes."

"Still worried about Manc?"

"You should be too."

"If we can just get into that dock and free the survivors, everything'll be fine."

Cassiopeia executed a graceless landing inside the massive, heavy-repair star dock. Tractor nets caught her, the tug and the tethered pods.

Medical equipment and its corresponding personnel waited beyond a wide transparent window at bay's end.

Tyne and her pilots landed in the four corners.

Ensuring I don't make off with some of the slaves. Alaric bound from his cargo bay to the repair slip and headed to the tug to disconnect it. He hurried from tug to pods, leaving his tether lie on the deck.

Gravity rose, shortening each leap.

Other suited workers helped him settle the pods gently down. Medical personnel and their helpers poured into the bay as soon as gravity and atmosphere normalized. Massive robotic titans plucked the pods. One grape at a time, they set them down at one of the medical stations.

Tinsley Yra strode up to him.

Alaric unscrewed his helmet and tucked it under one arm. "Thanks for this."

Tinsley shook his head. "You know, for a kid down on his luck when we met, you're giving away a lot of credits."

Alaric frowned.

"Still, it isn't about money, is it? It's about helping the less fortunate." Tinsley lowered his voice. "Just don't tell my executive heads of finance or public relations I said that out in the open. You should meet him, Alaric. He'd hate you."

"Who?"

"Binsen Plartmore, my finance and accounting exec," Tinsley chuckled. "Your good deed's giving him fits. He's convinced we've both been sucking vacuum."

"You absolutely have been," Tyne said.

"Tinsley Yra, Tyne Ren," Alaric said.

Tinsley's brows rose.

Tyne gaped at Alaric. "You know Tinsley Yra? *The* Tinsley Yra."

Alaric shrugged.

"A pleasure, Madame Ren," Tinsley said.

"Pleasure for you maybe, and it's just Tyne." She scowled at the rescue operation. "He's really just spacing all those credits...and I'm helping him."

"Feels good, doesn't it?" Alaric asked.

"No, it damn well doesn't!"

Tinsley chuckled. "Should set you up on a blind date with Binsen."

"You pay him well?" she asked.

"I imagine so," Tinsley turned thoughtful. "You'd have to ask him."

"High paid exec for Yra Era?" Tyne asked. "I'll take that date."

Tinsley drew out the word. "Okay."

Alaric clapped her shoulder. "It'll be over soon, Tyne. Once the pods are empty, Tinsley's buying them from us."

"Why?"

"As a favor," Alaric said.

"I'm converting them into a new experimental escape pod," Tinsley beamed.

"Great," Tyne said. "Just wonderful."

People emerged from pods one at a time. Occasionally a flurry of activity would indicate a struggle to bring back a sleeper from deep hibernation or a damaged pod. The refugees clustered near the walls in small groups, led to tables of fresh food, drink, and clothing. A wail occasionally punctuated the eerily still hum of activity.

Alaric's voice broke. "This is so hard."

Tinsley's lips pressed into a thin line. "Families torn apart, lives lost, so much sadness."

"All those credits," Tyne bemoaned.

"They only just escaped disaster." Alaric shook his head. "I wish I could do more, give them credits or something."

"You're not right in the head." Tyne stormed away.

"Still got my card?" Tinsley asked.

"Somewhere."

Hands settled on Alaric's shoulders. "You've a good heart, Captain."

Alaric touched one of them. "Thank you, Missus Frex. I'll have you on your way as soon as this is done."

"No hurry," Marita said. Another wail interrupted the bay. "Sad as this is, it does my heart good."

Jeslynn slipped her hand into Alaric's. Warm and soft, it reminded him of El. Emotion welled up inside him. *I wish she could see this.*

"We should lend a hand," Jeslynn said.

Marita led the other passengers into the crowd, leaving only the Frexs behind.

"We'd die of old age if we waited on you and your crusades," Mister Frex said. "We've made other arrangements."

A smile and a scowl awaited his gaze. "I'll be happy to refund you your shuttle costs."

"No need, dear boy, Uncle Elkner was happy to send his private shuttle." Her eyes fell on the freed refugees. "You've given us so much already."

Mister Frex lingered as his wife moved toward the crowd. "You'll pay yet, Captain. That's a promise."

Alaric sighed. "Can't please everybody."

Tinsley patted his back and joined the relief effort.

Alaric watched, heart broken and swelling at the same time. He looked back at Cassiopeia. She sat lopsided with one broken landing claw, worse off than she'd been when he'd first seen her on Earth. They'd crossed almost a dozen solar systems.

A dozen solar systems away from El...Jesse...home.

"You all right?" Cassii asked.

"I feel alone."

"You've still got me," Cassii said.

"I know, Cassii, but..." Alaric swallowed back tears. "It's just not the same."

"I'd wrap my arms around you if I could."

Alaric allowed himself a small smile. "I know. You're the greatest." His smile grew. "On second thought, you having arms might spell my doom."

"You've done a good thing here," Cassii said. "Nearly destroyed us to do it, but still a good thing."

Several refugees thanked Alaric. Others spat at him, focusing hurt and anger at him for not saving their loved ones.

He understood. He'd lost someone too.

Soon El, very soon.

An Ubori stepped up to Alaric. He seemed emaciated even for his extremely thin race. Blue tinted his transparent skin, casting his internal organs in a sickly hue where ripped clothes exposed them.

Alaric met both pairs of the Ubori's eyes. "They're replacing your clothing over there."

The Ubori inclined his head, green wisp pupils disappearing as he blinked tears away. He wrung four hands.

"Is there something else I can do for you?"

The Ubori's tenor chord carried the slightest echo. "You saved us?"

"It was a group effort."

He sighed. "I am yours."

"Uh, no, you're free to go," Alaric said.

"I owe you," he said. "My life's yours."

Alaric grimaced. "You feel you owe me a life debt?"

"Yes, I do."

"I'm Alaric, what's your name?"

"Tsin."

Alaric put a hand on Tsin's topmost shoulder. "You owe me nothing, Tsin. Lots of people helped. Maybe I'm even partly to blame. Can we just call it even? Please?"

Tsin studied him. "You are damaged."

"Pardon?"

"Your mind's broken." Tsin squinted one set of eyes.

"I think he's a biovoyant," Cassii said.

"You're a biovoyant?" Alaric asked.

Tsin wrung four hands and stared down. "I'm thus cursed."

"Cursed?" Alaric asked.

"They trained me." Tsin said. "It was required."

"You don't like being a biovoyant?"

"I hate it."

Alaric chewed his lip. "Oh, sorry my head made that worse. Get some food, you look hungry."

Tsin inclined his head and shuffled away.

"Glad he's gone," Alaric said. "Gave me the creeps."

57

STOLEN FUTURES

Alaric tripled Tyne's commission despite Cassii's objections. Tyne remained disgruntled, and Cassii snapped at him often. Repaying their loan and repairing Cassiopeia ravaged their reserves. Between Inhera, the savaged tug, and what Tinsley paid for the pods, they'd still ended up ahead, if not as much as before.

Alaric scoured Scrics's system market, cherry picking pieces and parts to rebuild Cassiopeia. He found a sonic shower unit, but decided hydro served fine—particularly with the image Tyne'd put in his head. Each purchase heightened his anticipation. He shuttled to Scrics Five's moon when not shopping or working with repair crews. He combed the moon's derelict ship junkyard—easily a wasteland the size of D.C. florentine frigates were never that common, but decades of Cassiopeia's fallen brethren offered up plating, systems, and weapons.

The escort fighters lingered, enjoying the free dock. Alaric didn't rush them away. *Might even achieve some sort of friendship that'd prove useful later.* He froze. *No. I'm not sure where that came from, but friends aren't for using.*

Satisfied he'd acquired all he could and that repair teams would put it to use, he booked a shuttle to Scrics Three.

"I don't know what's worse," Cassii sneered. "The mooning puppy on a hopeless crusade or your death wish."

"I have to do this," Alaric said. "I think I can help."

"Manc's out there, waiting for you to do something predictable."

"I can't stop living because he's angry."

"If you'd killed him—"

"No matter what he did to me, he's still my friend."

"That's great, ask for a hug before he splatters that solid bone skull of yours."

"I've made up my mind."

"Change it, evolve beyond your primitive origins."

"Hey."

"You saw Manc's message. You know he's coming."

"Manc can't anticipate my every move."

"He knows you better than you think."

"Damn it, Cassii...."

"Fine. Go. Risk your neck for some whore, but when Manc abandons your scorched husk in some alleyway, I won't shed one tear for you. Not one, you vacuum-brained, lust-besotted primitive."

Alaric stormed out of the ship, switching off his comm ring. *What is her problem? One centi she's praising me, the next she's calling me names. Ugh, why do they make computers so, so female?*

The shuttle dropped into Scrics Three's traffic patterns.

She doesn't understand. I need to do this.

<Right, princess, because saving a thousand slaves isn't enough. You have to challenge their whole damned system.>

He grabbed his head. *Why don't you keep quiet?*

Another voice laughed. *<Haven't you figured it out yet, runt? We're your imaginary friends.>*

I don't want you here. I don't need you.

<Except that's exactly why you created us from locked away memories, because you do. In all the trauma, you needed *someone.>*

The shuttle dropped him off several blocks from Twin Djinns. Alaric straightened his holsters and strode surface streets, squaring his emotional shoulders. The voice, memory, whatever, had left him shaken more than he'd been embarking on this venture.

At first, thinking of Eryss as only a Starburst had eased the ache he felt when he thought of her doing the things she was ordered to do. That sanitized thinking reduced her to an object, something people owned and forced to their bidding—like he'd forced her to listen. He embraced the pain, keeping it close to drive his mission to see her free.

He found her floor, taking a drink at the bar. He scanned the starbursts, but couldn't find her. A tall, red-feathered Eviarch strode up to him. It wore the same uniform as the Ongali who'd offered him credit.

"Captain Ignaree. How we pleasure you today?" A slight screech underpinned its voice.

"Thanks, I'm not into," Alaric looked the vulture-like umoid up and down, "guys."

It squawked. "I not pleasure slave."

Alaric scanned his neck but found no tattoos. "Sorry. I'm looking for a starburst."

It smiled, unsettling enough from any Eviarch, but this smile marked Alaric as carrion. It gestured talon-like fingers. A holographic menu of nude images appeared between them, each image accompanied by a line of stars above listed proficiencies.

"No, a specific one—"

"MiCola," He said.

Alaric frowned. "Huh?"

"Eryss MiCola," He said. "I'll summon."

"Wait, what's your name?"

The Eviarch frowned. "You call me Rusetor."

Alaric swallowed and played his hunch. "You're her supervisor right? Privy to her personnel file?"

Rusetor's head bobbed.

"Her father sold her to cover his debts. Did he owe you that debt or someone else?"

"MiCola defaulted on line of credit," Rusetor said.

Stars above, probably the same line of credit they offered me—if smaller. Note to self, don't go into debt to these monsters.

"She did or her father?" Alaric asked.

"Father owed," Rusetor's head bobbed. "He paid with girl."

"Some kind of indentured servitude? How much is left on her debt?"

"No, full sale."

"So she'll never work her way free?"

Rusetor's head eased forward, feathered brows pinched together. "Why you care? You want pleasure or not?"

"I want to...," His stomach tightened. "Buy her."

"She not worth much," Rusetor tapped the computer embedded in his forearm. He turned it so Alaric could read the display. "Slow earner."

Cold washed up Alaric's spine. His hopes shattered against the floor. *Holy Hedrin. Even if she was indentured, she'd be stuck here until she was a grandmother.*

"Can I buy you a drink while I think it over?"

Rusetor's head bobbed again. The bartender delivered Rusetor's drink, its composition worsening Alaric's discomfort.

The Eviarch raised its chin and poured the drink into its mouth. Its head bobbed and neck undulated as if shaking the thick drink down. A long sharp tongue licked its lower beak. It turned another smile on Alaric.

"You want MiCola, now?"

"No. You said she's a slow earner, would you consider a lower offer? Credits now rather than managing her long term."

Again, that vulture grin.

"Guess, we're done." Alaric lurched to his feet. The weight of inevitability weighed down his step. *How could I ever come up with that much—without selling slaves? Maybe Cassii'll have an idea.*

Consumed by his thoughts, he got turned around. He found his bearings and headed to the door. Eryss appeared between him and the exit single star aglow. A man draped over her, groping her breasts. Rusetor whispered in her tongue-empty ear.

Alaric's insides slithered.

Shock filled her expression until the man's hand groped between her legs. She reddened, tears trailing her cheeks.

Heat filled him, red edging his vision. His hand fell to his blaster.

Her eyes widened. She shook her head a fraction. Rusetor'd noticed his move too. The Eviarch spoke into his wrist computer, one hand on his own gun.

Alaric strode past them, eyes locked with Eryss. *I'm sorry. I've failed you twice now.*

Misery dragged out his return trip. He trudged into the repair bay. The escort fighters were absent. Tsin sat cross-legged before Cassiopeia's hatch. Four eyes rose at his approach.

Collecting problems today. Stars, can things get any worse?

Tsin rose.

"You're not going to leave, are you?"

Tsin offered an apologetic smile.

That'll lessen the tirades around her. He thought of Cassii. *Why do I think she'll be happy I failed?*

"Captain Alaric Ignaree?"

A small man in a dull brown suit stood behind him, tablet under his arm.

"Yes?"

A shark-like grin spread across his otherwise unremarkable face, complete with jagged teeth. "Considered yourself served. You're hereby compelled to appear before the High Court of Scrics Three, answerable for charges of piracy, slave trafficking, and reckless negligence."

"What?"

"Transit privileges through Scrics KIOSCs is prohibited, and any attempt to depart the Scrics system will be considered judgment for summary execution."

"What?!" Alaric clicked on his comm. "Cassii? Are you hearing this?"

The man pressed a small laminate into Alaric hand and exited before Alaric's shock wore off.

"Cassii?"

Silence.

He boarded, Tsin on his heels. The closest dome wasn't lit. Taloned claws gripped his heart.

"Cassii?"

An icy dread filled him. Alaric bolted for the bridge, racing through dim corridors under dark dome after dark dome. Cassii's main dome hung powerless on the bridge, surrounded by powered panels and displays.

A single angry red light blinked lies at him: AI Module Failure

He darted around Tsin and slid down the rail, stumbling when he hit the lower deck. He pushed off a wall and sprinted aft toward the computer core. Footfalls echoed off the tomblike halls. The core's door opened too slowly. He shoved himself through, ripping his jacket in the process.

He froze at the entrance, breath ragged. *No, no, it can't be.*

A gaping, black hole in the core's floor to ceiling components glared accusations at him.

She can't be gone.

He fell to his knees, fingers probing the AI module's empty bay, ignoring stripped wires even when they bit him.

No. He cast tear-blind eyes upward. *Please. Our last words were...*

The thought refused to complete.

The panel gaped, but less than the jagged wound in his soul, ripped out by the absence of Cassii...one of a kind computer...mother...friend...

Who could've? The vid of Manc and Tyne flashed to mind. Red narrowed his vision to a fiery tunnel. His face burned. His hands itched.

He snarled. "I'll rip the greedy bitch's heart out...."

THE END

Thank you for reading *Scion of Conquered Earth.*
I hope you enjoyed it as much as I did!

If you did, please help other readers find it by leaving a review.

If you want more Scion, keep reading for the excerpt from

SCION 2: STOLEN LIVES

1

DESPERATE FOR A FRIEND

Alaric raised his hands in surrender. The breathing mask pinching his ears muffled his voice. "This is a legal transaction."

The four traders—an Elcu, two umoid and a rilduron—dove for cover between towering heaps of space wreckage. They further complicated their late arrival by opening fire on the approaching Scrics authorities.

"You betrayed us, Ignaree," The rilduron's accusations carried on a biting wind. "We'll remember you for this."

"It wasn't me, Shtephe, I swear," Alaric said.

Vibrant orange spikes peeked up, an ear-to-ear bridge of cartilage cutting through them identified the trader's species as Ongali. He glowered at Alaric, shoved the credit stick Alaric'd just handed over into a belt and fired.

Alaric dove for cover as armored security men returned fire. The lighter gravity of Jerol—Scrics Five's moon—turned his dive into a glide that overshot his cover.

Damn it. What else can go wrong?

He scrambled behind twisted wreckage once vehicles for peoples' dreams. The corner nearest his head exploded, plinking garbage off his mask and bombarding his fighter pilot jacket with debris.

He swore. *I can't replace some of those campaign patches.*

An amplified voice filled the night. "I say again, this is Scrics System Security. Surrender immediately."

"I tried that," Alaric shouted. "You shot at me."

Two pulsewave scatter guns floated along the amorphous curves of the magenta Elcu accompanying Shtephe. The ovoid blob spluttered and hissed battle cries as cyan energy rings launched from its weapons by the pseudopodful.

Alaric's comm ring crackled to life with an oddly chord like voice. "What is happening?"

"Little busy here, Tsin," Alaric peeked around the debris. He ducked back as Shtephe blasted his cover.

"You're surrounded," Tsin said.

Tell me something I don't know.

Shtephe and his three companions traded blasts with SSS. The headless, waxy-leafed tangle of vines fired at him.

"Just a case of mistaken identity," Alaric said. "They think I'm some kind of pirate."

"You're under fire?" Tsin asked. "Corollas besiege you?"

"System Security," Alaric unholstered his blaster. He reconsidered, slamming it home once more.

Tsin's outrage carried on three words. "This is illegal?"

"No, it's mostly a misunderstanding." Alaric shot a glance at the AI module in the Ongali's other hand—the only even vaguely florentine-compatible module he'd managed to track down. "Wait, Corollas? Here?"

"Yes. They're surrounding you."

How the hedrin did they find me already? Alaric fogged his mask with profanities. "Get clear of the junkyard and lay low."

"Get clear where?" Tsin asked. "It covers Jerol."

Shtephe's rifleman screamed.

"Figure it out." Alaric chanced a look. "I'll be in touch."

The vanilla umoid clutched a cauterized stump that had been a shoulder moments before.

Lucky thing about energy weapons I guess.

<Real lucky. How about you leap out and try it for yourself, runt?>

The Elcu flattened itself fist-high and oozed over to the downed rifleman. It dragged him back as SSS rushed their position.

Alaric tossed a hunk of garbage toward Shtephe. He shot the debris out of the air and aimed at Alaric.

"Wait," Alaric whispered. "I'll surrender to them as a distraction, you run, just leave me the module."

Shtephe fired.

Alaric's cover disintegrated, forcing another dive for more. "You've been paid."

"Doubtless blank, typical turncoat precaution, betrayer."

Alaric bristled. "I didn't betray you."

Shtephe's answer filled the air with high speed but slowly falling shrapnel.

Think. He peeked around a cover for a look at the Scrics authorities. Shtephe and SSS sent Alaric deeper into the starship graveyard. He took cover behind a severed vultair wing. Their assault drove the Ongali and his purchased module closer to him.

What I wouldn't give to see Cassii fly down and scoop me off to safety. His gut churned.

Cassii, the AI that'd saved him from Welorin-invaded Earth was gone—stolen. He eyed the module again. *Without it, I'll never get her back. Without her, I'll never save El or Jesse.*

He scanned the wreckage labyrinth. Figures moved atop the surrounding debris piles getting into position to snipe them. *Corollas or SSS?*

He chewed his lip.

If I keep my head down and surrender, they can prove my blasters weren't fired. His gaze fixed on the module. *But I lose the only workable AI module in Scrics.*

He checked the battlefield and its skyline of mounded debris once more.

Where's that Elcu?

His brain caught up, recognizing the vultair wing under his fingertips. He dropped low and checked its underside. Hope swelled.

He yanked at the wing. It stuck fast. He pulled, giving Shtephe his head as target. The shot drove Alaric down. He cursed the rilduron, twice cursed the wedged wing, and thrice cursed the hell guaranteed by his plan.

He unholstered his blaster and fired it. *Not like the crooked bastards are going to hold me blameless after this anyway.*

It took several shots and a lot of wiggling, but he coerced the wing from its nest and flipped it over. He'd only brought a few tools to test the module, but it wasn't like he could go shopping while under fire. He made it work.

He stripped the fuel cells from both his blaster pistols, yanked wires from some piece of junk, and jury-rigged them to the photon bolt launcher still attached to the bent wing. He hesitated, the last wire hovering just off the weapon.

It's either going to keep firing until it runs out of juice or blow up in my face.

He positioned the wing to assault canyon walls of mounded junk between him, SSS and Shtephe.

Sure hope I'm due a little luck.

He touched the wire to the launcher. A hum rose. Sparks shot out of its sides. *Guess not, I'll--*

A blazing blue-white sphere of photons shot out of the cannon. Junk piles exploded, raining down sharp-edged chunks of broken dreams.

A glance showed him the Ongali's widened eyes and the rilduron's baffled arrangement of leaves.

Alaric touched the wire to the firing point once more and wedged it there with another wire. The launcher didn't take as long to warm up. It lobbed photon bolts one after another, bringing down an avalanche of destruction.

Alaric rushed the startled Ongali, slamming a fist into his jaw. "Sorry about this."

He snatched up the module and fled.

A yelp brought his attention back to the Ongali. Debris cut into the man's leg. Alaric cursed himself and rushed back to the injured man. He checked the bleeding and broken limb. *He'll bleed out before they get to him.*

The photon bolt launcher spat its last round.

He pulled the fighting batons from his belt, ripped the Ongali's pant leg off and wrapped it around the wound and makeshift splint.

"We know your name," the Ongali growled. "We'll get you for this."

My name? Alaric's eyes fell to the credit strip in the Ongali's belt. *If SSS doesn't know who I am, that'll tell them.*

"Can you walk?" Alaric asked.

"Not that I'd go anywhere with you, but no."

<Do it, kid.>

The shock of Manc Shepherd's voice in his thoughts brought him up short. "What?"

"No, I can't walk."

Alaric chewed his lip. "I'll contact you later to pay for the module."

The Ongali blinked at him.

"Sorry about this, too." Alaric brought the Ongali's discarded weapon down on his head with a sympathetic cringe. He snatched the credit strip and bolted.

The Elcu oozed out of a debris pile to block his path.

LOVE SCIENCE FICTION?

ADVENTURE INTO THE FARTHEST REACHES OF A WHOLE NEW VERSE

KEEP CONNECTED:

Keep up to date on book news, giveaways and expanded lore on my website:

- www.deliriousscribbles.com

Follow along on social media:

- http://www.twitter.com/TheDScribbler
- http://www.instagram.com/TheDScribbler
- http://www.facebook.com/DeliriousScribbler

GET INVOLVED:

While you're waiting for my next novel, get involved with helping your other favorite authors by being part of the little rectangular miracles called books. Here's how you help ANY author:

- Read our books and enjoy them. That's why we wrote them.
- Tell your friends about the book so they can enjoy it too.
- Follow an author on social media. Say hello. Writing is a lonely profession.
- Share links to reviews, posts, etc. on social media. The more the merrier!
- Post a review to help others find the book you enjoyed so much. This REALLY helps.
- Click "Like" on their Book and Author pages on Amazon
- "Share" links to their Book and Author Pages on social media.

ACKNOWLEDGEMENTS:

Let me acknowledge you, my reader, for reading this far—or skipping to the back like a cheater. Without someone to read these pages, this story's destiny would only be half fulfilled. You're in my thoughts as the story unfolds, keeping me motivated, driving revision and encouraging the best story I can muster. I genuinely hope you enjoyed it.

Being my first book released to the public, the list of people who helped it come into being is a long one. Some are still with me while others have replaced those gone off in different directions. Over this novel's history, it's carried several titles. Each of those titles and corresponding chapters has been subjected to proofreaders, sounding boards, editors, and people who contributed by simply ooo'ing and ahh'ing in the right places to keep me working.

First revision thanks go out to Johanna, Virginia, Jennifer, Parker, Karen, Shannon and Mike—my original core support. From there the cast of characters includes Bryan, Trint, Jon, Lynette, Michael, Kimberly, Katherine, Kelsey, Rus, Sean, another Mike, and of course B, B & J.

Professional writers with names you undoubtedly know played no small part in this project's completion. I've had many a harsh critique or guiding tidbit from the best you can read. I'm humbled and truly grateful to have gotten a moment of their time and hope to extend their kindness forward to the next starry-eyed writer too badly infected to flee for his life.

To Alaric, Cassii, Manc, Tyne and the rest of the cast. Thanks for a grand adventure. Stop nagging. We'll all see you in the next book.

Special thanks go out to Jason: proofreader, sounding board and all around SOB who demanded I acknowledge him first. He failed, however, to specify whether to construct these acknowledgements forward or in reverse.

Revision addendum:

Thanks to all the SharpEyes that sent in corrections: Dalton, Justin, Scott, and Bryan

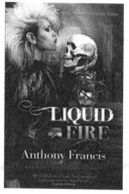

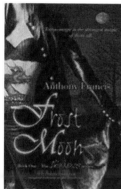

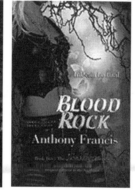

ABOUT THE SCRIBBLER

(Photo credit: Jim Cawthorne)

Michael J. Allen is a bestselling author of multi-layer science fiction and fantasy novels. Born in Oregon and an avid storm fan, he lives in far too hot & humid rural Georgia with his two black Labradors: Myth and Magesty. On those rare occasions he tears himself away from reading, writing and conventions he can be found enjoying bad scifi movies, playing D&D or the occasional video game, getting hit with sticks in the SCA or hanging out with the crew of Starfleet International's U.S.S. DaVinci.

To learn more about Michael, check out his website at www.deliriousscribbles.com

23518480R00252

Made in the USA
Columbia, SC
13 August 2018